Praise for *The Butcher's Boy*

"Brisk energy and confidence in the telling . . . complicated twists."
    —*Sunday Times* (London)

"A brilliant suspense thriller, reminiscent of Graham Greene."
    —*The Washington Post Book World*

"Clever, knowledgeable, inventive and suspenseful."
    —*The New York Times*

"Thomas Perry has hit the mark his first time out with the skill at storytelling that promises more successes to come."
    —*The Houston Chronicle*

"Original, clever, intricate."
    —*Publishers Weekly*

"An ingenious crime thriller."
    —*Library Journal*

THOMAS PERRY won an Edgar for *The Butcher's Boy,* and *Metzger's Dog* was a *New York Times* Notable Book. Perry's novel *Vanishing Act* was chosen as one of the 100 Favorite Mysteries of the Century by the Independent Mystery Booksellers Association, and his novel *Pursuit* was a national bestseller. Perry lives in Southern California with his wife and two daughters.

BY THOMAS PERRY

The Butcher's Boy
Metzger's Dog
Big Fish
Island
Sleeping Dogs
Vanishing Act
Dance for the Dead
Shadow Woman
The Face-Changers
Blood Money
Death Benefits
Pursuit
Dead Aim
Nightlife
Silence
Fidelity
Runner
Strip
The Informant
Poison Flower

The Butcher's Boy

The Butcher's Boy

A NOVEL

Thomas Perry

RANDOM HOUSE TRADE PAPERBACKS

NEW YORK

2003 Random House Trade Paperback Edition

Copyright © 1982 by Thomas Perry
Introduction copyright © 2003 by Michael Connelly

This work was originally published in hardcover and in slightly different form
by Charles Scribner's Sons in 1982. This edition is published
by arrangement with the author.

Library of Congress Cataloging-in-Publication Data

Perry, Thomas.
The butcher's boy : a novel / Thomas Perry.
p.   cm.
ISBN 0-8129-6773-9
1. Assassins—Fiction.   2. Murder for hire—Fiction.
3. Las Vegas (Nev.)—Fiction.   4. Government investigators—Fiction.
5. Legislators—Crimes against—Fiction.   I. Title.
PS3566.E718B8 2003
813'.54—dc21   200346507

Random House website address: www.atrandom.com
Printed in the United States of America

INTRODUCTION
Michael Connelly

It used to be that the quickest way for me to descend into a creative depression would be for someone to approach me and identify him- or herself as a fan of my work, but to then add the dreadful line "But your first one is still my favorite."

It didn't matter if the approach was in person at a bookstore or on the street, or through the U.S. mail or the Internet. I always took it very badly, and the compliment would serve to make me question what I was doing. This of course was completely unknown to the cheerful giver of the supposed compliment, because I was always able to maintain a frozen smile or the distance of mail, electronic or otherwise.

There was a time when I would actually respond, hoping to dissuade the reader of his or her own words, saying things like "That's impossible!" or "You don't really mean that!" But I soon realized it wasn't impossible and they did really mean it.

And that is the source of the depression; that's the rub. Writing, whether you consider it a craft or an art or both, is something that should get better with practice. It stands to reason. Writing comes from experience, curiosity, and knowledge. In short, it comes from life. The writer must improve with age and experience and life. So too the writing. Therefore, if I were to accept the compliment of the reader, wouldn't I be accepting the decline of my work? As of this writing, I have published twelve novels. If my best work was my first, what am I doing here?

Well, I don't feel that way anymore. I don't get depressed. It took me a long time, but I understand something now. First novels are like first loves. They are moments of discovery and celebration of things hopefully to come. They are windows. They carry with them the long reach of promise. Now when readers tell me they still like my first novel the best, I can take the compliment. I don't argue. I smile and say thank you.

All of this leads me to say that *The Butcher's Boy* might be my favorite novel by Thomas Perry. I say *might* because I am not certain—the man has written several very fine novels. (And of course I don't want to be responsible for making the author depressed in case he has not made the same journey and come to the same conclusion I have.) And I say *might* because I know there is still much good stuff to come from this writer.

But in rereading *The Butcher's Boy* in order to prepare for the writing of this introduction, I was struck over and over by the assuredness of this work and by its long reach of promise. I was amazed by what Perry knew when he knew it. I see it in the prose, the pacing, the choices. It's taken me a long time to learn what the cornerstones of this craft are, and yet there they are at work in Perry's first outing. Hey, *sure* he has gotten better since. But he sure started out near the top floor of the building.

Over the years and the millions of words, I have come to learn that it is all about character and velocity. A book is like a car. It pulls up to the curb and the passenger door swings open to the reader. The engine revs. Do you want a ride?

Once you get in, the car takes off, the door slamming shut and tire rubber burning in its wake. Behind the wheel the driver's got to be highly skilled, heavy on the pedal, and most of all, oh man, most of all, somebody you want to be with. He's got to drive near the edge of the cliff but never over. He's got to turn sharply just as you think you know where you are going. He's got to gun it on the final lap. And he's got to tell you the story all along the way.

If not, it is going to be a short ride.

I'm here to tell you that *The Butcher's Boy* is not the short ride. No matter whom you are cruising with in this story, you've got your hands braced on the dashboard. There is not a single throwaway character in this book. They are all real, they are all captivating. Perry approaches his people with a less-is-more philosophy, never confusing description with character, cutting all of that away and leaving only the telling details that open a window onto a true world.

This economy creates momentum. The story gathers speed and moves with an unalterable urgency. All characters, all action, relentlessly moving toward the same vanishing point on the horizon. They asked me to write a few pages here, but I think I could have covered it with one word: *relentless.* This book is a relentless journey in a car with no mirrors. No looking back.

This velocity is also created by the masterly intertwining of multiple narrative tracks. Perry came out of the gate with a narrative that would offer a great challenge to any writer. How do you bond the reader to a professional hit man? How do you get the reader to get in the car with a killer? Perry answered the call by creating a character who is meticulously detailed in all ways but his name. The telling details of life on the road and on the run connect him to us. His ingenuity and skills win the day.

Perry also balances the outlaw portrait with another strong character, that of the heretofore deskbound crime analyst Elizabeth Waring. She's unsteady in her new surroundings yet just as professional as her quarry. The juxtaposition of these two characters as they move separately but ultimately closer and closer is the gasoline that drives this car. It is rare that I have seen this pulled off successfully, and never with such success in a first novel.

Riding along all through this journey is Thomas Perry's command. The authenticity is on display on every page, in every paragraph. From how hot desert air feels on the skin in Las Vegas to how paperwork is shuffled in the Justice Department to how a hired killer slips into a locked hotel room to fulfill a contract, the author's skill in creating his world repeatedly awes the reader. Verisimilitude.

Every page is absolutely authentic, and that creates a velocity of its own.

Character, control, and momentum. Perry has pulled off a wonderful trifecta in this novel. It is a rare accomplishment. So unusual is a book like this that it reminds me of how its own character Elizabeth Waring viewed her search for an unnamed, unknown hit man.

> It was like trying to capture an animal that was so small and rare and elusive that you sometimes doubted that it existed.

Well, Thomas Perry captures the rare animal with this book. It exists. There are no doubts.

When *The Butcher's Boy* was first published, twenty years ago, it received many accolades. Among them was the Edgar Award for best first novel. This award is bestowed by the Mystery Writers of America and is not taken lightly. I think the book you are about to read deserved that honor hands down.

Time now for you to start the story. The car is at the curb, waiting. The door is open and the engine is thrumming as high octane moves through its heart. Get in and ride.

MICHAEL CONNELLY'S first novel, *The Black Echo,* which introduced detective Hieronymus Bosch, won the Edgar Award for best first novel from the Mystery Writers of America. Other Harry Bosch novels include *The Black Ice, The Concrete Blonde, The Last Coyote,* and, more recently, *City of Bones* and *Lost Light.* Among Connelly's other novels are *The Poet, Blood Work,* and *Chasing the Dime.*

For Jo

The Butcher's Boy

1 The union meeting, thought Al Veasy, had gone as well as could be expected, all things considered. He had finally figured out why the retirement fund was in such trouble all the time, when everybody else in the whole country with anything to invest seemed to be making money. And he had explained what he knew, and the union members had understood it right away, because it wasn't anything surprising if you read the newspapers. The big unions had been getting caught in similar situations for years. Low-interest loans to Fieldston Growth Enterprises—hell of an impressive name, but zero return so far on almost five million dollars. If the company was as bad as it looked, there would be no more Fieldston than there was growth. Just a name and a fancy address. When the union started to apply pressure some lawyer nobody ever heard of would quietly file bankruptcy papers. Probably in New York or someplace where it would take weeks before the union here in Ventura, California, heard of it. Just a notice by certified mail to O'Connell, the president of the union local, informing him of the dissolution of Fieldston Growth Enterprises and the sale of its assets to cover debts. And O'Connell, the big dumb bastard, would bring it to Veasy for translation. "Hey, Al," he would say, "take a look at this," as though he already knew what it meant but felt it was his duty to let somebody else see the actual document. Not that it would do anybody any good by then.

Or now either. That was the trouble and always had been. Veasy could feel it as he walked away from the union hall, still wearing his clodhopper boots and a work shirt that the sweat had dried on hours ago. He could smell himself. The wise guys in their perfectly fitted three-piece suits and their

1

Italian shoes always ended up with everything. The best the ordinary working man could hope for was sometimes to figure out how they'd done it, and then make one or two of them uncomfortable. Slow them down was what it amounted to. If it hadn't been Fieldston Growth Enterprises it would have been something else that sounded just as substantial and ended up just the same. The money gone and nobody, no person, who could be forced to give it back.

He kicked at a stone on the gravel parking lot. There probably wasn't even any point in going to the government about it. The courts and the bureaucrats and commissions. Veasy snorted. All of them made up of the same wise guys in the three-piece suits, so much alike you couldn't tell them from each other or from the crooks, except maybe the crooks were a little better at it, at getting money without working for it, and they smiled at you. The ones in the government didn't even have to smile at you, because they'd get their cut of it no matter what. But hell, what else could you do? You had to go through the motions. Sue Fieldston, just so it got on the record. A little machinists' union local in Ventura losing 70 percent of its pension fund to bad investments. It probably wouldn't even make the papers. But you had to try, even if all you could hope for was to make them a little more cautious next time, a little less greedy so they wouldn't try to take it all. And maybe make one or two of them sweat a little.

Veasy opened the door of his pickup truck and climbed in. He sat there for a minute, lit a cigarette, took a deep drag, and blew a puff out the window. "Jesus," he thought. "Nine o'clock. I wonder if Sue kept dinner for me." He looked at the lighted doorway of the union hall, where he could see the men filing out past the bulky shape of O'Connell, who was smiling and slapping somebody on the back. He would be saying something about how we don't know yet and that it's too early to panic. "That's right, you big dumb bastard," thought Veasy. "Keep calm, and you'll never know what hit you."

2

Veasy turned the key in the ignition and the whole world turned to fire and noise. The concussion threw O'Connell back against the clapboards of the union hall and disintegrated the front window. Then the parking lot was bathed in light as the billowing ball of flame tore up into the sky. Afterward a machinist named Lynley said pieces of the pickup truck went with it, but O'Connell said there wasn't anything to that. People always said things like that, especially when somebody actually got killed. Sure was a shame, though, and it was bad enough without making things up.

3

2 "Here's the daily gloom," said Padgett, tossing the sheaf of computer printouts on Elizabeth's desk. "Early today, and you're welcome to it."

"Thanks," said Elizabeth, not looking up from her calculations. She was still trying to figure out how that check had bounced. Even if the store had tried to cash it the next morning, the deposit should have been there at least twelve hours before. Eight fifteen, and the bank would open at nine thirty. She made a note to call. It was probably the post office, as usual. Anybody who couldn't deliver a piece of mail across town in two days ought to get into another business. They had sure delivered the notice of insufficient funds fast enough. One day.

Elizabeth put the checkbook and notice back in her purse and picked up the printout. "All those years of school for this," she thought. "Reading computerized obituaries for the Department of Justice for a living, and lucky to get it."

She started at the first sheet, going through the items one by one. "De Vitto, L. G. Male. Caucasian. 46. Apparent suicide. Shotgun, 12 gauge. Toledo, Ohio. Code number 79-8475." She marked the entry in pencil, maybe just because of the name that could mean Mafia, and maybe just because it was the first one, and the other prospects might be even less likely.

"Gale, D. R. Female. Caucasian. 34. Apparent murder. Revolver, .38. Suspects: Gale, P. G., 36; no prior arrests. Wichita, Kansas, code number 79-8476." No, just the usual thing, thought Elizabeth. Family argument and one of them picks up a gun. She went on down the list, searching for the

4

unusual, the one that might not be one of the same old things.

"Veasy, A. E. Male. Caucasian. 35. Apparent murder. Dynamite. Ventura, California. Code number 79-8477." Dynamite? Murder by dynamite? Elizabeth marked this one. Maybe it wasn't anything for the Activity Report, but at least it wasn't the predictable, normal Friday night's random violence.

"Satterfield, R. J. Male. Afro-American. 26. Apparent murder/robbery. Revolver, .32. Washington, D.C. Code number 79-8478." No.

"Davidson, B. L. Female. Caucasian. 23. Apparent murder/rape. Knife. Carmel, California. Code number 79-8479." No again.

Down the printout she went, letting the sheets fall in front of her desk to re-form themselves into an accordion shape on the floor. Now and then she would make a check mark with her pencil beside an entry that didn't fall into the ten or twelve most common murder patterns. It was Monday, so she had to work fast to catch up. One thing Elizabeth had learned on this job was that a lot of people killed each other on weekends.

It was just after ten when she reached the final entry. "Stapleton, R. D. Male. Caucasian. 41. Apparent murder. Revolver, .45. Suspects: Stapleton, A. E., 38; no prior arrests. Buffalo, New York. Code number 79-102033." Padgett, the senior analyst in charge of analyzing reports, would be on his morning break, she thought. The timing was always wrong, somehow. Whenever you got to the stage where you needed somebody it was either lunchtime or a break. She picked up the printout and carried it across the office to the glass-walled room where the computer operators worked.

She was surprised to see Padgett at his desk behind the glass, frowning over a report. She rapped on the glass and he got up to open the door for her without putting down the papers he was reading.

5

"I thought you would be on your break, Roger," she said.

"Not today," said Padgett. "Must have been a big weekend. Four of our friends bought airline tickets in the last three days." He always called them "our friends," as though the years of scanning lists for familiar names had prompted a kind of affection.

"All to the same place?"

"No," he said. "Two to Las Vegas, one to Phoenix, and one to Los Angeles."

"It's probably the weather," said Elizabeth. "They don't like it any more than we do. You still have to scrape the snow off your car if it's a Rolls Royce."

He looked impatient. "Okay, love. What did you find?"

"Eight possibles. The numbers are marked. The rest are the usual weekend stuff—rapes, muggings, and arguments that went a little too far."

"I'll have Mary get the details to you as soon as they're printed out. Give her fifteen minutes. Take a break or something."

"Okay," she said, and walked out again into the large outer office. She saw that Brayer, her section head, was just putting a few papers into a file, then throwing on his sport coat.

"On a break, Elizabeth?" he asked.

"Yes," she said. "Can't do anything until the computer spits out the day's possibles."

"Come on," said Brayer. "I'll buy you a cup of coffee. I'm waiting on something myself." They walked down the hall and into the employees' lounge. Brayer poured two cups of coffee while Elizabeth staked her claim on a table in the far corner of the room.

Brayer sat down, sighing. "I sometimes get tired of this job. You never seem to get anything worthwhile, and you spend an awful lot of time analyzing data that doesn't form a pattern and wouldn't prove anything if it did. This morning

6

I've been going over the field reports of last week's possibles. Nothing."

Elizabeth said, "Just what I needed—to hear my section chief talking like that on a Monday morning."

"I guess it's the logical flaw that bothers me," said Brayer. "You and I are looking for a pattern that will lead us to a professional killer, a hit man. So we pick out everything that doesn't seem routine and normal. The point about professional killers is that they don't do things to draw attention to themselves. What did you get this morning, for instance?"

"A shotgun suicide. One where they tortured a man and then cut his throat. One where a man was poisoned in a hotel dining room, one where the brakes failed on a new car. And a dynamite murder, and—"

"There!" said Brayer. "That's just what I was talking about. A dynamite murder. That's no hit man. It's a mental defective who saw a hit man do that on television. What we ought to be looking at is the ones that don't look unusual. The ones where the coroner says it was a natural death."

"You know why we don't," said Elizabeth.

"Sure. Too many of them. Thousands every day. But that's where our man will be. And you wouldn't be able to tell whether it was a hit man or pneumonia. Dynamite, shotguns, knives, hell. You don't have to hire a professional for that. You can find some junkie in half an hour who could do that for a couple of hundred."

"We help catch one now and then, you have to remember that."

"Yes, we do. You're right. We're not just wasting time. But there has to be a better way to do it. As it is, we find what we find, not what we're looking for. We catch lunatics, axe murderers, people like that. Once every few years an old Mafia soldier who wants to come in from the cold and can tell us who did what to whom in 1953. It's okay, but it's not what we're after."

7

"John, how many actual hit men do you suppose there are operating right now? The professionals we look for?"

"Oh, a hundred. Maybe two hundred if you count the semiretired and the novices who have the knack. That's in the world. Not too many, is it?"

"No, not many when you're trying to find them by analyzing statistics. From another point of view it's plenty. I'd better go call my bank while I've got a minute. They bounced my check unjustly."

Brayer laughed. "Typical woman," he said. "Mathematical genius who can't add up her checkbook."

Elizabeth smiled her sweetest smile at him, the one that didn't show that her teeth were clenched. "Thanks for the coffee. I'll have the activity report in an hour or two." She got up and disappeared out the door of the lounge.

Brayer sat there alone, sipping the last half of his cup of coffee and feeling vaguely bereft. He liked to sit at a table with a pretty woman. That was about as far as he allowed it to go these days, he thought. It made him feel young.

"May I join you, or am I too ugly?" came a voice. Brayer looked up and saw Connors, the Organized Crime Division head, standing above him.

"You're perfect, Martin," said Brayer. "You being the boss, this being Monday, and you being ugly enough to fit right in. It's a pattern."

"Thanks," Connors said. "How are things going?"

"Rotten, I'm afraid. Elizabeth went back to pick out the second-stage possibles, of which there are several. None very promising, but they all take time. The field reports from last week are all blanks except the one from Tulsa, which is three days late and is probably just as blank."

"I almost hope so this morning," said Connors. "We've got just about every investigator in the field, and Padgett's airline reports say at least four of the people we keep an eye on bought tickets west this weekend."

"Anything in it?"

"Probably the usual. Old men like warm weather. At least I do. And Roncone and Neroni have investments out there. Legitimate businesses, or at least they would be if those two weren't in on them. But there's always a chance of a meeting."

"Maybe we'll get lucky," said Brayer without enthusiasm. "Well, I think I'll go see if Tulsa phoned in. I'd like to close the books on last week before Elizabeth comes up with today's massacres."

"How's she working out, anyway? It's been over a year."

Brayer sat back down and spoke in a low voice. "To tell you the truth, Martin, she's a real surprise. I think if I had to retire tomorrow, she'd be the one I'd pick to replace me."

"Come on, John," said Connors. "She can't possibly know enough yet. There's a difference between being clever and pretty and running an analysis section. She hasn't even been in any field investigation yet."

"But I think she's got the touch," said Brayer. "She's the only one in my section that's smarter than I am."

9

3 Two this week, he thought. Too many. After the next one, a vacation. At least a month. The old lady in front of him stepped aside to count her change, so he moved forward. "One way to Los Angeles, the three o'clock."

"Five fifty," said the weary ticket agent, running his hand over the bald spot on his head as though checking to be sure nothing had grown in there while he wasn't paying attention.

He paid the money and waited while the man filled in the ticket. It would be no problem. After something like Friday, a man buying a ticket on Saturday morning for someplace far away might have stuck. A man buying a ticket for Los Angeles on Monday afternoon was nothing. He wasn't leaving the vicinity of a crime. He was just leaving. This man behind the counter wouldn't remember him. Too many people in line buying the same ticket, as fast as he could write. Not even time to look at them all. Not the men, anyway.

He stepped aside and pocketed his ticket. The clock on the wall said 2:45. Almost time to board. Not much time to hang around the bus station and get stared at. No reason for anybody to remember having seen him, because they hadn't seen anybody in the first place. No chance they'd check on the motel either. He'd registered Friday afternoon three hours before the truck blew up, and the truck had been thirty miles away in Ventura. Another county. All clean and simple. From Los Angeles, you could take any kind of transport to anywhere. You practically had to set yourself on fire to attract a second glance in L. A.

On Monday, February twelfth, at 2:43 P.M., a man not fat, not thin, not young, not old, not tall, not short, not dark, not light, bought a bus ticket for Los Angeles at the Santa Barbara bus station. He was one of twenty or thirty that afternoon that you couldn't have told from one another, but that didn't matter because nobody looked at any of them. If the police were looking for someone in the area, it wasn't on a bus coming toward Ventura on its way to Los Angeles.

ELIZABETH STUDIED THE SECOND SET of printouts on the day's possibles. The man who had been killed by the shotgun had left a note that satisfied his family and the coroner. The death by torture was linked to a religious cult that had been under investigation for a year and a half. The brake failure was officially attributed to incorrect assembly at the factory in Japan. That left the man poisoned in the hotel dining room and the victim of the dynamite murder.

The autopsy report on the unlucky diner convinced Elizabeth that there wasn't much point in following up with an investigation. Chances were that he hadn't even ingested the poison on the premises. It was a combination of drugs, all used for treatment of hypertension, and taken this time with a large amount of alcohol. Elizabeth moved on to the last one.

Veasy, Albert Edward. Machinist for a small company in Ventura, California, called Precision Tooling. Not very promising, really. Professional killers were an expensive service, and that meant powerful enemies. Machinists in Ventura didn't usually have that kind of enemy. Sexual jealousy? That might introduce him to somebody he wouldn't otherwise meet —somebody whose name turned up on Activity Reports now and then. Thirty-five years old, married for ten years, three kids. Still possible. Have to check his social habits, if it came to that.

Elizabeth scanned the narrative for the disqualifier, the one element that would make it clear that this one too was normal, just another instance of someone being murdered by someone who had a reason to do it, someone who at least knew him.

11

She noticed the location of the crime. Outside the head-quarters of the Brotherhood of Machinists, Local 602, where he had been for a meeting. Her breath caught—a union meeting. Maybe a particularly nasty strike, or the first sign that one of the West Coast families was moving in on the union. She made a note to check it, and also the ownership of Precision Tooling. Maybe that was dirty money. Well what the hell, she thought. Might as well get all of it. Find out what they made, whom they sold it to, and tax summaries. She'd been expecting a busy day anyway, and the other possibles had already dissolved.

She moved down to the summary of the lab report. Explosives detonated by the ignition of the car. She made a note to ask for a list of the dynamite thefts during the last few months in California. She read further. "Explosive not dynamite, as earlier reported. Explosive 200 pounds of fertilizer carried in the bed of the victim's pickup truck." Elizabeth laughed involuntarily. Then she threw her pencil down, leaned back in her chair, and tore up her notes.

"What's up, Elizabeth?" asked Richardson, the analyst at the next desk. "You find a funny murder?"

Elizabeth said, "I can't help it. I think we've established today's pattern. My one possible blew himself up with a load of fertilizer. You should appreciate that. You're a connoisseur."

Richardson chuckled. "Let me see." He came up and looked over her shoulder at the printout. "Well, I guess it hit the fan this weekend," he said. "But that's a new one on me."

"Me too," said Elizabeth.

"How do you suppose it happened?"

"I don't know," said Elizabeth. "I've heard of sewers and septic tanks blowing up. I guess there's a lot of methane gas in animal waste."

"Oh yeah," said Richardson, suddenly pensive. "I remember reading about some guy who was going to parlay

12

his chicken ranch into an energy empire. But you know what this means, don't you?"

"No."

"Brayer's a walking bomb. His pep talks at staff meetings could kill us."

Elizabeth giggled. "I knew I shouldn't have told you about this. I suppose I'll have to listen to a lot of infantile jokes now."

"No, I think I got them all out of my system for the present," said Richardson.

Elizabeth groaned. "Go back to your desk, you creep."

Richardson said, "I'm going. But you know what?"

"What?"

"I'd have this one checked out." Elizabeth made a face, but he held up his hand in the gesture he used to signal the return of the businesslike Richardson. "Seriously," he said.

"Checked out with whom?" asked Elizabeth, moving warily toward whatever absurdity he was anxious for her to elicit from him. "And why?"

"I'm not sure who. I guess the bomb squad. Maybe even somebody over in the Agriculture Department. Maybe this sort of thing happens all the time. Who knows? I'm a city boy myself. But if it does we ought to know about it. We might be sending agents out into the field once a week to find out some farmer blew himself up with his manure spreader."

Elizabeth studied his face, but he seemed serious. "I don't know if you're joking or not, but what you're saying makes sense. It'll take a few minutes to clear this up, and I've got some time on my hands this afternoon."

"Then do it," he said. "If only to cater to my curiosity."

IN THE LOS ANGELES AIRPORT there are some people who stand on the moving walkway, letting the long belt carry them to the end of the corridor. Others walk forward on it, com-

13

bining muscle and machinery into something over a dead run; and others, probably the biggest group, don't use the machinery at all. This group consists of people who have spent too much time sitting down and know they'll soon be sitting again for a few hours, or people who arrived at the airport an hour earlier than they needed to. Among them was a man not tall or short, not young or old, not light or dark, with a one-way ticket to Denver in his breast pocket. When the stewardess checks his boarding pass for the seat number a few minutes from now, she won't be able to decide whether he is on his way to one of the military bases in that area, or one of the ski resorts. And she certainly won't ask. After that she won't have time to notice. As soon as the lights go on she will be too busy to study faces. Once they are strapped in she will look mostly at their laps, where the trays and the drinks and the magazines will be.

THE MAN AT Treasury said, "That one's not in our bailiwick, I'm afraid. Have you tried the FBI?"

"Not yet," said Elizabeth. "I'd hoped to get something on it today."

The man chuckled. "Oh, you've noticed. But I'll tell you what you can do. There's a guy over there who knows just about everything about explosives. Name's Hart. Agent Robert E. Hart. If you call him direct you'll avoid all the referral forms and runarounds. He's the one you'd get to in the end anyway. He's at extension 3023. Write down that name and number, because it'll come in handy every now and then. Agent Hart."

"Thanks," said Elizabeth. "That'll save me a lot of time."

Elizabeth dialed the FBI number and waited. The female voice on the other end seemed to come from the soul of a

14

melting candy bar: "Federal Bureau of Investigation." Elizabeth retaliated, making her voice go soft and whispery. "Extension 3023 please, dear."

"That'll hold her," thought Elizabeth.

"Whom would you like to speak with, ma'am?" said the voice, now suddenly businesslike and mechanical.

"Agent Hart," said Elizabeth.

"I'll ring his office," said the voice.

The line clicked and there was that sound that seemed as though a door had opened on a physically larger space. "Hart," said a man's voice.

Elizabeth wondered if she had missed the ring. "This is Elizabeth Waring at Justice, Agent Hart. We have an explosives case and we need some information."

"Who told you to call me?"

"Treasury."

"Figures," he said, without emotion. "What do you want to know?"

"Anything you can tell me about fertilizer blowing up."

"About what?"

"Fertilizer. Er . . . manure. You know, fertilizer."

"Oh." There was silence on Hart's end.

Elizabeth waited. Then she said, "I assure you, Agent Hart, this isn't a—"

"I know," he said. "I was just thinking. What's the LEAA computer code designation?"

"Seven nine dash eight four seven seven."

"I'll take a look at it and call you back. What's your extension?"

"Two one two one. But does that happen? Have you heard of it before?"

"I'm not sure what we're talking about yet," said Hart. "I'll call you back in a few minutes." He hung up and Elizabeth said "Good-bye" into a dead phone.

15

She looked up and saw Padgett dash by with a cup of coffee in one hand and an open file in the other. Just then a loose sheet in the file peeled itself off in the breeze and wafted to the floor. He stopped and looked back at it in remorse.

"Got it," said Elizabeth, and sprang up to retrieve it for him.

"Thanks," said Padgett. "Too many things at once."

"Are your friends having a nice time out west?"

"Much better than I am," he said. "We've got to get a few investigators out there today before anything has a chance to happen, and I don't know where we're going to get them."

"You mean it might be something?"

"Probably not," he said, "but you never know. You can't take a chance of missing another Apalachin just because somebody's got the damned flu and somebody else is at an airport that's fogged in."

"How about holding the fort with technicians until the cavalry arrives? Locals even? Wiretaps and so on."

"You know what that mess is these days," said Padgett. "And we don't even have probable cause. Just four men we can't even prove know each other taking winter vacations within a couple hundred miles of each other. Want to go in front of a judge with that one? I don't, and I've been there."

"Well, good luck with it," said Elizabeth, not knowing what else to say. The telephone on her desk rang, and she answered it with relief. "Justice, Elizabeth Waring."

"Hart here," came the voice.

"Good," said Elizabeth. "What can you tell me?"

"It's pretty much what I figured," he said. "It's the fertilizer all right."

"You mean manure blows up?" she asked, a little louder than she had intended. She looked up and noticed that Richardson was watching her with a smirk on his face.

"No," Hart said. "Fertilizer. The kind they make in fac-

16

tories and sell in stores. A couple of the nitrate fertilizers are chemically similar to dynamite. If you know how to detonate them you can use them the same way. They're cheaper and you don't have to have a license to use them. If you run out you can go down to the store and buy all you want."

"That's incredible," said Elizabeth. "Do people know about this?"

"Sure," said Hart. "A lot of construction companies use fertilizer all the time. Been doing it for years."

"Then my case is closed, I guess," said Elizabeth. "The poor man probably just blew himself up by accident. But somebody ought to sue whoever makes that fertilizer. It could happen to anybody."

"No it couldn't," said Hart. "It doesn't blow up by accident. You have to use blasting caps and an electric charge. Theoretically the gasoline in Veasy's pickup truck is more dangerous than the fertilizer. More explosive power and easier to set off."

"So you think it was murder?"

"Or suicide. I haven't seen enough to tell, really, but I don't think it's likely he bought a bag of fertilizer for his garden and it just went off. I suppose if he was carrying blasting caps or shotgun shells or something, and the conditions were right, maybe. But the report says he was just sitting in a parking lot, not jolting along a country road, and something would have to set off whatever served as the detonator."

"So it is murder."

"I don't know. But if this is a case you're interested in I wouldn't write it off yet. I'd at least find out what he was carrying around in the bed of his pickup, and whether he even bought any fertilizer."

"Are you on this case too? What I mean is, is the FBI interested?"

"No. At least I don't think so. If the explosive had turned

17

out to be dynamite we would have been. There you have a federal statute having to do with a traceable substance. But as it is, unless it somehow ties in with another case, I doubt there'll be anyone on it. Local jurisdiction, no reason for the FBI to take an interest."

4 "Gentlemen, we're running this country like a goddamned poker game. The average man sees that he has nothing and somebody else has everything. He doesn't make trouble because he's optimistic enough to think that after the next hand he'll have everything. Watch out for the day when he figures out that the chips aren't changing hands the way they used to. And when he finds out that it's because the fellow with the chips is playing by different rules, we'd better be ready with our bags packed. You talk about a tax revolt, hell, there'll be a real revolt. See you next session, if there is one."

"It's the only game in town, Senator," said the senator from Illinois, putting his arm on the old man's shoulder and walking with him out of the committee hearing room. "Don't worry. We'll get a new tax bill passed next session. You put the fear of God into them."

They were walking down the quiet private hallway that led back under the street to the Senate office building. No one was now within earshot. The old man continued, "Hell, Billy. You're young yet. Boy senator from Illinois. But I may not even be alive next session. I'm seventy years old, you know. Six terms in the Senate. I'm not going to have a seventh, one way or the other, and when I go the chairmanship goes to—"

"I know, to Fairleigh. You watch seniority pretty closely if you don't have any yourself. But don't worry, Senator. Your tax bill is in the bag. Our esteemed colleagues aren't even dragging their feet anymore. Too much mail from home."

"I hope you're right, Billy," said the old man. "But I'd have felt a lot better about it if we could have gotten it all out on the floor this session. You know, I got a letter today from a woman who makes fifteen thousand dollars a year after twenty years working as a secretary. Her husband makes twenty-five thousand, so the first dollar she makes is taxed at forty-three percent. No tax shelters for them. By the time you figure state taxes, social security, and sales taxes that woman is losing over half her income. Maybe eight thousand dollars. Of the fifty richest people in my state, not one of them pays eight thousand a year in taxes. A lot of them don't pay anything and never have. And the recent tax bills gave the rich the biggest subsidy yet. We've got to make some changes."

"I know, Senator," said the younger man, patting him on the shoulder. "I've been with you on this since I got here. It's what got me elected. I said I'd try to work with you on income tax reforms that would help the average citizen, do whatever you wanted. They didn't vote for me, they voted for you."

"That's bullshit. You got here because you were the best governor they'd had in twenty-five years. And you'll get re-elected because you're the best senator for the last thirty. If something happens to me before we get this bill passed I'm counting on you to ramrod it. Remind a few people of what they promised us. You know who I mean."

"Well, here's my office," said the senator from Illinois. "Don't worry. We'll both be here to remind them, and we probably won't have to. Most of them will get an earful while they're home for the break. I leave myself in two hours. First speaking date is tonight."

"Oh, to be young again," said the old man. "See you in a few weeks, Billy." The younger man watched the older senator walk down the hallway toward his office. The familiar blue suit was hanging from the old man's stooped shoulders, but the white head was still held erect. The Honorable Mc-Kinley R. Claremont, senior senator from the great state of Colorado. He wasn't fooling anybody with that frail elder-statesman routine. Anybody who was interested could check his schedule and see he had a press conference set for eight fifteen tonight in the Denver airport.

"You're sure about all this?" asked Brayer.

"Of course I'm sure," said Elizabeth. "I'm sure of the facts, that is. I'm not sure about what interpretation to hang on them, because there aren't enough of them. Veasy was carrying two hundred-pound sacks of nitrate fertilizer in his pickup truck. He must have bought them that day according to the Ventura police, because nobody saw them before that. Somebody apparently came along while he was in a union meeting and did something to the fertilizer so it would explode. And the FBI agent said that was perfectly possible for somebody who knew how."

Brayer leaned back in his chair and tapped his pencil absently on the glass desk top. He stared off into space. Finally he turned to her and said, "I'm afraid I don't know what to make of it either, but it's sure not ordinary. Whoever did it was fast on his feet. He'd have to ad lib, if the fertilizer was only bought that day."

"So what do we do now?" asked Elizabeth. "Does it warrant an investigation or not?"

"I'm not sure I know what warrants an investigation these days. We're supposed to be keeping an eye on organized crime, not giving an Academy Award for the most imaginative performance by a murderer. Do you have any reason to believe this fellow Veasy might have had anything to do with the Mafia?"

"He didn't have a record, if that's what you mean, and his name didn't come up when I had Padgett run the Who's Who program on the computer. But who knows? Maybe he borrowed money, maybe he smuggled something for them— Ventura's got a harbor. Maybe anything. It could even have

21

had something to do with the union. We just don't have anything to go on."

"Except the fact that whoever snuffed him was clever about it."

"Right," said Elizabeth. "Clever enough to be a professional?"

"I don't know. Maybe a world-class amateur, maybe a lunatic with beginner's luck. But there's always the chance it's the real thing. Lunatics and beginners usually spend some time planning. They're not up to working with what they find."

"So you're going to dispatch an investigator?"

"I'm not sure yet. I'm not even sure if I have anybody I can send right now. What was that FBI agent's name, again?"

"Hart. Robert E. Hart. Extension 3023. Why?"

"I'll see if I can con his boss into sending him. If he's as good as the Treasury man said and I haven't heard of him, he's young enough and new enough to be eligible for legwork." He picked up the phone, then looked at her expectantly.

"You mean I have to leave?" she asked.

" 'Fraid so. It's hard to lie, cheat, and steal in front of an audience. Close the door on your way out."

5

Just one more before payday, and then a little vacation. Sometimes he wondered how long he would keep it up. At the beginning he'd thought five years was a long time, but now it had been six—no, almost seven, and still going strong. Living in motels and rent-by-the-week cottages could get to be pretty old after a month. It would be nice to be back in Tucson, where he could relax a little and get the old edge back. Eating in fast-food places and spending half your time traveling wasn't so good for your body. It had to catch up with you sooner or later.

Denver wasn't bad this time of year, though. Cold and clear. Later he'd take a walk down Colfax Avenue and see a movie. The plane wouldn't arrive until tonight, and the press conference would make the eleven o'clock news. For the first day or two the old guy'd be surrounded by reporters and home-town minor-league political hacks anyway. After that, when the rosy glow faded, there'd be time to work something out. Just a matter of seeing your best shot and taking it, like pool.

He turned off the television and walked to the dresser. He leaned over his suitcase and peered at the face in the mirror. A little tired from the plane ride is all. No lines, nothing, he thought. It would be ten years yet before it was the kind of face people remembered.

BRAYER OPENED THE door of his office and beckoned to Elizabeth, who was sitting at her desk glancing at a newspaper. She brought it with her into Brayer's office.

"Get down to Disbursement and pick up your travel

23

vouchers," Brayer said. "There's a plane at eight that'll get you to L.A. International by ten o'clock Pacific time, and a hop to Ventura that'll get you in by eleven."

"Me?"

"Do you see anybody else?"

"But I'm an analyst, remember? Good old Elizabeth? I'm no investigator. I haven't been out of this office since—"

"You're going, Elizabeth," he said. "You've got the rating and the qualifications. Just because you haven't done it before doesn't mean you can't do it, or if it comes to that, that I can't order you to. I checked it with Martin Connors. So you're going."

"So the FBI wouldn't do it?" she smiled slyly.

"Yes, they will. But they'll only guarantee to let us use Hart for two days. They can pull him back any time after five o'clock Wednesday afternoon. And they'll only send him if he's there to investigate explosions, not handle the whole case by himself. Now get down there to your friendly local travel agent in Disbursement so they have some chance of getting you both on that eight-o'clock plane."

"I'm on my way," she said, heading for the door. "I hate snow anyway."

"If you come back with a tan anywhere but on your face I'll skin it off you and nail it to the wall," said Brayer. "You're not on a vacation, Waring."

She stopped in the doorway and said, "I thought the usual thing was the Death of a Thousand Cuts?"

"Get going," he said. To himself he thought, Damn. The best I've got. Maybe the best data analyst outside the National Security Agency, off on a wild goose chase. The worst part was that he had needed to convince Connors to arrange it. He tried to remind himself there was no need to worry. The case and the timing could hardly be better for starting her in the field. It was the longest kind of long shot, complete with a trail

24

that was already cold. She'd have little chance to put herself in harm's way before she was ready, getting in on armed surveillance or arrests. With four of the capos suddenly showing up in the West on the same day, it hadn't been hard to convince Connors that it was time to try Elizabeth in the field. The department really did need seasoned field investigators, and if she worked out, who could tell? A female with her brains out in the field—hell, it might make a difference some time. But, he thought, if Connors ever got around to reading the preliminary reports and saw the kind of case he'd sent two people out to investigate, Brayer would have some explaining to do. He consoled himself by planning what he'd say to Grosvenor, when and if he finally bothered to report in from Tulsa.

As ELIZABETH STOOD IN THE ELEVATOR she was glad Brayer had said that about the suntan. California would be warm. It wouldn't do to show up wearing a heavy overcoat and wool skirts. It wasn't a vacation, as he'd said, but there was nothing in the rules that said you had to humiliate yourself in front of strangers, looking as though you'd arrived in California by walking over the North Pole. Besides, the bathing suit she had in mind didn't take up much room.

At the United Airlines desk there were two men. One sat drinking coffee, looking impatient, while the other did all the work. When Elizabeth reached the head of the line and handed the man her travel voucher, he nodded to the other and said, "Miss Waring, Mr. Hart is here waiting for you."

Hart dropped his cup in a basket and stepped around the desk to help her with the suitcase. "Good to meet you," he said, looking at the suitcase instead of at her.

"Same to you," she said. For once she meant it. He was tall and thin with a kind of delicacy about his hands and a rather unruly shock of light brown hair that probably made

25

him look younger than he was. He guided her away from the desk to a line of seats facing the loading gate like a man conducting a lady off a dance floor. This wasn't going to be so terrible after all.

When they were seated she noticed that he had somehow managed to pick a spot that looked as though it was in the middle of things, but wasn't close enough to anyone so they couldn't talk.

He said, "Before I forget, are you carrying a weapon?"

"Yes," she said. "They admitted there wasn't any reason, but regulations say field investigators have to. Are you?"

"Yes," he said. "Same regulation. We'll have to board early so we don't attract too much attention when they wave us through the metal detectors."

"I'm glad you came," said Elizabeth, venturing onto the most dangerous ground first so she wouldn't have it in front of her later. "What made the FBI decide to get involved?"

"Your Mr. Brayer. He asked for cooperation and the Bureau is being very cooperative these days. Ten years of bad press, all the political stuff, massive housecleaning after Hoover died—you can imagine. Brayer offered a fairly straightforward murder case with a chance of something bigger, and all he needed was two days of legwork."

"So the Bureau jumped at it? I hope it's not a waste of your time," said Elizabeth.

"No," said Hart. "The Bureau is re-establishing its usefulness, doing favors. So either way it's no loss to the organization. As for me," he said, and Elizabeth could see he was going to step out on the tightrope, "I've been on assignments that didn't pan out before, and none of them involved flying to Southern California with a pretty lady."

Nicely managed, she thought, if a little clumsy. So he too liked to cover the hard part first. She rewarded him with the best smile she could risk. No sense in setting him up for some

26

kind of embarrassment, but at least let him know we're friends.

The voice in the air said, "United Flight 452 arriving at Gate 23," and Hart looked at his ticket. "That's us," he said.

THEY SAT IN SILENCE and watched the rest of the passengers filing in and getting settled. Then the door slammed with a pneumatic thump and the engines wound themselves up to a high whine and the plane began to taxi out away from the buildings into the night. At the end of the apron it spun around and faced into the wind, the engines screamed, and they shot down the runway into the sky.

Elizabeth said, "You had your job long?"

"Four years, about," said Hart. "You?"

"Only a little over a year. It's interesting, though. What made you decide to work over there?"

"Came back from the service, went to an undistinguished law school where I earned an undistinguished record," he smiled. "Seemed like a good idea at the time. Either that or spend the next twenty years researching precedents and hoping to become a junior partner somewhere. This sounded like more fun."

"Sounds familiar," said Elizabeth.

"You too?"

"With variations. For me it was Business Administration, and the twenty years would have been spent doing market analyses," said Elizabeth, and turned to look out the window. They were above the clouds now, and she wondered how long she could keep looking out there before he remembered that all she could see was the tip of the wing.

MOVIES WERE ALWAYS a good way to spend those early hours of the evening in a strange town. A large crowd, a dark place,

27

and a built-in etiquette that kept people from looking too closely at each other or starting a conversation. By the time the lights came up in the theater and he joined the file of people pouring out onto the sidewalk, he was hungry.

Years ago Eddie Mastrewski had told him always to forget he was using a cover. You should be whatever you pretended to be, all the time except when you were actually working. That way there were only a few hours a year when anything could happen to you. The rest of the time you really were an insurance salesman or a truck driver or a policeman, and you weren't in any more jeopardy than anybody else. If you slipped once your other life would go a long way toward saving your ass. Besides, it gave you something else to think about. Eddie was a butcher.

Of course that had all happened in the days before the trade got so busy. Nobody had that kind of time anymore. You were crazy if you passed up the kind of business you could get. It was easier now too. Everybody was a stranger, and everybody traveled. The only cover you needed was to look like the others and do what they did when they did it. Right now people were eating. He walked down Colfax looking for a restaurant that was crowded enough.

"DON'T BE A JACKASS, Carlson," said the old man. "If I'm in any danger it's not from some guy with a gun, it's from some big corporation afraid of a bill that would take away its tax advantage. Criminals don't give a good goddamn about tax reforms because they don't pay any taxes."

"What I'm saying, Senator, is that things aren't that simple or predictable," said Carlson, a man in his thirties who was so tastefully dressed and well groomed as to appear abnormal. "You're a national figure now. Your picture is on the television every night. The exact composition of your politics isn't what we're talking about. It's the visibility in the media. That

28

alone makes you a target. If your picture happens to be on the screen at the moment some borderline case finally gets his big headache, you're going to need security."

"Fine," Claremont said. "Get me some security, then. Meanwhile get the hell out of my way and let me do my job."

"Right, Senator," said Carlson, opening the door of the limousine for Claremont and climbing in after him, still talking. The black automobile moved away from the curb and into the traffic so quickly that it looked as though the two men had barely caught it in time.

THE PLANE TOUCHED DOWN at Los Angeles International and Elizabeth began to prepare herself for whatever came next. Five hours in the air after a full day of work, and now at least one more hour before she could be alone and take her shoes off. She wondered what she must look like by now, then put it out of her mind. She probably looked like a woman who had just worked a thirteen-hour day, she thought, and there wasn't a whole lot she could do to hide it.

Elizabeth went over the notes she had taken during the long flight. First stop in the morning would be the Ventura police. Hart would handle the postmortem on the remains of the truck and the lab reports and the interview with the technicians. Elizabeth would read through the full report and interview whoever had written it, then follow whatever leads looked promising.

As the no-smoking light flickered and the engine wound down she wrote an additional note on her pad: *bank records*. If Veasy had a business relationship with organized crime there would be something that didn't fit. He would have made some surprising deposits or some surprising withdrawals. Or if not, there would be a discrepancy between the bank accounts and the way he had lived—maybe a sign that he had a source of money that didn't pass through the accounts. She added

29

safe deposit box? to her notes, then put the pad in her purse.

Elizabeth was glad to be able to move again. Airplane seats are small for a woman five feet five. She wondered what it must be like for Hart.

They joined the line of passengers moving past the stewardesses and out the door into the movable corridor that carried them to the terminal. Then they were in an airport lobby. Hart led her down another corridor to a second lobby, where there was a check-in desk for Golden West Airlines. He had a few words with the desk manager and then waited while the man picked up a telephone and turned his back. He hung up and said, "You can board at nine fifty-five at Gate Forty-one, Mr. Hart. Your bags will be transferred automatically, of course."

As Elizabeth and Hart wandered across the lobby, she checked the big wall clock: nine thirty. Not enough time to relax, too much time to wait comfortably in one of those blue plastic chairs. She was glad when Hart said, "How about a drink while we're waiting?"

They sat in a dark corner of the bar with their backs to the wall. The traffic was fairly thin, so the waitress was there for their order immediately. She scurried off to get them their drinks. She was back so fast that they hadn't said anything to each other.

"I've been thinking about this case," said Elizabeth. "It's going to be a little bewildering."

"They always are," said Hart. "This one is going to be more than that. You'll be better off if you think of it as preliminary research instead of a case of its own."

"What do you mean?"

"You're looking for professional touches. If you find any, that's about all you'll find, most likely. There's not much chance we'll make any arrests. If it's a professional there won't be anything to connect him with Veasy, and more likely than not we've never heard of him before. And this time there isn't even a case on record of anyone who works that way, so if it's a pattern this is the first of the series."

"So I shouldn't get my hopes up," said Elizabeth. "I haven't."

"Oh I don't know," said Hart. "Hope doesn't cost anything. But we've got very little this time. In a truck explosion like that there can't be any fingerprints. But there may be something connected with the method or the circumstances that'll be useful later."

"I've got a few ideas to start with," said Elizabeth. "Maybe we'll get lucky."

He nodded and sipped his drink. "Maybe, if we're thorough and careful and don't make any mistakes ourselves. But the best thing to do at the start of it is to forget about looking for anything in particular. Just look and write down everything you see or hear. It may make sense to somebody a year from now."

Elizabeth smiled to herself. He was a man all right—telling her not to get her hopes up, and then suggesting that it would all work out in a way that was too far off for anybody to predict. The endless replay of John Wayne handing the woman a pistol and saying ominously, "Save the last bullet for yourself" before he climbs over the stockade with a knife clenched in his teeth.

Elizabeth picked up her purse. "Nine fifty. Time to go."

He bolted the last inch of his Scotch, tossed some money on the table, and followed her out into the lobby. One more short flight, she thought, and then the chance for some rest.

HE WALKED OUT OF THE RESTAURANT and bought a *Denver Post* from the vending machine at the curb. Time to start doing some research on him. If they didn't publish his schedule, at least they might have a picture of him. You had to start somewhere. He remembered hearing a story about Dave

31

Burton trying to collect on a next-door neighbor once. Probably not true, but you never knew. Things like that could happen if you weren't careful, and the big ones like this were worth taking a little extra time with. For that kind of money, why not? And this was the last one for awhile. Another one of Eddie Mastrewski's proverbs. Always take it slow when you're tired. The police can be dumb as gorillas, make a million mistakes, but at the end of it they still get paid and go home to watch television. You make one and you're dead. If the police don't get you the client will because he'll get scared.

Getting out had to be the simplest part this time. He'd thought of that part right away, as soon as he'd heard the timing. A charter flight to Las Vegas, booked in advance. There was some kind of rule about that. Charter flights had to be advance booking, so the police wouldn't look closely for fugitives there. If you couldn't leave from another town, a charter flight wasn't bad.

ELIZABETH HELD HER EXHAUSTION in abeyance while the little plane flew along the coast toward Ventura. At first she could see the incredible lighted expanse below her, stretching down the long valley to fade into a feeble fluttering like stars. Then the plane moved out across the coastal range and over the water, and there was only darkness and calm on her side of the cabin.

It seemed like only a few minutes before the little airplane began to descend. The Ventura airport wasn't much. They put a short wooden staircase next to the fuselage for people to step on, and there was an eager young man in a gold sportcoat that seemed to belong to an absent older brother to serve as spotter for the deplaning passengers. He smiled and hovered, his hands held out silently announcing his intention to catch any passenger who might begin to fall.

The night was calm and warm, like late spring. The

airport reminded her of a small town bus station, but they managed to find a cab driver lounging out front who knew the Ocean Sands Motel, where Disbursement had made their reservations. She was pleasantly surprised to see the sprawling, vaguely Spanish stucco building half-buried in luxuriant, unfamiliar vegetation. She wondered at first if Disbursement had made a mistake, but then remembered that the economies were always inconsistent: the leather-bound notepads with the cheap, thin paper in the office told it all.

Hart took charge and registered for them. Elizabeth couldn't help wondering if it was just his faintly antiquated courtesy again, or if his experience of hotels was all of the sort where the woman didn't sign her own name. She didn't think about it for long, because as soon as the key to her room was in her hand she was on her way toward the cool, clean sheets. When she was lying there it occurred to her that she probably hadn't bothered to say good-night to him. She didn't think about that for long either.

HE ALWAYS MADE A POINT of staying away from women when he was traveling. It wasn't that any of the ones he was likely to meet would suddenly become suspicious and make inquiries to the police, or anything like that. It was just that it was too damned complicated. You had to make up something to tell them about yourself, maybe even make up a fake address and phone number, agree to be someplace at a particular time. Things like that took most of the fun out of it anyway, and added an element of danger.

So he walked more slowly to keep from catching up with the one ahead of him on the sidewalk. She was definitely trolling for someone—maybe him. He couldn't see her face, but her way of walking—her back arched slightly and her hips rolling a little as she strolled down Colfax Avenue—he had seen a thousand times. Women almost always walked fast when they were alone, especially on this kind of street. When they didn't, it was usually to say, I'm not going anywhere in particular and don't have anything to do: I've got all the time in the world. Another time, he thought as he watched her, his eyes moving irresistibly to the round, firm buttocks. A week from now it would be different.

She turned then and he knew that she was aware of him. She stopped to look in a store window, but he knew she was studying his reflection. He fixed his eyes in front of him and walked purposefully ahead at the same pace. As he passed her she began to walk again. If anyone else had seen it, it must have looked like an accident. A pretty lady window shopping, a man on his way to the parking ramp down the street to pick up his car. He heard her say, "If you like it, maybe you should try it." The voice was soft and confident at the same time, perfectly modulated to establish a kind of intimacy that said I know everything you feel and desire: I know you. He felt a wave of resentment well and pass over him at the violation, the casual assumption of knowledge like an assertion of possession.

He slowed and said, "Excuse me?" feigning a look of surprise.

She smiled the satisfied-cat smile they always had, with the lips closed and the amused eyes. Then she said, "If you're lonely, I'm not doing anything."

In one part of his mind he was thinking she was extremely tempting—huge, bright blue eyes that seemed to peep out from behind a veil of heavy brown hair. In another part all the danger signals were reminding him that this was neither the time nor the place. To have anything to do with her now would put him in jeopardy: she was risking his life and he was angry about it. So he said, "Oh, I'm sorry, Miss. I'm a married man." He did his best to look flustered, to make her think she'd been wrong this time, to convince her that this time she'd

34

picked a man who hadn't even seen her. And then he quickened his pace, behaving like a frightened businessman who wanted nothing more at the moment than to escape the place where he'd been embarrassed, but after thinking it over and smoothing out the rough edges, wouldn't be able to resist telling his wife and one or two close friends about it because he thought it magnified him: a real prostitute came up to me on the street and . . . well, she offered herself to me. I couldn't believe it.

He turned off on a side street and kept going, moving along in his preoccupied businessman's stride. Then he turned again onto a narrow street that ran parallel with Colfax—almost an alley, really. It was darker, and on one side were the backs of stores and taverns and restaurants, nestled together and indistinguishable from one another with their steel fire doors and loading docks and navy-blue dumpsters piled with cardboard boxes.

The girl had put him into a bad mood, reminded him of how impatient he was for this trip to end so he could go back to Tucson and relax. It wasn't easy to live for days at a time without so much as talking to anybody, and for weeks without saying more than "What's the soup of the day?"

He glanced at his watch. A little after ten. Time to head for the motel and read the paper while he waited for the eleven-o'clock news. Then the watch disappeared in a flash of pain, and he was aware that he had heard the sound of whatever had crashed into his skull even while he felt it. But he was on the ground now and his left kneecap seemed to hurt too. Dimly he could see a rock the size of two fists beside him as he rolled in the gravel. He didn't have time to decide whether that was what hit him. He just scooped it in and had his arm cocked when he saw a human figure bending toward him for the next blow. With all of his strength he hurled it into the darkness where the face must be, pushing off the ground with

35

his right foot at the same time. There was a sickening thump as it hit, and a high, tentative half-scream that never got all the way out before the shape crumpled.

He was up and moving now, whirling around because the other one would be behind him. This time he wasn't quite fast enough. A blow across his back with something long like a club electrified him with pain and terror, and he wasn't sure he could move himself. But then something hit him in the face and he was on the ground again and the other one was winding up for a kick. He grabbed the stable leg with one hand, pulling the man off balance, and punched up into the groin with the other—a quick, hard jab. This time there was no cry of pain, only the sound of the air leaving the man's lungs. Then the man lay on the ground doubled up like a foetus, rocking and grunting.

He stood up and looked for the others, but no, there had only been two. Muggers, he thought. Jesus! He looked down at them. The first one was probably dead. He wondered what he should do about the other. He didn't have anything with him—not even a knife. He couldn't leave them this way. They had almost certainly gotten a good look before they'd done anything. He walked over to the first one, picked up the bloody rock that lay by his head, and brought it down once, hard. Then he did the same to the other one. He dragged them by the ankles into the shadows behind the dumpster and moved away down the alley, limping from the pain in his left knee. His back was throbbing and he could feel a thin trickle of blood warming his right cheek, but he couldn't tell if it was his head or his face. The face worried him. Muggers. Jesus.

THE SENATOR SAT BACK in his chair and watched a commercial for new cars. There wasn't really anything in it about cars, but there was a small Japanese car there, and a lot of enthusiastic Americans cavorting around it, showing surprise and pleasure and amazement to a spirited musical score.

Then the news came on. Carlson went over and turned the volume up a little. Not enough so the Senator would have to take notice of the fact that Carlson knew he was old and probably didn't hear as well as he used to. Just enough to make explicit the view they shared, that commercials were a kind of atmospheric interference but the speech at the airport was the very essence of importance.

A newsman was saying, "Congress ended its regular session today and began its mid-session break. We'll have footage of Senator McKinley Claremont's return to Denver. There was a brief flareup of fighting in the Middle East, an earthquake shook Central America, and New England is wracked in the worst snowstorm in twenty years. More about these and other stories in a moment."

The Japanese car commercial came on again. "It's the same commercial exactly," said the Senator, peering at the screen in amazement as the enthusiastic Americans mugged and pantomimed their way through the song again. "Carlson! When did they start doing that?"

"Doing what, Senator?"

"Playing the same damned commercial twice in a row?"

"Are they? I didn't notice," said Carlson.

6 He moved as quickly as he could. There'd be plenty of time to baby the bumps and bruises later when there wasn't anybody to watch him do it, but now the important thing was to get back to the motel room and out of sight before anybody found the bodies. He made a quick inventory as he walked—there was a tear in the left knee of his pants, and the whole suit was dusty. With effort he brushed himself off. There was definitely blood on his face, but that was easily taken care of. He pulled out his handkerchief and brought it to his right cheek, but had to stifle a yelp at the pain.

"Damn," he muttered, wishing vaguely that there was something more he could do to them. There was no question it would show: by morning there would be a bruise, and the swelling had already started. He just hoped there wouldn't be a scar. Maybe all the blood was coming from beyond the hairline. "Damn!" he said again, under his breath. "Stupid. Rocks and clubs, like animals. Baboons!"

Down the alley he could see the pool of light of the motel parking lot. He stopped to listen for a car coming his way, but there was nothing. He was surprised to see that he still had his newspaper. He didn't remember picking it up. But a wave of relief washed over him. He opened the paper as though he had been reading it since he parked his car down the alley. Then he took a deep breath and came around the corner of the motel, heading for the back stairway. He heard a door somewhere in the other wing slamming but he kept on going, trying hard not to limp. His ears picked up the sound of keys jangling and muffled voices, but he kept on going, gritting his teeth against the pain. Up the stairs he climbed, using the handrail to keep the weight off the leg. He swung around with the paper under his arm, keeping his left side to the light as long as he could, then pressing his face so close to the wall it almost touched while he unlocked the door.

He was inside, and breathing hard. He carefully stripped off his clothes, leaving them in a pile on the floor, then walked into the bathroom. The mirrored wall told him what he had feared. He stared at it, and what stared back at him was a thin, nondescript man in his early thirties who looked as if he'd walked away from an airplane crash. The right side of his face was already beginning to blacken and swell, and a thin trickle of blood was beginning to snake down from his temple. He watched it saturate the sideburn and then quickly curve down the cheek to the chin. As he leaned closer to search the face, the drop reached the point of his chin and fell, making a bright blotch in the sink. He carefully washed his face, then ran the water in the bathtub.

He sat on the edge of the tub and stared at his knee while he waited. A scrape, a cut with a little dirt in it maybe. He flexed the leg, studying the pain as though he were finetuning it. No cracks or chips, he thought. Just a scratch is all. But the face—he wasn't ready to think about that yet. He padded out into the other room and turned on the television. The news was just coming on. He caught sight of himself in the other mirror, sitting naked on the bed. A small, whitish animal with a few tufts of hair. And hurt, too. As he watched, the injured face in the mirror contracted a little, seemed to clench and compress itself into a mask of despair. A sigh like a strangled squeak escaped from its throat. He said aloud to the face, "You sorry little bastard." And then the moment was gone. The people on the television screen seemed to be dancing around, celebrating something having to do with a little car parked behind them. He wished them all dead.

Then the newsman came on. He padded back into the bathroom to check the water. It was beginning to get deep

39

enough now, so he turned the tap off and tested the temperature. Too hot: time enough to watch the news.

When he got back to the bed, Claremont and his aide were descending the ladder of the plane. It was pretty much what he'd pictured—a white-haired, stiff-necked old coot in a three-piece banker's suit of the sort you could hardly buy in a store anymore, followed closely by a neat, short-haired, milk-complexioned young man who appeared to be the prototype of a new doll.

He studied their moves as they approached the terminal. The Senator looked old and frail and a little tired. Then there was a different scene, at a podium bristling with microphones. He was saying, "We're going to fight it through this time to the end. We've got key people from both parties working very hard in Washington and in their home districts."

Claremont looked old and vulnerable all right. Too old to run or fight, probably too old to even make much noise. He had that sharp-eyed hawkface look that old people got sometimes, and his temples were marbled with blue veins. The picture changed and the newsman was talking about something having to do with some dark, intense little men in olive-drab fatigues. He switched off the television, went into the bathroom, and slowly settled himself into the hot tub. He studied the knee again, watching the tiny pink cloud swirl away from the cut like liquid smoke. Then he settled back, relaxing every muscle in his body. In a minute he would submerge his head and try to clean those wounds too. That would hurt but it had to be done. No sense getting an infection.

He tried to think the situation through. He couldn't travel with a face like that. People remembered things like black eyes and bruised faces. And in the morning they'd find the two bodies, and start looking for somebody who'd been in a fight. The first place they'd look would be in the hotels and motels around here, starting with the cheapest first. It would look like a gang fight, but not enough like one to keep them

40

from checking out transients right away while they could still put their hands on them. He'd paid in cash for the room, three days in advance, like always. And then there was the charter flight for Las Vegas—paid in advance too. But that didn't leave until Thursday night. Too soon for the face to get back to normal, and too long to wait while the police looked for a man who'd been in a fight. So it had to be tonight. There was no other way. He had to be somewhere else before they knew what they were looking for. And then his mind stopped dead. There was still the Senator. How could he do the Senator and get out of Denver in one night with a face like that? He thought again about the two men in the alley. If only they hadn't picked him out, or picked that alley, or had thought of it another night. But there wasn't much he could do about it now. He started again from the beginning. How can I travel with a face like this?

MCKINLEY CLAREMONT SIPPED the last of his bourbon and watched the film of the Arab gun crew expertly loading and firing at a distant hillside. He wondered if it was stock footage, or if they were really getting that organized. In '67 he'd been to Egypt on a fact-finding tour and it hadn't been like that. After a couple of rounds, the ammunition they had with them had turned out to be the wrong size, so the crew he was with just sat down and started eating and drinking. Two hours later a captain told him they were waiting for the supply lines to get untangled, or for further orders, whichever happened first. Meanwhile they sat in the sun behind their useless cannon, waiting.

Carlson interrupted his thoughts. "I'd say it came off very well, wouldn't you, Senator?"

"All right, I guess," said the Senator. "On television they don't get the chance to spell your name wrong, anyway."

"Big day tomorrow," said Carlson tactfully.

41

"Right," said the old man. He set down his glass and raised himself slowly from his chair. "Call me at eight and while we're having breakfast we'll try to figure out what's got to be done. That is, if we've got time for breakfast?"

"Yes sir," said Carlson. "First appointment isn't until ten."

"Fine, see you in the morning then."

"Good night, Senator," said Carlson, already halfway out the door. "My room is right next door if you need anything. Four oh eight." The door shut.

Claremont shuffled over to the closet and brought out his pajamas. He tossed them on the bed and then took off his suit, carefully hanging it up so it wouldn't get wrinkled. If he didn't hate the idea of losing his privacy, he'd get a valet, he thought. Living out of a suitcase half of each year was bad enough. Then you had to decide whether to spend your time worrying about wrinkles or give up the few minutes of solitude you ever had.

He eased himself into the strange bed and tried out a couple of positions for comfort. Politics wasn't so bad for the young fellows, he thought. Trouble was, by the time you knew anything and had enough seniority to make anybody listen to it, you were too old. He peered through the darkness at his teeth soaking in the glass on the nightstand. Those things were older than some of the men in the House of Representatives. He chuckled to himself. Still plenty of bite to them, though.

HE FELT THE WATER around him loosening the taut muscles and soaking some of the hurt out of him. He began to feel stronger. Now and then he would take a deep breath and lean back with his chin tucked into his chest to submerge his whole head. Then he would wait until his breath came back and do it again for as long as he could. Finally he sat up, took the soap between his hands, worked it into a lather, then rubbed soap

42

over his head and face. It was as though dozens of hornets were stinging his scalp, his cheek, his temple. He gasped to fill his lungs again and ducked under. Slowly the pain went away.

He waited a few seconds, then climbed out of the tub and began toweling himself off, gingerly. When he came to his knee he dried around it. No telling what germs there were on a hotel towel, and no sense leaving blood stains. He looked in the mirror again. This time the face didn't seem quite so bad, with the hair combed and no clot of blood on it. It was the cheek and the eye that'd give trouble, but with the right pair of sun glasses, maybe not so much, at least until tomorrow night.

He knew what he had to do now. There just wasn't any other way. As he dried himself he walked out into the bedroom. He picked up his watch from the dresser and put it on. Eleven thirty-nine. It would be a long night, no matter what. If only this had happened when he was working on something normal. He could call them and ask them to send somebody else, or even farm it out himself to someone he knew—Eddie Mastrewski had done that with him a couple of times. That reminded him of something Eddie had said, and it brought back the nervous anxiety: "Never work when you're hurt, kid. If you don't feel good you won't think straight, either. And if people can see it they'll remember it. I don't mean major surgery either. I wouldn't work with a pimple." Eddie was full of reasons not to work.

He put on clean clothes and carefully combed his wet hair. There was one consolation, he thought. If anybody saw him and he did get away, what they'd remember about him was the bumps and bruises, and they'd be gone in two weeks with any luck.

The whole thing would have to be changed now. He had planned to get a high-powered rifle with a scope, and get him through a window in his hotel. That was the way the crazies whose fantasies didn't include getting their pictures in the

43

newspapers all did it. There wasn't time for that now, and he didn't have a gun, and—no use even thinking about it. He'd just have to live with the situation as it was.

He went to his suitcase and rummaged around for a few seconds, collecting some things. A pocket knife, a ballpoint pen, a clean handkerchief, a pair of sunglasses. He tried on the sunglasses and studied his reflection. It wasn't great, but it was something. He made a mental note to get a pair with bigger lenses, maybe the wraparound kind. Then he sat down to read the newspaper.

There was an article on the front page about the Senator's return. He studied it, but could find nothing that would tell him where the old man was staying tonight. He flipped through the paper until he came to a second article. This one had pictures of the old man and his aide getting out of a limousine in front of a building. Only part of the facade was visible, but it was a hotel, all right. They had said the old man had never lived in Denver. He had started out as a state assemblyman in Pueblo and still owned a place there. He studied the picture for clues. There was a doorman wearing one of those ridiculous comic-opera costumes, but no insignia on it, and nothing on the marble facade of the building except a number. He smiled. That would do it. 1905.

He picked up the telephone book and leafed through it until he came to a page marked *Hospitals–Hotels*. There were dozens, but it didn't take him long. The Constellation Hotel. 1905 19th Street. He went through the rest of the list to see if there was another one with a 1905 number—he had been the victim of enough coincidences for one day—but there wasn't. So that was it. He studied the section carefully, looking for the hotel's ad. There wasn't any. So he turned to *Restaurants*. In a few seconds he'd found what he needed.

He got up and packed his suitcase, then tore his bed up a little. He set the key on the dresser, and looked around one last time to see if he'd left anything before he turned out the lights. He walked down the back stairs and through the alley. The cold made his knee stiffen up a little, but he was walking better now. A few blocks down there was another motel, and a telephone booth at the gas station across the street.

When he came to it, he called a cab company.

"I'd like a cab, please."

"Where are you now?"

He read the sign across the street. "The Wee Hours Motel on Colfax."

"Where do you want to go?"

"The Pirate's Cove Restaurant on Alameda." He'd almost said Alameda and 19th. Never work tired or hurt.

"Right. He'll be there in about five minutes."

They always said five minutes, he thought. Now the suitcase. He couldn't ditch it here. The police might not recognize the rock as the weapon and go around to all the trash cans looking for something else. Never overestimate the police, count on them figuring out the obvious. He decided to hold on to the suitcase for the moment. The worst thing the cabdriver could think was that he was skipping out on a motel bill in the middle of the night.

He saw the cab pull up in front of the motel across the street. The driver was staring at the office window for his fare, so he didn't see the man with the suitcase until he was almost to the car. When he did he reached behind him, swung the back door open, and said, "Pirate's Cove?"

"Yep, that's me."

The cab was fitted with an oversized heater that blew a continuous rush of hot, impure air into the back seat. After the cold outside he figured he could tolerate it for a few minutes. He sat in the driver's blind spot.

The driver said, "Hell of a cold night, ain't it?" as he pulled away from the curb.

"Sure is. Glad you got here so quick."

"Not much business this time of night. Mostly dedicated

45

lushes who've lost their licenses. A few old folks out visiting each other. Now and then a whore or two."

"Must be hard to break even."

"Not too bad, really. When it gets slow we hang around the airport for the late flights. Nobody wants to call Aunt Mary to come pick them up at two A.M."

"I guess not."

They sat in silence for awhile. He could see one advantage to the late shift. Even on Colfax the traffic was light, and the cab was able to glide down the street catching each signal just at the moment when it turned green. He looked at his watch again. Just a little after midnight. He resented the way time was passing. He was going to need as much as he could get. At the Pirate's Cove he reached over the seat and gave the driver a bill. "Ten cover it?" he said, facing downward away from the light.

"Sure," said the driver. "Thanks." He'd tipped generously but not enough to be remembered.

" 'Night," he said and quickly got out, heading toward the glass door of the restaurant. When he heard the cab pull away he bent down to tie his shoe until the car was too far away for the driver to see him. Then he straightened up and moved off down the street toward the Constellation Hotel.

It was seven stories, shaped like a cereal box. He went around the block to approach it from the rear. There was a parking ramp and a broad loading dock. To the left of the dock he could see that one part of the back wall was pierced with ventilators and fans with screens over them and a number of pipes—the kitchen. Just in front of it he noticed a small wooden stockade. He walked up to it, opened the gate, and looked inside. There were two large garbage dumpsters. He opened the first, and the smell of it nearly gagged him. He tried the other, and it seemed to be mostly cardboard boxes flattened to save space. He set the suitcase on top and closed

46

the cover, then made his way to the back entrance of the parking ramp.

There was an elevator, so he entered it and studied the panel of buttons, then pushed *Lobby*, and waited. He hoped it wasn't too empty. The way he looked he couldn't afford much company, but if he were alone it would be worse. When the doors opened he stepped out quickly, keeping his head down and moving across the lobby at a slight angle from the front desk toward the only doorway he could see. There were two young couples, well dressed, lounging in the oasis of furniture in the center of the room. One of the women had her shoes off and was rubbing her toes wearily. The man with her said something about a nightcap and she rolled her eyes in distaste.

He knew exactly what he was looking for, but had no way of knowing if the hypothesis were correct. As he came abreast of the front desk he quickly stared at the mail boxes. Room 406, unquestionably, he thought. He had to try it, anyway. The person most likely to have written messages pile up in his mailbox this late at night in a hotel would be the Senator. He kept on going out the front door to the street, then walked around to the parking ramp again and pushed the elevator button for the fourth floor. This would be the hard part.

When the door opened he was prepared to see a uniformed guard, but the corridor was empty. As he searched for 406, part of his mind was taking note of which rooms seemed to be occupied. He heard voices behind one door, the background music from a television show behind another. There were Do Not Disturb signs hanging from some of the doorknobs. He went past 406 and down the corridor to take a look at the other elevator and the stairway. He had to get out of here afterward.

At the end of the hallway there was a room where the sign said, *Please Make Up the Room*. He wondered—it could just be somebody who'd reversed the sign by accident, meaning to leave the *Do Not Disturb* side out. He stopped and listened. There was no sound. He decided to chance it.

He took out his wallet and selected a credit card, then carefully slipped it into the door latch, easing the door open and waiting for the chain to catch. The door wasn't chained, so he moved inside and stood still, his back to the door, listening. He waited for his eyes to get used to the light, trying to sense whether there was anyone asleep in the bed. He crouched, trying to line up the surface of the bed with the dim glow of the window. When he succeeded he was sure. The silhouette of the bed was flat.

Quickly he walked to the window and out to the balcony. The Senator's balcony would be the fifth one over. He wondered if he could even do it now, tired and hurt and cold. He studied the row of identical, iron-railed balconies. Yes, he thought, that was the way in. They were far enough away from each other so a fat-ass architect would assume no one could make it from one to the other.

He went back into the room and closed the window. He looked around for something long enough to reach. There was a long, low table along one wall. He studied it—no, it was bolted down too securely, and it was too heavy to handle alone. Then he noticed the closet. It was a double closet, huge, for a hotel room. He looked inside and saw the shelf. Perfect, he thought. It was a good ten inches wide and eight or nine feet long. Thank God for good, substantial hotels. And it was screwed in, too. Working rapidly, he used his pocketknife to take out the screws, then brought the shelf out with him to the balcony.

He stopped to take one last look at the layout of the room, memorizing the location, size, and shape of each piece of furniture. Then he slowly and carefully extended the board across the void between his balcony and the next one. It reached, the other end making a light tap on the railing as he set it down. He lifted his right leg up and got his knee on the board, then the other one. He winced with pain. He had forgotten that. It would be a long, hard crawl. The shelf bowed in the middle as he eased his weight onto it, but it seemed safe enough. Four floors below him he could see the little fence with the garbage dumpsters in it, a tiny square in the corner of the parking lot. He thought about falling all that way; lying there in the cold, smashed on the pavement. But then he was at the end of the board. He swung his legs down to the balcony and turned to pull the shelf behind him. One down, four to go.

One after another he took them, not thinking about the rest of it now, not thinking about anything but crossing the cold, empty space that separated him from the fifth balcony. And then he was there. He leaned the shelf against the wall, then thought better of it. There might be some vantage, from some other building, where somebody could see it. He laid it down flat on the balcony, then ran his hand along the edge of the sliding window to feel for the latch. There wasn't one on the outside. Another security feature, he thought. Then he went to the other end of the window and checked that, hopelessly.

He would have to take the chance of leaving a sign. He opened his knife and slipped the blade under the rubber molding a few inches below the level of the inside latch, then slowly brought it up. The glass shifted minutely. He smiled, and kept smiling even though it hurt. It was just as he'd hoped. The latch was secure, but the glass wasn't fitted tightly to the aluminum frame. Using a gentle, steady pressure of his finger tips, he slid the large pane as far as it would go away from the latch, then stuffed his handkerchief into the crack to hold it there. He studied his accomplishment. He had about an eighth of an inch to work with now. Using his knife as a pry, he bent the aluminum frame a little to gain a few more thousandths of an inch. Then he took the knife and pointed the blade up under the latch. The spring was strong, but he managed to lift the hook clear of the catch and slide the window free. He stopped for a moment with the window open a hair, and pressed the molding and frame back into shape. He whisked his handkerchief over the glass and the frame, just in case. They wouldn't put it in the papers, he thought, but they'd send somebody to do it even if they thought he died of old age.

He took out the ballpoint pen he'd brought with him and held it up out of the deep shadows. He took out the clear plastic refill and looked at it. To any other eye it looked like nothing, a refill that only had about a third of its ink left. But the last two thirds were a clear liquid, like water only thicker.

Touching the window with his handkerchief, he quietly slid it aside and slipped into the room, closing it behind him and moving away from the light. He stood there, silent and unmoving, studying the room. Claremont was sound asleep, his slow, regular breathing faintly audible.

Now to find just the right thing, he thought. A bottle of pills, maybe. Or a laxative. Old people make a big deal out of taking a shit. He saw a glass on the coffee table, so he went over and sniffed it—liquor. That wouldn't do now. He could feel the seconds slipping past him, seconds he needed. He moved into the bathroom straining his eyes to find something for his purpose, but no—it was too dark. He thought of just forgetting the whole thing and smothering him with a pillow, but that was too dangerous and chancy. The bed was next to the wall, and all the old bastard would have to do was pound it once or twice in the struggle and that would be that. Old or not, he could make noise. He came out of the bathroom and stared at the sleeping figure. There was nothing—only the bed, the nightstand with the lamp and the glass. The liquor would have been great if he'd managed to get here in time to help with the mixing, he thought, but not now. And then he realized it wasn't the same glass. The liquor glass was on the coffee table.

Slowly and carefully, he drifted over to the bed and

stared at the nightstand. He had to look a little to the side to discern anything much in the darkness. He brought his face close to the glass and then almost laughed out loud. Of course, he thought. False teeth! He slowly reached over and poured the contents of the pen refill into the glass.

Then he drifted back out to the balcony and closed the sliding window behind him. In a few seconds he was already on the third balcony and putting down his portable bridge to the second. He looked down again, this time elated by the height, but he held himself in check. Always work slowly when you're tired, he reminded himself. He channeled his concentration into his work, moving along the shelf and then pulling it after him, setting it on the next shelf and easing himself onto it. And then he was there. He slipped back into the room and closed the window, this time letting it lock. Then he went to the closet and set the shelf back on its supports. For a second he considered just leaving it, but no. Later he'd regret it. He took out his knife and carefully replaced the screws. Then he forced himself to stand quietly for a moment. Did he have everything? Was anything out of place? He reached into his coat pocket and screwed his pen back together. Then he took a few deep breaths, listened, and stepped out into the hallway.

At the elevator he pressed the button for the parking garage. The doors sighed and opened immediately. That was a good sign, he thought. In all that time since he'd come up, nobody had used that elevator. He glanced at his watch. It was only one fifteen. And then he realized he was getting an erection. It struck him as funny, but he didn't dare laugh yet.

When the elevator doors opened again and he felt the cold night air he forgot about it. He moved across the parking ramp and out to the lot. At the fenced-in dumpsters he stopped and retrieved his suitcase, then kept on going. At the first public trash can he came to, he broke his pen in two and threw it in among the crumpled cups and napkins and bottles

51

and cans. He moved again, nursing his injured knee into exactly the right pace for a man disappearing into the night.

THE SENATOR STIRRED, then woke up. The room seemed awfully cold. The Constellation hadn't been the same since they'd remodeled it in 1972, he thought. It was those damned fancy windows and balconies and things. The workmanship just wasn't any good anymore. People didn't take pride in their work. But then he reminded himself that he was an old man, a cranky one at that, and it was probably just his bad circulation. He rolled over and composed himself to go back to sleep. "A goose probably just walked over my grave."

7 When the telephone rang it tore Elizabeth out of sleep, leaving her in an unknown place. After a second or two she remembered it was Ventura and a motel room, but it took four rings for her to see the telephone and one more to get her hand on it. The call was from Hart, who wanted her to be ready for breakfast in twenty minutes.

Elizabeth hung up and went to the nightstand for her watch. Seven o'clock exactly. Then she went off to the bathroom to brush her teeth and see about a shower. As she hurried through the morning rituals she tried to keep herself from becoming too excited. Even if there were a clue, something to go on, it would probably take months to follow it up, and by then the case would be common property. A hundred people in a dozen overlapping agencies would be involved. And there still wasn't any reason to believe she had finally crossed the trail of a genuine professional hit man or that he'd be of any use if they caught him. It was like trying to capture an animal that was so small and rare and elusive that you sometimes doubted that it existed, but if it did exist it would be capable of killing you. No, this was worse, because there wasn't any point in hunting it down unless you could keep it alive and teach it to talk.

WHEN THEY WALKED INTO the foyer of the Ventura police station, a sergeant carrying a mug of coffee was crossing the floor toward a corridor of tiny offices. He veered toward them, giving a reassuring half-smile. "Hi. Are you being taken care of?"

53

"Agent Hart, FBI, and Miss Waring, Justice Department, to see the chief," said Hart, flashing his badge.

"Okay," said the sergeant. "This way, please." He shot a look over his shoulder as he conducted them down the hallway. "Chief know you're coming?" he asked.

"Yes," said Hart.

Elizabeth said nothing, having reminded herself as they were coming up the steps that she'd learn more by listening and watching than by trying to take charge. But the fact that Hart had said FBI and Justice department hadn't been lost on her. Technically the FBI was just one of the divisions of the Department of Justice although that had been very easy to forget the few times she'd been inside the massive J. Edgar Hoover Building with its millions of files and hundreds of millions of fingerprint records and its museum. For the moment, anyway, she would leave Washington protocol for Washington.

The sergeant led them into one of the tiny offices, where an older version of himself sat behind a wooden desk, frowning over some papers as though he were translating them with difficulty from a foreign language. When he saw he had visitors he looked relieved. He turned the papers face down in a far corner of his desk and popped up, his hand held out. "You must be agents Hart and Waring," he said. "I'm Bob Donaldson. Always happy to cooperate with the FBI."

"Thank you," said Elizabeth, forestalling the correction Hart would probably feel was necessary. "As they probably told you on the phone, we're interested in the Veasy murder."

"Well now, ma'am," said the chief. "We're still not absolutely and completely sure it was a murder yet. We're coming around to that hypothesis, but we aren't sure."

"I'm sorry," she said, smiling. "I misspoke, calling it what we're looking for rather than what we're looking at."

He seemed appeased. "I've notified the homicide squad that you'd be here, and told them to be ready with the reports

54

of the investigating officers and so on. Beyond that I thought we'd just wait and see, let you look around and pick out the leads you want to follow."

"I'd like to take a look at the physical evidence, since that's what I do best," said Hart. "Miss Waring would like to study the reports. That way we can do two things at once."

"Good idea," said the chief, as though the idea struck him as revolutionary. "Sergeant Edmunds, take Agent Hart to the lab, will you? Miss Waring, I'll show you the reports." He took her elbow in a gentle but somehow weighty pressure, as though he were guiding a prisoner who wasn't quite dangerous enough to be handcuffed, and led her down the corridor.

There was nobody in the room marked *Homicide* when they got there, but Donaldson sat her at a table and gave her a stack of reports. "I'll be back in a minute," he said.

She heard his voice in the next office. "Where the hell are those guys? I told them these people were coming this morning."

Another male voice said in a bored monotone, "Out on a call. Found a Mexican lemon picker stabbed to death out on Telegraph Road about half an hour ago. Macaulay told me to let you know if you asked."

"Oh," came the chief's voice, now much quieter. Then there was a moment or two of silence. At last the chief said, "Well, when they come back in tell Macaulay I want to see him."

Elizabeth heard him returning from the other office. She looked up at him in the doorway and listened with an expression of interest while he recapitulated the substance of the conversation she'd just overheard. She wondered how he could not know the sound carried between the little cubicles, but apparently he didn't. Then he was gone and she was able to look over the reports in peace.

Until the instant of his death, Veasy hadn't been particularly noteworthy. He had a wife who'd been in his graduating class at Ventura High School, and three children born in the second, fourth, and fifth years of their marriage. They lived in a three-bedroom house in a tract which they'd been paying on for about eight years. Veasy was a machinist, making fairly good money working for Precision Tooling. The investigating officer had made a note at the bottom that his sources—the wife, the shop foreman, two fellow workers, and a neighbor—had not the slightest idea that Veasy had any enemies.

There was no indication that he owed anybody any money except the mortgage on his house. He didn't gamble except for an occasional poker game at the union hall and the beer frames in his weekly bowling league. He had never been arrested or had anything to do with known criminals. Elizabeth was more than disappointed. She was bored. The only thing about the man that made interesting reading was his death.

She turned to the interviews with the witnesses. The whole thing had been completely unexpected. The monthly meeting of Local 602 had adjourned, he had climbed into this truck and was blown up. That was all any of them seemed to know.

After an hour and a half of reading and study, Elizabeth had made only two notes: to interview Richard O'Connell, the union president, about the minutes of the meeting, and to request file checks of Precision Tooling and Local 602. The file checks would have to wait, because it would be lunchtime at Justice now. She went to one of the empty desks and dialed the extension at Precision Tooling that O'Connell had given the homicide man. Yes, O'Connell said, he could see her at ten thirty.

Elizabeth sat for a minute staring at the file. She got out her telephone credit card, deciding to take a chance that Padgett was still busy enough to be working through another lunch hour.

On the other end she heard Padgett's phone snatched up

and his voice say, "Justice Padgett" as though it were a title.

"Roger," she said. "I know you must be busy if you're answering phones at twelve thirty, but I need some background. I need a file check on a company in Ventura, California, called Precision Tooling, and on Machinists' Local 602."

"All right, but what specifically?"

"I'm afraid I'll need the whole thing on both. Any indication that anything isn't aboveboard. History, assets, cast of characters, everything."

"So you don't know what you're looking for." He said it without emotion, as though he wasn't surprised.

"I'm afraid not, Roger," said Elizabeth. "I'm fishing."

"I'll get somebody on it after lunch. Give them a couple of hours and call back."

"Thanks, Roger. I'll do that. You're a love."

"I'm that all right. But Elizabeth?"

"What?"

"Try to keep it within bounds. Fishing can get expensive."

She put her notebook away and went down the hall to Donaldson's office. She found him still pondering the same sheaf of papers. "Chief," she said, "I wonder if I could get a ride in a squad car. Agent Hart has the keys to our rented car, and I don't want to interrupt him."

"A ride? Sure," he said. He lifted his phone and said, "I'm sending Miss Waring to you. Get her a car and driver. Right."

THE FACTORY WAS A SMALL, rectangular aluminum building surrounded by a chain-link fence with an open gate. The place seemed to be all metal. Even the sounds that came from it were metallic, the noise of metal machines cutting and grinding and shaving metal, heating, bending, cooling it.

When she entered the shop, a man working a lathe lifted his safety goggles and walked over to her. "Are you Miss Waring?" he asked. He seemed to be about fifty, balding, and with the massive forearms of a man who worked with his hands.

"Yes. Mr. O'Connell?"

"We can talk out in the yard where it's quiet."

She followed him through the shop—where the whine of machinery was punctuated by an occasional ring of a hammer or the clank of chains—and out into a small asphalt square where there were a picnic table and benches. "Is this where you eat lunch?" she asked.

"That's right," said O'Connell, sitting down. "Now what can I tell you?"

"Mr. Veasy's death was rather unusual, as you know, and so we're working with the Ventura police to find out whatever we can about it. If there's anything at all you think should go into the record, I can guarantee that it will." She watched him for a moment, but he was just waiting for her to continue.

"I'd like to know what went on at the union hall that evening. Do you have the minutes of the meeting? I understand you're president."

"There aren't any minutes of that meeting. We didn't vote on anything, so there wasn't much to write down," said O'Connell.

"Do you remember what was said?"

"We were talking about the investment of the pension fund. How to get the best return for our money, how to keep it safe, you know. The usual things." He looked at her through clear, empty gray eyes.

"Did Mr. Veasy say anything that you remember?"

"Al? Sure," he said, beginning to smile as he remembered. "He was a great talker all right. He was complaining about the quarterly statement from our biggest investment.

58

Said we weren't getting anything back for our money, that we were speculating instead of saving, and that we were gonna lose it."

"Do you agree?"

"No," he said. "Not at all. A union has to do something or inflation will eat up the pension funds before anybody has a chance to use them. You have to put money into things that'll produce profits in the long run, even if nothing much happens the first year or two."

"What investment bothered him?"

"Well," said O'Connell, "we have a lot tied up in an investment corporation called Fieldston Growth Enterprises."

"Mutual funds?" Elizabeth wrote down the name.

"No. Land, mostly. Resorts, golf courses, retirement places. Al didn't like it one bit. Said he'd tried to find out about them and couldn't. There weren't any resorts or anything that they owned, so he panicked. They're new, so they haven't done any of that yet. But I've seen brochures with the designs and layouts, and it'll be big. I'm sorry Al couldn't live to see it."

"What else happened that night? Did he argue with anybody?"

"No, not really. He and I went round a little about the pension fund, but it wasn't personal."

"Did anything else seem to be on his mind? Was he depressed lately or nervous?"

"Al Veasy didn't commit suicide," said O'Connell. "His truck blew up is all. Must have been a leak in the fuel system. Could happen to anybody the way they make 'em now. If I was his wife I'd sue General Motors."

"So it looked to you like just a tragic accident?"

"What else? Murder? What for?"

"I just have to cover all the possibilities, Mr. O'Connell."

Elizabeth thanked him and walked back to the waiting police car. Both doors were open and the officer was leaning

59

against the trunk gazing off down the road through his mirror-lens sunglasses. He was probably nice looking, she thought, but you'd have to get him out of uniform to tell. They always seemed to be covered with bits of metal. "Where to?" he said.

"Twenty-seven twenty-four Grove Avenue."

"Veasy's house?"

"That's right," said Elizabeth. All the stops were routine, she thought—no way to break out of it, nobody new to ask.

The rest of Elizabeth's morning was just as unproductive. What she got from Mrs. Veasy was inarticulate grief. At least the investigating officers had managed to find out a little about the dead man's habits. But they did this kind of thing every day, and were probably pretty good at it—ignoring what people were trying to say—their theories, opinions about people and life and death—and listening for what they had to throw in to make it comprehensible to an outsider—specific information about the victim's habits, behavior, friends, and enemies.

Elizabeth was suddenly tired. She glanced at her watch and saw that it was almost noon. "Let's go back to the station," she said. The policeman drove with a special kind of authority, a tiny bit faster than anyone else on the straight, level highway, so the other cars would move aside to let them cruise by. She looked out on the rows of low suburban houses as they slid past, now and then surprised by a squat date palm or a row of towering eucalyptus trees. If it weren't for the plants this could be Indiana. Or Virginia, anyway. Just about anything seemed to grow here. But not on Grove Avenue. The houses were built so close together there wasn't even room for a decent lawn.

When they reached the station she asked to use the desk sergeant's telephone and called Padgett in Washington. "Hi, Elizabeth," he said. There was something odd about his voice, but she couldn't identify it. Amusement? Spite?

"Hi, Roger," she said. "What have you got for me?"

"Precision Tooling isn't going to help much. They're purer than Caesar's wife. Started in 1936 by a couple of master machinists who hired a few friends, then grew when the war came. Made airplane parts, patterns for drop-forged ship fittings, things like that. Been a minor defense subcontractor ever since."

"Any chance of new stockholders? Unusual loans or anything?"

"Elizabeth, these people have been on our books for thirty-five years. They get a new clearance every time a contract comes up for renewal. If they moved the water cooler we'd know it. They're in perfect health."

"Well, save the file for me anyway. What about the union?"

"Clean too, at least so far. They're part of the file, but we're still checking with the Department of Labor. All we know at the moment is there aren't any shady characters hanging around the factory; that was all Defense was interested in. Labor should know something."

"When they answer ask them for information on the pension plan."

"The what?"

"The union's pension fund. And oh, yes. I'm afraid I've got a new one. Fieldston Growth Enterprises. The union invested in it."

"All right, but keep the fishing to a minimum, okay?"

"Sure, Roger. Whatever you say," said Elizabeth, without conviction. "I'll call you early tomorrow."

"Wait a minute, Elizabeth," said Padgett. "Brayer wants to talk to you." The irony was back in his voice.

Then Brayer's voice said, "Elizabeth, have you heard the news about Senator Claremont?"

"No. What about him?"

"He died in his hotel room in Denver last night. It looks like a stroke or a heart attack, but the autopsy will take a while. There's going to be an investigation, so I'm taking you off what you're working on. I want you in Denver by late afternoon or early evening."

Elizabeth couldn't help herself. She said, "What for? It's crazy! I've been on this case exactly four hours, not to mention the fact that there's nothing for me to do in Denver when I get there."

"No use arguing about it, you're going. It's orders from the Attorney General's office. We've got to send a field agent, and you're the closest one that I can spare today. This thing Roger's working on looks big, and everybody's tied up."

"You trying to tell me the FBI doesn't have a field office in Denver?"

"Damn it, Elizabeth! I'm not going to stand here for the rest of the day justifying my decisions to you. There are reasons, that's all. Now get moving." He hung up, hard.

Elizabeth whispered to herself as she hung up the telephone, "Yes, sir!" When she looked up, Hart was coming down the hall with the chief of police.

"Chief, thank you very much for your cooperation," he said. "We'll be in touch." It was all very cordial, but there was an edge to his voice as though he were trying not to sound angry.

As they walked down the steps to their rented car he said, "Was that your call from home?"

"Yes," she said. "Did you get one too?"

"Of course. A little while ago." The anger was definite now.

"I don't understand it."

"I do," he said. "Politics. Pure politics. They have to reassure the senators who vote on budgets that we take it seriously when one of them dies. Even if it's a heart attack."

"But I'm not even a field investigator. I'm a data analyst."

"Who cares? There's not going to be anything to investigate. We're just there for the roll call."

62

"That still doesn't explain why they pulled us off an actual fresh murder when there must be thirty or forty teams closer to Denver who are better qualified than I am at least—"

"How do you know this was a murder?" he asked.

"Well it is, isn't it?" she said. "Nothing else makes any sense at all. I was at Veasy's house this morning. They have a yard you could cover with a bedspread, and he was supposed to be carrying big sacks of fertilizer around in his pickup truck. What for? And the other thing is that you're really angry and I don't think you would be unless you thought it was a murder too, so we can at least agree on that even if nobody else does. If you didn't think the case was important—that is, a murder—you wouldn't care if they took us off it."

As she spoke, the words came faster and faster until Hart could hardly follow her. He took his eyes off the road for a second and saw Elizabeth was staring straight ahead with her brows knitted a little, which meant she had settled that part of it and was already launched into the next stage, whatever that might be, so before she got too far he'd better tell her. "Do you want to know what I found this morning in the union hall parking lot?"

She turned to him again and smiled. "Of course, Bob." He wasn't sure if she was humoring him or not, but he went on.

"A few bits of wire and a fragment of the jacket of a blasting cap. Both charred. So I guess we know that much, anyway."

"Yes," said Elizabeth. "That much is for certain. Now if only we didn't have to go on a side trip to Colorado. I wonder what it's like there this time of year."

"Cold, clear. Now and then some snow."

"Terrific," she said. "And all just so the Senate staff can look at a report in two months and see that two people from Washington were there."

"Oh, I'm afraid it's worse than that, Elizabeth. They

63

won't have to wait more than a day. There'll be reporters, photographers, probably national television. Senator Claremont was a very important man. That's the real reason why they sent us, I think. After tomorrow's newspapers whoever's there won't be of much use in undercover stuff, and we're home office."

"Oh, God," she said, and slumped back in the seat. She thought, wonderful. Elizabeth Waring on national news in her thin California clothes investigating a death by old age. On national television. While somewhere in Southern California there would be two clerks, both of them busy forgetting what the man looked like that bought the hundred-pound bags of fertilizer and the blasting caps last Friday around supper time. Probably they'd be watching television. And what they'd see was . . . Elizabeth Waring. In Denver, Colorado, there, by her official presence alone to reassure ninety-nine men over sixty that there was no such thing as a death by old age.

8 By now most of it had probably happened, he thought. Just after daylight somebody would have gone through the alley and seen the two of them lying there. Around 7:30 or so whoever owned the car would have come out expecting to drive it to work. And the Senator—hard to say what time a senator would get up in the morning, but it would be before now. There was no question he was already dead.

It had been a long, cold night, he thought. It wasn't so bad now—almost a different world. But he was tired, and some of the aches and pains were beginning to feel as if they might be more than that. He went over it in his mind again. He had waited to get a couple of miles away before he'd even looked for a car to hotwire. He'd found a two-year-old Pontiac parked on the street and taken it north on Route 87 to Cheyenne, Wyoming. Cheyenne had been the only choice, really, and that worried him a little—only two hours of driving time from Denver. But he'd have a long lead before anybody noticed it, where he'd left it. He was proud of that one, and it cancelled out the fact that Cheyenne was too obvious. It takes someone a day or so to decide that a car in a parking lot attached to a housing complex not only doesn't belong to him, it doesn't belong to anyone else either. Then it takes a day for somebody to get up the nerve to complain about it. The walk to the airport had taken some more time, but at least it had been too dark for anyone to see him.

HE HAD MANAGED to get on the 7:00 A.M. flight from Cheyenne to Salt Lake City, and now he was on the noon plane to

Las Vegas. He'd phoned in a reservation to Caesar's Palace from Brigham Young Airport. The warm, clean air of the plane was a foretaste of what would be waiting for him in Las Vegas. And then, he told himself, it would all be over. No more fear, no more cold, and a chance to rest and take care of his wounds. This had been the worst trip he'd ever made. A nightmare. But at least the worry was over now—that had been the worst—the hot, physical fear, and the other part that knew you were going too fast, probably making mistakes because you were scared. That was all over now. Right now there were probably policemen searching for one or two young men who looked as though they'd been in a fight, but if they were, they were looking in the poorer sections of Denver, Colorado. They might be looking for a stolen Pontiac Grand Prix, brown, with a white vinyl top. If they were, they probably weren't looking for it in an apartment complex in Cheyenne, Wyoming. None of these things had anything to do with the man who would be checking into Caesar's Palace this afternoon, limping a little, and wearing dark glasses that hid a few bruises and a cut or two. A man who had suffered for taking a chance on a ski slope that was beyond his capacity wouldn't raise much comment in Las Vegas. The inexhaustible supply of people of that sort was what paid the rent.

THE ENGINES CUT BACK and the blunt nose of the giant airplane seemed to run head on into a more solid medium, slowing and falling at once. Hart looked over at Elizabeth, who was peering out the window over the craggy formations of the Rockies, her forehead pressed against the glass. There was something special, almost intoxicating, about being close to a beautiful woman. There was a space around her, a few inches, that belonged to her and seemed to be permeated with her smell and sound. And something else, like an electrical charge, that seemed to tug you closer to her, but set off a

66

warning signal that reminded you not to let yourself drift any closer, because in a moment you would touch, brush a sleeve or a shoulder against a soft arm, and then it would be too late. You could never relax inside the charged zone that belonged to a beautiful woman unless there was some kind of prior understanding between you that made it all right to touch because you had touched before. He wondered if Elizabeth was aware of the tension too, sitting there thinking about it and wishing the plane would land so she wouldn't be forced to think about it anymore, wouldn't be held in enforced immobility while each of them hovered in suspension at the border of the other's personal space.

Beautiful women like this one were a special problem. The big, almond-shaped green eyes, the tiny waist, the impossibly thin wrists and long, graceful fingers made her seem as though she belonged to a superior species, smaller and more delicate than ordinary mortals and yet quicker. The impression might have been of an insubstantial creature, but it wasn't that at all—what he felt was astonishment, almost as he might for a small antelope or an ocelot, an animal, a miraculous thing unconscious of what it was. He sensed in himself an overwhelming desire to touch, to verify that she was real and had the feel, the surface, and weight that his eyes told him she had.

She turned her face to him. "I hope we can get through this quickly and get back to work."

Hart said, "Do you think the case is the real thing? I mean, we know it was no accident, but we also know Veasy probably didn't buy the fertilizer himself. It seems to me the theory that it was a pro hinges on his being able to work with whatever he found."

Elizabeth frowned. "Yes, there is that. But we don't really know what we're looking for, so anything we find out is to the good. The fact that it took a day for the local police to come up with the theory that it was dynamite, and another day to figure out that it wasn't, and then it took another day for us to prove that the explosion was planned seems to me to show that whoever it was knew what he was doing."

"But that doesn't make it much more likely that this is a case of the sort that your section would be interested in, does it?"

"No, but I've got a couple of other things I'm checking on. The method isn't what's worrying me right now. I'm satisfied that he's good enough at what he does. What's missing is a reason for anybody to hire him to do it. And I still think he was hired. There's nothing about Veasy to give me an excuse to believe it, but I do. People who just get mad at each other use guns or knives."

The airplane whistled down to meet the runway, then thumped to a stop before taxiing to the terminal. Elizabeth and Hart sat still while other passengers filed out, then slipped into the queue when there was an opening. As soon as they were in the carpeted tube that stretched from the airplane to the terminal Elizabeth spotted the man. He wasn't obtrusive enough to come to the attention of the other passengers. He could have been an airline employee, but he wasn't. He stood there beside a wall ignoring everyone who went by him, looking straight at Elizabeth. She said to Hart, "We're being met."

"What?"

She leaned into him so her face was close to his ear and said, "They've sent someone to meet us."

Hart said, "I see him. It's good. Maybe we'll get this over fast."

They walked up to him and he said, "Mr. Hart? Miss Waring? Come with me, please." They followed him, and Elizabeth was surprised to see him open a side door at the end of the tube. Then they were in a small room with an entrance on the other side.

"Right on time," said the man. "I'm Pete Turnbull, FBI Denver." He held out his hand for each of them to shake. Elizabeth studied him and decided he couldn't have been more than twenty-five, but was trying by means of his neat, banker's blue suit and the serious, competent look on his face to cross the line into the thirties. It made him look precocious, like an overeager junior executive.

"Good to meet you," said Hart. "What now?"

"I'll take you to the office, where they'll fill you in on the case. Give me your baggage tags and I'll arrange to have your suitcases catch up with you there."

They handed him the tags, and he disappeared through the other door for a second, then reappeared, smiling. "There's a car waiting," he said, and they followed him out the door and down a corridor to the main lobby.

At the big swinging doors Elizabeth felt a gust of cold wind, so she wrapped her light-weight coat around herself tightly and plunged after Turnbull into the open air. In a second they had passed through it into the waiting car, which was parked in a loading zone with its motor running. Turnbull took the wheel and maneuvered them expertly into the circular drive and away.

"What can you tell us about it?" asked Elizabeth.

"The Senator?" said Turnbull. "Not much, really. You'll get the full rundown. I'm not on it. What I know is he died this morning, early, and was found by his legislative assistant a short time later. That much is in the papers. The rest of it, if there is any more, they're keeping quiet for now."

Elizabeth looked at Hart, who seemed to be deeper in thought than the case would warrant. Then he said, in a voice that was too casual for the expression on his face, "Do you know if they've ordered an autopsy?"

"I haven't heard. I suppose they have, though. I know about five agents were put on this case today, and they're on overtime as of two hours ago, so they'd probably at least do that much."

Hart's expression didn't change. He sat back in the seat and said nothing.

The federal office building was a relic of the era when politicians liked to remind themselves and their constituents that this was, after all, the U.S. government. The building was huge, with lots of Corinthian columns that weren't there to support anything except the public's awe and reverence.

Elizabeth and Hart entered through the broad portal, expecting to see the place had been empty since five o'clock. It was true that the dozens of smoked-glass doors off the foyer seemed to be locked up for the night, but there were still people coming and going, and off to the left there were five men who were unmistakably reporters sitting on one of the massive oak benches.

At the far wall was a directory of offices. The FBI was on the second floor, so they walked up the marble staircase. Elizabeth identified what had been nagging at her since she'd seen the place. It was like the buildings in Washington, with everything on a scale larger than people. The railing was too thick for a human hand to grasp, the doorways were at least ten feet high, the benches in the foyer made the reporters look like lost children. It was as though someone had taken great pains to make it clear that this was an outpost of Washington, and by no means a minor one. When they reached the second floor there was no question where they should go next. The cavernous hallway was dark and empty except for a single lighted office at the end.

Inside the office there was a single desk where a receptionist sat during the day. Agent Turnbull ushered them through the outer office and opened the door to a small room with a long conference table, where three men in shirtsleeves were talking across open file folders. Behind her Hart said, "Hello, we're Waring and Hart." Elizabeth decided it sounded like a company that sold expensive clothes to British gentlemen.

The men stood up and shook hands while the one at the end of the table said, "This is Bill Greenley. And Joe Mistretta. I'm Mike Lang. Have a seat, and we'll get you caught up. It won't take much time, because we don't know a whole lot yet. I think Bill can do it quickest."

Greenley was a man in his middle thirties who sounded to Elizabeth to have spent some time testifying in courtrooms. He had seemed a little uncomfortable during the obligatory amenities, and now he launched into his recitation as though it had been prepared and rehearsed in advance. "We've placed the time of death between 0630 and 0800 today. There was no one with the deceased at the time, but the Senator's legislative assistant, Mr. Carlson, came to meet him for breakfast at 0800 and found him dead. The preliminary report from the autopsy says the body temperature was eighty-six degrees at 1000 today, which would mean no more than four hours. Claremont was partially dressed at the time of death." He added parenthetically, "As though he were getting ready to go to breakfast. The preliminary report contained the observation that the cause of death was heart failure. Not damaged. Just stopped." Greenley set aside the sheet of paper he'd been looking at and took up another.

"The secondary report indicates that the Senator's blood contained traces of an unidentified toxic substance, which was probably introduced orally." Greenley paused to look at Elizabeth and Hart as though he wanted to let his statement blossom in their minds before he pushed on to the next level. "The toxic substance has been determined to be the probable cause of death."

"Does it have any competition?" asked Hart.

"No," said Greenley. "No lumps, bruises, cuts, or signs of a struggle. Heart and circulation okay for his age, according to the coroner."

"Have you got a lab analysis of the substances found in the room yet?"

"They're still working on it," said Lang. "But if you mean a simple overdose, I think not. Here's the list of the stuff

71

they found. The only medicine was aspirin." He handed a sheet from another file to Elizabeth, who held it so that Hart could read it too: "Rolaids, one roll, unopened. Listerine mouthwash, four-ounce size. Polident, one box, seventeen. Aspirin, Ascriptin brand, one-hundred-tablet size. Empty glass, probably from alcoholic beverage. Glass for soaking false teeth. Deodorant, Mennen stick."

For the first time, Elizabeth spoke. "Who's actually in charge of the case? The Denver police?"

"Right," said Lang. "They knew we'd be interested, and so they called us in at the start. But at least for the moment it's theirs."

"What are the ground rules?" asked Hart.

"As close to full cooperation as we can make it. Right now all we're doing is laboratory work, and they're doing the rest of it. We've agreed to share all information both ways. If somebody finds something that points away from Denver we take over that part of it."

"What if it turns out to be murder?" said Elizabeth.

"The unidentified toxic substance is making that look like a possibility," said Lang. "I don't like it, but there's no use hiding from it, and that's why we asked for reinforcements this morning." Elizabeth and Hart exchanged glances, but Lang continued. "If that's what it is, we take full responsibility. Assassinating a senator is a federal crime."

Elizabeth sat quietly and felt a wave of weariness come over her. Ventura seemed to be far behind her now, receding into some impassable distance composed of complications rather than mere time and space. For a while the Ventura case had begun to look hopeful, she thought. No, not hopeful, really, but so peculiar that there had to be something to it. She promised herself she wasn't going to forget about it. But now there was this. It would have to be gotten through somehow before she could start learning about her own killer. She was surprised to find herself thinking of him in those terms, but

72

now that she had, she accepted it. That was what he was—her own. Her first.

"So WHAT WOULD YOU like us to do while we're waiting for the lab work?" asked Hart.

"That's one of the things we were trying to decide when you arrived. We've asked for everything Washington could send us on the Senator—friends, enemies, habits, even old news stories. It'll take time for them to dig it out, though, and it probably won't give us anything we didn't get from Claremont's assistant hours ago. The best we can do at the moment is probably to put together as much of the background as we can, and figure out what to do if that toxic substance turns out to be arsenic, say, or cyanide. It might be best if you just went to your hotel and got some rest. No use all of us sitting here."

"Or maybe to the Senator's hotel," said Hart. "I suppose it's still being held pretty close by the local police. Would we step on their toes if we went over to take a look?"

"No," said Lang. "That's part of the deal. Joe, can you take them over? I'll call you if the lab work comes in."

Hart and Mistretta waited at the doorway for Elizabeth to go first, but then Mistretta edged out in front, striding down the hallway and struggling into his coat. They followed him down the stairs and along an unfamiliar back corridor that opened on a parking lot with only about a dozen cars scattered at varying distances from the building, looking forlorn and stranded. A light snow had begun to fall.

As Mistretta turned out of the lot and drove down the side street toward the Constellation Hotel, Elizabeth said, "Joe, where do you think this case will end up? Murder?"

"When you see the room you'll be able to make up your own mind, Elizabeth," said Mistretta. "But I won't hedge, because an hour from now you'll have reached the same conclusion anyway. The door was locked from inside, the window

73

was locked from inside, there is no reason to believe anybody saw the Senator from midnight until 8:00 A.M. I think before the night is over we'll have a lab report that the toxic substance was some kind of poison you can buy over the counter. And I think tomorrow by noon we'll have a confidential report from the Senator's doctors at Bethesda Naval Medical Center saying he had terminal cancer, or an even more confidential report that he was being blackmailed, or something of that sort. Because whatever happened to him, the chances are pretty good that he did it to himself. And if I have to make an early call, I'll go with the odds every time."

Elizabeth thought about this for a few seconds, and then Mistretta added, "And it was poison."

"So?" she asked. "Unusual, I'll admit, but it happens."

"True," he said. "But it's hard to find a poison that doesn't leave the victim feeling pretty awful for an hour or two before he dies. And if he doesn't expect to feel that way he picks up a phone and calls somebody."

The hotel room looked as though it had been the scene of some unusually messy kind of mechanical failure. Every smooth surface was covered with a thin film of greasy black dust. The bedclothes were churned into a pile at the foot of the bed. On the rug in the center of the floor was the chalked silhouette of a human form, caught in an attitude suggesting a grotesque dance.

Elizabeth found an empty spot in the room and stood, looking around without touching anything. It was hard to imagine what the place had been like when it was occupied by living people. The police had apparently looked at everything, dusted the whole room for fingerprints, taken everything that was movable back to the laboratory for study.

Her trained mind shifted into its analytical mode and concentrated on the elements before her. The absent cups and glasses were taken care of; the body; Claremont's luggage. She looked into the closet. His clothes were gone too. All that was left, really, were the four walls and furniture, covered with fingerprint dust. She walked to the bathroom. The U-shaped trap was gone from beneath the sink; the drainpipe ended abruptly a foot below the fixture. Even the toilet had been tampered with: the tank cover was on the floor covered with the ubiquitous black dust.

"This isn't doing me much good," said Elizabeth. "It doesn't look like a hotel room anymore."

"I know what you mean," said Mistretta. "If there ever was anything to find in here, it'll turn up in the lab reports. The forensics people were in here for six hours. It looks like they've covered everything."

"Do you mind if we try something else?"

"Why not?" said Mistretta. "Until the final autopsy report comes in, anything's as good as anything else."

"Then I'd like to see another room like this one. The best thing would be an empty one on this corridor," said Elizabeth.

"Good idea," said Hart. He had been silent the whole time, walking around the room making notes on a pocket pad, tearing off sheets, and stuffing them into his pockets.

"Take your pick," said Mistretta. "They've closed off the whole floor for the time being. They're all empty."

They tried the next room, but it was torn up too.

"The assistant's room?" asked Hart.

"Right," said Mistretta, who closed the door and led them to the next one.

Inside, Elizabeth's imagination felt comfortable again. The room was designed to be exactly the same as the Senator's, but it still had that peculiar air of suspension that hotel rooms seemed to have, as though somebody had been there so recently that if you turned your head quickly some relic or remnant of their personal lives would be visible for an instant. She walked around the room, opening drawers, peering into the closet, finally, focusing her attention on the bathroom. Everything gleamed with a precarious expectancy that made

75

her want to open the seals and move things around, like walking on fresh snow. But her mind moved for her, counting and calculating and remembering.

When she returned to the bedroom Hart was kneeling in the open doorway scrutinizing the locks. He said, to nobody in particular, "Not much to stop anybody if the deadbolt wasn't in."

Mistretta said, "No good. The assistant says their bags were with them from the time they left the airport, and they didn't go out after they got here. When he left the Senator threw the bolt. In the morning they had to call the maintenance man with an electromagnetic gizmo to open it up. That didn't work either because the fit was too tight, so they drilled it."

Elizabeth wondered why she hadn't seen that, but apparently Hart hadn't either. It wasn't much comfort, she realized, as she walked to the window.

Mistretta saw her fiddling with the latch and said, "That's been checked too. There's a little wear on the molding, but the lock is working perfectly. No prints on the inside handle, and no handle on the outside."

Elizabeth went out onto the balcony. It was really night now and an icy wind clutched at her hair and the skirt of her coat. She looked around at the identical balconies, beside her and above and below. No, it was probably too farfetched. Four floors below her was the parking lot, where the cars were only shiny-colored rectangles with no depth to them. Somebody who wanted to kill a senator could do it in a thousand ways that didn't involve swinging on a rope that high up in the cold. Might as well ask, anyway.

Elizabeth came in and shut the window. The air in the room seemed unnaturally still and quiet and warm. "What about the balcony?" she asked. "Any way to tell if anyone was on it?"

76

"Not much point to it, since the lock would have kept him in the cold anyway," said Mistretta, "but they checked it. There wasn't anything much. No prints on the railings, no rope marks, nothing on the glass except the usual smudges and a couple of spots where the maid had given it a quick swipe with a dustrag."

Elizabeth said, "Wait a minute. Let's go take a look."

Mistretta shrugged and followed her back to the Senator's room. Hart appeared to be unaware of them; he was now in the bathroom, kneeling beside the bathtub and studying the drain.

Elizabeth went directly to the Senator's window, walked out to the balcony, and looked back into the lighted room. There was a thin film of dust over the whole surface of the glass, dappled with lighter dots where fingers had touched it. But in two places about two and a half feet apart, there were clean spots, where someone had brushed a cloth in a circular motion. She came back inside.

"Joe, the whole window is covered with prints and smudges and dust, except those two places. The one we were in before doesn't have any clean spots."

The telephone rang, and it startled her. "Hello?" she said, far too loud.

"Mike Lang here."

"Yes, Mike," said Elizabeth.

"I think it's going to be a long night. The poison turned out to be curare, of all things. It's in the glass where he soaked his dentures, in the dentures, and no place else. No container anywhere, either, and the Polident box is clean."

"So it is murder," said Elizabeth.

"I hate to pin it down that tight, but I'm damned if I see any other explanation. He couldn't have carried curare in without a container, and a man doesn't kill himself with his own false teeth. At least not if he's got any sense of dignity."

"No. But curare? Are you sure? It's not exactly the American murderer's favorite form of poison, is it?"

"Of course I'm sure. And I don't have anything else to tell you that'll make it seem sensible. But at this point I'd be willing to listen to anything anybody else has."

"I think there's a chance somebody came in from the balcony," said Elizabeth. "We're not sure yet, but it looks as though somebody had both hands on the glass, about chest high."

"You mean they got prints on it?" asked Lang. "Terrific!"

"No," said Elizabeth. "That's just it. Somebody wiped the glass off. Nobody who works for a hotel would wipe two spots on a six-by-eight-foot window. They'd wash it or forget it. And no guest would wipe the outside of a window for any reason."

"Is Mistretta with you?"

"Yes, he's right here."

"Then let me talk to him."

Elizabeth handed the phone to Joe, who listened intently for a few seconds and then said, "Yeah, it's possible she's right, but we're still looking it over."

He listened again, then said, "The police didn't think so. No. Too obvious, I guess. The window latch was the first thing they went for after the corpse was moved. They said no indication of forced entry."

He was silent for a moment. "Yeah, that too. Of course. We'll keep you posted."

Mistretta hung up and chuckled. "That's something, isn't it?" he said to Elizabeth. "We earn our pay on this one all right. Which do you want to work on first? Proving a man came in through the locked fourth-floor window because there are no fingerprints, or figuring out how he arrived at the idea of using curare on the old guy's false teeth when he got here? I don't suppose the MO file will help much on this one, unless it

78

was a South American pygmy we're looking for." He shook his head and the false bravado began to fade.

Elizabeth wasn't looking at him, though. She was standing before the window with both hands in front of her. "Pygmies don't live in South America," she muttered absently, staring at her reflection.

"I suppose we'd better get the forensics people back up here," he said, picking up the telephone again.

Elizabeth didn't turn, just said, "Yes. I'd like to be here when they come." She'd never noticed that before, she thought. When you press your palms against a flat surface, the tips of your fingers are just exactly shoulder height. If you allowed for shoe soles, five foot ten? Six feet? They'd measure it, though. You could always count on them to measure.

Hart came into the room, bringing with him his notepad, still scribbling on it. He said, "I heard a phone ring. Was it the lab report?"

"That's right," said Elizabeth. "It was curare that was put into the glass where he soaked his dentures, believe it or not. Mixed with his Polident."

"What's the report on the rest of his stuff? Any curare or containers for it?" He seemed to Elizabeth to be hiding his surprise at the poison and it annoyed her a little. How could he not be surprised?

"No," she said tonelessly.

"Then I'd say we have only a few things we can check on," he said. "One is that somebody close enough to him to get into his luggage put poison on one of the Polident tablets and only one. Maybe his assistant or whoever packed his bags. Another is that somebody tampered with them between Washington and here." He hesitated for a moment, but Elizabeth wasn't going to help him, since he hadn't had the decency to be surprised. Then he said, "But I'd say the least unlikely thing is that somebody came in through the window."

"The forensics people are on their way up now to check the window out," said Mistretta. "Elizabeth figured it out a little while ago."

"Good thinking, Elizabeth," he said, with apparent sincerity.

Elizabeth wasn't ready to accept the compliment. Patronizing bastards, all of them. She was past that part of it anyway, thinking about the killer. He had to be athletic, or at least fit, to be able to go from any other room to this one. No matter how it was done he still had to get from one balcony to another in the cold and dark. That probably meant he wasn't over forty. He was between five foot nine and six feet tall. And he was sneaky. God, he was sneaky.

9 There was something clean about the
sun in Las Vegas. Even in February
there was a searing, blinding white light
that made you feel as if you were being sterilized, even cauter-
ized, so there wasn't a germ that could stick to you. Everything
extraneous would be burned off your skin, desiccated and
sucked dry, its empty husk blown clattering away in the hot
wind out of the desert. Even the air itself felt like that—a
breeze that carried with it tiny abrasive particles of ground-up
quartz and topaz too small to see. You could feel them buffing
and polishing away at you.

He rolled over on his stomach. Better be careful the first
time out. Getting a sunburn on top of all those scrapes and
bruises would be about the limit of what he could endure. He
could already feel the sun gradually heating up his back and
shoulders, breathing its energy into them so that moment by
moment the temperature of his skin rose in infinitesimal gradi-
ents. In a few more minutes, he decided, he'd go back to his
room and get cleaned up, then take a nice long nap before
dinner. Your body heals faster while you sleep, he thought.
There was no reason to think about anything at all until Friday night. Friday was payday.

The soft electronic female voices were alternating on the
public address system: "Telephone for Mr. Harrison Rand.
Harrison Rand, telephone. Telephone for Princess Karina.
Princess Karina, telephone," a steady murmur going out
across the swimming pool from nowhere in particular, the
volume just high enough to flicker across the corner of your
consciousness. There was no more urgency to it than the con-
stant whir and click of the slot machines in the casino. This, he
thought, was the only place he knew of where clock time

didn't matter. You measured time against the size of your bankroll—unless you were lying on a chaise longue next to the swimming pool, he remembered. Then the sun would damned well remind you what time it was if you weren't careful. Enough for today.

He sat up and put on the dark brown terrycloth robe and zoris he'd picked up in one of the hotel stores this afternoon. Then he changed his mind again. The vast empty surface of the swimming pool sparkled at him. There was time enough for one more dip in the water, he thought. There was no reason not to do exactly as he pleased, and swimming was good for you—the best thing in the world for damaged muscles, and it would be time to stop when you didn't feel like it anymore.

The water was warm, almost hot, like a gigantic Roman bath. He swam lazily from one end to the other, testing the flex and fluidity of his muscles against the solidity and support of the water. It had always struck him as funny that they should have a heated pool that was twice the size of the ones they used in the Olympics, and that he should be alone in it every time. People who were serious about swimming didn't drive through the desert to do it. He stopped at the shallow end and let himself go limp in the warm water, feeling the deliciousness of it, held there as though by a broad, gentle hand. He floated on his back, surveying the people sprawled on lawn chairs, absorbing the sunlight. Most of them had probably been up all night, he thought. Gambling, drinking, fucking, and now they were recharging their batteries by the energy of the sun. No, they weren't swimmers, but it seemed to comfort them to be near all that water. Something to look at through your polarized sunglasses while you waited for night.

He swam back to the deep end, acutely aware of the workings of his muscles as he stroked. He was going to be all right. Everything felt exactly as he wanted it to. At least his body did. His head was going to take longer. It felt big and soft and sensitive today, a peeled pumpkin held in anxious balance on a neck too thin for it. Just so there weren't any scars on his face. The pain he could live with.

He pulled himself up out of the pool and flopped down on his chaise longue. In a few seconds he could feel the water on his body disappearing into the parched desert air, leaving his skin feeling tight. He let the sun settle its gentle pressure on his face for a few moments before he put on his sunglasses. Then he closed his eyes and let himself slip into a state that felt as good as sleep but wasn't quite a relinquishment of consciousness. "Telephone for Mr. Arthur Walters. Arthur Walters, telephone. Telephone for Mrs. Natalie Beamish, Natalie Beamish, telephone," crooned the soft unanxious voices in monotonous alternation.

"You do all that to yourself or did you have help?" said a voice above him. His eyes flicked open for an instant like camera shutters behind the sunglasses, and brought back with them into the darkness an imprint of the familiar, hulking shape. Little Norman.

"You know how it is, Little Norman," he answered. "You want something done right, you have to do it yourself." He heard the scrape as Little Norman dragged a lawn chair across the pavement to his side. Little Norman. The first thing anybody said when he heard the name was that he never wanted to see Big Norman. Little Norman was six foot four without his hand-tooled Mexican cowboy boots, and must have weighed in at two-fifty without the two rolls of quarters he always had in his pockets. As if those fists needed the extra weight. And Little Norman was no longer young. He had to be at least fifty-five and semiretired, so that wasn't it either.

"What brings you to Caesar's Palace, Little Norman?" he said. "I thought you hung around at the Sands."

"Nice sunny day out," said Little Norman. "Good day to get a tan." Little Norman was wearing his usual tailor-made suit and stiff-collared white shirt with pearl studs. Little Norman was also blacker than the bottom of a coal mine.

"You're right there. Been getting some myself, and doing a little swimming."

"That's good, kid. That's what you need for those thumps you got on you. A little sunshine, a little exercise, a lot of rest." He said it again, "A lot of rest."

He just nodded and let Little Norman go on.

"For excitement there's always the tables. You don't have to do anything spectacular to keep your blood circulating, you know what I mean, kid?"

"Sure I do, Norman." He smiled. Then he said, "I'm not working. Nobody works in Las Vegas, you know that."

Little Norman's long face broke into a broad grin. "That's real sensible, kid. Coming in here with a face like that, people wonder. I'm not asking where you got it, you understand. But people do wonder where you got it and whether you're maybe a little mad about it."

"If you see anybody like that, will you do me a favor?"

"Sure, kid, if I see anybody like that."

"Tell them I'm not working."

"I'll do that."

"Thanks, Little Norman. I wouldn't want anybody worrying about my health."

Little Norman stood up, straightened his tie, and said, "If you've got some time on your hands you might stop by for a drink. You know where to find me, don't you?"

"Sure," he said.

"I'll see you, then."

He watched Little Norman's huge back moving along the edge of the pool toward the entrance near the casino. It hadn't taken long, he thought. He reached in the pocket of his robe and pulled out his watch. Four hours. He'd been in Las Vegas less than four hours before someone had noticed him and told Little Norman. But at least Little Norman seemed to be satisfied. For the next hour he'd be scurrying all over town telling rich, powerful old men that there was nothing to worry about this time. Their deaths hadn't been purchased yet. It really was a vacation. And the uneasy truce would hold until the next thing came up. He should have looked up Little Norman right away, he thought, and made sure the word got out before any of them got nervous. It was the polite thing to do.

10

In his room he closed the door, bolted and chained it, then took off his robe and walked into the shower. Little Norman worried him because it hadn't occurred to him that the way he looked would cause them alarm. It was never a good thing to come to the attention of any of the dozen nervous old men who lived in the fragile sanctuary of the open city. Each of them had survived to his present vicious senility through predatory cunning and the instinctive preference for striking first. And they wouldn't forget that. No matter if you were eighty-three years old and propped like a sack of rags in a wheelchair like Castiglione, you would remember that much.

As long as Little Norman did what the old men paid him for, it would be fine. And there was no reason to think he wouldn't. But now a slight trickle of fear had begun to mix itself into his bloodstream. It wasn't enough to spoil the pleasure of being safe and comfortable in Caesar's, but it was there. He decided that maybe it wouldn't be such a bad idea to go have that drink with Little Norman. He had told him he was on vacation, and now he'd damn well better act like it. Besides, he was on vacation. At least until Friday night.

WHEN HE WOKE UP the room was dark and he could hear the voice of a man outside the door of his room saying, "System, my ass. You see this place, Alice? It's made out of systems thought up by dumb women from Fullerton." Then a door closed and he heard footsteps receding down the hallway. He couldn't hear what Alice said in reply, but the man's voice said, "So you won once. That doesn't . . . ." and then they were out of earshot.

He rolled over and looked at the luminous dial of his watch. Nine thirty. Perfect, he thought. Just the right time to start the evening. He lurched to his feet, turned on the lights, and went to the closet to lay out his clothes. The nap had done him more good than he'd dared to hope. He felt cheerful and clearheaded. If he hadn't caught sight of himself in the mirror he'd have said he was 100 percent.

It was Eddie who'd taught him about rest. Eddie had been the undefeated world champion of resting. He could still hear the quiet, patient voice: "Never work when you're tired, kid. You have to be able to think straight, and you have to have the physical edge too. Each time it's a contest and if you don't come in first place every time you're dead." Eddie Mastrewski had kept the physical edge all right. That frigid winter night in Philadelphia when the building contractor had spotted them on the street and tried to run away he'd seen it. All his mind had told him was that they couldn't shoot, and so he was paralyzed for a minute. But Eddie had just muttered "Oh, shit," reached over the seat to the back of the car, and taken off on foot after the contractor with the tire chain. He ran him down and garrotted him.

But Eddie'd had the build for it, he thought. A Pennsylvania Polack from the coal mining country—probably the toughest physical specimens on earth except for maybe central Asian goatherds who were supposed to live to be a hundred and forty. He could hear Eddie correcting him, "I'm not a Pole, I'm a Lithuanian. There's a difference, kid. I just don't know what it is." But Eddie had sure known how to sleep. He seemed to sleep whenever there wasn't some definite reason why he shouldn't. Even then Eddie seemed a little resentful and suspicious that the reason might not be good enough. He'd seen Eddie sleep on trains, buses, and airplanes; in stations and sitting up behind the wheel of a parked car. Over the years he'd learned that there was something to Eddie's theory. Sleep really did make a difference. Maybe Eddie hadn't had

87

enough sleep the day he got it. Or maybe when you got to a certain age there just wasn't enough sleep to make up for all the years.

He put on the sport coat he'd bought in the hotel store this afternoon, took another look at the knot in his tie, closed his door, and began to walk down the hall toward the elevator. Then he hesitated. No, he thought, it's stupid not to. He returned to the room, bent over, and pulled a few tufts of lint from the bright azure carpet. He stuffed them between the door and the jamb about two inches above the surface of the red carpet of the hallway. It's always better to know than to wonder, he thought as he stepped into the elevator.

He made his way through the crowds and noise of the casino and out to the front entrance. The doors gave a wheezy sigh and opened automatically to pull him forward into the warm night air. The absurd magnificence of the oversized fountain along the drive seemed to be the focus of the unanimous eyeless contemplation of the genuine Carrara marble copies of classical statues that stood sentinel. Sammy Cohen had once called them The Stupefied Losers, but that wasn't what they looked like. It was as though they were staring in dumb amazement at waking up and finding themselves so far from the gentle, reasonable proportions of home.

He glanced at the line of taxis waiting in the loop, but dismissed them in favor of the stroll. There were hundreds of people walking up and down the sidewalks of the Strip in light summer clothing that changed colors as they passed under the garish incandescent auras of the gigantic marquees and glittering facades of the casinos. He stepped in among them, into a herd that was flowing along in the direction of the Sands. As they passed each doorway, came into the glowing circle of each new complex of lights and neon signs, a portion of the herd would be drawn off by the magnetism of it. Others would issue forth from the doors to replace them.

They were moving toward the center of the city, and as they did the white river of automobile traffic in the street seemed to slow down and constrict, the signs and lights to cluster together more tightly into a general undifferentiated blur and dazzle, until the doorways were just holes in the light.

Then there was a pause in the glitter, as though it were gathering itself up for some major effort, and then the monolithic marquee of the Sands burst forth to dominate the night. He peeled himself out of the moving crowd, walked up the steps, and crossed the boundary into the air-conditioned cool of the casino. Inside the light, the air, the colors, the sounds were all different and belonged to the special exigencies of this place, where the world consisted of a low-frequency hum of unflagging agitation, like an itch or a hope.

He made one slow circuit of the casino, past the banks of winking, buzzing, clattering slot machines that spun gyroscopically on the periphery, then past the zone of roulette wheels and crap tables and along the rank of fan-shaped blackjack games ascending in order of wealth toward the roped-off sanctum of high-stakes baccarat, where the croupiers wore black tuxedos and the reverential faces of French financial consultants.

Little Norman wasn't in evidence in the casino, but he knew that someone would tell him. One of the unseen beings Norman kept on his personal payroll would probably be talking into a telephone right now. He made a leisurely path to the doorway of the Regency Room and slipped through the doors into the candlelit red-and-gold silence. He always had the sense that this place was insulated from the cacophony of the city by something more than walls, as though everything outside could explode into screaming atoms and you'd never know it by so much as the wavering of a candle flame. The maitre d' conducted him to a booth in the far corner of the room, where a waiter nodded his respect for the wisdom of beef Wellington and a middle-range Bordeaux with two glasses.

He had almost finished the beef Wellington when Little Norman came in and sat down at his table. "Hello, kid," said Little Norman. "You come over here looking for me?"

"That's right, Norman. I thought I'd take you up on that drink. I suppose you've already had dinner?"

"Yeah, but since you got an extra glass I'll help you with the wine." Norman poured it himself, sniffed the bouquet, and said, "Not bad at all. Your idea or the waiter's?"

"Mine," he said and kept eating.

"Then you've picked up a lot since you worked with old Eddie. I always heard that travel broadens you." He chuckled.

"I've always heard that too."

"Something on your mind, kid? You're not looking too cheerful. I mean besides the thumps on your face."

"I'm fine. Nothing wrong that a few days of rest won't handle. How about you, Norman? You have a hard day? Run into anybody that was nervous about anything?"

"No," said Little Norman, and smiled. "I ran into one or two who used to be nervous, but I seem to have a natural talent for reassuring people. Should have been a psychiatrist, I guess. I'd probably have a lot more money."

He eyed the heavy gold ring on the finger Norman had wrapped around the stem of the glass. The diamond, he calculated, was around five carats. It looked big even on Little Norman. "I doubt it," he said.

"I guess you're right," said Little Norman. "White folks don't want a big black psychiatrist, and black folks don't have the money for one. They just have to stay crazy, like I did, and learn to enjoy it."

He pushed his plate away and noticed that Little Norman had emptied the bottle. "Well, how about that drink, Norman?

You want it here, or you want to go someplace else?"

Little Norman leaned back in his chair to let the waiter deposit the check where the plate had been. He paused to savor the last inch of wine in his glass, then said, "You know, I think you've been working too hard. Seems to me like you're in a hurry all the time, like you forgot how to relax. I'm gonna have to take pity on you and remind you how it's done." He waited while the waiter whisked the money away. Then he stood up and said, "No sense in being crazy if you're not gonna enjoy it."

"I know you wouldn't want me to learn it on the street, Norman," he said, and got up to follow.

ELIZABETH SAT ON THE EDGE of the bed watching the forensic team going about its work. It took an extraordinary act of patience even to watch them. They crawled around on all fours, sighting along the edge of each smooth surface for latent prints, then wrote in pads, took photographs, stretched tape measures from one point to another, and made more notes.

It was already clear that they weren't going to find anything new in the room, she thought as she watched a sergeant crawl up to the coffee table and stare at the same spot for the third time. She said to Hart, "Let's try something different."

"Got anything in mind?"

"How about the other rooms on this floor? Do you have the list of who was in what room? Maybe we could start with the hotel register."

"Mistretta's got it and he's checking them all out now. Not just this floor, either."

"Well, it looks as if we've hit the point of diminishing returns in here." The forensics people were packing their equipment in black metal boxes and preparing to leave.

"Whew!" said the sergeant. "This has been a long day."

91

Elizabeth said, "Oh?" She was still a little resentful because they hadn't seen the importance of the absence of prints on the window.

"Yes, ma'am," he said, "two murders this morning besides this one, three breaking and enterings, all within a mile or two of here."

The resentment came back without warning. Ma'am and sir were what policemen called outsiders. Whatever sympathy she had been prepared to feel for a tired cop who'd been crawling around straining his eyes for invisible marks went out of her. But she just said, "Please have copies of those reports sent to us at the Bureau office, with the precinct log."

"No possible connection, ma'am," said the patient sergeant. "The other two had their skulls crushed. Nothing subtle about it. Just a gang fight in an alley. The B and E's were all just the usual—an auto parts store, a housebreaking, and a stereo shop."

She matched his patience. "I want them anyway. It's important to learn everything that we can about what went on in this part of town last night." At last she succumbed: "If nothing else, it may tell us where the squad cars were when a murderer was swinging like Tarzan from balcony to balcony on the outside of this building."

"Yes, ma'am," said the sergeant. He picked up his fingerprint kit and stomped out the door.

Elizabeth became aware of Hart standing there watching her. She turned on him and said, "I know it wasn't nice. But it happens to be true."

Hart shrugged. "The local police can be very helpful if they want to."

"So I'll be extremely sweet to him when he gives me the logs and the investigation reports, and we'll be fast friends forever. But the local police might not be the kind of help we're going to need on this case. Has anybody—"

"Yes," said Hart. "The CIA was as surprised about it as

92

we were, and they've spent the day trying to match it to their standing list of possibilities, apparently without success. Mike told me they've probably cabled their field offices and are waiting for something that sounds plausible to come back. He also told me it doesn't look as if anything will. McKinley Claremont was in the Senate for almost thirty years without doing anything very controversial in the area of foreign policy."

"I suppose all we can do tonight is wait for the forensics people to work their way through the other rooms, then."

"That and wait for our replacements to arrive," said Hart. "As of an hour ago we're no longer here just to establish a presence."

"So they'll send in the first team?" said Elizabeth. "We haven't done so badly, considering we've hardly had time to begin."

"No, we haven't," said Hart. "But just the same, I'm not going to do much unpacking."

"Speaking of that, has anybody told you where we're supposed to be staying?"

"They had our bags sent here a little while ago." He reached into his pocket and fished out two room keys. "That way we're easy to get hold of if they turn anything up."

Elizabeth reached for the telephone and dialed a familiar number. An unfamiliar voice came on and said, "Justice."

"This is Elizabeth Waring. I want to leave a message for Roger Padgett," said Elizabeth.

"I'll see that he gets it," said the voice. "What's the message?"

"I want his airline reports for last night and all day today wired to the Denver field office of the FBI. Everything within a five-hundred-mile radius of Denver. The information I requested previously I want telephoned to me at the Constellation Hotel."

"That in Denver too?"

"Yes," said Elizabeth, "I'll give you a number." She read

93

the number on the telephone dial slowly. Then she held out her hand, and Hart placed one of the keys in it. "Room 256."

"Got it," said the voice. "Anything else?"

"No," said Elizabeth. "Thanks."

Elizabeth sat on the bed feeling exhaustion beginning to flood into her mind, taking possession of whole sections of her brain at once like water rushing into a sinking ship. Too many things were going on at once, and she was beginning to lose the strength of will that kept them separate. Everything was beginning to get muddled together and hazy. She couldn't remember anymore whether she was collecting information that was supposed to lead in some particular direction, or just collecting information. Pervading all of it was an impression, a sense that an awful lot of people seemed to be dying. There was something unreal about it.

You knew they were dying because somebody told you so over the telephone, and by the time you got there, there wasn't even a body. At most there was a chalk outline like the one on the floor at her feet. The discreet efficient functionaries had already cleaned everything up, so there wasn't the palpable and substantial residue of an act of violence, just a question; the murder itself just an intellectual postulate and you were supposed to deduce its causes and corollaries starting with an infinite range of things that could have preceded it in time. All you had to work with was your ability to see the relationships, to pick the single thread of logic that might lead to the one who'd done it, and then follow it slowly forward, trying hard to take each step faster to bring yourself closer and closer to the present moment, where the murderer would be waiting for you. And all the time, the act itself was moving backward, further and further into the past. Everything you chose to look at put the act farther from your reach—trace the poison? check the airline records for suspicious travelers? check the police reports? the other rooms in the hotel? the Senator's personal life? the CIA's foreign agents? the world?

94

She was aware that Hart was saying something to her that had just battered against the tired receptors in her brain without their being fast enough to decipher it. "Huh?" she said.

"I said I think we ought to go to bed."

"So do I," she said, and sensed in herself a tiny warm tremor of joy. Then she realized that part of her mind had heard him differently, and had rushed upward to meet him without being held back or delayed by the restraints. She caught it in time to keep it from blurting out, "Oh, you mean each of us, not both of us." She smiled to herself as she stood up and walked out the door. All the barriers seemed to be going at once; things were tearing through them without warning, things she hadn't suspected were there. This one would take some thought. Not that it meant anything, but it was interesting, like a dream.

THEY WENT OUT TO THE parking lot and got into Little Norman's white Mark IV, then drove to the Marina Hotel.

At the bar, which was set back and above the casino, Little Norman said, "Grab a table where I can see the action; I'll be back in a second."

He said, "Where are you going?"

"Just a quick phone call, kid. I'm looking after your interests."

He waited as Norman plowed through the knots of gamblers to a bank of telephones near a men's room. When Norman got there, he dialed and then turned back to face him, smiling as he talked.

The waitress leaned across him with Little Norman's drink, actually placing a breast on his shoulder for an instant. Everything here was different, he thought. It was calculated to put things that secretly delighted just out of reach, always as though it had been a fortuitous chance. They probably had a

95

class that taught them to do that, as the last girl in the line of the dinner show at the Lido had her G-string snap, always in the last few bars of the performance.

Little Norman said, "To your health, kid," and took a drink.

He responded, "And yours," and drank too, but only enough to wet his mouth and let the ice click against his teeth. There wasn't much point in overdoing it, and he would overdo it if he had to drink one for one with Little Norman. Besides, he had been on the road for over a month, and he never drank on the road. You had to keep your head clear on the road.

On the other side of the casino the crowd around one of the crap tables was two deep and growing. The man who was rolling was wearing a sport coat, but had stuffed his tie in a pocket and opened his shirt at the neck. He rolled again and a little cry went up from the table that was just loud enough to reach the bar. More people strolled over attempting looks of detachment, but joined the crowd and riveted their eyes to the table. From where he sat in the bar it was hard to tell whether they were betting or watching. The quick, mechanical movements of the croupier didn't reveal anything to him. From this distance they all just looked hungry.

"You a gambler?"

"I may try my luck a little later," he said. "Why?"

"Some people in that line of work are, some aren't. Henckel once lost twenty thousand in one night. Personally I didn't like it much until after I quit. Couldn't see the point in it. When you're old you need some kind of excitement that doesn't involve your body."

Another cry reached them from the crap table across the casino, not a cheer, exactly, but a wordless, spontaneous howl from all the throats gathered around the table, as though it were the collective sound of their blood pressures going up in unison.

"You're no more retired than I am, Norman," he said. "Just got a steady job now."

"It ain't so, kid," said Little Norman, his eyes suddenly open wide and his smile gone. "I'm sixty-one years old. But once I was good. One of the best. Quiet and reliable. Maybe the best button man in the Midwest." Then his eyes narrowed and the opaque smile returned. "Not as good as you, though. I was real surprised to see your face like that. I never expected to see you looking like that. Not ever."

"It happens," he replied.

"I didn't say it couldn't happen," said Little Norman. "What I said was I didn't think I'd see it. That's a loser's face."

Across the casino the man rolled again; this time he rolled into a silence, a deep-drawn inbreathing like a wall of anticipation. From the bar it was hard to tell whether he made his point, but the silence seemed to draw spectators even faster, like particles rushing to fill a void. When the stickman leaned across the table, bestowing and gathering in single economical movements, the man was still visible, standing with his back to the bar. But then the crowd shifted a little and he disappeared behind it.

"Maybe so," he said. "Hard to tell about winning until you count the money."

"That's a fact," said Little Norman. He gulped down the last finger of Scotch in his glass and stood up. "Be seeing you, kid. It's always a pleasure."

"Thanks for the drink, Norman."

"Any time," he said as he stepped down to the casino floor. For a long time it was possible to watch his head and shoulders moving along above the crowd, but then he was gone.

11 He finished his drink and left the hotel. There wasn't any particular reason to leave. He wasn't hiding from anyone and didn't have anywhere else as a destination. It was just the normal thing to do, as automatic as the urge to blink his eyes, as automatic as going outside and then waiting beside the door to see if the next one out paused for a second to see which way he'd gone. He was on vacation for two more days. That was no time to let himself slide into a position where he'd feel uncomfortable.

He walked across the parking lot to the street, and joined the anonymous hundreds moving along the Strip from casino to casino. Just before they got to the MGM Grand Hotel he parted from his companions and took a shortcut through a closed gas station, then stopped in the shadows behind it. Nobody came after him, so he went on. If there was a watcher, he at least had sense enough to keep his distance and not be annoying.

He went in the front entrance of the Grand Hotel and moved quickly to the other end of the gigantic casino, where the blackjack games were proceeding in an atmosphere of spurious calm. At one table a man piled his remaining chips on the square in front of him and waited, one foot already on the floor to push his chair away from the table. The dealer's deft fingers peeled cards out of the shoe and made them rematerialize in front of the players, and the man found himself sitting behind a ten and a four. He didn't seem surprised or disappointed by it, just watched while the second ten appeared and the dealer's hand snatched away the chips. Then his foot pushed off and he relinquished his chair.

The dealer's face didn't seem to notice that the man was

gone, or that he'd ever been there. Only his marvelous hands took note of the fact that there were no chips on one of the betting spaces, and passed by without leaving any cards. The face didn't acknowledge it when another man sat down in the seat to wait for the next deal. One of the hands snatched the five crisp twenties and tamped them into the cash slot, while the other left a stack of chips where the money had been. If the dealer's eyes had passed across the new face with its terrible bruise and the cut just above the hairline, they didn't linger there. The eyes were only there to direct the hands, and there was plenty for the hands to do.

When he sat down at the table he checked his watch. It was eleven thirty. It didn't make much difference to him where he spent the next few hours, but it was important not to lose track of things. He set out a single five-dollar chip and watched the hands of the dealer deposit his cards on the table. They were a queen and a ten, so he stood pat and waited while the dealer's king and five drew another king and busted. The hands fluttered over the green felt surface of the table, rearranging chips and cards, rewarding and punishing with the same even, imperturbable movements, but in any case obliterating the decisions that had just been made along with the combinations of numbers and symbols that had prompted them. Each time there was a new set of decisions, and then the hands performed their mechanical reckoning and dealt again. He kept a rough tally of how well he was doing, and it was no worse than he'd expected. The dealer had started on a losing streak, and busted about half of the first twenty hands. After that the normal order of probabilities had reasserted itself and the house's regular five-percent advantage had resumed. When he glanced at his watch again it was one thirty. Two hours was enough. He gathered his red chips and headed for the cashier's cage. When he went out the front door he had six twenties and a ten in his shirt pocket. It was mildly pleasing to him. He was no gambler and the minimum bets he had

99

stuck to had just kept him there passing the time. But he figured it was better than losing.

Outside, the last big crowds of the evening were spilling out into the parking lots from the late shows. Caesar's Palace was practically across the street, so he joined a group walking in that direction and began looking for the watcher, who would have been alerted when he left the blackjack table. Hadn't he seen that older man in the gray suit who joined the crowd at the corner? Earlier, at the Sands. Only before there had been a woman in a white dress with him. People always went in pairs to the shows. He looked for her, but the man was alone, looking a lot like a middle-aged businessman from someplace else who'd left the tired little woman in the hotel room and gone out for some action on his own. If he wasn't, she'd turn up again in time.

He kept the man's location in mind without looking at him again. Then a portion of the crowd streamed into Caesar's and another portion split off into the parking lot to search for their cars. Once inside the casino he moved off along the edge of the forest of slot machines. There she was, a nice silver-haired lady from Missouri with that hypnotized look they all got, intently pumping dimes from a paper cup into a slot machine as though the wheels and gears couldn't spin fast enough to digest the coins. Only this time she was wearing a blue dress. The man in the gray suit walked past her and over to the elevators without either of them making a sign.

That was just fine. As watchers went they were tolerable. They didn't hang around close enough to be annoying, and now that he'd spotted them he could relax. He went to the second row of elevators and pushed the button for his floor.

The hallway was empty, so he made his way to his room and checked the space between the door and the jamb. The little ball of blue fuzz was still stuck there, an inch or two above the bright red carpet. Good. No surprises. They must be satisfied for the moment.

100

He swung the door open and for an instant struggled to remember if he'd left the bathroom light on. As the door swung wider he caught a glimpse of the television screen, which was casting a bright variegated display of moving colors into the dimness. He stepped aside and waited. Then a woman's voice said, "Come in, baby. You've got the right place."

He stepped across the doorway and caught sight of the whole room at once. She was kneeling in the middle of the bed and she seemed to be wearing nothing. He poked the door all the way open and moved warily inside. There didn't seem to be anyone else. He ignored her for the moment and searched the room for hiding places. There was nobody in the bathroom or under the bed. He checked behind the curtains, then out on the balcony, but there was nobody. He retreated to the doorway and looked at her. "What are you doing here?" he said.

"I'm a present, honey. Compliments of Little Norman." She crawled toward him across the big bed and he took a closer look at her. She was small and dark, with long black hair and skin like cinnamon and big black eyes. Mexican or Puerto Rican, he thought. She couldn't be much over twenty.

"How did he get you in here?" he asked.

"Little Norman knows somebody," she smiled. Then she stopped, poised for a second in a parody of thought, kneeling with her knees apart and her body erect to let him get a chance to look at her. "No," she said, "Little Norman knows everybody."

He locked and bolted the door, then leaned back against the wall and looked for something to block the window latch. Now she was off the bed and standing in front of him. "Relax, honey," she said. "I thought you were supposed to be here to enjoy yourself." Her voice was cool and soothing. Her hands were fiddling with his belt. "So loosen up a little." And then she was down on the floor, murmuring something in a soft, kittenish voice, but he couldn't understand it because she was also taking his penis into her mouth.

He stood with his back poised against the wall, careful not to let his mind go completely out of his control, keeping back the tiny part he needed to look and listen, while she took possession of the rest of him. So now there were two of him—one that gave in to whatever she did and seemed all mindless yearning, a rush forward from some dim distant place, and the other part that looked over her shoulder for a flicker of shadow behind the curtain, and shut out the soft cooing sounds of her voice to hear a footfall in the hallway or a click of metal.

After a few minutes the one who kept watch was no longer tense and fearful. It didn't go to sleep, but it let the other part relinquish the safe wall, shed its clothes, and take the girl to the broad, ornate bed. It didn't stop listening and watching, partly because it couldn't, and partly because there was still the marker left in the door that somebody besides the girl had seen and replaced.

HE LAY SPRAWLED on the bed pretending to be asleep. He had been pretending to be asleep for a long time now but she still hadn't moved. Maybe she wasn't the adventurous type. But how could she not be? Taking in every penis that pointed in her direction, just so long as it had an endowment of a hundred bucks or so to go with it—a few chips the dealers had missed. So now if she thought he was sleeping she'd leave, try to turn one or two more tricks before daylight.

Then he realized she had moved. One minute he had been touching her and the next he wasn't. He tried to sense her movement; he couldn't open his eyes, because he knew she'd be watching his face all the way out the door. She'd done this before, he thought. She knew enough not to crawl on the bed with her hands and knees; just seemed to slide across the sheets. It was probably a talent that was worth a lot to her: when she'd managed to temporarily exhaust a particularly

102

difficult client, or at times like this when she'd been paid for the whole night in advance. He heard a very quiet swishing sound as she pulled on her underpants, but not even a snap of elastic. A few seconds later he heard the click of a clasp or a button, but that was all. Then he could sense her presence near the door, and more whispers of cloth. It seemed to take a long time. What the hell was she waiting for? Oh yes—the wallet in his pants. She was the adventurous type.

Then the door opened and closed so smoothly that he didn't hear the click of the latch, just felt it. He opened his eyes and looked around the room. It was as though she'd never been there at all. Perfect. He went to the wall by the door and looked at the pile of clothes he'd left there, picked up his pants and felt for his wallet. Good. At least she hadn't taken the whole thing. He looked inside and counted his money—still better. She had been smart. She'd only taken about four or five of the sheaf of twenties and left everything else intact. Most of the time when she met the trick at two A.M. and smelled liquor on his breath, she could assume he wouldn't even know she'd taken anything. At least he wouldn't be sure. He threw the wallet on the bed and smiled while he chose fresh clothes from the closet. He didn't begrudge her the money. He'd have given her almost that much as a tip if she'd stayed all night anyway. Then his smile turned into a chuckle. If he'd been able to trust her, he'd have given her three times that much to leave now and not tell Little Norman. And as it was, he knew she'd never let Little Norman know she hadn't stayed with him in the room. Not if Little Norman had paid her. Not ever. Not on her life.

103

12 He was dressed and ready in a few seconds. It was time to make some quick arrangements. If someone spotted the girl before daylight they'd check to be sure he was still in the room. He slipped out the door and down the hall to the back stairway. Then he was outside again in the mild, sluggish night air, making his way down the street. He did his best to look inconspicuous, but he knew that walking slowly with the few late gamblers wasn't enough. If he was seen at all they'd recognize him and after that their curiosity would be insatiable.

The crowds thinned out and straggled as they moved out on the Strip toward the Hacienda, and he felt his protection slipping away from him. Then the last of his companions turned off into one of the small motels and he was alone again. It was no use trying to do it on foot—he'd have to take a chance on a taxi. He strolled up the walk to the parking lot of the Hacienda. At this hour there were no cabs waiting in the loop, but he knew there would be one in a minute. He kept to the shadows near the street, strolling toward the front entrance as slowly as he could without attracting attention. Then a cab swung into the drive, bobbed to a stop at the top of the loop, and unloaded a young couple. He broke into a trot and reached the cab just as the driver was getting back in. "Can you take me to the airport?" he said, leaning down to speak so he would be practically shielded from the hotel.

The driver shot him an appraising look and said, "Sure. Get in." There was only a mile or so of empty highway between the Hacienda and the airport, and the driver accomplished it with a grim confidence. They still seemed to be accelerating when the cab swung into the drive.

The Avis Rent A Car agency was near the front entrance, the part of the airport dominated by candy counters and telephone booths. There would be two sets of watchers at the airport, he knew. The other set would be the one the police stationed there to see if any familiar faces were arriving under false names. But they would all be grouped around the ticket counters, baggage checks, and entrance gates; two sets of watchers, staring most of the time at each other. Now and then a face would appear that was a surprise to one side or the other, and then there would be a flurry of activity, one side attempting to surround the new face with disguises and distractions and whisk it away into obscurity while the other attempted to follow it unobserved.

But all of that was going on in the other part of the building, and the car-rental counters were as remote from that activity as any other part of this town could be. There was no trouble with the car. The Indiana driver's license and Mastercard in the name Frederick G. Ackermann weren't forged, after all. The bills were mailed to a post office box in Gary and forwarded. The fact that a nonexistent man paid his bills was sufficient identity.

He drove with a feeling of elation. There was no chance that they had noticed him at the airport, he could sense that. Now he did a few quick turns and then pulled over to the curb on a side street to be sure. After ten minutes he had seen no other vehicle, so that was that.

He drove the car back to the Strip and scanned the buildings and signs. It had to be now, so the stores were out of the question. The pawnshops were too dangerous because you could never tell what silent partners there might be—and what pawnshop would be open at four A.M., even in Las Vegas? No, the only chance was a gas station, the right kind of gas station, and the only way to tell if it was right was by location. He described it in his mind and using that description as a map, he drove out of town and straight through the moonlit desert to it and pulled up beside the air pump. If it were the right place there would be some opportunity. He got out and walked around the car staring at the tires with a look of puzzlement. Inside the lighted cubicle of the station a man in greasy work clothes sat reading a magazine with his feet up on the desk. Faint sounds of a radio floated above the occasional drone of a solitary vehicle rushing past on the distant freeway.

He checked the tires and added a pound of pressure to one of them, now and then glancing at the gas man in his cubicle. The gas man never moved, never looked up throughout the whole operation. He got back into the car and moved it to the gas pumps. He was glad that the car-rental companies had stopped filling the tanks before they rented them. He topped off the tank and entered the station where the still-motionless gas man sat reading. Now that he could see the magazine he noticed that it was a *Newsweek* dated June 15. That didn't seem to matter to the gas man, any more than it mattered that he hadn't turned the page. He must have found one that he liked.

"I owe you four fifty," he said, waving one of his twenty-dollar bills.

To stand up the gas man only lurched forward, still bent slightly at the hips, as though something about the desert had baked the fluidity out of him while he was sitting there waiting for something to happen important enough to propel him out of that chair. He scuttled to the cash register and stood with his face close to the drawer and his shoulders hunched around it in an unconscious attitude that resembled an embrace.

In a second or two the gas man would be scuttling back to the chair, so there was no choice but to ask him. "Is this place a store, too?"

"Store? Hell no. All the stores're in town," said the gas man. "Buy nearly anything there, lots of things you'd be better off not having." He turned around and laid the bills in the stranger's hand without counting them, as if to say a grown man can damn well count his own change, and if he doesn't do

106

it he's a fool. The stranger didn't move, so the gas man's eyes flitted longingly at his chair, but he didn't follow them: he stayed where he was between the customer and the cash register.

"Oh," he said. "Looked like a store, with all the stuff you've got sitting here."

"That?" said the gas man. "That's something, all right. It's not merchandise. It's security."

"Security?"

"That's right. Folks leave Vegas sometimes without enough gas to get home to L.A. They drive a few miles and then figure they're out far enough to find somebody dumb enough to give them a tank of gas on credit. I'm it."

He only nodded and gave a knowing smile, so the gas man went on, well launched on his favorite proof of the utter folly of mankind.

"I've seen 'em all. Brand-new Cadillacs pull in here and no money at all to buy gas. So they'll leave things. Watches, diamond rings. Damn near anything. They'll swear up and down they'll be back in a day to give me the money and pick up what they left. Once in a while they do, but mostly not. Even had one once wanted to leave her two kids here for security."

"So all this stuff was traded for gas?"

"No," said the gas man, shaking his head and looking down at the floor. "Security." He pointed at a man's wrist-watch hanging on a utility hook next to a crescent wrench. "That watch was left over two years ago for a tank of premium. Fifteen gallons, it was. About ten bucks. Watch is worth two hundred easy, and I still got it."

"Amazing," he agreed. "You ought to sell off some of this stuff. Probably make a hell of a profit."

"You're right," said the gas man. "I ought to, but I don't get much chance. On the way into Vegas they don't stop out here, and on the way out they don't have any money. Just this

107

stuff. Radios, suits, jewelry, guns, suitcases, whatever they brought with 'em and haven't figured out how to trade for chips. You see anything you want, make me an offer."

"Maybe I will," he said. "What have you got?"

"Lots of things. All in the next room here, waiting for 'em to come and buy it back. Take a look."

In the back room, which was also the gas man's toolroom, an entire wall was covered with the miscellaneous belongings of the travelers. It looked like the lair of a burglar. There were piles of suitcases, a rack of expensive clothing, and a pegboard covering the back wall that was hung with cameras, radios, binoculars, jewelry, guns, and even a painting of breakers crashing onto the beach at an imaginary Malibu that had been supplied by the artist with a few indomitable gray rocks. He casually surveyed the hoard, looking more closely at a pair of binoculars and a camera before he let himself turn to the guns.

"I'll give you a hundred for this one," he said, tapping his finger on the graceful walnut stock of a thirty-ought-six with a scope.

"A hundred?" said the gas man. "That won't do it. The scope's worth eighty. Man who owned it got a bighorn sheep with that rifle just a week or so before I got it."

"He tell you that, did he?" he smirked.

"Well, it's a good rifle. I'll take two hundred for it."

He studied the rest of the guns hanging on the pegboard for a second, then said, "If you'll throw in this pistol I'll give you two-twenty."

The gas man looked more closely at the rifle, then plucked the pistol off the wall and tested the action. It was a thin .32-caliber Beretta. He thought for a second and then said, "Cash?"

He nodded and the gas man handed him the pistol. He put it in his coat pocket and counted eleven twenties from his wallet. The gas man counted the twenties a second time before

108

he folded them and put them into the pocket of his overalls. Then he started to turn away, but stopped and added, "Sell you some ammunition for those? I got no use for it."

"People leave you cartridges too?"

The gas man chuckled. "No, just one. Fellow had a whole case full of it. All kinds. Guess he was a collector or something. I'll give it to you for half the marked price."

"I'm not really interested," he said. "I wasn't out here on a hunting trip, you know, but I'll take a box of each if it's not too old."

"About a year, no more." He was already bent over a crate in the corner, reading the small cardboard boxes he pulled out, one by one, until he'd found what he wanted. "Let's see. That'll be eleven dollars."

When he paid the gas man and took the two cartridge boxes he noticed the date on them was almost three years ago, but he'd only looked out of curiosity. It made no difference. At the car he set the rifle and the cartridge boxes in the trunk, taking only the Beretta and a dozen rounds into the front with him. He glanced at his watch as he pulled out onto the highway. Only twenty-five minutes—less time than it would have taken to fill out the papers in Los Angeles.

There was only one problem left, and that was where to put the car. It had to be available, close to Caesar's, and in a place where it would attract no notice. If you put it that way, there was no choice. He glided up the drive in front of Caesar's Palace, pulled to a stop in the middle of the only part of the parking lot that was still crowded at this hour, and got out. He opened the trunk as far as he could without letting the light go on, loaded the rifle by the light of the moon, jammed it into the wheel well beside the spare tire so it pointed to the rear, and closed the trunk.

He was in the hotel's back hallway a moment later, skirting the casino and shops, and taking the back stairway to his room. There was no sign that anything had been moved. His clothes were still in a heap on the floor by the door, and the television was still glittering noiselessly into the darkness, throwing colored shadows across the crumpled white sheets of the bed. There was little chance anyone knew he had been out, and whatever searching they were going to do had been done early in the evening. He had managed to build himself an edge—not much of an edge, just a car and some guns that they wouldn't know about. But then he probably wouldn't need an edge. He was on vacation.

He loaded the pistol, went to his bag, and took out six large Band-Aids. He used them to tape the pistol tightly to the wall inside the closet above the doorway, the one spot where nobody ever looked. Then he took his pocket knife and cut a thin slit in the lining of his left coat sleeve just above the cuff and pushed the two car keys into it. It wasn't much of an edge, he thought, but at least it was enough to let him go to sleep. It was almost five in the morning, and it had been a long day for a man who wasn't working.

13 Senator Claremont's papers had been stuffed into a battered brown leather briefcase and flown to Denver in the baggage compartment of the airliner. They sat apart from the rest of his belongings on a little table in the corner of the laboratory, the latch of the case burnished to a dull gold sheen by daily handling.

Elizabeth sat sipping her morning coffee and staring at the soft, wrinkled leather. "Has anybody gone into the papers yet?" she asked, her voice catching a little in her throat so that it came out almost a whisper. It reminded her it was the first full sentence she'd said this morning. Hart had left a note under her door telling her to take a taxi to the FBI building. She had yet to see him, and wondered vaguely where he was. Elizabeth cleared her throat and prepared to try again, but Mistretta had heard.

"Not yet. We're checking with the White House first. Protocol. The theory is you never know what might be in there. There's always a chance it might be something they don't want turning up as physical evidence at somebody's murder trial."

"Are they sending somebody?"

Mistretta shrugged and went on with his work, which consisted of studying a long typewritten list and making a shorter list on a pad beside it. Elizabeth decided against asking him what the list was. It looked too much like the sort of drudgery he might want to share.

She left him and went down the hall to the main office. As she came in the receptionist said, "Miss Waring, this is just in for you over the line from Washington." It was a computer printout. Elizabeth accepted it without bothering to look. She

111

had seen Padgett's airline summaries too many times. "Is there a place I can spread these out?" she asked.

The receptionist glanced at the sheaf, appearing to calculate its length and apply it to all available spaces. "The best place is the conference room," she said, indicating the room where Elizabeth had been the night before.

Elizabeth stepped into the room and considered closing the door, but didn't. It wasn't that the airline reports didn't require concentration, but that the concentration probably wouldn't produce any useful results anyway. She unfurled the long, continuous scroll on the conference table and then walked back to the head of the table where it began.

FLT 205 UNITED. DENVER CHICAGO: DEP: 0503. ARR: 0647. Underneath were the names and addresses of the passengers. She wasn't sure what to do with them. Padgett used the reports to spot the particular two or three hundred names he referred to as his "friends." All that took was programming the computer to remember the names, addresses, credit card numbers, and usual aliases. It was done in a second a day. But this was different, and would have to be done by elimination.

The murderer worked alone—one set of marks on the window, a single person sneaking around in the darkness trying not to wake up a sleeping victim—it had to be one person. But would the person travel alone? It would be less suspicious to travel with someone else: a family, children and all. No, that couldn't be. If he traveled with someone else his companion would know. The camouflage wasn't worth the risk. So it had to be a single reservation. And it was probably a man, most likely between twenty and forty. The marks on the window were too high for any but the tallest women, and the climbing around on the balconies in the cold would require the kind of flexibility and stamina that began to disappear early even in athletes.

She went through the passenger list of Flight 205, cross-

112

ing out all the obviously female names and the men who traveled with them, all the half-fare children's seats, all the men who were traveling in pairs on one reservation. That part worried her, so she thought it through again: who would the second man be? A partner? But if it were a partner, he would have to be responsible for doing something that was worth a share of the money, if there were money involved. But if the murder was political, there wouldn't be any distrust, and no money: he might be a contact, a controller, a spymaster. No, that was unlikely too. There was no reason for any organization to risk a second agent where he had no particular function. Then she remembered that there was still the Senator's briefcase. If something were missing from the briefcase the second man would be the one to take the handoff. If that were it, though, they wouldn't be on the same plane. They'd be on two different planes going in different directions, or no plane at all. The handoff would take place before anybody left town, and probably very soon after the murder. So he had to be alone. A young man alone. Elizabeth moved down the long conference table, crossing off the names on each flight. She lost track of the time it took, and when she reached the foot of the table and straightened up, her back was stiff. She noted it and forgot it as she walked back to the top of the list.

The next thing had to be the times. The Senator hadn't gone to bed until after 11:30 Monday night. That meant nobody could have come in until midnight at the earliest. If everything went supernaturally well he could have been out by 12:30 and caught a 1:00 A.M. flight out of Denver. She sat down on the nearest chair and worked out the rest of it: a 2:00 A.M. flight from Cheyenne, a 3:00 A.M. from Pueblo, a 3:30 from Laramie, a 2:30 from Boulder, and nothing earlier than 6:00 from Salt Lake City. There was something else about times, but she couldn't quite identify it yet. It was too vague, just a feeling that she was missing something impor-

113

tant. She opened her mind but it wouldn't come, so she stood up and walked down the list again, this time crossing out the flights that were too early.

Elizabeth studied the list and thought for a minute—of course, the addresses. If somebody had killed a senator and gotten on an airplane afterward, it meant he didn't live in Denver. That let out about half the remaining names, which she spent the next half hour crossing off. The list was getting short now, and she was able to tear out whole sheets and set them aside.

She sat there and thought it out again from the beginning. There were still around five hundred names, too many to do anything with. But there was something else—it was all too neat, too logical, and she was getting farther and farther along, each step depending on the others, and if one step was wrong he could slip through the mesh. It all depended on his being logical too, setting everything up just as Elizabeth would herself. All he had to do to escape her logic was to do something foolish—have a companion he trusted enough to travel with—something of that sort. But there was still something else and she was near it now. She could feel it. He wasn't foolish. He'd done too much too carefully already, taken too many steps to get to the Senator and get out without faltering or wasting time. He made all the right choices, and some of them were crazy. They were crazy, but they were logical.

Elizabeth looked at the list and it was suddenly clear. She was looking at the wrong list. What she needed was the reservations list. She knew now that she understood him. He was a man who made choices. He hadn't climbed into the hotel room of a U.S. senator knowing he was going to poison his dentures. That was what had bothered her from the beginning. It was too absurd. It was just that he carried with him a range of options in case he needed them. He wouldn't take a chance on not getting out, missing a flight or having it cancelled,

114

and he couldn't be sure he'd succeed on the first try. If it was the first try. He'd be double-booked. He might have reservations on a flight every hour for several days. And there would probably be a car, and a bus ticket too. It didn't matter which one he finally used, whether he'd gotten on a plane or driven out or disappeared into thin air or stayed put. The point was, he'd have given himself all the options. Whatever he'd finally done didn't matter at all, and there was no sure way to resurrect it now anyway. The only thing she was sure of was that he'd be on more than one list. Elizabeth snatched up her printouts and walked out of the conference room.

"Where's your computer terminal?" she asked the receptionist.

"Room twenty-one seventeen," said the receptionist.

Lang, the FBI man she'd met last night, was in the terminal talking to one of the programmers when Elizabeth arrived. He listened carefully as she tried to explain what she wanted. The programmer saw her theory immediately. He said, "What's the flag?"

"What do you mean?" asked Elizabeth.

"What do we ask the computer to look for to establish a match?"

"Names, addresses, credit card numbers if there are any. Anything that comes up more than once. The idea is, he'd want to use several airlines, probably several nearby points of departure, and certainly several times, beginning with Monday night and ending when the Senator was scheduled to leave Denver. When was that, Mike?"

"This Friday night," Lang said.

"Okay," said the programmer. "I'll begin with the airlines. You want car rentals, buses, Amtrak. Anything else?"

"No," said Elizabeth. "If that doesn't produce at least a double, then I'm wrong in the first place."

"Right," agreed the programmer, and began to type in

115

codes with rapid, jittery fingers as though Elizabeth and Lang had ceased to exist or had somehow been switched to another circuit that had nothing to do with him.

An electric voice that Elizabeth recognized as the ghost of the receptionist said, "White phone, Agent Lang," through the intercom. He went to the wall and picked up the telephone. Then he listened for a moment, said "Understood," and hung up.

He headed for the door before turning to Elizabeth. "We can get started on the papers now, if you'd like to be in on that."

"I suppose I would," said Elizabeth. "The reservations lists will probably take most of the day."

In the laboratory Elizabeth expected to see the others already peering into the briefcases, but when she and Lang arrived the room was empty. "Where is everybody?" she asked.

Lang said, "Hart's on the poison with the forensics people. They're taking the samples to the Air Force's toxicology lab today and then hanging in for a theory on where it came from. Mistretta's investigating the people who stayed in the Constellation Hotel. The theory now is that whoever it was must have checked in, but not necessarily while the Senator was there. Anybody who would want to kill the Senator would have known enough about him to know that's where he'd stay when he came to town. Hobson's sweating through the police reports for all the precincts in Denver beginning last Friday. Davis is doing the same for state police. MacDonald—I don't think you've met him—is coordinating all the inquiries to other agencies, trying to get them to squeeze their informants —Alcohol, Firearms, and Tobacco; Narcotics, CIA, and so on. I've got other people collecting hotel and motel registrations all over the city, watching airports and train stations for old faces, and others transmitting everything to Washington for interpretation. So we're stretched damn near the limit around here. Within a couple of days we're going to have about all the raw data we're going to get. If we don't get a break or an inspiration pretty soon, somebody's going to have an uncomfortable time in the Senate.

"What do you mean?"

"There's bound to be a special committee of inquiry set up to find out what happened. Somebody from the Bureau— probably the director himself—is going to have to go in there with whatever we can give him. If he doesn't have a culprit, he's going to have to prove there's such a thing as a perfect crime."

"You don't really have much hope for it, do you?" she asked.

Lang turned to study her for a moment. A look of tired amusement seemed to flicker across his face, but he stifled it, took off his glasses, and peered closely at the lenses before taking out his handkerchief to clean them. "No, I don't. I didn't at the start. Somebody who pulls off something like this and manages to get himself out of sight afterward without leaving a print or a witness is practically home free. He doesn't look any different from anybody else." He put on his glasses again, as though illustrating his point, and added, "What it amounts to is a burglar who didn't take anything."

Elizabeth thought about it and sighed. It really was a lot like that. She was beginning to feel tired again, and it wasn't even noon yet. "So we're just covering now, trying to look thorough, is that it?"

"Oh, no," said Lang, suddenly flustered. "We're not dogging it and neither is Washington. They're doing a real number on that end; looking for a motive, sending out their own people to follow every lead. I just meant we've got two things to worry about—doing our job and preparing to prove we've done it. So let's get going on that briefcase." He went to the corner of the lab and picked up the briefcase. He stopped at a desk and pulled a printed form out of the top drawer and brought that back with him to the table.

"Here's how it goes," he said. "We take down an itemized list of what's in here, and then each of us signs it. Just a standard procedure when the owner isn't around to sign the slip, but let's be sure we don't make any mistakes on this one. A year from now I don't want a man from the National Security Agency to show up with this in his hand asking me how some document the Senator once initialed turned up for sale in Berlin or Hong Kong or Zurich."

Lang took out the first thick sheaf of printed matter. He said, "I'd say this is a copy of the *Congressional Record*, pages 1098 through 2013, twelve January through one February. With—let's see—penciled corrections and notes. Agreed?"

Elizabeth glanced at it, and nodded as she wrote down the description.

Next there were an address book, a set of airline schedules, an issue of *Time* magazine, a draft of a speech on income taxes. It felt uncomfortable and strange, not because she was going through a dead man's belongings, but because they didn't feel as if they belonged to a dead man at all. Everything was half finished, cut short: the magazine fresh and still smelling of printer's ink, the speech still lacking a conclusion as though someone had just stopped talking to answer the telephone in the middle of a sentence. But then she remembered that was all murder was, once you got beyond the blood and the pain and the momentary unpleasantness.

She wrote rapidly as Lang formulated the descriptions. They seemed overly precise, silly almost if you allowed yourself to think about them that way: "Spiral-bound notebook. Quantity, one. Blue. Gem Corporation. Eight and a half by eleven, numbered pages to two hundred. Pages eight, nineteen, seventy-three, and one hundred and six missing. One, no, two packs of cigarettes, Sobranie, unfiltered. Wrappers unopened. Memorandum, dated February third, addressed to All Senatorial Offices from Mr. Deering of the General Services Administration, Re: Unnecessary Use of Electricity."

As she scribbled the word "electricity" she was saying, "Got it."

"That's it," said Lang. "Oh yeah . . . briefcase, brown leather with brass fittings. Initials MRC."

They both signed the list and Lang held onto it. "I'll go call this in to Washington now," he said. "They can reassure the White House that we're not sitting here looking for fingerprints on the plans for a new ICBM."

"Can I get started on these papers?" asked Elizabeth.

"Sure thing," he said. "The only things that look promising are the address book and the notebook, but you might as well get started." He went out and closed the door behind him.

The first few pages of the notebook were enough. She leafed through the hundred and seven other pages with writing on them, and they didn't get any better. The notebook was a sedimentary deposit of all the things the old man had wanted to remember. Appointments with other senators and appointments with his doctor crowded lists of groceries and fragmentary cryptic memoranda. *Bannerman Act—call N.G. Remind Carlson to invite d'Orsini et al. Sunday.* She wondered if she had a clue when she saw the double exclamation on *Clayburn!!* until she saw the triple exclamation on *Pretzels!!!* There were phrases from what appeared to be political orations: *The trouble is, they're trying to run the country like a poker game*—but there were no notations as to who had said it, where, why, or when.

ELIZABETH SAT AND THOUGHT. There would have to be some kind of systematic grid that could be constructed to unravel it. It was rather simple, actually. Since the reminders and appointments would have to be written in before they happened, the exact dates could be pinned down by checking with the

119

other people involved. The notations on each page would have to be transcribed in thematic divisions—to start with, the categories could be *appointments and reminders, political references, personal references,* and *miscellaneous.* There had to be a *miscellaneous.* It might be possible to retrieve almost all of it—whom he saw or spoke to, what he was doing each day of the past two months, what he was thinking about. It would take some time, though, and might not be of any use. After all, if there had been anything there, wouldn't the Senator have noticed it in time to save himself?

But there were shortcuts available. He'd had a staff, and they would be able to translate most of the notations, maybe all of them. There was the legislative assistant. What was his name? She leafed through the notebook again, and it was everywhere: *Papers on Calloway Bill—Carlson. Have Carlson call N.G. Re: Oil Depl. Allow.*

Elizabeth walked to the wall and snatched the white telephone. It rang immediately and then she noticed it had no dial. The voice that said "Yes" was that of the receptionist. My God, she thought, doesn't anybody else work here? But she said, "This is Elizabeth Waring in the Forensic Lab. Can you get me an appointment with Mr. Carlson, the Senator's aide, as soon as possible?"

"I'm sorry, Miss Waring," said the receptionist. "Mr. Carlson is on his way back to Washington. I'm sure we can put through a call to him this evening."

"Damn!" said Elizabeth. "Who told him he could go and why in the world would he want to?" She regretted it instantly, but already the receptionist's even, measured tones were answering, "Mr. Lang spoke with him on the telephone only a short time ago before he left the hotel."

"So he may not be gone yet?" said Elizabeth.

"His plane leaves this afternoon at twelve thirty and arrives in Washington at seven fifteen Eastern time."

Elizabeth glanced at her watch. It was just noon. "I'm

120

sorry, but there's no dial on this phone. Can you call the airline and ask them to get him to a phone? It could be important." She was glad she'd said "could be." Her control was coming back.

"Yes. If we locate him I'll ring you in the lab."

The telephone rang again in a few minutes and Elizabeth said, "Waring."

"I have Mr. Carlson on the line," said the receptionist.

"Mr. Carlson?"

"Yes, Miss Waring," he said. Behind his voice there was a huge hollow where random noises echoed. He spoke tonelessly and loudly as though he had his free hand pressed to his ear.

"I have a number of questions that you seem to be the only one who can answer, and I—"

"Miss Waring, I'm sorry, but I have a flight to Washington that's already boarding, and I'm about to miss it as it is. Can I call you back when I get home this evening?"

"I'm afraid that won't do. You see, I have something you'd have to look at to be able to explain. If you could take a later flight, I'd—"

"I've already been interviewed and grilled and investigated for over twenty-four hours, and—oh. Just a second." Elizabeth could hear that another male voice was droning just outside the range of understanding. Then Carlson said something too. It went on for a few seconds, and then she heard him sigh into the receiver. He said, "I've just missed my flight. I have to wait four hours for the next one." He sounded sad.

"Where can I meet you?" asked Elizabeth.

"How about here, if it's just a few questions? I'll be at the American Airlines desk in about twenty minutes. I'll be in a light gray suit, looking impatient. And you?"

"I'll be the lady carrying the Senator's notebook."

* * *

121

WHEN SHE SAW HIM HE was standing at the ticket counter staring at his watch, then craning his neck out of the stiff shirt collar with his mouth slightly open as though to demonstrate to anyone in his vicinity that he was a man who was being unjustly delayed by petty matters. When he spotted her striding toward him with the notebook, he leaned back against the counter and pursed his lips in a look of sardonic displeasure.

Elizabeth tried to remind herself that he probably *was* being delayed by petty matters—by a piece of evidence that wasn't likely to be evidence of anything in particular—but she knew that the people in the ticket line were thinking that she was an incompetent secretary who had misplaced an important document and made her employer, the efficient-looking, carefully tailored and barbered man in the gray suit whose glasses were even now glittering little semaphores of disdain at her, late. She couldn't forgive him that. So when she was still seven feet away she said, "Relax, Mister Carlson, you're not under arrest. We just want to have a talk." She spoke in a voice that sounded as though it was meant to reassure a man who was essentially a coward.

His reaction brought to birth a smile she had to stifle: it was as though he had been prodded from behind. He was off and walking and she almost had to run to catch up. He didn't stop until he was no longer visible to the people at the counter. He was definitely annoyed. "Miss Waring, I thought you people were much more discreet."

Elizabeth just gave him a puzzled look, then appeared to dismiss his odd behavior by placing it in some category well known to professional investigators who were accustomed to seeing people at their worst. She said, "Well, shall we get started? I'd hate to have you miss the next flight." It was said with what could almost have been taken as sympathy if they hadn't understood each other so well.

"All right," he said. "Where?"

"I've made arrangements to borrow a conference room."

They were expected at the airport courtesy desk. The room was off the main lobby and contained ten chairs, three of which looked comfortable, and a long wooden table. There were no windows, but a painting of an undifferentiated landscape was hung along the far wall. They both chose utilitarian chairs at the table. Elizabeth opened the Senator's notebook and took out her own.

"Mr. Carlson, why were you going back to Washington today?"

"Because Senator Claremont is dead. There didn't seem to be anything I could do about it and Agent Lang said I might as well go. You people were through with me. Am I under suspicion?"

"No, of course not," said Elizabeth, as though the idea had never crossed her mind.

"That's good, because if I am, we'll stop this right now while I get my lawyer."

"I'd thought of that," said Elizabeth, "but that would be time consuming, and we didn't want to delay you any longer than necessary. If you'll just give me the best cooperation you can, I'm sure we can get through this quickly.

"Tell me what you know about this notebook."

"It's not really a notebook. It's a scratch pad. The Senator liked to keep it by him so he could jot down things that occurred to him when he didn't have time to do anything about them," said Carlson. "He had a rotten memory and had the sense to know it, so he wrote things down."

"Did it work?"

"Most of the time he'd remember to keep the rest of us informed. The appointments would get transferred to his calendar and so on. Sometimes he'd forget. Sometimes he'd even forget where he'd put the notebook—leave it in some hearing room or a press conference or someplace. But it always turned up."

"I'd like to go through a few portions of it and see if you can help me understand it," said Elizabeth.

123

"Sure," said Carlson. He glanced at his digital wristwatch as though he were going to charge for his time beginning now. Then he opened the notebook and began to read it aloud. "Dinner the seventh–S.A. That's the dinner the Saudi Arabian ambassador gave on the seventh of January. He never could remember the ambassador's name, which is Ruidh, so he gave up trying. Call R.T.T., that's got to be Ronald T. Taber, the congressman from Iowa. They were in on a farm bill a few years back, and now and then one or the other would call to compare notes on how it was working."

Elizabeth wrote quickly, trying to catch as much as she could, and hoping that the order of it would help her put it back together later. Carlson went on, looking and talking as though it were a family album full of vaguely familiar faces. He was good, she had to admit. He seemed to know what everything was and how it came to be that way.

Finally he came to the list and stopped. "I don't know what all this is," he said. "It must relate to the tax hearings that he was planning for the fall."

"Relate in what way?"

"Well," said Carlson, "there was a special staff for the committee, which handled details for the hearings. They're more likely to be able to tell you for sure than I am. This isn't anything I handled."

"But what does it look like?"

"It's a list of corporations—all sizes and shapes. See? Bulova, General Motors, Eastman Kodak. Then you get ones nobody ever heard of—Gulf Coast Auto Leasing, Standard Hardware. North Country Realty. A few that are utilities: PG&E, Commsat, FGE, Con Ed."

"What do you think he was going to do with them?"

"Maybe use them in a speech, maybe subpoena their books, maybe call somebody to testify. I don't know. They have a staff for that."

"Who would know?"

124

"Justin Garfield would. Staff counsel. This list is over a month old and if it has anything to do with the committee, he'd probably have been in on it by now. You can't call in General Motors and tell them to be there next week with a shoebox full of receipts and tax forms. It takes time to get it together in a form that one person can look at."

Elizabeth turned the notebook toward her and glanced down the list. "What does PG&E stand for?"

"Pacific Gas and Electric. Oh, yes, I forgot. You're from the East."

"And FGE?"

"Probably Florida Gas and Electric."

"Where do I get in touch with Justin Garfield?"

Carlson pulled a leather address book out of his inside pocket and read, "(202) 692-1254, extension 2. Should we go on?"

"Please."

Carlson returned to his translation, moving from page to page with renewed confidence. It was clear that senators didn't get much time for solitude or much privacy either. Carlson knew whom the Senator had seen, whom he'd called, and what they'd talked about. Twice he had to turn to his own address book and match a telephone number with an initial, but that was only to verify. At last they reached the end of it and Carlson said, "Is that all you wanted from me?"

"Yes, Mr. Carlson. Thank you for your cooperation. Where can I reach you if we need to ask anything else?"

"For now, in the Senator's office. If my situation changes, I'll let the FBI know." He glanced at his watch again and said, "Good-bye." They didn't shake hands before he went out, closing the door behind him.

AT THE CONSTELLATION HOTEL the only sign that there was anything that hadn't been planned and provided by a solici-

125

tous and efficient management was that the elevator wouldn't stop at the fourth floor.

It wasn't until she closed the door to her room that Elizabeth realized she had forgotten to stop at the Bureau to return the Senator's notebook to the lab. She cradled the telephone in her lap while she rummaged through her purse for Lang's number. When the telephone rang she felt it and heard it at the same time. Her startled jump knocked the phone to the floor.

"Hello?" she shouted into it.

"Hi, clumsy," said the voice.

"Hello, Padgett," she said. "What have you got for me?"

"A sore finger. I've been calling all day."

"I was at the FBI working."

"You don't have to tell me. I don't handle travel expenses. Making any headway?"

"We've got a little to go on, but it's mostly hunches and shaky physical evidence. Enough to keep us busy. Have you got anything new on the Veasy thing?"

"Just what you asked for. The company pension fund has been mishandled, from the look of it."

"Ah—"

"Just mishandled. Stupidity, not crookedness. They've dumped most of it into pie-in-the-sky stuff, hoping for a killing. A lot of it's gone to the outfit you asked about—Fieldston Growth Enterprises. It looks legitimate, but they're speculators, pure and simple. Buying up a lot of undeveloped land in resort areas, things like that. Been at it about eight years, picked up a lot of paper profit but not a dime you or the union or the IRS for that matter could put your hands on."

"Where's their office?"

"Las Vegas."

"Why did I ask? Who owns it?"

"Biggest stockholder is Edgar Fieldston himself, at forty-two percent. There's not much information on him. No arrests, pays his taxes and all that. He's chairman of the board and draws a salary of seventy-five thousand. Second is the Machinists, who own fifteen percent. The rest are individuals, a couple of banks, all small percentages."

"Where'd you get all this?"

"It's all public information—their annual report, 'FGE for the Future.' Then I checked with a few people in the SEC and the FTC to corroborate—"

"FGE."

"Sure. Fieldston Growth Enterprises."

"Is Brayer nearby? I've got to talk to him."

14 He woke up to his own face; as though it were a separate entity that had moved into the room during the night and now filled a corner like a piece of furniture that would somehow have to be moved aside before anything else could happen. It was dry and angry and hot to the touch. He made his way to the mirror and confronted it.

It wasn't as bad as it felt, he thought—not infected, anyway. But it was going to take some time and even then it would leave a scar. The bruises and bumps would go away in a couple of weeks, but not the cut. The knee was stiff, but he could feel the blood beginning to course through it and loosen it a little.

He looked at his watch. Eleven o'clock already. He carefully shaved, ran the shower over his wounds, put on clean clothes, and went out into the corridor. It was time to pick up the watchers and get something to eat. They'd probably be waiting near the two most likely exits. He strolled along, testing the knee for hitches, but the elasticity of it seemed to have returned. He crossed the casino and made one circuit of the lobby before he turned to join the line at the ballroom. There middle-aged women in PTA dresses were ranged along a cash register to admit candidates for brunch, which they did with a stony and repellent efficiency, spotting hand signals from the waitresses with the impassive eyes of casino pit bosses.

The watchers weren't easy to spot this time. He didn't see any familiar faces, and he didn't see anyone who made a habit of staring past him into the distance. He had known the old couple would be gone, but it hadn't occurred to him that they might not be replaced by someone as obvious. He flashed a glance down the line for someone. If the watcher weren't very good, he would pick that moment to turn away or adjust his glasses or at least touch his face; nobody did.

Inside the ballroom he found a banquet laid for the purpose of proving to the eye that any paroxysm of human greed or voracity could run its course and still be buried in inexhaustible plenty. Pyramids of champagne glasses filled beyond the brim towered over mounds of scrambled eggs and sausages; bleeding slabs of beef were being expertly shaved into pink pages by shining blades. Piles of chicken breasts seemed in danger of spilling over their silver bins to crush the ornately decorated layered pastries. People of all descriptions assaulted the tables in celebration of their acceptance into this place where there could be no such thing as lack or unfulfilled desire.

Mothers piled extra squares of pastry, oozing globs of hollandaise, and slabs of paté on the plates of their children; elderly people balanced second plates on their skinny forearms as they picked their way back to their tables.

They drank and ate and then rushed to the serving trays to accumulate more while their first plates still were heaped with untasted food. All around the ballroom the obsequious starch-coated functionaries circulated like gentle spirits, filling glasses, deftly clearing spilled food and broken crockery from the aisles, and always, unceasingly and untiringly, replenishing the splendor of the serving tables—all of it calculated to foster in each guest the illusion that he had somehow managed to encompass the whole banquet with the amplitude of his desires and to engulf all of it in his insatiability; the pitiful rodent-inroads he had accomplished on the feast were made to stand in his mind for the fulfillment of Gargantuan yearnings in the soul of a restless and heroic being. As it always did, the management had succeeded in concocting a substantial form to stuff into the yawning emptiness of the clients' dimly perceived insufficiencies.

He had to wait a little longer because he was alone, and the management always balked a bit before devoting a table to one person. But he knew there would be a waitress who remembered that a man alone tips more generously than he does when his wife is watching. It took a few moments before one of them noticed him, cut him out of the gaggle of detainees, and conducted him to her region of the ballroom. It was a tiny table for two along the far wall, where he could survey the entire room without seeming to.

It wasn't until he saw Orloff that he knew where to look for the watcher. Orloff's short, corpulent body bobbed up into the line of people waiting for a table, and a man in a light blue cowboy shirt nodded to him and left. It was typical of Orloff, he thought—always in a hurry, always running three minutes late for an appointment somewhere else. He'd waste a face so he didn't have to stand fidgeting in a line, his pudgy fingers wandering over the immaculate surface of his gray suit coat as though something important were in one of the pockets.

He watched as Orloff's fat white hands fluttered impatiently at a passing waitress, then pointed at his table next to the wall. The waitress nodded and Orloff waddled rapidly down the aisle toward him. When Orloff reached the table there was a dewy mist of sweat on his face, as though he had just passed through a cloud. He was a little out of breath, but it sounded more like agitation than exertion. He was taking gasps of breath through his thin red lips and blowing them out his nose in nervous little snorts.

He pushed the chair opposite him away from the table with his foot and Orloff settled into it, his elbows already on the table.

"Have you lost your mind?" said Orloff.

"Why, have you found one?" he answered.

"It's Wednesday, the fifteenth of February," Orloff hissed, then paused to snort twice for emphasis. "Our agreement was that you would pass through here on Friday the seventeenth in the evening."

"I finished early."

130

Orloff's face seemed to bloat suddenly with suppressed anger. At that moment a waitress appeared with a jug of coffee, which she poured with cool precision in a stream from the height of about a foot. When she disappeared Orloff pronounced with malicious triumph, "You've made a serious mistake." Then he shook his head, making his jowls wobble. "It was not discreet. Not discreet at all."

"Don't worry," he answered. "They don't give a shit about you. They just wondered if I was here working, and I've taken care of that." He took a sip of his coffee, which he decided was rather good. It was a shame Orloff was here to distract him. He was getting hungry.

"Oh, I'm sure you have," Orloff sighed. "You show up three days early looking like that and then give me your assurances that everything's fine. You'll pardon me if I don't bubble over with confidence in your judgment."

"Sure. I'm not your psychiatrist."

Orloff almost smiled. "The condition of your face would indicate you've miscalculated before."

"If you're worried about it pay me now and I'll go away."

"It's not that simple," said Orloff, his hands beginning to flutter about in his suit coat again before he located his handkerchief and mopped his brow. "It's a sizable sum and it isn't here yet. Which, if you had lived up to our agreement, would have been here at the moment you arrived."

"Don't start talking breach of contract," he said. "You may be a terrific lawyer, but save it for a court. Nobody refuses to pay me."

"You've made it much more difficult. How do you imagine it'll look to them when a large sum is passed from us to you? It's much more difficult." He shifted his eyes to his coffee cup, staring at it as though he were surprised to see it. "Much more difficult, more difficult and more expensive."

"You'll get it. Nobody refuses to pay me," he smiled.

Orloff cocked his head and stared at him. "No," he said.

131

"I suppose they don't." He pushed his coffee away as though afraid he would spill it, then ascended to his feet like a freed balloon. "Friday," he said. He rushed back up the aisle, glancing at his watch.

He watched the fat man out the door, then went to the serving area to select some food. It was too stupid even to think about, he told himself. Orloff was afraid because he knew they would see the connection as soon as the money came out. But the first thing Orloff had done was walk right up and sit down with him in a public place where they were sure to be seen. What was that for? Maybe to prove to someone he wasn't afraid. Afraid of what?

None of the old men should care about it one way or another. It was a straightforward set of contracts between outsiders on outsiders. He carefully picked out fresh vegetables from the platter with a pair of silver tongs. Maybe it had something to do with the money: he'd said there was trouble getting it together. But they always said that, the lightweights and small timers—as if they were afraid he'd want more if they didn't pretend that was the last dime. Still, it didn't make any sense. Orloff was genuinely worried about something.

He moved along the serving line, picking small portions of food that looked as though they'd be good for him. By the time he had returned to his table he had worked enough of it out. There was a third party involved in it somewhere, a third party Orloff was afraid of. And if Orloff was more afraid of the third party than he was of him, he guessed maybe he'd better start worrying a little bit too.

ELIZABETH TRIED TO CONSOLE herself as she struggled to get the airplane seat to lean back at the proper angle. There wasn't much material to work with, but she tried. She'd been away long enough already, for one thing. It would be nice to sleep in her own bed and not have to worry that she was

132

running out of ways to recombine the few outfits she'd had time to throw into the suitcase. She looked at the profile of Hart in the seat beside her: of course, his time was up too. The FBI had jerked him back to Washington as they'd said they would. Wednesday was the limit. It didn't matter that the two of them had spent most of the time shuttling from disaster to disaster like a pair of reporters, always just a few hours too late to do anything but visit the spot where something was supposed to have happened. And there would be lots of work waiting for her when she got back to the office; Brayer had made that clear. It might not be work that made any difference, but somebody had to do it no matter what, and she was drawing the salary so it would be she. Elizabeth watched the stewardess making still another circuit of the cabin with her tray of drinks, offering each passenger one more chance whether he or she showed any interest or not, awake or asleep, alive or dead for all Elizabeth knew. Every station had to be treated with exactly the same leisurely solicitude, even if the stewardess knew the next five didn't want to be bothered and the sixth was waving a twenty with one hand and an empty glass with the other. Standard procedures had to be followed and there was always a logical reason for them that had to do with statistics. Organizations did things with the long run in mind. It was only individuals that jumped at momentary advantages, took short-cuts, made mistakes. Then Hart was talking to her.

"It's not as bad as all that," he was saying. "You look pretty depressed for somebody who's going home."

"It is as bad as all that," said Elizabeth. "I could tell we were getting closer to it. I could feel it. And now we'll go back and the whole thing will be buried in the files."

"Sure," he said.

"What do you mean?" said Elizabeth. "Is it as simple as that? No results because they didn't feel like letting us do a real investigation? That's great."

133

"I mean that we did what we were supposed to do—we looked around and got some information on two different matters, and it'll go into the files and maybe contribute to the handling of those matters. That's what it's all about."

"Matters?" said Elizabeth. "Jesus."

"You can't think in terms of solving these problems yourself. What you do is contribute to a systematic information-gathering effort, and you'd better realize that or you'll find yourself being unhappy and frustrated most of the time. Maybe a decent dinner would cheer you up. We'll be in Washington at five thirty and I could pick you up at eight. I might have enough clout to get us a late reservation at Le Provençal or Sans Souci on a Wednesday. I've always made a point of grossly overtipping just in case of an emergency like this."

She smiled as kindly as she could. "No thanks," she said. "I'm tired and I want to see what I can do tonight about the way I look before I stagger back to work in the morning."

He didn't seem daunted. There was something to be said for men who didn't seem daunted, she decided, but it wasn't enough to change anything. She listened as he tried to make his way back to neutral ground as gracefully as he could: "It's a solitary hamburger for each of us then," he grinned. "Some other time."

"Some other time," she agreed. But would there be another time, she wondered. There was a mystery to these things too. Sometimes something happened and sometimes nothing happened. Whatever controlled it was too subtle and indistinct to make rules about. She settled back in the seat and watched the approaching stewardess. There was no reason not to have a drink, she thought. She wasn't going anywhere.

134

15

Thursday morning. He stared into the mirror and worked his fingertips over the skin of his cheeks. It wasn't too bad. He was still young enough to heal quickly, he thought. In another day or two the suntan and the soft life would take care of the worst of it, and he was beginning to think there might not be a scar. He lingered in the shower for fifteen minutes, trying to decide how to manage the next stage of it. There was too much he didn't know. He dressed carefully and inspected the results. Not bad—a real estate man from Phoenix having a little side trip on the way home from a business meeting or a winter vacation, if it weren't for the bruises. But the sunglasses helped.

At the end of the hallway he waited for a moment to see if another door opened, but there was no sign of anyone. It would be the maid, probably, who would be under orders to ring someone she thought must be an assistant manager as soon as Room 413 was unoccupied. He took the stairs to the casino and moved through the crowds in the direction of the front entrance. The telephones here were too closely flanked by slot machines. There was no way of telling who today's watchers were, or even if there were some electronic eavesdropping system. It didn't matter because if they could video-tape every hand at every blackjack table they could probably pick up a number dialed on the house phones too, and there was no way for him to know what happened to the tapes afterward.

On the street he stopped to buy a newspaper at a vending machine, then walked into Uncle John's Pancake House. He waited at the door to see if the watchers were following closely

135

enough to be seen, then went to the telephone booth and placed the call.

He counted six rings before the voice on the other end said, "Dapper Dry Cleaners."

"Mr. De la Cruz, please," he said.

A voice shouted "De la Cruz" over the hum of machinery.

"Cruiser, I don't want to talk long, so listen. I have a little work I need to subcontract—maybe two days' worth and nothing noisy, so it can be any rummy as long as he doesn't stand out. Can you sell it for me?"

"Well, hello to you too, amigo. I heard somebody seen you but I didn't believe it. Bring me some shirts." The line went dead. He said good-bye to the dial tone and went back to the line of patrons waiting to be served for breakfast.

He sat down at the counter and ate quickly, scanning the paper. It wouldn't do to keep the Cruiser waiting too long: his other interests might take him away from the laundry. As soon as he could get out without seeming hurried, he was back on the street.

It didn't look as though the maid had been to his room yet; at least she hadn't cleaned it. He built a pile of his dirty shirts and fitted the hotel's plastic bag around it. Once outside he walked the two long blocks to the Flamingo to lead whatever watchers there might be far enough from their cars before he got into a taxi. To his disappointment he didn't see anyone rushing for a car as he drove off. That had been one of Eddie's favorites: "Always look as though you're doing one thing and do another; but do it smooth. Don't look as though you changed your mind. A stupid watcher will commit himself too early and walk right up your ass. If they're set up to cover you with a switch they'll usually look at each other, just like one was handing you off. They can't help it." But that was only if they weren't good. If they were, you might see them and you might not.

When he came through the entrance to the laundry he could see the Cruiser waiting for him in the center of the dry-cleaning section. Clothes on hangers suspended from the conveyer track on the ceiling whisked past the Cruiser's dark, slouching form like frantic ghosts. Abruptly the moving track stopped and the dresses and coats swung forward once, then backward, then stopped too, and hung opaque like a curtain. The Cruiser stepped from among them.

"Hello, amigo," he said, snatching the bag and shaking the shirts out onto the counter. "What's happening?"

"Just some watching until tomorrow night. Nothing special."

"How much?"

"Four hundred do it?"

"What's the bonus?"

"Another four for the best. One if I'm just sure he was awake and nobody saw him."

The Cruiser smiled and thumped the counter once with his fist and said, "Sold" and then returned to sorting shirts. "What's the name?"

"Harry Orloff. He's in the phone book. Want something up front now?"

The Cruiser nodded his head. "All but the bonus."

He looked up as he took the four hundred. "You know I can't do anything without something to at least flash at them, amigo. And if you're not around Friday when I deliver these shirts—I'm not saying you wouldn't want to pay, but things happen—I'd be out that much. I gotta live here, man, and—"

"It's all right. Just get on it as soon as you can. I'd like the shirts at seven on Friday. That okay?"

"Sure, amigo. See you then. Earlier if there's something to talk about. You at Caesar's?"

"Yes. Four thirteen."

"Okay," he said, and disappeared behind the hanging curtain of clothes.

137

When he was back on the street he glanced at his watch. It was 11:30 already. The best time to return to the Strip would be after twelve when the first of the DC 10's and 747's from the East arrived and dumped their hundreds of passengers at McCarron Airport. Every day the taxis streamed onto the Strip to deposit them, disoriented and burdened with luggage too heavy for them to carry, under the gigantic roofed porticos of the big hotels. And then each taxi would roar out the driveway again to try for one more piece of this flight or the first passengers off the next one—the man who was first to the taxi stand because he was in a hurry and didn't mind tipping big to get to the casinos.

He decided to walk. Sunshine and exercise were the best medicines in the world. He was feeling stronger already, even though his leg still didn't feel right. And maybe by evening he'd know what was bothering Orloff. It was probably just that somebody had seen him with Little Norman and gotten scared, but it could be anything. And for that matter, Little Norman hadn't behaved right either. As soon as he showed up with a bruise or two everybody had changed—as if he were an eyesore that was going to lower the going rates on hotel rooms or spoil the customers' appetites.

He reached the Strip at Sahara Avenue and crossed to the other side of the street. He passed Circus Circus, the Stardust, the Silver Slipper, and settled on the Frontier. It was a little quieter this time of day, and it was mostly blue inside. He established himself in the dark bar off the main casino and ordered a Bloody Mary. He didn't much like them, but if you were going to drink in the daytime you had to have what other people drank in the daytime.

As he sipped the Bloody Mary he could see that the midday flights must have begun arriving at the airport. Already on the other side of the casino the lobby was beginning to fill up with people wearing too many clothes for this weather, who apologetically stepped aside to avoid carts of baggage pro-

138

pelled with relentless efficiency toward the elevators by bell-men who seemed unaware of obstacles. In another half hour the first planes would be fueled and ready to take off again, and the scene would be complicated by the husbands in line at the hotel cashiers while the wives pumped the slot machine handles a few more times. If there were still watchers they would have to fight the crowds.

It was just about right, he thought. He wouldn't stay out of sight long enough to worry anyone; just long enough so the watchers would have time to pick him up again and pretend they hadn't lost him in the first place. Then he noticed that the bar was slowly beginning to fill up around him. In a few minutes more waitresses would appear, and when that happened the lights would begin to brighten imperceptibly so they could push the drinks without bumping into each other or losing track of anybody.

He edged farther into the shadows and watched the people coming into the bar. There were the usual couples—some middle-aged, husbands in sport coats and looking secretly pleased at the unfamiliar feeling of not wearing ties on a weekday. The wives in spotless unwrinklable pants outfits that were designed and manufactured to say money—some young, the pair not quite used to each other yet, the man still looking younger and greener than the woman in spite of what he thought of himself. Then there were a few solitaries, both men and women, all fortyish, who would sit down where they could get a good view of the casino. Usually they smoked heavily but didn't drink much—drank at all only because it was the price of the seats they occupied while they collected themselves from the long flight and scanned the casino to see which tables seemed to be paying off. After the first drink most of them would have to get change because they didn't have anything smaller than a hundred.

Then he noticed three men who didn't look right. Two were wearing business suits like junior bankers or insurance

139

men, and the third was dressed like a cowboy in a magazine ad—boots and jeans and a blue shirt with snaps on the pockets. They all came in together, but sat alone in different corners of the bar. He couldn't decide whether they were inspectors from the Nevada Gaming Commission or the troubleshooters the casino planted to keep the whores from hanging around and distracting the gamblers.

And then he spotted the old man crossing the lobby toward the elevators, his accountant in front of him to shield him from the possibility that anyone could come within eight feet of him, his lawyer beside him, eyes sweeping the surrounding area for any sign that something was out of place, and then, five paces behind him the porter pushing the luggage cart. It didn't matter who paid the men in the bar for watching the old man. Just the fact that Carlo Balacontano was here was enough reason to be somewhere else. The old man was an industry. There would be bodyguards, courtesy envoys from the semiretired Dons in the area, influence peddlers, favor seekers, business partners, all trooping in to get an audience with Carl Bala. And probably there would be cops, here to be sure he wasn't in town because he had a secret interest in a casino; and just as much, to be nearby if any of the people who hated him finally managed to have him killed—not to stop it, but to clean up afterward so the public order wasn't derailed too brutally or for too long. It wasn't a good place to be.

The old man had passed through and disappeared in a moment. He waited while the three men finished their drinks and left, then finished his own more slowly. He headed out through the aisles of jangling, buzzing, winking slot machines toward the side entrance to the parking lot.

ELIZABETH WAS NOT FULLY awake and it was ten o'clock already in Washington. It was her third time zone this week;

the fact that this was the one she was supposed to be accustomed to didn't help any. And being pulled away from her activity reports before she'd had fifteen minutes to burrow into the three-day backlog destroyed any illusion that she was settling back into the routine. As soon as he'd noticed her, Brayer had said, "Drop that. Padgett needs your help."

So now, as drudgery specialist for the entire office, damn them, she was doing Padgett's field reports while the computers in the room behind the glass wall ticked out more to be piled onto her own desk. Sometimes she imagined she could hear it, though she knew that was impossible. It wasn't just the work. It was that she was always at the mercy of contingencies, at any moment available to be pulled away from her own work to become what amounted to a clerical assistant to Padgett or Richardson or somebody. They were all supposed to be on a par: senior analysts. But when Elizabeth was in trouble you didn't see Brayer pulling them off anything to help her. And they didn't see it and wouldn't see it if they outlived the Washington Monument. It was just the way things were. Every time one of Padgett's "friends" felt his hemorrhoids acting up and decided to see a doctor in Des Moines, Elizabeth had to drop everything and monitor field reports or do background checks or something. And when the "crisis" was over and even the file report was already done because Elizabeth had done it for him, did anybody worry about Elizabeth's work? No, dammit, they didn't. They stood around in the lounge or took a much-needed day or two off.

This time it was going to be worse. There were four of Padgett's old mafiosi out of their neighborhoods at once, all in the Southwest, and now two had turned up in Las Vegas. These were old men, rich men. What else would they do in the winter but go to a warm spot? And of course they'd stop in Las Vegas. What on earth did John think? That they'd sit alone in the middle of the desert reading Gibbon's *Decline and Fall of the Roman Empire*, no doubt. And when Elizabeth

141

had worked two or three weeks as Padgett's lackey, they'd all four have had enough of the big hotels and gambling and golf and hookers and go back home to rest up and so would Padgett.

But not Elizabeth. She'd go back to her own desk and work three more weeks of twelve- and fourteen-hour days to catch up. But she wouldn't say anything to them, because there wasn't anything to say that was sufficient to overcome the massive stupidity of it. If she tried they'd wink at each other behind her back and tell each other it was probably just that she was having her period. Well fuck them, she thought. And you can't even get the satisfaction of saying that because if you do they'll decide you're a slut and have that to hold over you too.

Suddenly she realized she hadn't been doing any work for some time—just staring at the field report and feeling sorry for herself. It wouldn't help. It just meant there was that much more to do besides her own work. She forced herself to read it: "There are none of the standard indicators of friction or animosity at this time. Balacontano has been placed in a celebrity suite at the Frontier Hotel, which, although it has security design of B class, does not appear to indicate undue fear of violence. The suite also has superior facilities. The normal price of the suite is six hundred dollars per diem, and it is often used to house entertainers appearing in the hotel shows. As of this time there is no indication of the length of Balacontano's stay. The Learjet (leased from Airlift Transport, Inc.; Nutley, New Jersey, Registration Number N-589632) was refueled immediately after landing. No flight plan for another destination has been filed with the FAA, however. There has been no communication with persons outside the suite since arrival at eleven forty-five A.M. Thursday."

Big deal, thought Elizabeth. Flew in and checked into a hotel room, in a thousand words or less. But they were edgy, she could tell. They always did that until something happened

142

and then they snapped to. Every word would count then, but now it was just chattering to make the time pass, to keep the sense that there was somebody back here listening.

She looked up and saw Padgett rush by with a worried look on his face, carrying a voice transcript in his hand. So important—Man with a Big Job to Do—he was really in his glory now, she thought. Probably one of them ordered a martini from room service and the agent in place called for help. Padgett rapped urgently on Brayer's door, then passed in.

Elizabeth returned to her reports: "Toscanzio is at the MGM Grand Hotel, where it appears he has been for at least twenty-four hours." So that's part of it, she thought. Somebody lost track of one of them, and now the whole organization is supposed to compensate for the lost day by watching them all twice as hard, as though they could bring back that day.

"Elizabeth," said Brayer from his doorway. "Come on in. I think we've got something."

Sure thing, Mr. Brayer, thought Elizabeth as she set aside the sheaf of reports and stepped to the inner office. It had to be an isolated farmhouse, she thought. The agents were getting edgy and it was about time for a farmhouse. Field agents seemed to live with the vision of an isolated house in the backs of their minds because they were weaned on the Apalachin conference and Boiardo's private graveyard. It was like the Holy Grail to them, and you knew they were getting eager when it started turning up.

"What is it?" she asked.

"All hell seems to be breaking loose," said Padgett. So it wasn't the farmhouse. Maybe they were already up to the Man With A Rifle, always amended in final reports to man with a long, thin parcel (or golf club or broom or cane or pool cue).

"What, exactly?"

"Three murders in Las Vegas in the last two hours—at least two of them odd-job types. The other one seems to be some kind of businessman who just got in the way while they were taking out the first of the others. We're checking, of course."

"What makes you think it's significant?"

"Because Balacontano made his first appearance in public while it was going on. Went down to the hundred-dollar tables and started betting the farm at the crap tables, not even looking to see if he'd won or lost, flashing a lot of money and attracting attention."

Elizabeth noted that the farm had made its appearance in a new avatar, but didn't let it distract her. "What about other people? Toscanzio? Castiglione?"

"All in an uproar for the first few minutes, then quiet. Shut up in their houses and hotels. But no soldiers in evidence anywhere, almost as though somebody got word to them and convinced them there was nothing to worry about. Like they were ignoring it for now. Or maybe they knew in advance. It's hard to tell at this distance, and the reports are all of the 'we're standing by' variety."

Brayer was still silent, staring at the transcript on his desk. Elizabeth waited for him to say something, but he didn't. She asked Padgett, "Any idea yet on how it was done?"

"No," said Padgett. "Give me ten minutes. There's a call out for the report of the LVPD as soon as the homicide team gets back in."

She glanced at her watch: twelve o'clock. That meant nine o'clock there. Friday. Too early for much of the reaction. Some of them probably weren't awake yet. The hourlies later in the day would be more reliable.

"What do you think, Elizabeth?" Brayer finally spoke up.

"I think we should check on the other two and see where they go. If there's a conference in Las Vegas and this is really Balacontano, I would guess they'd head for home. If they show up in Las Vegas this was nothing. If they don't, it doesn't prove they'd ever planned to, but it's still worth checking."

"Agreed," said Brayer. "And Padgett, be as thorough as you can when you're checking on those victims. Don't give up easy. If you can establish a connection with somebody in particular it'll tell us what's going on. We might as well know who's mad at whom." Then he added, "Even though it probably won't do us any good or them any harm."

Padgett wheeled about and headed for the door and Elizabeth followed. Brayer sat immobile, staring at the transcript. Elizabeth almost asked for it, but thought better of it. There would be another copy at the monitor's desk. Brayer was either planning his next three moves or contemplating the vanity of his last three. If it helped to stare at a paragraph he'd long since memorized, so much the better.

145

16

"Amigo," he said. "I got some shirts for you."

"I'll go pick them up."

"Not a good idea, amigo. I'm on the road already. Ten minutes, no more."

"Right." The line went dead.

Shit, he thought. Any news had to be trouble, and it was—what? ten hours? before the shirts were supposed to be back. He looked at his watch. Nine o'clock. The Cruiser never did business at nine. Most of his customers wouldn't be up for hours. Even the cleaning business didn't open until ten thirty.

He scarcely had time to dress before he heard the knock. When he swung the door open the Cruiser slipped inward with it as though attached to it, then tossed the box of folded shirts on the bed.

"Amigo," said the Cruiser. "You really fucked me up." The Cruiser was smiling, the first time he could remember having seen that exact expression: he was showing his bad teeth and his breath seemed to come in short gasps.

"What happened?" he asked.

"You said it was no big thing but it was. All you had to do was tell me it was. You know better, amigo. You should never have done it to me."

"It's no big thing. Orloff owes me money."

"Not now. He's dead."

"How?"

"I sent a man to his office to watch. He was in a parked van all night and then I was going to send somebody else this morning. He was my cousin. Not smart, but I thought I'd let him have this easy one to make some money. But he wasn't smart, so I sent my boy Jesus at seven to see if he was awake.

146

He was. God. Something to do was such a big deal he hadn't even lain down all night. Sat there in a chair staring at an empty office through a peephole he drilled. He sent Jesus to get him something to eat. Jesus got back to the block in time to see it. Orloff drove up to the office and started to get out of his car. Then three of them just appeared from no place. Jesus said he thought the one with the shotgun came out of the building, one came from someplace on the other side of the street where the van was parked. The other might have been in the bushes, but he couldn't tell. They just were there. Orloff just stood there next to his car shaking, and the one with the shotgun blew his head off. Jesus said my cousin panicked and jumped into the driver's seat and tried to start the van. He must not have seen the one near him. Jesus said the guy didn't look surprised or anything, just stepped to the side of the van and put a pistol to the window. He fired five or six times. After that Jesus didn't see anything else. He was already running."

"I'm sorry it happened. Where is Jesus now?"

"Outside in the car waiting for me. I've got to get us all out of town."

"Will a thousand do it?"

"I think so. You know I'll have to tell if they corner me, though. With Jesus and Ascención——"

"Sure. But try to give me time. Leave now and keep going. I wish I could tell you something that would help you spot them, but I don't know anything. He just owed me money and looked nervous. Did the kid tell you what they looked like?"

"No. Just three Anglos. One dressed like a cowboy and the other two in suits. They didn't even look like they came together."

"Thanks for the shirts," he said.

"Yeah," said the Cruiser. "See you sometime." He slipped out the door and was gone.

He locked the door and sat down on the bed. It wasn't

good. There was no way to tell if it even had anything to do with him. Anybody who had any dealings with Orloff would probably consider doing it sometime. Orloff was cunning and greedy, and he sometimes got nervous. But the three who did it had to be the ones he'd seen in the Frontier, and that meant it had something to do with Carl Bala—but what? They'd either been watching for Bala or just watching him. And there was the money too—a lot of trouble for nothing. His leg started to ache a little at the thought of it.

And now he couldn't leave. If he did, they'd think he'd done it—broken the rule and violated the truce the families had agreed to among themselves and imposed on everyone else for almost thirty years. Especially the way his face looked, and the fact that Orloff had been seen with him—the fat, stupid pig. Now he'd have to stay put and hope that would convince the dozen old men locked in their houses and hotels that he represented no threat or inconvenience to them. At least with Orloff he could be sure whoever had wanted Claremont dead didn't know about him. Orloff had never been stupid enough to make his services as middleman unnecessary. He'd known his life depended on it. So he could forget about the three men unless somebody saw the connection between the pile of dead meat in the van and the Cruiser and had the resources and the persistence to find him. And Cruiser would probably be in Mexico by late afternoon.

The ringing of the telephone startled him. He snatched the receiver off the hook and snapped, "Yes?"

"Hi, kid. It's Norman." The deep, velvety voice was quiet and imperturbable.

He collected himself. "Hello, Norman." So it was starting already, the test. "What can I do for you?" He added, "It's pretty early yet for either of us, isn't it? What time is it?"

"Almost ten, kid," said Little Norman. "I figured you'd be up for hours by now. Maybe playing tennis. You like to keep in shape, don't you?"

"Sure, Norman."

"Well come downstairs and I'll buy you breakfast. I'm in the coffee shop."

"I'll be there."

He quickly got undressed again, showered, shaved, and put on a coat and tie. At the closet he lingered for an instant, thinking about the gun taped to the wall, then felt ashamed. Whatever happened he wouldn't need a gun between the room and the coffee shop. This wasn't the time to indulge his nerves.

In the coffee shop Little Norman seemed to take up one side of the booth, his arms spread out along the top of the seat in a gorilla's embrace so that the camelhair sport coat looked like upholstery. When he sat down, Norman didn't smile. "You're having ham and eggs, kid," said Little Norman. "I ordered them while I was waiting."

"Thanks, Norman. That'll be just fine." He added, "Sorry to keep you waiting, but you pulled me out of the sack."

"I came to tell you something," said Little Norman.

"What's that?"

"I just heard Harry Orloff died." His dark eyes didn't flicker; they seemed to sharpen and hold him for impaling.

"So?" he said. "Sorry to hear it. He should have lost some weight."

"Don't play that on me, kid," hissed Little Norman, leaning forward on his elbows so his big face loomed only a foot away over the table. "I was the best before you were born. You were with him two days ago."

"Sorry, Norman," he said. "What now?"

Little Norman leaned back again to give the waitress room to set the plates on the table between them. Finally he smiled. "That's better."

"I didn't do it, you know," he said. "I don't work in Vegas."

"I know you didn't," said Little Norman. "I heard he owed you money."

149

He picked up his knife and fork and started to saw at the slice of ham. "Easy come, easy go," he said.

"Not this time, kid," said Little Norman. He leaned forward again and his voice dropped. "You're gonna get paid, and then you're gonna leave. Tonight at nine you play blackjack at the Silver Slipper." He didn't wait for an answer. He was already standing by that time, and then he was moving off toward the door, the broad tan back of his perfectly tailored coat swaying slightly as he leaned to the left to avoid a scurrying keno girl whose stacked wig barely reached his shoulder.

"WHAT THE HELL DOES that mean?" said Padgett. The computer clicked and the lines of green print swept into view across the screen. "A car stopped at a red light, was blocked in by two others, and three men walked up and shot a whole family inside it."

"That supposed to mean something?" asked Brayer.

"That's the fourth, fifth, and sixth," said Padgett. "It has to mean something. How can it not?"

Elizabeth pressed the hard-copy button and waited for the machine to roll out the warm, damp sheet. She scanned the report of the Las Vegas police, and it suggested nothing at all. A husband, a wife, and a boy of ten. Stopped at a corner waiting for the light to change. "If we had a little more it might tell us something," she said.

"What do you want?" asked Brayer.

"Anything. What he did for a living, where they lived. What they had with them, I guess. And maybe which direction they were going." She looked out the window into the second heavy snowstorm of the month, and tried to picture it: a bright, sunny morning in Las Vegas and the car stopped in traffic. Maybe the man and woman in the front seat, and the little boy in the back. And then screeching tires, cars lurching

150

to a stop at odd angles, and the sound of guns blasting in the windows, the impact of the slugs at first punching circular spiderweb shapes into the glass, then spattering the glass into tiny crystals like diamonds spread all over the bodies. "I guess that would be first," she said. "Which way was the car going?"

HE WAS AFRAID. It was as if fear were a thick, oily liquid that had somehow seeped into his entrails and stuck there, holding him in a kind of paralysis. Somehow his body had stopped digesting; his food had turned into a greasy, immovable mass. He could feel it—his body wanted to do something, fight, run, turn light and fly—but the thing was in there, holding him down.

No. He'd seen it too many times. They'd sit there staring at him, maybe their fingers fluttering involuntarily like birds while their eyes went stupid. After it was too late they'd do something—the hands would reach for whatever was nearest, or the leg muscles would tense for a spring, but by then they'd be dead. It wasn't going to be that way with him. He sat on the bed and thought about it. Little Norman had said they were going to pay him. That was something to think about.

He felt a little better. They were going to pay him. That meant that they acknowledged the debt and that Orloff had done something else. No, that didn't work unless they thought Orloff had told him where the money was going to come from. And that he had some way to make it worth paying him. He looked at his watch—almost noon. Nine hours left, so he might as well reassure them now.

He reached for the telephone and asked for the United Airlines number. Even as he made his reservation he wondered who would take an eight-o'clock flight from Las Vegas on a Saturday morning. Probably the other passengers would all be people passing through—or maybe it was just that so

151

many people arrived here on Saturday mornings that the only other choice was to fly the planes out empty. He'd probably never know, he thought.

It was going to be tough to give himself an edge in nine hours, most of it daylight. They'd be watching him too closely. He knew he'd have to get started if he was going to make it.

He looked about the room to see what there was to work with—the bed, the shower, the telephone, the air conditioner —all standard. It would have to be the Magic Fingers machine on the bed. He studied it carefully. The metal box had an electric alarm clock besides the mechanical massager. The coin box was impregnable, but the wiring was easy enough to get to. Once he had the back open it was fairly simple. The wires that went to the alarm buzzer fit through the crack in the back once they were stripped of insulation. He set the alarm for noon and tested the wires. The spark wasn't much, but it would do. He put the Magic Fingers machine back together and trailed the wires beside his pillow. Then he went to the dresser and brought back his bottle of after-shave lotion and read the label: 98 percent alcohol. He set the alarm, poured the lotion into a paper cup, set it on the bed, and arranged the wires. It wasn't much, but it might help. If he wasn't back by two A.M. there would be a fire in Room 413.

That was one of the things Eddie had been able to give him. "Know everything. If there's nothing you can know that the mark doesn't know you better make something happen." The main thing would be getting out. He had the car, and there was the off chance that he might use his plane reservation. Then there were trains and buses. He'd have to get those set up during the afternoon. But that late at night there wouldn't be many of them, and he might not be able to get where he had to be to get on one.

It was probably just nerves, he thought. They weren't going to kill him in the Silver Slipper, and they weren't likely to pay him two hundred thousand and then kill him. But noth-

152

ing else about this seemed right either. There was no question that something big had gone very wrong, and now they were trying to clean it up. Whatever it was made it worth what they'd done to Orloff, and they'd never have done that in Las Vegas unless it was necessary.

Whatever it was, he'd have to stay out of sight until it was time for the payoff. If they were going to kill him it would probably be before rather than after. He checked the lock on the door, chained it, then moved the dresser in front of it. Then he went to the closet and pulled the pistol off the wall and checked the clip. Then he turned on the television.

17 The air was cold now that the sun had
been down for a couple of hours. The
hot, steady current of the desert breeze
had changed into something harsher and more petulant that
whirled down the Strip in icy eddies, then pawed at him and
buffeted him from above as he waited to cross the street. He
hunched his shoulders and moved closer to the center of the
crowd of people. It was as though the frigid emptiness of the
mountains was rushing in to correct some imbalance that had
been precariously asserted by all this light and noise and motion and color—as though some fragile barrier had been swept
away. He pulled his coat tighter around him and felt the pull
of the tape on his belly. The hard, sharp edge of the safety
catch on the pistol irritated his skin a little, but there wasn't
anything to be done about it now. There would be watchers
around him already. It was the only place for it anyway. It had
to be near his center of gravity, where he could forget about it.
There was no way to carry an extra pound of steel attached to
your side or your leg without involuntarily carrying yourself
differently. One of the first things he'd learned was to watch
for the man who held one arm an inch farther out than the
other, or the man who stepped a little stiff-legged.

Before the light changed the first two lurched forward
into the street, and the rest of the people scurried after them.
He stayed among them, measuring his steps to keep himself
surrounded by their bodies. He looked at his watch again. He
was still on time. It was just the cold that had made the walk
seem endless. Above him in the dark night sky the gargantuan
lady's high-heeled shoe beaded with white light bulbs spun
absurdly.

In a moment the pneumatic doors huffed closed behind

him like an air lock, and he stepped forward into the warm brightness of the casino. He kept moving deeper into the place. There was no question they had picked him up by now. Somewhere out of sight a telephone would have lit up and a voice would be saying "He's here," and that would be all.

He strolled along the line of blackjack tables, his eyes sweeping the green felt surfaces for a sign, then straying upward to the private, emotionless eyes of the white-shirted dealers. He spotted it without difficulty. A new brigade of dealers filed down the aisle from wherever their break room was, but this time one of them stationed himself behind an empty table, fanned the deck of cards across the felt, and stood with his arms folded on his chest in the customary pantomime of ostentatious idleness that announced the opening of another table. The placard at the dealer's elbow said ten-dollar minimum bet. So it was not to be private—it would be duly witnessed and recorded. The minimum was low enough to ensure that the table would fill up quickly. He waited to take a seat until two other players had rushed in front of him. The dealer swept his hand across the felt and the fan of cards closed into a thick deck. While the hands expertly performed the ritual of shuffling, the rest of the seats at the table were claimed.

The dealer's empty eyes seemed to stare out over the heads of the gamblers at some distant focal point as his fingertips tapped the fat deck into the shoe. The dealer looked young, his carefully sculpted hair blond from the sun, but already he had the ageless look of detached competence they all seemed to have worn into them. He clapped his hands once, held the perfect fingers up, turned them to show his palms, and said, "Good luck, ladies and gentlemen."

The cards seemed to fly from the shoe and appear in perfect order before the gamblers. The gamblers paid little attention to each other as each played his hand in turn, assessing the threat implicit in the dealer's up-card. He watched the dealer's hands float above the felt, collecting cards and moving

155

chips with relentless. unhesitating efficiency. He looked at the cards in front of him, a queen and a ten. The dealer's nineteen won the chips on four of the betting circles, and paid off one other bettor. The cards appeared on the felt again and the dealer busted; the hands moved in an arc along the semicircle, duplicating five of the stacks of chips. The cards appeared again and the dealer's seventeen had to pay four of the gamblers. As the game went on, the trend became clear. He was winning three hands out of four at minimum bets. Three of the others were getting random pairs of cards, sometimes good, sometimes bad. The dealer was using the other two.

One was a fat man in a blue plaid sport coat who was dealt an ace and a ten-point card every few hands. The other was a small, pinched-looking woman about forty-five years old who was playing a mysterious intuited system that seemed to be paying off. He wondered which one the dealer was going to bust first. He collected his steady income, letting the dealer deftly pay his winnings in larger denomination chips to keep the stack in front of him from looking too big, and watched the other two winners to see if he could sense it coming.

When the fat man began to double his bets, he knew. Slowly the trend changed. When the man lost, he doubled again. In a few minutes the chubby pink fingers extracted another pair of hundred dollar bills from the plaid sport coat and bought more chips. The cards kept coming, each pair the fat man got costing him more. Then he got up and left. When he pushed his chair back another man left too. By now the little woman was winning so steadily that the others took an interest. Nobody noticed that the nondescript man beside her was winning almost as steadily, or that he was now betting twenty-five-dollar chips. Two of them shrugged in sympathy when her luck ran out. One of them said, "Good move," when she climbed down from the stool while she was still ahead. One by one the rest of the players dropped out and were replaced by new faces, until he was the only one of the original players who remained. The new people won or lost and moved on, none of them allowed to remain long enough to notice that the quiet man in the gray tweed was on a big winning streak. And then the dealer paid him off for a hand just as a new dealer arrived to relieve him. The dealer clapped his hands once, held his fingers up and said, "Good luck, ladies and gentlemen," and walked away.

Instead of watching while the new dealer began to shuffle, he looked at the last stack of chips. The third one down was slightly smaller. He pretended to restack them and palmed the chip so he could look at it. In the center, where the others had the legend *Silver Slipper*, this one said *Flamingo*. He put it in his pocket, collected the rest of the chips, and moved away from the table. At the cashier's window the teller gave him almost ten thousand dollars.

IT SEEMED EVEN COLDER outside now. The Flamingo was several long blocks out on the Strip, but he didn't take a taxi. As soon as he had made his way to the blackjack tables he spotted the invitation. This time it was a middle-aged woman who looked a little mannish in the dealer's white shirt. The evening was approaching its peak now, and seats were scarce at the tables. The twenty-five-dollar minimum bet at her table didn't discourage anyone when she laid out the fan of cards. The game proceeded as it had in the Silver Slipper. Time after time he got nineteen or twenty. The dealer's seventeen or eighteen took most of the chips on the table; about a quarter of the time she went over twenty-one. He won steadily while the faces around him changed. After about an hour the dealer paid him with a chip from the Dunes. This time when he cashed in the teller gave him forty thousand dollars. As he walked to the Dunes he was beginning to wonder where he would carry the rest of it. But by the time he left the Dunes it was almost midnight, and the Friday evening gamblers were

157

too busy to notice that the teller had counted out sixty thousand-dollar bills to the man in the gray tweed. At the Aladdin it was the same. By the time the dealer at the Tropicana gave him the chip from Caesar's Palace he calculated that he must have the whole two hundred thousand. His pockets were full of money and they were sending him home. He had to admit it was sort of funny: they'd actually found a way to ring in their own dealers without the solid-citizen management types of all those big hotels even suspecting it. Anything happens, the hotels get the heat.

At the front entrance of the Tropicana the wind was now blowing in an unvarying, merciless rush up the street into the city. He checked his watch and saw that it was after one thirty. The fire he'd set up in his room would start at two if he didn't stop it, and the pedestrian traffic had died down at the outer end of the Strip. He took the doorman's offer of a taxi. "Caesar's," he said and the car roared down the driveway to the street, then stopped. The driver said, "Excuse me, sir," and got out. He bent down as though to check the left front tire.

It was a second before he realized what was happening, but when the two cars pulled up on either side of the cab he recognized the face of the man in the cowboy shirt. The man was out of his own car and reaching for the door handle of the cab already. The one on the other side was a pace or two slower. He chose that one.

He didn't feel the pain when he tore the pistol off his belly, just a sensation of cold where the tape had covered him and his shirt was open. The gun blast jerked the man backward a few feet, but he was out the door and had the pistol in the cab driver's face before the body toppled on its back. The cab driver's face had an expression of surprise when he squeezed the trigger. He knew the cowboy was on the ground somewhere behind the car, but there was no time. He jumped into the front seat past the steering wheel, threw the cab into gear and hit the gas pedal hard with his left foot. The cab jerked forward as he struggled to control it without showing his head above the seat. He heard shots as he wheeled out onto the Strip, but the sound of the cab's engine accelerating drowned out whatever he could have heard of the bullets smacking into the side of the car. He took the first right turn off the Strip and waited to see if the other cars had followed. After a few seconds he knew they had stopped to pick up the bodies, so he drove the cab into a parking space behind a closed gas station and got out. "Jesus," he said aloud. "So it was the taxis." They had offered him one outside each casino. And that was why they'd picked the casinos so far apart.

Damn them!

There was nothing he could do now except get out quickly. He'd have to make his way to the car in Caesar's parking lot and get out. But damn them! They hadn't needed to do it in the first place. He wouldn't have been a threat to Carl Bala, sitting up there in the Frontier surrounded by a dozen concentric circles of hotel security men and policemen and the syndicate faithful, all watching each other watching him. And he didn't even know if Bala was the one who'd ordered it. He loped along behind the buildings, moving parallel with the sidewalk out on the Strip, looking out at each alley to see if there was anyone to walk with, but each time seeing only empty sidewalk and the flash of passing cars. God! The stupidity of it! They could have sat there and done nothing, and he wouldn't even have known who owed him the money. He sure as hell wouldn't have shown up with his hand out at Carl Bala's door. If he had, he would have deserved this, for being a fool. They had wasted his life for nothing at all, as if he were some poor sucker who'd happened to be standing too close when a numbers runner came in for a handoff. It was a joke.

He was now behind the MGM Grand. Caesar's parking lot would be just a block up and a block over, but there didn't

159

seem to be any way to get there. It was just too much empty pavement to cross alone and on foot if they were cruising the Strip in cars.

Behind the MGM Grand he had a thousand cars to choose from. He selected one he would feel comfortable with if he got stuck with it for the night, a dark blue Chevrolet. He hotwired it. He was out of the lot in a few seconds. At Caesar's nothing looked peculiar. There were still gamblers wandering from aisle to aisle looking for their cars, and even a few late arrivals pulling into the lot. He knew that for the moment they would be searching for him on the freeway only. They would think he was still in the cab until they found it behind the gas station. In a little while if it didn't turn up they might have the cab company report it stolen.

He glided up the driveway and found a parking space near his rented car, sat there and waited. Something about the place made him hesitate to disentangle the ignition wires of his stolen Chevrolet. The rented car was only thirty feet from where he sat, but that thirty feet would be enough for them if they'd thought to wait for him. And if they'd managed to find out about the rented car sometime during the week, it was all over anyway. They'd be sitting somewhere out of sight waiting for him to turn the key and blow himself into a hundred thousand spoonfuls of hamburger. So he sat there with his lights off and his motor idling, staring into the darkness around him for any of the signs—a parked car with the silhouette of a head in the driver's window, a man alone and on foot who didn't find his car right away, a car that circled instead of swinging out into the driveway at the end of an aisle.

He glanced at his watch. It was two ten already. By now the fire should have started in his room. The smoke sensor should have gone off. The fire engines should arrive in a few minutes. At this hour they'd roar down the Strip at fifty or sixty, their flashing lights visible for a mile or more, not downshifting once until they were abreast of the giant sign that said Diana Ross. He tried to spot the window of his room, scanning the fourth strip of glass up from the parking lot for a flicker of light. Damn them! They weren't thorough, they weren't smart, but there was no way to make yourself a break with them because there were so damned many of them, lumbering around like so many baboons. It didn't matter what you did, the weight of their stupid single-minded brutish persistence would advance behind you—either slowly like a glacier or fast like an avalanche and obliterate all your tricks and contrivances and you with them. It was too late to be cautious, too late even to be afraid. Somebody powerful, maybe Carlo Balacontano sitting in his suite in the Frontier, had become annoyed with Orloff, so Orloff and everybody in his vicinity must cease to exist. It was a miracle they hadn't torn Orloff's building apart the same day to eradicate every sign that such a person had ever walked the earth.

It was time to move. If he didn't do something soon there wouldn't be time to get out. He felt in the lining of his sleeve for the keys to the rented car, and clutched them in his left hand. He killed the engine, reached under the dashboard until he felt the line of fuses, and plucked them out of their clips one by one. There was no time to figure out which circuit controlled the dome lamps. When he opened the door he didn't want to be bathed in light.

He was out the door and moving quickly now. He heard no engine start, no sign of life as he accomplished the thirty feet to the car. If they were about, they hadn't moved. He bent down as though to tie his shoe or check a tire or pick something up, and scanned the surface of the asphalt around him for feet. While he was down he unlocked the door and waited.

Suddenly he could hear the thin, whining sound of the sirens somewhere down the Strip, screaming into the vast night sky that practically swallowed their shriek into its emptiness.

161

But there was no question what it was. "The cavalry," he chuckled to himself. "The fucking cavalry." From here on it would be timing.

The sound of the sirens swelled as the trucks approached. He crouched, straining to prepare. At the moment when the first of the trucks flashed into view he slipped into the car, the interior flickering with light for only a second. If there were watchers they would be staring at the trucks, if only for that second; there was no way they could stop themselves. The first truck, a long hook-and-ladder rig, bounced up the driveway doing at least thirty, its siren wailing to a stop as though out of breath as the truck pulled up in front of the covered portico. Another like it burst into the parking lot by the side entrance and pulled around the building out of sight. Smaller trucks were materializing now, but he didn't watch them. Instead he scanned the parking lot.

He saw them at once. Three cars lit up to reveal the shapes of men swinging out to their feet. He ducked down and listened for the sound of running, but the noise of the big diesel engines was now flooding the air to replace the sirens. He saw one of the men dash past his window, but the man's eyes were fixed on the doorway of the casino. Now the fire trucks were all in place according to some prearranged contingency plan the fire department worked by. The watchers would be at the hotel entrances waiting for him to try to slip out with the frightened guests.

He had a moment of residual terror when he turned the ignition key, but he already knew there was no bomb. They would never have sat in the parking lot to watch it go off. He backed out of the parking space and drove onto the Strip. If any of them noticed him it was too late for them to be sure what they were looking at, because already there were four or five others driving away from the hotel as he'd known they would. The hotel guests would stay to clog the sidewalks and the parking lots and crowd the firemen, but the visiting gam-

162

blers would be heading for their cars to go someplace where there damn well wasn't a fire to close down the tables just when their luck was about to return to them.

He was out now, in a clean untraceable car with a full tank, carrying about two hundred thousand dollars stuffed into his coat. But as far as they were concerned he was dead already. He had been from the moment some old man's mind had settled on him and declared him a possible irritant. All that had remained was the mechanical, automatic translation of the thought to accomplishment, and the old man had probably lost interest in specifics of that sort years ago. Having given his frown or his nod or said, "Take him out too," his mind would have moved to other matters.

So he was dead. Well fuck them. He wasn't going to take that. They were damned well going to know he wasn't dead.

18 She stood in front of John Brayer's desk with the computer copy in her hand. "Fieldston Growth Enterprises," Elizabeth said. When Brayer didn't react, she set the sheet in front of him and touched her finger to the line. He could hear her pointed nail tapping the glass top of the desk. "Fieldston Growth Enterprises is the name of the building where this lawyer Orloff was murdered. It's also the name of the company that turned up in the investigation of the Veasy murder in California."

"Oh, yeah. You didn't get anything much on that one, did you? Too bad we had to pull you out so fast. You're keeping up with what the locals are doing, aren't you?"

"John," said Elizabeth, letting just a hint of the exasperation she felt seep into her voice, "this company has turned up at least twice now in murders that might be professional within a week. It's a match as it is, and I think there's a third." She waited until she knew he had to speak.

"All right," said Brayer. "It's slim, but I'm willing to pursue it, to a point. The third, if I remember, was that the initials turned up in something of Senator Claremont's, right?"

"You know it is," she said.

"What's the name of the staff counsel on Claremont's tax committee again?" He matched her impatience with a fair imitation of sluggish complacence, but she saw that he already had the telephone receiver in his hand.

"Justin Garfield," she said in a sweet alert voice he would probably have believed in another conversation.

"You might as well go wait for me at your desk," said Brayer. "If this guy says FGE is Fieldston Growth Enterprises, I'll want a report I can use to get a subpoena for their

164

records before you get on the plane." He started to dial the telephone.

"What plane?"

"To wherever this company is—oh, yeah," he said, staring at the computer copy she'd laid on his desk. "Las Vegas."

HE KNEW WHAT HE HAD to do without stopping to think about it. When he drove past the Frontier he spotted two watchers without even turning his head. One was in a Mark VI parked in perfect position to block the front exit of the parking lot if he slipped the hand brake and let it roll forward five yards. The other was just inside the lighted front lobby, waiting for a taxi within a few feet of a half dozen of them. He drove eastward toward the other end of the city.

There was no simple way to do it without making a lot of noise. He wouldn't have the kind of time it took to be clever, and there were sure to be a lot of people around who were ready to avert just this kind of thing. Castiglione was old, but he was old the way a retired president was old, living behind a high fence in a house that was built like a fort and cost somebody plenty. If you had a reason to see him it was hard enough to get in, but if you didn't have a reason it was worth your life to try. Still, it had to be Castiglione. He was the only one. He was the elder statesman, the one who had always had the juice to keep Balacontano and Toscanzio and some of the others in check. If he was out of the picture there would be confusion. None of the capos would ever believe that one of them hadn't done it, and the only reason to do it was to make a bid for ascendancy.

Eventually one of the others would come out on top, but it would take time for them to devour the losers. If he couldn't be sure of getting the one he wanted, this was the next best thing. He drove up Grayson Street slowly, a good citizen of Las Vegas trying not to wake up the neighbors after he got off the eight-to-two shift at the Thunderbird or somewhere. Grayson Street was a ruler-straight parkway with a hairpin turn at the end of it dominated by the imposing adobe facade of Castiglione's house. As he swung past the house he studied it carefully. There was nobody outside patrolling the grounds. It had probably seemed unnecessary to have somebody freezing in the cold desert wind to protect a man whose personal enemies had been dead for decades. The adobe wall around the yard didn't obscure the view of the house, which sat on a little rise in the center of a vast lawn. No shrubs had been allowed to grow within a hundred feet of the house, so anyone who approached it would be in the open all the way back to the street. And there would be lights, although at a glance he couldn't see them, big floodlights that would change night into day in the first seconds of danger. The windows of the place were negligible squares cut into the adobe of the house's Spanish-style facade, more because a blank wall that size without some variation would offend the eye than because old Castiglione would want to look outside at the shimmering heat waves of the desert floor.

It wasn't promising, he thought. Castiglione had been in too much danger for too many years before he'd come West. Besides the front entrance, there was a side door that opened on a stone walkway to the swimming pool. He parked the car in the driveway of a neighbor, facing the street. He took the rifle and began to walk the circuit of Castiglione's wall. Now that he could see the place clearly, it was even more forbidding. There were only the two doors he'd seen from the street, and at the back of the house even the small windows had been eliminated. He began to wish he had some dynamite. He couldn't see any lights burning in the house, but he knew that the old man who lived here would have someone awake, if only to be sure the telephone didn't disturb his sleep.

He felt frustrated and disappointed. It was going to be a pain in the ass. He carefully climbed the fence and approached the house, watching where he placed his feet. It wouldn't be out of the question for the old bastard to have the lawn booby-trapped. He cautiously walked around the house looking for points of vulnerability until he found what he needed. There was a barbecue pit big enough to roast a side of beef, and near the swimming pool were two cabinet doors built into the wall. When he saw them his heart began to beat faster. It could be done. He took his pocket knife and quietly jimmied the first of the doors. Inside was the hot-water heater for the house. Behind the second door was a collection of miscellaneous objects: garden tools, charcoal and a can of fire-starter for the barbeque pit, bottles of chlorine for the swimming pool, a long hose already attached to a faucet. He leaned his rifle against the house.

In the darkness it was difficult to work silently, but he moved with care and deliberation. First he took the charcoal and the can of fire-starter and moved around to the front door of the house. He banked the charcoal against the gigantic wooden door and soaked it with the odorous liquid, getting as much as he could on the door itself. Then he left it to sink in and moved back to the patio. He took all of the garden tools and spread them on the pavement in front of the door. The hose he propped between two gallon jugs of chlorine so that it aimed from the side into the doorway. He checked the loads of his rifle and pistol and set the rifle on the deck next to the swimming pool. He looked around to see that everything was ready. The hot-water heater was the key to all of it, so it would have to be first. He turned off the gas valve and then disconnected the heater from the gas pipe. He went around to the front door and started the charcoal fire.

He trotted back to the patio, turned on the gas and lit the jet, then turned it up so the flame was high enough to lick the top of the cabinet. Then he turned on the faucet and adjusted the pressure so that a steady, hard stream of water rushed across the doorway. Finally he retreated to the swimming pool. He lowered himself into the water at the shallow end of the pool and gasped. It was colder than he'd imagined. He ducked down to wait, holding the rifle above the surface and shielding himself from the growing glare by clinging to the gutter of the pool nearest the house.

It seemed to be taking a long time. He peered over the edge of the pool at the house. There were still no lights on, but he could see the glow of the fire in the front of the house, and the gas jet was flaming steadily. The eaves had caught, and part of the roof. Already the facade of adobe was crumbling, and the plywood siding beneath it crackled into flames almost instantly. He began to shiver, whether from the cold of the water or the cruelty of the night wind he couldn't tell. It suddenly occurred to him that Castiglione might not be home. What if he wasn't even home?

But then the lights went on, one after another, each window now glowing. The fire from the hot-water heater must have eaten its way into the back of the house. He ducked down again. When they were ready to leave, the outside lights would blaze on. He listened to the muffled shouts inside the house, trying to gauge how many voices there were. There were doors slamming and the sound of running feet. He knew when someone reached the front door, because he heard a yelp that escaped into the night air, then footsteps back toward the rear of the house. The pool, he judged, was about seventy feet from the side door. He steadied the rifle on the cement deck and lined up his sights.

At last the side door burst open and a man ran out onto the patio. When he was sprayed by the hose he turned and shot at it, then swore when he stepped on a rake. He ran toward the hose, since it seemed to his dim, confused, frightened brain to be somehow the source of the trouble. He was easy to hit because when he got near enough to see that there was no one holding the hose he stopped short, silhouetted in the growing light of the fire behind him. Another man made it

168

far enough to kneel over his fallen comrade, then looked around him for someone to kill, before the rifle's sights leveled on him too.

Inside the house they couldn't tell what was happening. There had been shooting outside, and water coming from somewhere, but there was no way to put it together into a coherent idea that would tell them what to do. Somebody must be trying to put the fire out with the hose: he could tell that was what made sense to the two who rushed to the door next, because they weren't armed. He let one of them get almost to the gas jet before he cut him down. The other stood inside the doorway, unaware that his companion was dead.

From his spot in the dark swimming pool, he decided to take a chance. He shouted, "Get the old man out!" then ducked down into the shadows and waited. There was the sound of movement inside the house and then he saw what he had been waiting for. A man in pajamas carefully eased a wheelchair into the doorway, and moved it out onto the patio. He aimed the rifle at the center of the chair's back and prepared to squeeze a round into it. Then he sensed something was wrong. When the attendant got the chair to the patio he moved away from it toward the front of the house, his gun drawn. It wasn't right. They wouldn't leave the old man alone, no matter what happened. He studied the chair through his telescopic sights. There was something in it, but now he was sure it wasn't the old man. Some hero? No, there were shoes on the footboard, but the leather back of the chair didn't bulge in the right places. He thought quickly. It couldn't be the front door. He could see that the front of the house was blazing now. There must be another way out. But where was it?

It had to be the garage. They'd want to get him away. The garage was behind him, too far to walk an invalid in an emergency. Suddenly it made sense. The place was built like a fortress, and yet the garage was a hundred yards away from the house. There had to be a tunnel under the yard. Then he

169

realized that as soon as the ones who were left had made it to the garage, the old man would be driven away and then the floodlights would come on. He had to get out of the pool before they reached the safety of the garage.

He calmed himself and aimed at the only man he could see, the one in the doorway. He watched him fall backward. He dropped the rifle into the water and heaved himself out of the pool and began to sprint for the garage. He made it just as the electric door began to whir. He heard the car's ignition, and then the dark shape of the car, its lights out, slid forward beside him, inching ahead behind the rising door. He froze and waited until the driver was abreast of him, then fired the pistol into his face. The car kept sliding slowly forward of its own volition, no living foot on its brake to halt it. When the back seat slid into view beside him he saw the old man's face, held for an instant in a mask of surprise and terror like a photograph. When he squeezed the trigger the head jerked sideways as though it had been kicked. He walked along beside the drifting car and shot the old man twice more before he relinquished his place beside it.

He knew there would be only seconds now before someone turned on the lights. He sprinted for the nearest place the driveway ran along the wall and clambered over it. He didn't look back, just kept running, turning the seconds of remaining darkness into whatever distance he could purchase. As he came to the end of the wall he saw a crouching shape waiting for him, both hands extended in front of it as though to steady a pistol. He heard the man shout something just before he fired into the crouching shape. The man's gun went off in a last spasm of the fingers and he ran over the body before he realized that the man had said, "Hold it." Hold it? Why would he say that? He kept running, but glanced back for an instant and realized the body was wearing a white shirt and tie under its coat. Strange, he thought. At three o'clock in the morning? But he didn't have time to think about that. He was running

170

hard along the house fronts. Behind him the floodlights went on and he heard the driverless car crash into something. When he reached the driveway where his car was parked, he jumped in, started it, and gave it as much gas as he dared without turning on the lights. In the rearview mirror he could see half the sky was lit up, a chaos of white floodlights and orange fire, and he could hear the first barking of guns back and forth across the deserted lawns and into the empty night. As he turned the corner and urged the car to fifty-five, he smiled to himself. He didn't feel so angry now.

19 There was the climate-controlled humming tube of the airplane's interior; and then the two stewardesses standing at their station next to the Formica kitchenette like a pair of dancers from the chorus line brought out for a last bow in front of the curtain; and then the white, searing sunshine of the Las Vegas Saturday morning. Elizabeth squinted as she stepped down the portable stairway, staring down at her feet to avoid a glaring sun that seemed to explode at her from every direction at once.

There were no knots of happy relatives waiting at the terminal entrance for the passengers to arrive—everyone was a stranger here—only sober-faced preoccupied porters. As she looked about her for some sign that would tell her where to find her suitcase, a man's voice came over a loudspeaker.

"Elizabeth Waring, please come to the United Airlines Courtesy Desk, Elizabeth Waring. Elizabeth Waring, please come to the United Airlines Courtesy Desk, Elizabeth Waring."

Brayer. No question about it, she thought. No doubt he'd forgotten to tell her something, and it wouldn't occur to him to wait until she got to the hotel. She approached the desk, and said, "Elizabeth Waring."

The man handed her a note, which said, "Please telephone John Brayer as soon as possible." The please had to have been the airline's amendment. She went to the bank of pay telephones on the wall across the lobby and dialed. He answered on the first ring.

"Something's going on there, Elizabeth," said Brayer. "I'm not sure yet what it is, but we've got an agent down."

"Oh God," said Elizabeth. "Are you sure? Who is it?"

172

"The Las Vegas police phoned a half hour ago. They found DiGiorgio this morning when they were going over a burned-out house. He's alive, but there were five dead men in the yard, and they're not sure if there were others inside."

"What do you want me to do?"

"Sit tight for a few minutes. There'll be a police officer at the United desk to take you to the hospital. If they'll let you talk to DiGiorgio find out what you can. If they won't, get everything the police have and get back to me. When you've done that I should have a better idea. For the moment work through me. Don't try to get in touch with any of the field agents. I don't know what the hell is going on and I don't want anybody spotted until I do."

"John," said Elizabeth, "I see the policeman at the desk now. I'd better get going."

"Fine. Get back to me when you can. We've got people all over Las Vegas and if they're in danger we've got to know it."

Elizabeth hung up and moved toward the desk just as the policeman turned to approach her. "I'm Waring," she said. The policeman nodded and touched the polished brim of his hat as they set off toward the door. He was tall and his first two strides left her a yard behind.

"My luggage," she said apologetically. "I haven't picked it up."

"Where are you staying?" he asked.

"The Sands."

He looked a little surprised, but said, "If you'll give me your stub I'll have it sent on." He returned to the desk and gave the stub to the United man. He joined her at the curb outside, where his patrol car sat idling, its front door open and the radio squawking and sizzling.

She got in beside him and he swung out into the drive. "How's DiGiorgio?" she asked.

"Critical," said the policeman, his face stony. She de-

173

cided that he didn't like women, but that it didn't matter whether he did or not, so she forgot about it. "He lost a lot of blood before they found him. Upper chest. One shot from close up, small caliber."

Elizabeth thought about it for a moment, but it didn't mean much. "Does anybody know what happened?"

The policeman's eyes shifted to her face for an instant, then flickered back to the road. "We'd hoped you might help us there, ma'am." There it was again, she thought. The exaggerated politeness reserved for outsiders. Outsiders and women. "He's your man." It sounded like a reproof.

"He was assigned to surveillance," she said. "But it was supposed to be remote. He wouldn't have initiated any contact."

The policeman nodded. "That's what we thought." Then he added, "Of course, we didn't know he was here. We were pretty surprised when we found his identification." So that was it, she thought. A federal agent turns up and the local police didn't know he was there—the implicit assumption that somebody is probably on the pad. She let the thought lie there between them, because there wasn't anything she could do with it. It was just the way things were done and they both knew it and neither one was responsible for it, though it carried with it an insult to what he was and what he did.

He seemed to have thought through it before she arrived, and so he recovered first and determined to do his job. He went into his recitation. "The house belonged to Salvatore Castiglione, so we're assuming that was who Agent DiGiorgio was observing."

"Belonged?" she said. "Is the house destroyed?"

"No," he said. "Castiglione is dead. So are five other men who were apparently staying there. Four of them were shot with a high-powered rifle. We found the rifle in the swimming pool. Agent DiGiorgio and Castiglione and one other man were shot with something smaller. Maybe by each other. We

174

won't know until they finish with the ballistics reports and the autopsies."

Elizabeth thought for a moment. Castiglione dead. She tried to put it together. DiGiorgio is spotted, Castiglione orders him killed, and DiGiorgio puts up a fight, killing—six men? And besides, there was the rifle in the swimming pool. And Castiglione had been watched for years. It was a fact of his life. He wouldn't panic now. No. Try again. DiGiorgio is watching Castiglione's house, and for some reason a fight breaks out between the men in the house. Shooting starts, one of them has a rifle; DiGiorgio goes to stop it and gets hit. But what about the fire? Try again. DiGiorgio is watching the house. Men come and try to burn the house, to kill Castiglione. Castiglione's men fight back. DiGiorgio is there, tries to stop it or at least to apprehend somebody, and is wounded. She kept trying the combinations, trying desperately to ignore the one that kept coming back into her mind: DiGiorgio is standing outside the darkened house with a high-powered rifle in his hands, waiting for the old man to come through the door to escape the fire. DiGiorgio has spent too many years sitting in cold cars outside fancy restaurants, checking license numbers on parked limousines, translating taped conversations into English. DiGiorgio is an avid hunter.

The policeman had the microphone in his hand and said, "Go ahead."

The radio clicked and farted, then the voice said, "You may proceed to the hotel directly."

The policeman said, "Copy," and slipped the microphone into its slot.

"What's that about?" said Elizabeth.

"I guess your man didn't make it."

"THAT WAS QUICK," said Brayer. "What have you got?"

"Not much," said Elizabeth. She was standing at the glass

175

door to the balcony. It overlooked the swimming pool, where people were lying immobile in long deck chairs, their bodies glistening with oil as though they were being rendered for their fat. But what she was thinking about was that the layout was just like the room where Senator Claremont had been killed. She edged along the wall to catch the light so she could study the finger smudges on the glass. "DiGiorgio died before I could get to the hospital. I just got off the line with the local homicide people and they said he'd been in a coma since shortly after they brought him in." She waited, but he didn't say anything. She added, "I'm sorry."

"So he didn't tell them anything either." Brayer's voice was gruff.

"Nothing anybody can use," she said. "In the ambulance he was just raving. I think what he said was 'a fucking war.' "

"What?" said Brayer.

"A fucking war. Over and over again. It could have been that it reminded him of something in Viet Nam. I didn't know him well, but he was an ex-marine, wasn't he? Although from what I've been told, that wouldn't be too far off. You wouldn't have to be delirious to make the connection. There were six besides DiGiorgio, and the house was a ruin."

"Including Castiglione," said Brayer. He paused for a moment. Then he said, "Look, Elizabeth. There's the possibility that he was just describing what it looked like. Agreed. But there's also a chance he was describing what he thought was happening. What if this Orloff character was involved in something? Say he was working for Castiglione, and somebody, maybe Toscanzio or Carl Bala, decided to take over and killed him? Then there was that family killed in their car. A reprisal? And there was another shootout in front of the Tropicana last night. Nobody knows what happened because when it was over the ones who were left standing put the ones that were hit into cars and drove off. But there was blood all over the pavement. So far nobody has been reported missing and

176

no doctor within a hundred miles of Las Vegas has treated anybody for gunshot wounds. We're monitoring for it. What's it sound like to you?" He didn't wait, just kept talking. "I'll tell you what it sounds like. 'A fucking war.' "

"You think so?" asked Elizabeth. "But who? And what do we do about it?"

"Well, obviously Castiglione was on one end of it. And I'll bet whoever comes up top dog is on the other end. God knows what we're supposed to do about it. I'll tell you what I'd like to do. I'd like to pull all our people, you included, about a thousand miles eastward and let those bastards kill each other off. If it weren't for the chance that it has something to do with Senator Claremont I think I'd damned well do it."

She said, "That and your curiosity." She heard him give a humorless little chuckle.

"You're probably right," he said. "And DiGiorgio."

"Yes," said Elizabeth, "I'm sorry about that, John. I didn't know him well, but I guess you must have."

"Oh. Yes," he said, without inflection. Then his voice became animated again. "Jesus," he said, "I think what bothers me most about it is that he had no business there in the first place. He was supposed to sit tight and watch, no matter what happened. He probably died trying to save that old piece of scum from something he had coming to him for years."

Elizabeth said nothing. She didn't see any reason to remind him that DiGiorgio was the only one found at the scene who hadn't lived there, that he'd been found in the yard, not in his car, where every regulation, every procedure of the department insisted he should be. She knew Brayer had been thinking about that since he'd received the telephone call in the early morning.

"Now we've got to find out as much as we can without wasting time," said Brayer. "But don't do anything stupid." He said it as though he had something specific in mind. "You

177

find out what you can about the company and that's all. The minute you see or hear anything that might be illegitimate you report it. And if it looks like it might be more than that you get on a plane and talk to me about it in person. You got that?"

"Got it," said Elizabeth. "Don't worry, John. I'm no hero."

"I'll be satisfied if you're not a fool." He hung up.

20 The building didn't look like a place where there had been a murder. It looked still less like a corporation that would appear in the notebook of a United States senator. It consisted of a single one-story cinderblock structure with a small sign that read *Fieldston Growth Enterprises*, and a tiny lawn protected by a frail cordon of thirsty geraniums.

When Elizabeth walked in the front entrance the receptionist stopped typing and smiled with some sincerity, and Elizabeth believed the smile. This had the look of a place where a receptionist could get lonely. There were only the wood-paneled walls, the typewriter, and the telephone.

"Hello," she said. "I'm Elizabeth Waring of the U.S. Department of Justice." She held out her identification, but the woman didn't look at it so she dropped it into her purse.

The receptionist was in her mid-forties but her hair was already tinted with a blue rinse, probably, Elizabeth decided, to draw attention to her vacant blue eyes. The eyes didn't flinch or flicker. Any visitor was obviously a treat.

"May I help you?" asked the receptionist, her smile broadening. Elizabeth revised her estimate when she saw the tiny crinkles at the corners of the mouth—mid-fifties, she thought, but takes care of herself.

"I'd like to speak with Mr. Fieldston, please."

"Oh, I'm sorry, Miss Waring," said the receptionist. She seemed moved by the disappointment she was about to inflict. "Mr. Fieldston isn't in today."

"I wonder if you could tell me where I can reach him? I'd like very much to speak with him."

"Mr. Fieldston is out of town this week," said the recep-

179

tionist, as though he had vanished into a realm that was out of reach to any form of human communication.

"Do you have a number for him? I'm on a tight schedule."

"I'm sorry," said the receptionist. "Mr. Fieldston is meeting with a client, and I'm never permitted to tell anyone where he is when he travels. I'm sure you understand."

Elizabeth didn't, but she was interested now. "Why is that?"

"The investment business is a difficult one. If Mr. Fieldston's competitors knew in advance what he was buying, the negotiations might be complicated by other bids. If people knew he was acquiring a particular holding, the price of all surrounding holdings might be artificially inflated." The way she added, "And so on," signaled that the receptionist had either run out of imaginary excuses or reached the limit of her understanding of the business, but Elizabeth couldn't decide which it was.

"Let me leave my number then," she said. "I'm staying at the Sands." She fished in her purse and found a calling card, and wrote on the back of it *Sands Hotel, Room 219.* "If Mr. Fieldston calls, please ask him to get in touch with me." She turned to go.

"What can I tell Mr. Fieldston?" asked the receptionist, already prepared with a message pad. "Is it about Mr. Orloff?"

Elizabeth hesitated, but she supposed that it was about Orloff, partly. "Yes it is," she said.

"A shame," said the receptionist. Elizabeth could see her write *Re: Mr. Orloff* on the note, then watched, fascinated, as the receptionist stapled her card to the note and placed it in her *Out* box. It was the only piece of paper in the box.

SOMEONE HAD BROUGHT her suitcase into the room during the day. Taped to it was a note on the front desk's stationery:

Please call Mr. Bechtman, Room 403. The time on it was only four thirty. Two hours ago.

Elizabeth dialed 403 and the voice said, "Elizabeth, stay where you are. I'll be there in a minute." She sat down on the bed with the dead telephone to her ear. Brayer!

Brayer's seersucker sport coat and sunglasses weren't a disguise so much as a radical change in his personality. After more than a year of getting used to the dark, conservative suits that got shiny and wrinkled in the back from the long days he spent sitting at a desk, Elizabeth was fascinated.

"Great outfit, John," she smiled. "You look like a Cuban spy." But she was thinking something else; he was perfect. He looked like another version of what he was—a middle-aged man from somewhere in the East. A man who had spent most of his years working too hard and not getting enough out of it to soften the signs of wear—but who wasn't at the office today and meant to make the most of it. Maybe he was here for a convention; maybe he'd come with the little woman and managed to slip away from her for a few hours to look for some action at the tables.

But the voice was Brayer of Justice. "What have you got so far?" he said.

"Still very little to go on," she answered. "Edgar Fieldston is out of town checking out some kind of investment. The secretary pretends she can't tell anyone where he is but she's probably lying and doesn't know herself. After that I went to the police station to see what they had. It wasn't much either."

"You didn't ask them about FGE, did you?" Brayer snapped.

"No," said Elizabeth. "But it was just because there didn't seem to be any reason to. I figured you'd want to know about DiGiorgio—"

"Right," said Brayer. "What's new on that?"

"The place was clean. If Castiglione was doing anything special it was miles from his house. Except for Castiglione the

181

men killed had no criminal records and were legally entitled to carry the guns found there. They were officially employees of a private security company—there's no question what they were but you couldn't have proven it in court. The rifle that killed them was manufactured over twenty years ago, and the last time it was recorded as sold was at a gun shop in San Diego in 1967. It'll take time to track down the man who bought it, if he's still alive. DiGiorgio, Castiglione, and the driver were killed with a .32-caliber pistol. What they think now is that it was done by three men—one near the pool with the rifle, one near the garage with the pistol, and one somewhere near the front of the house who started the fires and then probably stayed with the getaway car to control the front door, driveway, and street."

Brayer listened intently, then nodded. "Okay. So it's probably the three who got the Mexican family. And Di-Giorgio saw what was happening but didn't see one of them or got distracted at the wrong moment." Elizabeth could see he was imagining it, re-creating what must have happened, as a man re-creates the scene where he lost something valuable.

He sat down on the bed and took off his sunglasses. His eyes looked tired. "Okay," he said again. "That's probably all we'll get on that. The rifle will turn out to have been lost or stolen years ago. The pistol was already at the bottom of Lake Mead or sawed into fifty pieces hours before the police got around to investigating. No surprises anywhere."

She said, "Sorry, John. I guess your trip was a waste of time."

He looked surprised, his gaze suddenly widening, but turning sharp and predatory. "No, we're just beginning," he said. "The reason I came is Fieldston Growth Enterprises. All your chickens have come home to roost."

"What do you mean?" asked Elizabeth.

"I mean that there's something wrong with it. When I got

182

through to Justin Garfield, I didn't see much in it. The list was only a statistical fluke. They programmed a computer at IRS to spit out the names of companies that had earned unusually high incomes last year but had reinvested most of them to avoid showing a big profit on the balance sheet at the end of the year—plowed the money back under. Senator Claremont was looking for instances where they might have disguised investments as operating expenses. He wanted to amend his tax bill to close the loophole. Fieldston Growth Enterprises had a high ratio of gross income to net profit and so it went on the list. It was no big deal. Garfield said it was possible the Senator might have decided to call in somebody from FGE to testify in next session's hearings, but it was just as possible he'd have deleted it. It might not be big enough to use as an example. The Senator had a preference for the dramatic." He pulled a notebook out of his coat and stared at it.

"So what makes it look interesting?" asked Elizabeth.

"Garfield's people started poking around, doing groundwork for the committee. They came up with some odd facts. Edgar Fieldston started the company in 1971, so they began with him. He looked good. An old California family. They owned ranch land that got bought up in the thirties. They took a loss, but it didn't matter much because the money involved was still enough to make them as rich as anybody needs to be, and in those days nobody would have believed what the land would be worth in fifty years, or cared much either. Fieldston looked fine, except for one thing, and it wasn't much. In 1969 and 1970 his income taxes were in arrears. He was building up penalties."

"So he started a business in 1971," said Elizabeth, "and came out okay." She shrugged.

"Right," said Brayer. His mouth turned up into something like a smile, but colder and harder. "He couldn't pay his taxes for two years. In the third year he had enough money to pay the taxes, penalties and all, and start a business with an initial investment of, let's see—" he glanced at the notebook. "Four hundred and sixty thousand dollars."

"A silent partner?" said Elizabeth.

"Has to be." Brayer closed the notebook and slipped it back into his breast pocket. "And nobody got suspicious. He was the scion of an old family with money. Maybe he sold some land they had left somewhere, maybe a rich aunt died, maybe a friend loaned him the money. The rich have rich friends. Nobody asked any questions."

"Until the name of the company started turning up around murders," said Elizabeth. "Until they got careless." She was warming to the hunt now, her mind racing ahead for the next stage of it, but Brayer stopped her.

"No," he said. "Just the opposite. Until Garfield's computer spit it out by accident. I think Fieldston's silent partners got wind of it somehow and reacted to protect the company. Garfield's people weren't light-footed. They did credit checks, talked to bank officers, and so on."

"But they wouldn't do that," said Elizabeth. "No. It doesn't make sense. We're off the track." She was up now, pacing the hotel room. "First, there's Veasy. A machinist in Ventura, California. He might have been a threat because he was critical of the union's investment in FGE, but not much of a threat unless he got in touch with the Senator's committee, and there's no way he would have known about it. And if by some chance he did, the last thing they'd do is kill him because that would bring the police and maybe the FBI." She walked back and forth, as though each step brought her closer to what she was looking for. "And killing the Senator wouldn't do it either because there was still the committee, and Orloff was their man, their lawyer. No, John, it has to be something else. Something is missing." She stopped and stared at him, but he was smiling that strange, cold smile, still sure.

He said, "You're right about part of it, but wrong about the rest. Veasy was the first in time, but not in logic. That's what you're missing. The Senator was the main thing. If they got rid of him, the committee wouldn't go after FGE, because he was the only one interested in it. Garfield told me today the information on Claremont's inquiries has already been packed away. At the end of the next term it would have been shredded because it wasn't part of an official, permanent record and it wasn't part of an ongoing project. And nothing had happened yet. There was no reason for anybody to wonder if the Senator's death was linked to FGE, certainly not the police, because the only ones who knew he'd ever heard of FGE were the committee staff, and they'd never hear about Veasy or Orloff or the rest of it. All they'd ever know was that it was one of a hundred or so that they were supposed to check out for a hearing months from now."

Elizabeth was still shaking her head. She said, "There has to be more. A lot more. They knew they wouldn't get caught, agreed. But that was because no reasonable stretch of the imagination would connect them with the Senator—but that's still true. Because nobody would kill a U.S. senator just because he might subpoena their books or call clean, upright Edgar Fieldston to testify."

"I'll go the rest of the way for you," said Brayer. "And they wouldn't kill a machinist in Ventura because he was criticizing his union's investment in a company he'd never even seen the outside of." But the smile was still there, still sure and maybe even a little smug.

"And there's still Orloff," said Elizabeth. "That has to be something different."

"It's all the same," said Brayer. "It doesn't matter how it was done or in what order. The time doesn't matter at all for now. They were plugging leaks, getting rid of every liability they could think of at once. Maybe it was all done to protect something that was very important to them and might come out as soon as any government agency started to look closely at the company. Something close to the surface."

"What?" asked Elizabeth. "It can't be the silent partner. And yet it has to be."

"There's a vulnerable point somewhere, and they knew it. And right now they're trying to cover it up. They'll succeed if we don't get to it soon. The one thing we've found that fits the pattern is that they've got a number of complicated investments—subsidiaries, really. One is an oil consulting firm. We're concentrating on that one for the moment. It'll take time to track everything down."

"Why that one?" asked Elizabeth.

"Because it involves moving people and small amounts of sophisticated equipment from one place to another. A lot of it to other countries. There are a hundred possibilities: smuggling, a money-laundering operation, drugs, or maybe just an excuse to have somebody in particular on the payroll with a legitimate reason to travel."

"A hit man!" said Elizabeth.

"Don't jump to conclusions," said Brayer. "That's the least likely of a hundred possibilities. For one thing, it would be the hardest to spot, and whatever they're worried about is more obvious. Maybe it's just an excuse to have bank accounts or investments in foreign countries."

Elizabeth sat down again. "So that's why you're here," she said. "It's a full-court press, isn't it? You're going to put the pressure on and watch to see who squirms. Who else is in on it? The FBI?"

Brayer's smile broadened a bit as he nodded, but then it disappeared. "I'm afraid it's a little bit different this time," he said. "It's a full-court press all right. I didn't know you liked basketball, by the way, but it fits. The only thing is, we can't let them see all of it at once."

She could tell that something was bothering him. It was a

moment before she realized what it was. She said, "And they've already seen me."

He nodded. "They've already seen you."

She sat there for a moment, thinking about it. Then she stood up, straightened her skirt, and said, "All right. What do I do first?"

"We've already requested a subpoena for their ledgers. It should be ready by morning. It lists you as officer of the court."

21

The trees lifted naked branches toward a sky that seemed to be made of stone. Now and then an icy gust of wind would tear down the street bringing with it a scurrying herd of wrappers and dead newspapers. He had been on this street before. Three, maybe four years ago. That time he hadn't stopped, just checked to be sure he had the right address and then driven on. He'd been alone that day too, and he'd had some time and had promised Eddie he'd look. Eddie had been careful enough to last for a long time. It would have been stupid not to do what Eddie said. "This is an address you might need sometime, kid. Don't ever write it down. Go there when you're in Buffalo and remember where it is. Chances are if you ever need to see him you're gonna be in a hurry."

Most of the snow had been pushed off the sidewalks into the gutters, so he had no trouble walking if he avoided the thin patches of ice near the curb. There were only a few bundled figures leaning into the cruel wind as they walked. They scuttled close to the storefronts for shelter, veering outward only to avoid each other, their faces turned down out of the wind. Sliding steel cages accordioned across the doors and windows of the buildings. No business was open on Sunday morning on this stretch of Grant Street. He moved more quickly. The coat he'd bought last night was warm, but his ears were already numb. The collar wasn't high enough to do anything for them.

One more block. He wished for a moment that he still had the car. But that would have been foolish. He wouldn't be here until tomorrow night or the next day at the earliest—and in a car with Nevada plates. You couldn't drive through places like St. Louis and Cleveland in a car with Nevada plates and not attract attention.

188

There were houses now and he knew he was getting close to it. The houses were set farther back from the street and he missed the shelter of the storefronts. There it was. 304. He remembered what Eddie had said. "Knock and ask for directions to someplace. It don't matter where. Don't ask for him or you won't get in the door."

He made his way up the icy walk and then up the steps to the porch. He knocked and listened, but the wind was the only sound. "His name is Harkness," Eddie had said, "and he's a nigger. Don't hang around out front for too long because your white face will attract attention." There was still no sound, but the door swung open.

An old black man in a white shirt that was buttoned to the collar stared out at him, saying nothing.

"I wonder if you could tell me how to get to the Albright-Knox Art Museum," he asked.

"It's cold out there," said the man and stepped back. He followed him inside into the dark, warm hallway. The floor was carpeted but underneath he heard the creaking of hardwood floorboards where he stepped. Along the wall to his right there was a row of rubber boots; above them a row of pegs where thick, damp coats hung like effigies. It was quiet here, so quiet that he sensed there must be others in the house, waiting.

"Who told you to ask me?" said Harkness.

"Eddie Mastrewski told me to ask here if I got lost," he said.

The old man stared at him, then spoke quietly. "How is Eddie?"

"Dead," he said.

The old man only nodded, then walked on into a large, dark living room and lowered himself into an overstuffed chair. The old man looked like a shrunken child in the dark embrace of the chair. After a moment Harkness said, deliberately, "I know you."

189

He waited, and the quiet voice came again from the half-invisible man in the chair. "I know who you are."

He shrugged. "I can pay."

The quiet voice said, "I know you can. What do you propose?" Suddenly he knew why it had all seemed so familiar —this house, this old man, the furniture—it was the formal, quiet way his grandfather had moved and talked when he was a child. It was the way the men of that time discussed serious business.

He said, "I'm in a lot of trouble—"

Harkness interrupted, not harshly, just talking into his sentence. "You don't need to tell me that. Nobody comes here except he has his troubles. What you want from me?"

"I have to disappear, but I have to do some traveling first. It may take time."

The old man sat motionless and silent, staring at him. "I see," he said. Then he said, "It'll cost twenty thousand dollars. More if it's longer than a month. That's if I can do it at all."

He waited and the old man went on. "Only two thousand is for me. The rest is to keep you alive while you go."

"Why so much?"

"I said I know you. I don't want to know why you have to disappear, but I know it's not the law. If anybody found out how you traveled, the ones who helped you wouldn't go to some nice warm cell."

"What do I get for it?"

"A bodyguard. Enough cover, if they're not too eager to find you."

He frowned. "A bodyguard? Hell, I can't travel with a bodyguard. They'd spot us."

"You can with this one. She's the best I know of."

ALL IT AMOUNTED TO was going in with the FBI's auditors and taking possession. You just handed the subpoena to whoever was there and let the auditors do the hard part. They'd know where to look and what to look for. That was what Brayer had said. "Just stay out of the way. Don't worry. Those guys know exactly what they're doing. Pick up the search warrant and meet the auditors at the FGE office."

She wondered what one wore to a raid. That's what it added up to. She got out of bed and tested the shower. The stream of water was hot and strong—where did the water come from in the middle of a desert? Oh, yes. Lake Mead. She slipped out of her nightgown.

The telephone rang and she turned off the shower—seven A.M.—it had to be Brayer.

Brayer's voice said, "Elizabeth, are you awake?"

"Yes, barely," she answered. "What's new?"

"I just wanted to check. I don't want anything to interfere with the schedule. It looks good so far. They haven't got the slightest idea what's going on. The place has been watched since yesterday morning, and nothing has been moved out or destroyed."

"Are you sure?"

"Of course. We've been through their garbage and their outgoing mail. There are only about four employees who work weekends, and they left empty-handed."

"You've thought of everything."

"Yes, I have," he said. There was no irony in his voice. "Just take care of your part of it and we'll be fine. Even if there isn't anything in the company records the raid's got to trigger some action from the silent partner. He'll have to wonder if there is."

Elizabeth returned to the shower. She'd had just enough time to get wet and enjoy the sensation of waking up when the telephone rang again. She wrapped a towel around herself and scampered out into the bedroom. Brayer had changed his mind about something, no doubt.

"Agent Waring," said an unfamiliar male voice. "This is

191

John Tollar, FBI Las Vegas." It sounded like an address. God, they were a humorless bunch.

"Yes?" she said.

"We've been informed of a change. Can you meet me at the front desk as soon as possible, please?"

"I'll be there." It didn't sound as though Brayer had just gotten impatient, she thought. Something was up. They must have panicked and made a move. Elizabeth dressed as quickly as she could and made her way to the desk. There wasn't any problem locating the FBI agents. There were two burly men in business suits at the elevator when she emerged. Their broad, tanned faces reminded her of a football player from the Pittsburgh Steelers she'd seen advertising cologne on television. They made her miss Agent Hart a little, but only for an instant: they were perfect for this job. Brayer had probably handpicked them because they looked like what they were; their beefy, unlined, and untroubled faces had a quality of merciless and efficient innocence that would terrify whoever saw them show up with a search warrant.

"Miss Waring?" said one. "I'm John Tollar and this is Bill Hoskins. We have our car waiting."

Elizabeth let her hand be engulfed twice by their hard, clean palms, then followed them down the corridor away from the casino and the lobby. John and Bill, she noted. Easy enough to remember the names, but hard to remember which was which. John had the dark gray suit and Bill the dark blue suit. She let one of them open the car door for her while the other assumed the driver's seat.

As the car moved out to the street, Elizabeth said, "Why so early? Did something happen?"

Tollar said, "I don't actually know if anything happened. We just got a call from the Bureau to move now."

Something must have happened. It was typical that the Bureau office wouldn't have told them, and that they would refuse to speculate in front of her. But it wasn't like Brayer to

192

pass up another chance to interrupt her shower with a telephone call. But this was their show, really. They were the auditors and she was only—what? The decoy.

At the courthouse they pulled up to the front entrance and Bill got out to open the door for Elizabeth. For the first time she noticed he was carrying a gun in a shoulder holster. She felt a wave of affection for John Brayer. He was always cautious, always protecting his people. DiGiorgio's death must have torn him apart, but he wouldn't let anybody know how it felt; he'd just make damned sure it wouldn't happen again.

She quickly found the chambers of Judge Stillwell. The judge's clerk was already waiting with the warrant, and as soon as she'd flashed her identification he simply handed it to her. More of Brayer's work, she thought. All preparations made with quiet efficiency. Elizabeth scurried down the empty corridor and out to the car.

She glanced at her watch. Almost eight o'clock. They'd arrive just as the office was opening for business. John maneuvered through the morning traffic expertly and without visible effort. There was obviously nothing special about this job for them. It was just another warrant to be served, another set of ledgers to examine. They were probably a little jealous that other agents always made the arrests and felt the excitement. In a little while they'd be sitting in an office in their shirtsleeves tapping away at calculators. They took a shortcut to the Fieldston Growth Enterprises office, a long straight street that passed warehouses and lumberyards. They bumped over three sets of railroad tracks, past a junkyard piled high with the wrecked and stripped carcasses of automobiles. This was another side of the city, she thought, a place so foreign to the hotels and casinos that it didn't seem that the same name could be used to refer to both. She wondered if this was what truck drivers and railroad men thought of when they said Las Vegas—a gigantic depot in the middle of the desert where you delivered tons of liquor and bed linen, food and cigarettes,

193

and then pushed on to Kingman, Arizona, or Albuquerque, New Mexico, before the sun got too high and began to overheat your engine.

But then they turned a corner and she recognized the squat building with the Fieldston Growth Enterprises sign. John parked the car in the rear of the building and the three walked in on the receptionist just as she was uncovering her typewriter. Her purse was still in her hand. She said "Good morning" and looked pleased.

Elizabeth handed her the warrant and waited for her to read it. "What is this?" she asked.

"It's a search warrant," said Elizabeth, trying to manage a soft, kindly tone. "We'd like to see your accounting department, please."

The receptionist stared at Elizabeth blankly. Then it occurred to her that something she'd heard meant something to her. "Last office," she said, waving the warrant at the corridor behind her.

The auditors were two steps ahead of Elizabeth before she had time to move. They walked down the corridor and into the accounting office and flashed their identification wallets at the three clerks in the room, then immediately began opening file cabinets and taking out files. She left them to it and turned to the astonished clerks. She said, "We're here for an audit. It won't take very long to get what we need and then we won't disrupt your office any further." She tried to be reassuring, but she felt like the one in a bank robbery who says, "Don't move and you won't get hurt."

The two FBI men were working quickly, piling files on the nearest desk and then rummaging for more. Elizabeth felt too uncomfortable to stay. She wandered back up the hallway toward the front of the building. The receptionist was staring at the warrant, her purse still in her other hand.

Then Tollar emerged from the office carrying a stack of files, followed by Hoskins. "Can I help you?" she asked.

194

"No, thanks," said Tollar. "Only one more load." They went to the car. They returned to the accounting office and then appeared with another set of files. "That's it," said Hoskins.

Driving back to the hotel Elizabeth could think of nothing to say. They had the files and all she could do now was wait. The people in the office hadn't been criminals, she was sure of it. Whatever the files revealed to the FBI's experts wouldn't be anything that those startled clerks knew anything about. It was a little depressing.

In front of the Sands she got out. "Let us know as soon as you have anything."

Tollar said, "We'll call," and they drove off.

Elizabeth felt like having breakfast, but even more like going back up to her room to finish her night's sleep. She decided in favor of breakfast; it would be impossible to sleep, wondering what they were finding in the files. She looked at her watch again. It was only ten thirty now, and the raid was already over.

She was relieved to see that the Sands had a coffee shop. It was more in keeping with her mood than a full-scale restaurant would have been. And it was quicker. She sat down at the counter and ordered a prune Danish and a cup of coffee. It was the coffee she wanted, but it seemed somehow more respectable to eat something. When she finished she moved through the casino to the elevators and headed for her room. Brayer would want to hear from her.

When she opened the door to her room she nearly screamed. Brayer was sitting opposite the door. "God, you startled me," she said.

"Good," snapped Brayer.

"Well, I'm back, anyway. It all came off as ordered."

Brayer looked angry. "What came off? And where the hell have you been? The auditors have been waiting for you for damned near half an hour. I said ten thirty, dammit."

195

Elizabeth's heart stopped. What if—no, it wasn't possible. Just a communication snarl at FBI. She said, "John, I served the warrant at eight and the auditors dropped me off here at ten thirty. If that's not what was supposed to happen we—I—may be in big trouble."

Brayer looked both angry and confused, but said, "No. Who told you to do that?"

"The auditors. Hoskins and Tollar from the FBI."

Brayer sprang from the chair and picked up the telephone, his face now set in a look of maniacal concentration. He dialed a number and almost shouted into the receiver, "Ray, do you have two agents named Hoskins and Tollar?"

Elizabeth searched her memory. She'd seen their identification cards, hadn't she? No, she had seen them flash something in the FGE office at some frightened civilians. She hadn't seen the cards herself. She started to feel light-headed.

But Brayer was saying, "Then we need an all-points bulletin on two men as soon as you can get it on the wire. Here, I'll put someone on who can give you a description." He handed Elizabeth the phone. She wasn't sure, but she thought she could get through this, through these moments, and even through the next hour. But sometime, she knew, she was going to be by herself, and then she was probably going to cry.

22 The faces in the room were not accusing. They were empty and cold and attentive like the faces of the men around the green felt tables downstairs. They weren't judging her for what had happened, she kept telling herself. But each time she tried to believe that, she remembered that she had already been judged by each of them in the first seconds and forgotten. They weren't thinking about what had happened except as it revealed to them what they must do next. It was just a fact, something that had to be taken into account—an agent had been lost because he hadn't followed standard procedures. A second agent had been stupid enough to hand over essential evidence to two men she'd never seen before because they looked like FBI agents.

Everyone was waiting for Martin Connors to speak. It was his prerogative as the head of the Department of Justice's Organized Crime Division, senior to everyone else in the room by virtue of his rank and his white hair, but also because he had been the last to arrive, taking a special flight from Washington because one of his units was onto something big and blowing it.

Connors sat back in his chair and puffed hard on his pipe. "All right, I think I understand the situation. The element that seems to connect the murder of the Senator and this man Veasy is Fieldston Growth Enterprises. Then this lawyer, Orloff, is killed in front of Fieldston. An examination of the tax records seems like an interesting enough idea to warrant study, but two impostors steal the company's files: I guess that's clear enough. The question, then, isn't whether FGE was the place to look for the evidence that would connect the

197

murders of Veasy, Senator Claremont, and Orloff, but whether it still is."

"That's right, Martin," said Brayer.

"That's not too good," said Connors. "Bad showing by both sides, I'd say." He sucked his pipe again, and said, "There's not much reason to doubt that whatever was on the premises that would help us is gone—they selected the files themselves." Elizabeth could feel herself blushing.

The FBI Las Vegas field headquarters chief interjected, "Of course we might find the two men, and we'll probably be able to put some of it together in other ways."

"True," Connors nodded. "But it wasn't that kind of move. They were buying time, and they've got it, as far as I can tell. What are the chances you'll get them? I mean ever, not just while the files are still in their possession?"

The FBI man shrugged. "Not much, and every minute means it's less likely. They could have parked the car in one of the hotel lots with the files in the trunk and it'd take a week to find it. And every third man in Nevada looks like a football player." He looked a little like a quarterback himself, thought Elizabeth.

Connors said, "Right. So for now we've got to forget what we've missed out on, and concentrate on what they've given us. What they've done is conceded that FGE is the connection. Somebody very important is, or was, vulnerable in at least two ways. First, the lawyer Orloff knew something—maybe just who the silent partner is. That's a dead end because they got to him. Second, the company records held some information they thought we could use. The point is, they got it in a very special way. They took a hell of a chance, for one thing. They should have been spotted going into the building. Why weren't they, by the way?"

Brayer answered, "Just a screw-up, Martin. Our surveillance team saw Waring and figured the men with her had to be FBI, and the FBI thought they were ours." He looked embarrassed. His superior stared at him but didn't say anything to reassure him.

Instead Connors turned to Elizabeth. "All right, Waring. You've been in on most of this. What do you think is their next move?" Elizabeth stared at the carpet. She had to admire Connors' perception. Always ask the lowest-ranking person first, because the others won't be afraid to contradict. Once you ask a person's boss, you won't hear a peep out of him.

"I'm not sure, Mr. Connors," she said. "I agree that they're trying to break a connection. If that's true there are several people we ought to look for. The first is Edgar Fieldston. The others are the ones who have been doing the killing. And I think the murder of Castiglione ought to be included in this."

"Why?" asked Connors. "Of course we're interested. We've got a lot of people on it, but he wasn't the silent partner."

"Because it's an enormous event for the people we're interested in. Why did it happen just now, and in this town? It doesn't make any sense unless it has some connection with these other murders."

Connors shrugged and puffed on his pipe. "Give me a hypothesis."

"All right, here's one. Castiglione was using FGE as a front for various operations, including a cover for professional killers. He had dealings with other powerful people—maybe heads of the other families. When the Senator's committee made inquiries Castiglione had him killed. The others whose dealings with him could have come out got nervous and decided to get rid of him and the company's lawyer and the company's records."

"Plausible," said Connors.

"Of course it's plausible," said Brayer. "Everything is plausible if you haven't got the answer. You have to go on what we know. What we know is this: somebody killed Clare-

199

mont and Veasy and Orloff, and FGE is the common denominator. Somebody also killed Castiglione. Maybe it's connected, and maybe not. In any case the hits were all done by professionals, and the chances are we won't get professionals unless we get very lucky. So what's left?"

"You tell me," said Connors. "And make it good, because when we're through here I'm going to have to either ask the Attorney General's office to authorize the expenditures you'll need to pursue it or tell him I've scrapped the operation."

"But it's not that simple, Martin," said Brayer, his hands now clenched on the arms of his chair.

"I know. But this is an expensive operation, and what have we got to show for it? You've lost a man and spent a lot of time and money."

Elizabeth could stay silent no longer. "That's not how to figure it, Mr. Connors," she said. "What we've got is nothing but FGE. What we might have in a week is the man who killed a United States senator. Something big is going on, and this is just the start. They can cover their trail on FGE for a time, but we'll know more eventually. What we ought to be doing in the meantime is watching all of the candidates to see if we can catch one while he's trying to cut off the links with FGE."

"Martin, look," said Brayer. "They're shooting each other down on the street over this. If we watch closely enough we've got a hell of a chance, and it won't be tax evasion or stock fraud."

Connors sat immobile, still puffing little clouds of smoke into the room. Finally he spoke. "I suppose there's no alternative. I'll speak with the Attorney General himself if I have to." He stood up and nodded to the others in the room. "John, my plane leaves in an hour, and I'd appreciate a ride to the airport. I'll arrive in Washington at nine thirty, and I'll expect a call with a list of what you'll need. You might as well include what it would take to find Edgar Fieldston and if necessary

200

extradite him from wherever he is. I expect he's probably dead, but the extra funds will give you some leeway."

HIS EYES OPENED and he was alert and present, as though he'd stepped through a doorway from sleeping to waking. It had been years since he'd allowed himself the luxury of even momentary uncertainty about where he'd been when he'd closed his eyes. Had he heard something? No, it was just his instinct telling him it was time. The shadows in the room had deepened and melted together into darkness. He sat up and strained to see the dial of his watch. It was six thirty; the old man had been gone for over five hours.

He stood up and listened to the breathing of the empty house: the faint hum of the furnace in the cellar, the soft substantial sound of the clapboards standing up to the bitter wind. It brought back the feel of the house in Pennsylvania when he was a child, not so far from here, but too many years ago. It was as though he'd walked out, and when he looked back that world had been gone for so long that there wasn't anyone else left who even remembered it. The house was probably still standing, like this one was, but now someone else lived there.

"It's a safe house," Eddie had said. "Nobody talks about it because they might have to use it someday. But I know. People have gone through that door and nobody's ever seen them come out the other side. For all I know he turns them into niggers."

He heard a sound outside the house. He drew out the Beretta and floated slowly and carefully into the kitchen, his ears tuned to the pitch of the first noise. It was the sound of footsteps making their way to the back door. He crouched at the kitchen door and leveled the pistol on the back hallway. He heard two pairs of feet, one scraping the pavement—probably the old man—and another harder and faster, clicking on the walk. That had to be the woman, taking shorter steps. But he didn't move. What was to keep the old man from selling him? In five hours he could have found out who the buyer was.

The key turned in the lock and the old man called into the darkness, "It's me," then opened the door.

"Come on in," he said, and stepped back behind the doorway away from the sound of his voice. The light came on in the kitchen and he could see them. While the old man was struggling out of his overcoat, he studied the woman. She looked right. She was about five feet eight, not tall enough to be noticeable and not too small. She was pretty, he decided, but she was smart enough to be the kind of pretty that didn't strike the eye at first glance—she had done something to herself. It was the hair and probably makeup. The dark, shining hair was cut short and then waved so the angles of the face were softened into a kind of unremarkable pleasantness. He couldn't tell much about her figure, but she seemed slim even in the thick coat she was wearing. As long as the coat wasn't hiding gigantic breasts or a seventeen-inch waist she'd do—an attractive schoolteacher or maybe a secretary traveling, but not the kind that traveled with the boss—a secretary on vacation with her husband.

"This is Maureen," said the old man.

He nodded to her, and she acknowledged it but said nothing. He said, "She looks okay. When do we leave?"

The old man said, "That's not up to me. I'm going in the other room to watch a little television while you work that out. After that I'm going to bed. Just leave my two thousand on the counter and lock the door when you go. If it's there when I get up tomorrow morning I never heard of you." He walked through the kitchen door and closed it behind him.

"We can go any time now," said Maureen. "Everything I need is in the car."

"I'll get my suitcase," he said, and went back into the living room. The old man was gone, but he could hear the television in the bedroom. His suitcase was in the front hallway where he'd left it. When he returned to the kitchen he set the two thousand dollars on the counter and placed a coffee cup on top of it.

He let her out first, and followed her into the cold night wind. She took a different way, up the driveway and past a tiny garage. On the far side of the garage was another garage and a driveway leading to the street behind. He followed her to a three-year-old Chevrolet parked at the curb.

She handed him the keys and waited while he stowed the suitcase in the trunk. He let her in and took the wheel. The car's engine sounded well-tuned and healthy, and he could feel the heater warming the interior. As he pulled away from the curb and down the street, he could tell that it had gotten colder by the way the tires wobbled and crunched over the ice chunks.

"Do you know where you're going?" she asked.

"Yes," he said.

"Good. Then we can talk while you're driving. You don't have to tell me anything. That isn't part of our deal. But if there's anything that will help I'd like to hear it."

He thought for a moment, then made his decision. She was in all the way already. Even if she had an inclination to betray him she would know they probably wouldn't be able to get him without taking her out too. He decided to clinch it. "I had a deal with a man who was working for somebody else. After I delivered, they killed him but made me think I was going to get my money anyway. I got out. That was two days ago. It could have been anybody, but Carlo Balacontano was there when I was."

"Carl Bala," she said. "Shit." She was lost in thought for a moment. Then she said, "I just have to know one more

203

thing, and I won't ask any more. How bad do they want you? Is it just the money or do they have some reason to be afraid of you? The old man said you were a pro."

He looked over at her, but her face was obscured by the shadows. He drove on through the night. After a few minutes he found the entrance to the expressway and swung the car up the ramp into the rushing stream of southbound vehicles. It was over an hour before either of them spoke again. She asked if it was all right if she smoked, and he said it was.

23 Elizabeth studied the report. It could hardly be called a report, because it told her nothing she hadn't known for a week; in fact, there were two paragraphs that she had handed in as field notes for the Ventura police. Veasy, A. E. Death by detonation of explosives carried in vehicle. Probable murder. No suspects, no motive, no identification of the source of the explosives, no witnesses to the wiring of the truck, no similarities to other cases. Projected course of investigation: none. They were cutting it loose. No case with a report that said *Murder by Persons Unknown* could ever be closed, but the report had the neat and polished appearance of a document done for the archives. They knew this was a sheaf of paper they were going to have to live with. Damn.

She turned to the Senator's file. It was already five or six hundred pages of field reports, chemical analyses, interviews, and transcripts from consulting agencies. It wasn't really different from Veasy's file. It would just take longer before they could give up. But already the additions were beginning to take on that peculiar archival quality. Here and there she could see notations that said *substance not traceable* or *checked without result* instead of *investigation in progress*. It was just time, that was all. A week for a machinist, and how long for a senator? A month? A year? It didn't matter, because in another week or two the real investigation would have ended—maybe it had already. If there was evidence about the murders it had to be at Fieldston Growth Enterprises. And that meant it was gone. Because of Elizabeth Waring.

When Elizabeth looked up, Brayer was back. She returned to her work without speaking to him. Since Connors had left, the sight of John Brayer had been an irritant. She had placed him in a vulnerable position by her mistake, and he had accepted it and supported her. Now he was an irresistible temptation, the only possible source of approval that could assuage the guilt and humiliation of the last twenty-four hours, and she couldn't ask for it or even take it if it were offered. It wouldn't be offered because then he wouldn't be John Brayer, who approved what was efficient and productive, and disapproved of everything else.

The file had been kept up. After she'd left Denver the FBI had even followed up on Elizabeth's theory that the killer would have multiple sets of reservations. If he had, he'd been clever. He'd used more than one name, and possibly even used other blinds nobody had thought of. He was home free, she thought. He could run for senator himself, now that there was a vacancy.

"Elizabeth," said Brayer. His voice sounded normal—happy, almost. She closed the file.

It couldn't be, she thought. They hadn't caught Tollar and Hoskins.

"We've got some action. I just got a call from the Flamingo. They've asked for a bellhop in Toscanzio's suite. It looks like he's headed for home."

HE WOKE UP and looked at Maureen. She was still moving the car down the highway, her eyes peering through a pair of saucer-shaped sunglasses at the traffic. She'll do, he thought. Even if all she knows is driving a car and staying awake when I can't. I'm a respectable businessman on a trip with his wife.

The first stop would be the one that would tell him how to handle the rest. He'd worked in Detroit. There were people who knew him by sight. It had to be first, it had to be the test. He looked out at the bleak, rolling hills, a few trees between

patches of old gray snow. Even like this it was familiar—
especially like this. It reminded him of the man standing alone
on the hillside, a man so alone he could have been lost on the
surface of Jupiter or drifting in the darkness and silence at the
bottom of the ocean. And as soon as the man had seen his face
he'd known. The man had been a numbers runner, or was it a
bookie? But the man had come up short. He'd been given
chances, but he hadn't used them. But as soon as they'd gotten
close enough for their eyes to meet, the man had known that
this wasn't a warning. That was when the rest of the world had
dissolved and he'd become the man alone on a hillside, a dark,
motionless vertical object standing on the gray, empty snow.
He hadn't bothered to say, "Wait, I can pay." He hadn't bothered to say anything, because when he saw who they'd sent to
meet him he'd known that restitution and repentance and even
money were things that pertained to people on a world a million miles away from him, a world that he was no longer a
part of. He had stood there and then the bullet had smacked
into him and toppled him over. The man lay there against the
empty hillside, already dead with his blood leaking out into
the snow, and he'd stood over the body and pumped the trigger until the clip of the big .45 automatic was empty. Later
he'd dropped the gun in the river, a heavy military-model .45,
inaccurate beyond a few feet, all square edges and with a kick
that jerked his forearm when he fired it.

In Detroit he had let them use his face. He'd been young
in those days and hadn't known any better. It hadn't occurred
to him that this day might come and there might still be people
around who had thought about that face during the long winter nights, wondering if it would be the last thing they ever saw.

They were nearing the city. He said, "I'll drive now. Find
a place to pull over."

Maureen nodded and turned off at the next exit. It was a
rest stop that consisted of a parking lot and gas station and a

207

Howard Johnson's with a tiny souvenir shop attached to it. They got out and separated to the rest rooms, then bought gasoline before he swung back onto the highway.

He drove for another half hour, the traffic heavier now, as more and more cars poured onto the highway from the roads that converged on the city. At the Woodward Avenue exit he slipped from the current and guided the car down the ramp to the stoplight.

"What do you want me to do here?" said Maureen.

"Nothing," he said. "We make one stop and move on. In and out as fast as possible. I'm going inside and you stay with the car so we don't get a ticket."

He inched the car down the familiar street from stoplight to stoplight, past large department stores and office buildings and banks. It hadn't changed much. He searched for a place to leave the car. Anyplace would do now. He passed the Midwestern Bank and turned right.

Maureen said, "What about there? You just passed a parking lot. There's another one coming up."

"No," he said. "Some of the parking lots downtown are owned by people I don't want to see. I can't take a chance."

Just past the next corner a delivery truck was waiting to pull out. He stopped and waved the driver on, then pulled into the empty space. "Stay here," he said, and got out. He walked back up the sidewalk to Woodward Avenue and looked for a likely store. It took only a block before he found the side entrance to Hudson's Department Store. He had no trouble finding the right kind of briefcase. It was the kind that the men in this district carried—hard sides and a combination lock.

In ten minutes he was crossing the street in front of the Midwestern Bank. "There is a magic elixir to make you disappear," Eddie had said. "It's money. If you have enough of it you can go anywhere and do anything and nobody will ask you where you got it. But that's only if you've got enough of it so you don't ever have to do anything to get more."

208

At the teller's cage he said, "I'd like to get into my safe deposit box, please." He made sure she saw the briefcase. A man with a briefcase might be bringing something to put in the box, or might be making an exchange. You never knew. But he was probably taking a minute off from work, and might be pressed for time.

The teller said, "Your name, please."

"David R. Fortner."

She made a move with her left hand and a man appeared beside her. He said, "Please come with me." The man conducted him to a tiny cubicle with one chair and a table in it, then took his key and reappeared with the box. He asked the man to wait outside; he'd only be a second.

When he was alone again he opened the box. Inside were the bills, exactly as he'd last seen them five years ago. There was no point in counting them; it took time to count a hundred thousand in hundreds. They fit neatly into the briefcase. He watched the man lock the box into its place in a wall of identical boxes, then took the key.

As he walked back to the car he looked at his watch. One thirty-five. It had been less than a half hour, and now he could move on, leaving Detroit behind.

Maureen sat in silence as he drove back toward the freeway. Every third block she glanced behind them at the traffic, but after they were on the highway she settled back and lit a cigarette.

He had planned to drive for an hour and then stop, but when the hour was up he kept driving, putting the monotonous miles between him and Detroit. It had gone beautifully, he knew. It had been in and out with little chance anyone could have seen him. But he still didn't feel what he wanted to feel, so he drove on, checking the mirror every few seconds to see if there could be a car that had been behind them for too many miles. It was just his nervous energy, he knew, and not the sure and reliable sense of caution he'd acquired over the years. But he drove on into the afternoon sun, building up the count of miles between him and the days he'd spent accumulating the stack of money in that box.

He drove past South Bend and Gary and was on the broad eight-lane expressway that poured the westbound cars into Chicago when Maureen said, "I think we'd better find a place to stop for the night."

He said, "Not for a while yet. We can move faster at night."

Maureen said, "I'm tired and I'm hungry, and I think we should. A vacationing real-estate man from Syracuse doesn't drive all night, and his wife doesn't have to look as though she slept in her clothes. Why don't we stop at a motel in the right price range and eat supper in the right kind of restaurant? We mustn't look as though we're running from something. Use your head."

Of course she was right. Besides, he thought, they probably wouldn't want to try for us where it'd cause an uproar. They'd rather have us on a dark highway. If they spotted me. And they couldn't have. It might be a week before the word reached places like Detroit that a sight of him was worth money. And nobody had ever known about the safe deposit box.

He saw a Holiday Inn sign drifting toward them beside the highway. It was as good as anyplace: the right location for a couple who had been on the road all day and didn't want to get enmeshed in the city traffic, the right price. And there would be food nearby. He suddenly realized that he'd been hungry for a long time.

In the parking lot Maureen put her hand on his forearm and held him back. "Here's where I start to earn my keep," she said. "Do what I say, and you'll be all right. I've been doing this for a long time, most of it with people who weren't much more than dead weight."

"What do you want me to do?" he said.

210

"The cover is my responsibility. It's part of what you're paying for and I know it's good. We're Mr. and Mrs. William Prentiss of Syracuse until we're alone again. From now until we're on the road tomorrow the curtain is always up and you're always on stage."

He smiled. "That's a little extreme, isn't it?"

She shrugged. "You're paying for it, you can decide. If the troubles you've got involve Carl Bala, it probably isn't. But you know more than I do about that, too. All I can say is I haven't lost a patient yet."

He sat still for a moment and thought. Then he said, "How thick is the cover?"

She said, "It's about as thick as anything I've ever used. The car is registered to William Prentiss, the license is good, the address exists. If we use the credit cards the bills will get paid on time."

"All right," he said. He took out his wallet and examined the driver's license, the car registration, and the credit cards again. They were either very good forgeries or genuine. He got out and started walking toward the motel office.

"Wait for me," she said, and caught up with him. "From here on we stay together."

In the office, he went to the registration desk while Maureen wandered to the other side of the room and pretended to look at a rack of postcards. When the desk clerk asked what kind of room they wanted, he hesitated for an instant, and Maureen said, "A double bed will be fine."

Once inside the motel room, Maureen walked all around, looking under the bed and behind the mirrors and in the bathroom until she appeared to have satisfied herself of something. Then she turned on the television, came close, and whispered in a voice he could barely hear, "You haven't worked with a woman before, have you?"

He shook his head.

"You've got to think differently now. Look at me. If you

211

were my husband, a young real estate man from Syracuse, would you want twin beds? You might take them, sure. But you wouldn't ask for them. That's just the kind of thing that creep would snicker about, and maybe mention to a friend or two."

Then she brightened and said, "Give me a minute to make myself look human and we can go eat. Check the phone book and see if you can find a restaurant." She leaned forward and brushed his cheek with her lips, and then disappeared into the bathroom.

The kiss startled him, but he did as he was told. He found a restaurant that appeared to be just the thing; the address was on the same street as the motel. The ad in the Yellow Pages was only mildly pretentious. There was no mention of entertainment, and that was the main thing they'd have to avoid. In some clubs in the Midwest, it was hard for singers and comedians to work unless they were sponsored by the Italians. There was always a quiet man in the audience studying the act, judging the applause, watching for the moment when the performer was ready to be booked into the big clubs in Los Angeles or Las Vegas or New York.

In a moment she was back. "What did you find? I warn you, no more hamburgers." He was starting to feel a little foolish. They hadn't eaten anything since they'd left Buffalo.

"This place," he said. "The King's Coach. It's just down the road, and it looks okay."

Then she took on a look of concern that amazed him. "Can we afford it?"

"I don't know," he said. "It doesn't look too fancy. But hell, we're on vacation now, you know." He felt even more foolish, like a man who had been enticed out of the audience to blurt out a single line on stage.

"I won't argue," she assured him, already making for the door. "Come on. I'm starving. We can bring the bags in later."

212

He locked the door and joined her in the car. "What the hell was that all about?" he said. "Weren't we alone?"

"I don't know," she said. "Get us moving." He started the car and pulled onto the road. She said, "I checked as well as I could, and didn't find anything. But we can't afford to stumble into one of those places that they wire to blackmail businessmen getting a little on the side. The best way to listen in is through the telephone or the TV, especially if the TV is on a cable instead of an antenna; but they're practically impossible to check unless you take them apart. A video camera is harder to hide. I don't think they have one in there, but they might."

"If you thought they could be listening, why did you talk in there?" he asked.

"I had to make sure you knew enough to act the part. The TV will cover a whisper, but if you'd blurted something out in there we'd have been taking a chance to go back. If the place is a trap they didn't see or hear anything unusual yet. They'll pay attention to somebody else." Then she laughed. "Maybe a suspicious-looking couple who really are a real-estate agent and his wife."

He said, "You know a lot about it."

Her brightness faded again. "I didn't ask you where your money comes from, did I?"

"Okay," he said. "Then tell me about Prentiss. How much money do I make selling real estate? What can I afford to order in a restaurant?"

She thought for a moment, staring judiciously at him, and said, "Well, you're pretty good at it, but no world-beater. I'd say you make between twenty and thirty thousand. You can afford to eat just about anything on the menu if it's the kind of place I think it is. But don't be too imaginative. You don't want escargot, for instance, because you don't eat things like that. As long as you stay on the steak-and-potatoes side of things you're safe. Wine is okay, but not anything extraordinary if your natural inclinations are in that direction. And take it if it's good or not. And don't overdo it on the other side either. Don't try to mispronounce the name of it while you're ordering. You're an ordinary guy, not a dunce. Just use your head. And straighten your tie."

When he pulled into the parking lot at the King's Coach, Maureen said "Perfect. Pretty ordinary and there are plenty of cars in the lot. Maybe the food will even be good."

He nodded. It looked safe enough.

"One more thing," she added. "If we have to wait for a table we'll go into the bar. I'll have a martini and you'll have a bourbon and water, or Scotch, if you like that better. Do you feel up to talking about our kids, or do we have to invent something? I don't imagine you're up to much real estate, are you?"

"I think I can handle a little of each if I have to. What are the kids' names?"

"Tom is four and Jo Anne is two, so no talk about Tom being the captain of the football team or anything. Now let's eat. I really am starving."

The meal proceeded uneventfully. They talked for a time, staying with their two subjects. By the time the waiter brought the check, he was reasonably comfortable as William Prentiss. That was the major part of a cover, Eddie had always said. "You have to be who you say you are." But he wasn't used to working with a woman, and it worried him a little. There were too many ways to get caught in the open.

At the car he said, "All right, you're in charge. Back to the motel?"

She thought for a second, then said, "Yes, I guess so. But be careful. When we go in I'm going to check the place out to see if anyone's been there. If they have, it'll probably be bugged. If I brush my hair with my right hand, it's probably all right. If I use my left, watch out. The next thing I do will be to walk over to the place where I think the problem is. Watch me and do anything I say to do. In any case, don't say or do anything out of character."

"How will you know?"

"The usual things. You sat on the bed when we came in. There were wrinkles on the bedspread. I balanced a hair on the bathroom doorknob, inside. When I closed the curtains I left them a thumb-width apart. The first thing a small-time blackmailer will do is close them the rest of the way. He may remember to open them a little bit before he leaves, but he won't measure it. When I turned on the TV I put a smudge on the screen with my other hand. If they've put something in there they may change it, or even wipe it off."

"Anything else I'll need to know?"

"Only the commonsense things. I'll have a gun in my purse. Use it if you need it." She smiled. "I know. I'm putting you through a lot when the chances are a million to one against trouble. But you know it's not wasted effort."

"I know," he said. The practice was never wasted. He had to learn to work with her, and it would have to be her way, if she was to provide the cover.

At the door to the motel room, Maureen prepared to enter first, her hand shuffling busily in her purse as her eyes darted about. He carried the bags, but set them down at the door to search for the key. He watched Maureen as she settled her eyes on the slightly opened curtains behind the window. She nodded and he opened the door, and then she pushed in ahead, her hand still in the purse. He breathed a sigh that he fancied could be the sigh of a husband setting down heavy luggage. He locked the door, regretting that there was no chain, then watched as Maureen made her inspection. She brought a hairbrush out of the purse, walked over and knelt in front of the television, and turned it on. Then she began the talk again, stood up, and walked into the bathroom, still carrying her purse.

215

He listened to her, waiting for some signal that all was well. "And that waiter," she was saying. "I was waiting for him to pour your coffee all over the table and wipe it up with your tie. How can they always get the orders switched when there are only two people at the table?" The bathroom door closed.

He forced a chuckle, and stared at the screen, where a detective was grandly wrapping up his case, as he did weekly, by accusing his client of the crime. The client, as always, produced a pistol from nowhere, and jeered as he admitted everything in detail. In a moment the client would be running away from the detective, stopping occasionally to fire a shot or two in the general direction of his pursuer, then turning to run again, always up a stairway or fire escape, higher and higher until he was trapped. At the top he would run out of ammunition, hurl his pistol at the head of the detective, and lose the ensuing fistfight. In any case he would be on the pavement below in time for the commercials. He glanced idly at the bed as he took off his coat and loosened his tie. There were wrinkles on the bedspread. Were they the same?

In a moment the bathroom door swung open and Maureen came out, her head cocked to the side. She said, "I'd like to have the recipe for the stuff they put on the asparagus, though." He didn't bother to answer. As he watched, she gave her head a toss, and began brushing her hair with her left hand. He had to force himself not to whirl his head around to look for it. What was it? A microphone? A camera? What? Watch her. He grunted and waited for her to move.

She stood firm in the doorway brushing her hair, but she seemed to be pondering. She said, "I'm going to try to make it myself. But you'll have to help test it, because I want to get it right on the first try." Then she smiled a too-broad smile, almost a wince, and added, "God, the way the prices have gone up, we can't afford to miss the first time." She still hadn't moved from the bathroom doorway. Then that was it. It had

216

to be in there. He could see that light perspiration stains were beginning to appear under her arms. But still she held the grin and went on talking and brushing.

He said, "I'm no cook. You said so yourself."

She answered, "Yes, but everybody should learn. It'll keep you alive if the real-estate business falls apart and you can't eat out anymore."

Did she mean the cover was no good? She must. But that they wouldn't be able to run. He said, "Okay, now let me in the bathroom." He picked up his toothbrush and toothpaste and headed for the door. She stepped aside and said, "All right, but save the shower for morning, okay?"

He froze in the doorway, not believing at first what he knew he felt. She had stopped brushing her hair. He looked at her eyes, which now held an approximation of a coquettish half-lidded sidelong glance, but there was behind it a kind of terror. The hand that held the hairbrush was trembling. He didn't bother to look down at the hand that was fondling his genitals.

He smiled and said, huskily, "Jesus, I think I'll get that recipe myself. Give some to the girls at the office."

Maureen turned and slipped away, and tossed the hairbrush on the table. As he brushed his teeth, he looked around him with an air of casual curiosity. The only thing that looked like a possibility was that there was no medicine cabinet. The mirror was attached directly to the wall. She had made a point of the shower. Was there something in it? Better not look. But it didn't make any sense. If there were a camera and microphones, they would be trained on the bed. And they would both have to be there in a minute.

When he returned to the bedroom he was still confused, not knowing where to look. He was afraid that his eyes would rest on the spot, and they would know he was looking for something. Then he wondered if they would notice he was moving his eyes around too much. Only Maureen was safe to

217

look at. She was sitting on the bed with her legs tucked under her, still brushing her hair with her left hand and smiling faintly to herself. He picked up his coat and started to hang it on the chair next to the bed. It had to be near, or he would never reach the Beretta in time. Maureen was busily turning back the covers, when she seemed to notice him again. She said, "Mind if I check our finances?"

"Not at all," he answered, and she sat back on the bed and whisked the coat to her. She fumbled for a moment in the pockets, then found the wallet. She dropped it on the floor. As she leaned down to pick it up, keeping the other hand on the bed for balance, he thought he saw a swift movement under the coat. Then both hands reappeared and she was peering into the wallet, moving her lips as though counting.

"Not bad," she said. "We should be okay at least until we get to Miami. Then we can use the traveler's checks."

"That's what I figure," he said. Miami. What else was there to say? He engaged himself in unbuttoning his shirt.

She tossed his coat back to him. When he caught it he was sure. The gun was gone. "How about my wallet?" he said, and she tossed it to him. He set it on the nightstand and continued to undress. Somehow his mind resisted. For some reason his alarm had eddied and swirled around inside him and had finally solidified as a reluctance to be trapped naked. Yet he knew that the surest way to convince whoever Maureen thought was watching that he was something out of the ordinary was to remain fully dressed. He knew Maureen must have slipped the gun into the bed somewhere, but now she was on the other side of the room, rummaging in her purse.

For a moment he was terrified. She couldn't reach the gun, and he would need precious seconds to find it. If she had seen something, what—but then he remembered the gun in her purse. She hadn't forgotten. She was standing guard over him until he could get into the bed and find the pistol. He quickly finished undressing and slipped in between the cool, fresh sheets. He pretended to stretch, and in one motion grasped the Beretta in his left hand and pulled it down next to his thigh. Then he lay on his back with his arms folded behind his head, looking at Maureen.

She moved to her suitcase, then took out a filmy white negligee. He had forgotten about that—that it was her turn now, and it must be harder for her. If someone was watching, it was a man. He resolved to make it easier for her if he could. He turned out the lamp beside him, leaving only the one on her side. If she wanted that out, she could turn it off easily and naturally. He said, "What do you think we ought to do first in Florida? I mean besides shopping."

"I thought you were so excited about going deep-sea fishing," she said, looking at him as she began to unbutton her blouse.

"Yeah," he said. "But what about you? What will you do while I'm out there hauling in the big ones?" He wanted to keep her talking, busy playing the part until the hardest moments were over and she could slip into bed and pretend to sleep. He tried not to stare as the blouse came off and she stepped out of the skirt.

She looked into his eyes from across the room, her lips turned up in a little smile as though she knew what he was thinking and thanked him for his two contradictory wishes. "Oh, I'm going with you," she said as she reached behind her and unhooked her bra. "I'm the bait." As she spoke she shrugged it down off her shoulders, and he couldn't help watching her firm round breasts jiggle slightly, the pink nipples standing out like tight little buds. When she slipped the silk underpants down her thighs he tried unsuccessfully to keep his eyes off the dark triangle of hair.

He said, "And what if the fish don't like girl meat?"

She stopped in the middle of reaching for the wisp of nightgown, smiled again, and said, "Then there's always the fisherman." He could feel himself blush hotly as he realized that she was looking at the place where the thin covers rose over his erect penis.

She stepped to the bed in time to stop him as he reached across to turn out the other light. "Leave it on tonight," she said. As he started to turn she was already pressing against him, sprawled atop the covers, kissing his neck and giggling. She began to claw back the blanket, and he understood. She actually intended to go through with it. He snatched her wrist and said, trying to make it sound like a joke, "Wait a minute, Miss. I'm a married man."

She held his face in both her hands, still smiling her false smile, but her eyes opened wide in a kind of pleading. She said, "I know it. And if you don't start acting like one you won't live until morning."

He pressed himself to her, fondling her breast and kissing her deeply. She gently drew him on top of her, one hand clenching and unclenching on his back, and the other moving about under the covers. When she had found the gun he knew it. The hand stopped and she opened her legs. And then he was inside her, feeling at once the warm moistness of her, and the cold, hard impression of the gun on his leg. She began to give low, whispered cries, and kicked back the covers, keeping only one side veiled.

Whenever he opened his eyes, he could see her open eyes rolling about, as though in a kind of rapture. Her cries were coming more quickly now, and she moved almost with violence, her head rocking from side to side. He could see nothing but her head on the pillow beneath his, her hair spread like a flaming halo about it. At last the lids came down and she shuddered. A real orgasm, he thought. For a moment he was lost in the surprise of it, but he forgot it as her hips began to move again. He looked down at her face. There were tiny beads of perspiration now on her upper lip. Again she was moving her head from side to side. Finally her eyes narrowed for an instant before closing and they were both lost, falling weightless as the throbbing pressure exploded out of him.

For a moment they lay still, and her hand flattened on his back, while the other moved down it, then stopped. The hand raised slightly, and he heard the deafening bark of the pistol and felt a flash of heat. In an instant he had rolled clear, and found himself crouching like a wrestler beside the bed. At the foot of it he saw the figure of a man standing with an expression of pained surprise on his face, his eyes bulging and his mouth hanging open. As the figure tottered, two more shots slammed into his chest and he toppled backward like a felled tree.

"Shit," he muttered, and looked at Maureen, who was still pointing the pistol under the covers, where there was now a singed and smoking black hole. She said, "See if he's dead."

He bent over the body, but there was no uncertainty. There was no pulse, no heartbeat, no breathing. It was as though the thing on the rug had been part of the furniture of the unfamiliar room, or a bit of luggage left there by a slovenly porter. He looked at the face, frozen in its instant of outraged amazement. Then he said, "We've got to get out of here."

"Uh-huh," she said. He looked up to see that she was already at her suitcase, taking out a fresh set of clothes. She turned to him and said, "But we'd better make him disappear."

He began to dress. "Not much point in that," he said. "It'll slow us down, and it won't help."

"What do you mean?" she said. "We can't just leave a—"

But he interrupted her. "I knew him."

221

24

"Twelve five P.M., Tuesday, February 20, Las Vegas: Subject Vincent Toscanzio. At 11:50 subject boarded TWA flight 921 for Chicago. He was accompanied by three persons: One registered as William Capell, positive ID Guillermo Montani. Others listed as Daniel Chesire and Richard Greene not identified. Photography will be forwarded to Justice.

"2:30 P.M., Tuesday, February 20, Las Vegas: Subject Carlo Balacontano. At 1:30 subject boarded private aircraft at McCarron Airport. Aircraft took off at 1:45. Flight plan filed for Nutley, New Jersey. No ETA.

"9:15 A.M., Monday, February 19, Palm Springs: Subject Antonio Damonata, AKA Tony Damon. Subject checked out of Royal Palms Hotel at 7:00 A.M. Wife, Marie Damonata, took Sun Aire connecting flight to Los Angeles, 8:30 A.M. and Pan American flight 592 at 9:50 A.M. Destination Miami, Florida. Subject and two other men in Cadillac El Dorado, Blue, California license 048 KPJ, left vicinity at 8:35, probable destination Los Angeles.

"5:40 P.M., Monday, February 19, Miami: Subject Marie Damonata arrived Miami airport flight 592. Flight was met at 5:20 by four men. One positive ID Martin Damonata, son of Marie and Antonio Damonata. One probable ID Stephen LaTona."

That was enough, thought Elizabeth. Brayer was right, and the last one clinched it. What the others were doing might have been open to question, but Tony Damon was scared to death. The murder of Castiglione had stirred them all up, and now they were on the move, scurrying back to their strongholds and getting the women out of sight.

It was coherent, she thought. Everywhere it was the same. The news had traveled quickly. "Five eighteen P.M., Tuesday, February 20, Seattle: Subject Joseph Vortici. Vortici has not left his home since Sunday, February 18. Vortici's children have not been in school."

They were all waiting for the next thing to happen, and it was clear they all expected it to be ugly. She put down the sheaf of reports and walked to the window. Las Vegas was a strange place. Even this building, FBI headquarters, felt like some sort of temporary structure thrown up in the middle of the desert. One-story, cinder blocks painted government green, an air conditioner every few yards. The only buildings that looked as if they were built by people who intended to stay were the giant hotels and casinos clustered around Las Vegas Boulevard like dinosaurs crowding up to drink at a stream. It was ludicrous, really. It was everything that everyone had always told her. What had Brayer called it? "A monument to the Mafia's ability to cater to the lowest forms of lust in the souls of the American people; to give the suckers what they want. It's the biggest joke that's ever been played on the United States." "Take a good look at it," he'd said. "You'll learn something. It'll show you why the best we can ever hope to do is yap at their heels." It was true. It wasn't a regular city. All around were the most bizarre and outlandish temptations to do things you couldn't do at home—eat too much, drink too much, stare at naked bodies in feathers and sequins, but mostly, gamble. But you had to admit there was something about it. It wasn't exactly beautiful. It was—dazzling. For all intents and purposes, a place that grew up overnight, the night Bugsy Siegel arrived in 1946. Vanity Fair. If John Bunyan could have seen it he would have recognized it.

"Miss Waring." She turned and saw it was the local FBI division chief. It was the first time she'd seen him since the meeting in the hotel. Where had he been?

"Yes?" she said.

223

"These gentlemen are agents Grove and Daly from Justice." He left the office and closed the door.

She waited for them to say something, but they were busy pulling out chairs for themselves and shuffling papers in their briefcases. They looked vaguely familiar. She had probably seen them some time in a Justice hallway. She smiled and said, "What can I do for you?"

Grove said, "Miss Waring, we're from Internal Security. We'd like to ask you a few questions."

She struggled to hold the smile, but she knew it must be fading. "Sure. What about?"

Daly, a chubby man with thick glasses and a crew cut, spoke first. "It's about the incident concerning Fieldston Growth Enterprises. Please sit down." He sounded kind, soothing, almost the way some men did who had always been chubby and worn thick glasses.

Grove cleared his throat, and she suddenly realized that this was going to be something she wouldn't like. The men were distinctly uncomfortable. "To the best of your knowledge, who knew you had been ordered to serve a warrant on Fieldston Growth Enterprises?"

"John Brayer, of course," she said. "The FBI. There were two Bureau auditors, but I didn't get to meet them. I suppose the local FBI division head, the man who was just here. And there were two or three agents on surveillance at FGE." Grove scribbled on a yellow legal-size notepad.

He said, "Who else?" He seemed to know the answer.

She remembered. "The presiding judge and I suppose his staff."

He repeated, "Anyone else?"

This time she was sure. "Nobody I know of."

Daly spoke up. His eyes looked apologetic behind the round magnifying lenses—big, sad, puppy eyes. "Please try harder to remember, Miss Waring." It seemed to be very im-

224

portant to him. "Did you mention it to anyone? Family? A boyfriend, maybe?"

"No, of course not," she said. "I spoke to no one."

He smiled. "All of us who work in this field deal with a hundred details every day, a lot of them sensitive. We'd never intentionally reveal anything, but sometimes we make—" he paused, then chose "errors. Maybe we have plans that have to be cancelled due to our responsibilities at Justice." What in the hell was he getting at?

He smiled again. "You know. You get a call from the boss—your Mr. Brayer, and then you have to break a date. My wife has gotten used to it, but believe me," he chuckled, "it took many years."

She saw it coming, but had to wait. He said, "You call your boyfriend and say, 'Sorry, can't go. I've got to serve a warrant.'"

Elizabeth said, coldly, "I just told you I spoke to no one. I have an excellent memory. Now tell me what's going on."

This time Grove answered. He was a large man about fifty years old, with small, sharp eyes and a broad, expressionless face. "We're here to find out why the people you're investigating seem to know in advance what the next move is. Your superiors consider you bright and perceptive, Miss Waring. Surely that must have crossed your mind."

"Yes," she admitted. In fact it had kept her awake until after two last night, but she wasn't going to tell him.

His expression didn't change. He said, "Well, it occurred to Mr. Connors too. He's asked us to find the problem."

She wondered whether she would be able to keep herself under control. Her head was beginning to throb. "And so you're asking me."

He nodded. "And so we're asking you."

She said quietly, "But I don't know. I was just told to do it, and when I got a call from the two agents—but they

225

weren't agents, were they?—I served the subpoena. I spoke to no one."

Daly said, "Do you have any suggestions for us, Miss Waring?" So there it was: the chance to serve as the anonymous accuser. "We're not making much progress." The methods of interrogators were always the same.

"No," she said. "I only know I'm not the one. I don't have any idea how they know what to do or when to do it. It might be they just figured it out. I was the agent in the open. I'd been to FGE the day before and gotten nowhere. The next logical move was to audit their records. Maybe they just put the pieces together."

The two were already standing up and putting their notepads away.

Elizabeth felt a sudden desperation. She knew it was part of their craft, that they were trained to make her tell them things because she wanted to know what they knew, but she couldn't help herself. "Wait," she said. "Whom else are you talking to?"

Daly's chubby face turned to her in a look of bright hope. "All of the agents, I suppose. The judge and his staff. Are we missing someone?"

She said, "No, I don't think so." Watching them leave, she regretted having said anything.

Elizabeth shut the door and dialed Brayer's room at the Sands. When he answered she said, "John, I've just been grilled by two men from—"

He interrupted, "I know, I know. Internal Security. Don't let it bother you. They're looking for a leak."

"I know they're looking for a leak," she said in frustration. "But I'm not it."

"No," said Brayer, "and neither am I. But I had to put up with it too, and so does everyone else."

"Then it's not because I was the one who—"

"No, dammit," he said. "It isn't. So forget it. I've got

things going on here and I can't take the next hour to hold your hand. So get back to work."

"What's going on?" she asked.

"More killings." He hung up.

ELIZABETH SAT WITH THE DEAD TELEPHONE in her hand. The field reports were still in a pile on the table, set aside to make room for the Internal Security men. But killings. Brayer had said killings. That made the field reports obsolete, she thought. Half of them were more than twelve hours old. The petty chieftains had been running for cover for two days. By now some of them could be anywhere—given twelve hours Damon could be in Hong Kong. Or dead. But Elizabeth had been assigned to the field reports, and the only way back into Brayer's good graces was to do what you were told. And she had been told to analyze the field reports. But how did Brayer know there had been killings? She picked up the pile of reports and leafed through them quickly. They were almost uniform. There were no reports of murders among them, just the opposite: what she held in her hand were thirty or forty individual ways of saying that nothing was happening. If there were killings, Brayer hadn't gotten the information from the field, because as soon as a call came in, the typescript was run off and distributed to everyone on the case. Her heart stopped. Oh, God, she thought. Was it the mistake or the suspicion that she was the security leak?

Elizabeth sat motionless for a moment, then remembered she was still holding the telephone, and set it back on the cradle. She thought it through again. No, it wasn't like Brayer to take someone off a case and say nothing. He wouldn't leave her in a quiet office with a pile of out-of-date reports to keep her out of the way while the others handled everything sensitive, would he? But then why hadn't he explained what was going on? Then it hit her. There was another possibility. That

227

was if the killings were local. The field agents would be reporting directly to the local controller. And the controller right
now happened also to be the unit head. John Brayer.

There was one way to find out, she thought. If the agents
were in the field the controller would call in the report to the
FBI office, even if the controller was John Brayer himself.
And if Brayer had called in and the report had been with-
held from her, she decided, she was damned well going to
know why.

228

25

The car's headlights threw a bright wedge of light into the dark Illinois fields and the car rushed forward to occupy it, never quite fast enough to catch up. He drove in the silence of intense concentration. He knew he had to figure it out, but no matter how he arranged the facts, there was something he didn't know how to account for. It was the thing that was most dangerous.

Maureen spoke. "I didn't sell you."

"Huh?" he said.

"I said I didn't tell them where you were." Her voice, coming from the darkness, sounded frightened. Of course.

"Oh, don't worry," he said. "No, do worry, but not about that. I know you didn't. You might be stupid enough to sell me to them and then panic when you realized they would take you out too. They're not stupid enough to send a face I knew. Not unless they didn't know where I'd be. You did fine. Your fee just doubled."

He sensed in the darkness that her body relaxed from a rigidity that must have gripped it for some time. Stupid, he thought, both of us—her for being afraid and me for letting her sit there like that and not noticing. And the gun she must have near her hand will disappear now. She won't let me see it, and she'd deny it if I said it, but I know it's there. Probably under her skirt, between her legs.

"What now?" she said.

"Now we've got trouble," he said. "Did the old man know the cover?"

"Yes," she said. "But he didn't blow it. He wouldn't and anyway he couldn't be sure they'd get us both."

229

"I suppose," he said. "But the cover is blown. We'll get rid of the car in a bit."

She was silent, so he went back to his concentration. Something was going on. He thought about the comical surprise on Crawley's face when the slugs had ripped into him in the motel room. But that was just a distraction. Crawley was Bala's creature. What was he doing in Chicago? Chicago belonged to Toscanzio. It was Toscanzio's responsibility to get the man who'd killed Castiglione if he was in Illinois. It shouldn't have been Crawley; they'd never hire an outsider for the one who'd gotten Castiglione. It should have been Toscanzio's soldiers, maybe half a dozen. And they wouldn't have sneaked in to do it quietly. They'd have smashed in and demolished him, torn the whole motel down if they had to. It didn't make sense unless killing Castiglione had worked. He smiled to himself. There was no question about it. The bastards were at each other's throats.

"He looked just like that when we found him, Miss Waring. We haven't moved him yet because of the—the way it was done."

"I see," said Elizabeth. She walked back toward the front of the gift shop where the other one had been, the girl. She stepped behind the counter and stood at the cash register, then scanned the room. You couldn't see the dressing cubicles from the counter. The tall racks of china objects in the center of the room were too thickly crammed for that—coffee cups that had *Las Vegas* and a pair of dice on them, ash trays that looked like roulette wheels. The killers had probably stood behind the rack of coats in the back. The front of the gift shop was where all the likely objects were placed: the jewelry, small carved figurines, and even the junk that wasn't worth stealing. In the back were the bigger things, the clothes and the imported coffee tables. They were too big for a shoplifter. There was a round convex mirror on the wall, but the girl at the cash register couldn't have seen behind the rack of coats. God, what a place. A rack of coats—sable and mink and silver fox, none of them to be had for less than seven thousand, and next to it a rack of T-shirts. Something for everybody.

The girl's body was gone, but the usual chalked outline was on the rug where she fell. Not that anybody needed it. It was amazing how much blood you had in you.

"Miss Waring, we're getting ready to move him now."

Okay. One last chance. It wouldn't accomplish anything, probably, except to give her one more image for a nightmare. But you had to look. You always had to look, because they might have made a mistake, gotten too confident, let their flair for the dramatic get them into trouble. She left the counter and made her way back around the racks of souvenirs to the dressing rooms.

The police lieutenant was waiting for her. He pulled open the curtain and stood back. A gentleman, she thought. Absurd. She stared in at the body. It was sitting on the bench, leaning in the corner of the little cubicle, the head lolling sideways as though he were trying to look over his own right shoulder. She could see the face in the mirror, the open eyes bulging, and a T-shirt stuffed in the mouth. It was hard to tell what he would have looked like when he was alive. He was big: fifty-three years old, they'd said, but he was broad shouldered and with a barrel chest. She looked down at his waist. Not much of a paunch—he had stayed in shape. A hard man to take into a busy gift shop and do this to. He'd been strangled and they'd broken his neck. She looked down to examine the shoes, but she couldn't get past the abdomen without stopping. For some reason that was the most horrible part of it. The joke.

The china figurine of a baby rabbit had been stuffed into the fly of his pants, so only the head and shoulders stuck out, the little face smiling shyly at nothing. She looked down at the

231

shoes. They were beautifully polished, with no scuff marks. What was the leather? Lizard. At least two or three hundred dollars, she thought. A good match for the suit. She'd lost track of what men's clothes cost, but this one was expensive.

"Do you know what he did?" she asked.

"Did?" said the police lieutenant.

"Yes," she said. "What he did for a living. You know."

The lieutenant shrugged and let the curtain swing across the body. "Not really. Ferraro was from New York, and the response from NYPD didn't tell us much. The first round just said he was a probable. When they sent the rap sheet to us the last they had was 1958, assault, three counts. Nothing recent, but he's obviously come up in the world." He nodded, and the ambulance men shouldered their way into the cubicle to begin maneuvering the body to their cart.

"What do you think happened to the girl?" said Elizabeth.

"Hard to tell," he said. "At the moment I think she probably saw something or heard something, and started toward the dressing room. But it's possible they wanted her too. She was shot four times. There must have been a silencer because nobody heard anything, and this is a big, busy hotel."

It didn't matter, Elizabeth knew, because Brayer had been right all along. They had probably killed the girl because she'd seen their faces. There must have been two of them. It was Ferraro they wanted. But why in a gift shop in a bottom-level corridor of the MGM Grand Hotel? She looked out through the glass display window at the crowds moving past. It was easy to see how they'd done it, slipped in and done their work, maybe one of them at the door to pull the curtain and put up the *CLOSED* sign. Then in a few minutes they'd just come out and dissolved into the flowing current of people. And it might have been an hour before anyone had checked the door or wondered aloud why a hotel gift shop was closed at ten thirty on a Wednesday. But why? The only possibility was that Brayer was right. It was a struggle for primacy, and the opening gambit would have to be like this, terror tactics, each side telling the other that it would be best to submit. They were saying we can get you whenever and wherever we want to.

HE RETURNED TO THE CAR and carefully wrapped the money in the newspaper so that it made a neat, tight bundle. He wrapped the masking tape around it and slipped it into the padded book mailer, then sealed the mailer. Maureen watched, but said nothing, just stared out across the broad expanse of the parking lot while he worked. He left the car and returned to the post office, then printed boldly across the package, *P.O. Box 937, Tonawanda, New York 14150,* and dropped it into the mail slot.

When he was back in the car Maureen said, "Is that what this is all about?"

He started the car and drove out of the lot. "What do you mean?" he asked.

"You're collecting your nest eggs, aren't you?"

He nodded. "That's part of it."

"And you're mailing them somewhere."

"It would be hard to deny that, wouldn't it?" he said. "So what? I've got to travel light."

"Nothing," she said. "I just hope you're not one of those guys who has a wife or a girlfriend somewhere waiting to pick it up."

He chuckled then said, "Maureen, are you jealous? I mean, you're a lovely lady and an outstanding fuck, but come on."

"That isn't what I mean and you know it," she snapped. "I mean if wherever you mailed that isn't secure I want to know about it, and I want my money now, because I'm getting out of this. If there's somebody at that address they'll have the money and they'll have the place it was mailed from."

233

He looked at her. She was staring at him and her jaw was tight. He said, "Relax. It's a post office box. I've had it for some time. I've got several of them, all over the place. Some I've used for people to get in touch with me when they had a job to offer. Some I use as addresses for the covers I need: a place to send bills for credit cards, license renewals, and so on. There's somebody behind all those boxes—me. This address is a money drop for me. I've only used it three times since I've had it, which is about that many years. I've never given the address to anyone, and nobody knows I've been there. Is that secure enough?"

Maureen didn't answer at first, just stared ahead at the road. Then she brightened and said, "You're not such a terrible fuck either. Nothing special, but adequate, I suppose."

He said, "Then it's settled."

She looked puzzled. "What's settled?"

"That we get rid of this car, scrap Mr. and Mrs. William Prentiss, and disappear into the sunset. We're going to make a jump and then go under for a bit."

They made Peoria at almost two o'clock. This time Maureen drove the car around the block and waited while he went into the bank. The money didn't fit in the briefcase, so he put the rest of it in his pockets. This, he decided, would be enough. There were savings accounts in seven banks in different parts of the country, but they could wait. None of them was large enough to be vulnerable, and the money would keep until it was safe to transfer it in small payments to the account of his next identity. In the meantime it would even draw interest. If he left it for a few years it would double.

The proportion was about right. He had at least eight hundred thousand dollars in those accounts, three hundred thousand in the post office box, and two hundred thousand with him when he returned to the street. He could wait. He could wait until Toscanzio and Balacontano and the others died or went off to retire in Italy, until Little Norman and

234

everyone else who'd ever known him had died and been forgotten. Because he didn't have to work again. He was a rich man. He could take it day by day, living comfortably but not comfortably enough to draw anyone's attention. And each day he bought himself would make it less likely that the Italians would ever find him. Each day he would seem less dangerous to them, and each day would bring them something new that they'd rather think about because there was a profit in it. Someday they'd have forgotten all about him. In five years he'd be one of those problems that had solved itself. In ten, it would be hard to find anyone who could remember whether or not he'd been found and killed. Crawley had played a hunch and waited for him in Detroit and followed him. He'd have done the same himself. A sucker who had to disappear would try to get on a plane for someplace far away that he'd never been to, but you had to figure a pro would go to ground in a familiar place. But Crawley was dead. The only thing that still worried him a little was that Crawley had seen the car, and managed to find it again in the motel parking lot outside Chicago. Crawley had never been that lucky. Had he managed to do that alone?

He stood in front of the bank looking for the car. Maureen would keep circling the block until she saw him. The traffic downtown was heavy, he thought. It might take a few more seconds before she came around again, so he watched the people on the street. It wasn't a bad way to do things, he thought. There were other people standing in front of buildings across the street waiting for buses or the arrival of friends. He knew he didn't look appreciably different from the others, if you took them as a group. He was wearing a sport coat and carrying a briefcase. The only difference was that his was full of money.

He even counted two who looked a hell of a lot more suspicious than he did. One of them was a short, dark man with curly hair who was just standing on the corner across

235

from him. He was wearing a gray three-piece suit and carrying a briefcase. He wasn't waiting for a bus, because he was right at the corner. Whenever the light changed, a herd of people would scurry across the street, but he'd still be there. Whatever he was waiting for, he didn't look impatient about it: he never looked at his watch and he never looked up and down the street to see if it was on the way. Maybe he was early. The other man was about a hundred feet from the corner, in front of the display window of a travel agency. He was waiting for someone too, but he was getting impatient. You could tell because he had been staring into the window for a long time, the way people did when they had been standing in one place long enough to wonder if they were attracting attention. It made them feel as though they had to be absorbed in doing something, or people would notice them. People would think, look at that schmuck standing there. He's been there for twenty minutes. She stood him up, and he's too stupid to know it, the poor bastard.

Where the hell was Maureen? His sense of time must be off, because it seemed he'd been here long enough for her to go around the block at least twice. There couldn't be trouble, not real trouble. He hadn't been in Peoria in a year, at least. There was no way anybody could anticipate that he'd be coming to pick up an old contingency fund. The one thing they would believe was that he wasn't worried about money. They'd given him two hundred thousand less than a week ago. But what was keeping Maureen? Unless she'd decided to sell him after all, now that they were separated and he could be had alone. No, that didn't fit. She would wait for the forty thousand he'd promised her, because she could never suspect that he was worth more than that to them, not on what he'd told her. So where was she?

He began to feel a prickling sensation at the back of his scalp. He was vulnerable. He had to stand here in the open as long as it took. There was no plan to cover the possibility that one of them would get into trouble. He'd only been in the bank for ten minutes—what trouble would there be? But there must be a problem. And here he was. He didn't even have a gun. You didn't walk into a bank with a gun on you because it wasn't worth the risk.

Suddenly he saw the car swing around the corner. He felt the muscles in his neck and shoulders relax. He could see Maureen behind the wheel now, coming toward him. It was all right. Then he thought, if she stopped somewhere and went into a store to buy a new pair of panties or something I'll make her wish she hadn't. As the car approached he took a step forward toward the curb to meet it.

The car didn't stop. Maureen didn't even look in his direction, just drove on past him and kept going. His practiced reflexes took over and he completed his stride and made another step forward. He looked down the street into the distance as though he hadn't recognized Maureen. His mind worked at the problem. She had seen something and come here to warn him.

She was being followed. It had to be that, because nothing else would make leaving him here less dangerous than picking him up. Somebody was following her, and she thought they wouldn't make their move until the two of them were together in the car. So it had to be the car. Crawley hadn't been alone after all, and someone had spotted the car a second time. And now she would have to keep driving, leading them somewhere else until either she shook them off or they realized she'd seen them. That meant they'd backtrack until they found him, or they'd take her and ask her questions. He didn't bother to think about that. She'd tell. His forty thousand wasn't worth what they'd do to her. Nothing was.

So he had—what? Five minutes? Fifteen if she bought it for him. He looked at his watch, and then started walking down the sidewalk. The important thing would be to get off these streets as quickly as possible. He wished Peoria had sub-

237

ways. A taxi might do it, he thought, but he didn't see any. A bus? No, a city bus was too dangerous. If anybody saw you get on, he'd see the route number and he had your schedule for the next hour. He walked briskly, varying his pace to the hurried strides of the people around him. He was getting cold. He hoped it didn't show. A businessman wouldn't hang around on the street long enough to get as cold as he felt.

Across the street and ahead of him was a Sears store. That looked like the most promising place. He stopped at the corner to wait for the light to change. Then he saw the man. It was the short man in the gray suit. He had moved down the block across the street, and now he was standing at the corner. He looked to see if there were a second man. Maybe the one who'd been staring in the travel agent's window? He couldn't see anyone who looked familiar. But the man in the gray suit was looking at him.

He started walking again. The man in the gray suit walked too, moving parallel with him across the street. So that was the way it would be. The man in the gray suit had intended to let himself be seen. He was herding him somewhere; it must be to a place where a second man waited in ambush.

He considered the situation. Something up ahead was a trap. The man in gray was herding him forward. He didn't look over his shoulder, but he knew that there would be somebody following at a distance to keep him from turning around if he recognized the tactic. If he went into a store, so much the better for them. They'd have time to prepare for him while he waited for an advantage that would never come. He knew the strategy, but it had a flaw. It depended upon the victim's natural inclination to wait while his chances slipped away. The ones who were following him, guiding him toward the pocket, would converge on him until it was too late for him to move, because any one of them was close enough to kill him. So he had to move now.

He watched the cars gliding past in the street. A taxi

238

would be perfect, but his luck didn't seem to be running today. Still, it had to be that way, a jump that would put him outside the triangle that was closing on him. Then he'd have a chance. He stopped at the next light and waited. The light changed and all the other people crossed the street, but still he waited. The man in the gray suit was stopped across the street from him, and he knew whoever was behind him would be coming up fast.

The light changed again and the first car across was a Volkswagen. He waited for the station wagon behind it, then made his move. He ran forward and flopped onto the long, flat roof just as the car began to move. The driver seemed to know that something had happened, because he started to brake, but then horns sounded behind him, so he speeded up again. The horns were louder now, because the other drivers were alarmed. Then it must have occurred to the driver of the station wagon that he'd hit something. He pulled over to the curb, opened his door, and got out, but what he saw made no sense. A man was running away, carrying something—a briefcase, maybe. But he wasn't concerned about that so much as he was about whatever he'd hit. He started the long walk back up the street to the light. Jesus Christ, he thought when he saw the two men running down the street toward him. It must have been bad. He just hoped to God it wasn't a kid or a doctor. If you ran over a kid or a doctor they made you pay for the rest of your life. When the two men sprinted past him at full speed he felt a giddy relief. Then he thought, Oh, God, don't let it be a pregnant woman. Even a doctor would be better than that.

26 The afternoon had been exhausting. For once it wasn't that they didn't know anything. They had too much information from too many sources. It was too complicated to be coherent. It was just as Brayer had said. "We're not looking at some gang fight. We're looking at a disruption in one of America's biggest industries. We don't even know what the hell to look at. Ferraro gets killed in a gift shop. Castiglione at his house. A guy named Crawley gets it in a Holiday Inn near Chicago—Christ, we don't even know what he was or who he worked for. But there was a booby trap in the shower of the room where he was killed—wired to electrocute whoever used it. The killing is what we're seeing. But how do we know that what we ought to be looking at isn't that one day the ice cream doesn't get delivered to a baseball game in Cleveland, or a chain of shoe stores in Massachusetts goes bankrupt because the banks won't give the company a loan?"

Brayer was right. It was ridiculous. The Organized Crime Division of the Justice Department was—what? three hundred people? And there was no way even to sort out the information that was coming in now from every agency whose jurisdiction included some avatar of the Mafia. Because that was everybody.

Elizabeth walked across the casino toward the corridor with its waiting elevators. When she opened the door to her room, she managed to stifle the scream before it got out, but not the jolt of adrenalin that seemed to pump into her veins. She could feel her temples throbbing as she said, "What are you doing here?"

Grove was the one who spoke. He said quietly, "Please come in and close the door."

240

Elizabeth came in but didn't put down her purse. She remained standing. "What are you doing in my room? Searching my luggage?"

"Oh, no, Miss Waring. You're in the clear. Completely. We're here for another reason." It was Daly who spoke.

Then Grove again, "We're here because there's a tap on your telephone. We've had a team in here half the day looking for bugs, but all they had was a remote on your line."

Elizabeth sat down in the chair beside the desk. "So you've found the problem." It wasn't a question, it was a statement. She was relieved. They were here to tell her she wasn't under suspicion anymore. For a moment she almost felt grateful, but then it didn't seem appropriate. "You've taken care of it?"

"Yes," said Daly, "we've detected the tap. But it isn't feasible to remove it. We don't know where it is, and we can't take it off without compromising other . . ." he paused, searching for the right word, "sensitive parts of the investigation."

"So what do I do?" asked Elizabeth.

"Nothing you wouldn't do otherwise," said Grove. He looked at his watch, then said to Daly, "It's almost six fifteen."

Daly said, "Miss Waring, in a minute your telephone will ring. Just answer it and say the things you would normally say. But don't ask for more information than you're given, and don't volunteer anything."

Elizabeth said, "All right. Who is it, though?"

"It'll be Mr. Connors," said Grove. The telephone rang and Elizabeth jumped. It was too quick.

"Answer it," said Grove.

Elizabeth obeyed. "Hello?"

"Agent Waring?" came a female voice.

"Yes."

"Please hold for Mr. Connors."

Connors came on immediately, and the secretary was gone. Elizabeth had the sensation that there were numberless

241

people listening to him as he spoke. Her mind ticked off the ones she knew of. The secretary, Daly, Grove, a team of technicians trying to follow some electronic signal that could tell them where in the circuitry an extra milliohm of resistance occurred. And the wiretappers themselves. She couldn't picture them, of all the invisible listeners. There was no face, no idea what it would look like—there was just the sense that there was a person, an intelligence waiting between her and Connors, not breathing or moving, not necessarily even capable of breath or movement. Maybe it was just a tape recorder. Connors said, "Miss Waring?"

"Yes, sir."

"We've found the leak in the operation."

What was he saying? Was he telling the wiretappers that Internal Security had found the tap? Why? "Really?" was all she could say. And why was he telling her?

"That's right. And I'm positive he'll tell us everything he knows. We've finally got the break we needed."

He? A person? She said, "That's great, Mr. Connors." She wasn't sure how enthusiastic to be, so she tried to modulate her tone to imitate his.

"We've got it set up so he'll have to talk. Immunity from prosecution, money, resettlement. If he doesn't talk we've got enough to charge him. So the problem turned out to be a bonus."

"That's wonderful," said Elizabeth. She almost asked him what he wanted her to do next, but she remembered that Daly had told her not to ask questions. She said, "Thank you for letting me know."

Connors said, "Quite all right, Miss Waring. You can go on with the investigation from your end, and we'll handle the rest from here. Good-bye." He hung up.

Elizabeth put down the receiver. "Do you think that was long enough?" she asked Daly.

Daly was standing up and beginning to move toward the

242

door. "That was fine, Miss Waring," he said. He seemed to be speaking to the carpet.

"But I always heard it took a long time to find a tap—ten or twenty minutes," she said.

Grove and Daly were moving toward the door, but she stepped in front of them. "Wait," she said. It couldn't be the way it looked, but what else could it be? And if it wasn't, what was all that nonsense about finding a leak? She said, "Tell me what just went on here. They weren't looking for the tap at all, were they? It was something else."

Grove's face remained impassive. "That's right. We're leaving the tap in place."

Elizabeth's heart was pounding, and she could feel her temples beginning to throb again. She understood, but she was going to make them say it. "So that's it," she said.

Daly's eyes fluttered to her face and then back to the carpet. "It was necessary," he said. "There is a leak, we're sure of it."

"So you decided to set him up?"

"That's right," said Grove. "You did a good job. Now we've got to leave here and get on with our work. Thank you for your cooperation."

"But you know what you did. They'll kill whoever it is."

Grove nodded. "Maybe they will. Judging from the rest of the case, they'll probably try, anyway. Good night."

She said, "But that's—"

Grove interrupted, his voice suddenly harsh. "Who do you think that was on the other end of the line, lady? It was Connors. He authorized it, he made the call himself. So forget it. You've done your part. Thanks to you the leak has been neutralized."

"You—we—just made sure somebody in Justice would be murdered," she said. "Maybe somebody in my office. And he won't even have any warning because there wasn't any real investigation. Nobody was even accused of anything."

243

Grove's face didn't change. He said, "What do you think this is, anyway? Do you think it's a game? Whoever it is was doing the same thing to you. Ever think of that? And if we got lucky and caught the bastard he was dead already. In jail or out of it his friends would have gotten him." He stopped, and seemed to remember something. "And by the way, don't stop using that telephone. Just remember not to say anything you don't want them to hear."

Elizabeth sat down on the bed and watched them leave. She tried to decide what she felt. Then she identified it. She knew that a shower wouldn't wash it off, but she also knew that the shower was waiting for her in the next room and absolution was not.

"WE'VE FINALLY GOT SOMETHING on Edgar Fieldston," said Brayer. "The SEC called a few minutes ago, and they think they've gotten a glimpse of his coattails." He was smiling, but it wasn't his enthusiastic smile. Elizabeth waited for the rest of it.

"Yesterday a loan was approved at the United Free Bank of the Bahamas to an Edgar Fieldston—four million dollars' worth."

"What was the collateral?"

"A portfolio of stocks. A lot of blue-chip stuff to sweeten the deal: IBM, Commsat, Xerox, ITT, but the main part was FGE stock. Almost five million dollars' worth, if you take it on today's market."

"How did the SEC get wind of it? The Bahamas aren't subject to our reporting regulations, are they?"

"No, but the United Free Bank wasn't up to the transaction. They had to get in touch with First National in Miami. You see, the deal was for cash."

"Oh, God," said Elizabeth.

But Brayer continued. "Even that wouldn't have done

244

it, because bank-to-bank transactions aren't subject to reporting regulations. But First National couldn't spare that much cash, so they got in touch with the Federal Reserve Board. Federal Reserve likes to keep an eye on deals involving banks in the Bahamas, because some of them exist mainly for the purpose of moving dirty money. When they learned about the collateral they got in touch with the SEC to see if somebody happened to notice that he'd misplaced some stock certificates. The SEC didn't pick it up until it was too late. The stock wasn't stolen, and Fieldston owned it, so—"

"So he's wandering around in the Caribbean," said Elizabeth, "with four million dollars in cash. At least he's alive."

"Maybe," said Brayer. "If he is, I'd say he doesn't intend to come back. If the FGE stock collapses, as I expect it will when we're through investigating their operations, he's just picked up four million dollars for about two hundred thousand in legitimate stocks and a whole lot of worthless paper."

"But there's another possibility?" asked Elizabeth.

"Yes, I'll admit he could be on his way to someplace like Paraguay or Costa Rica or Haiti, where he can't be extradited and can live like a king on his 'loan.' But it's more likely he was getting the Mafia's investment out of the company."

"If that's true, what then?"

"Then it may not even be the real Edgar Fieldston the bank gave the loan to. In any case, he's not likely to run off until he's paid whoever's behind him. They're not interested in niceties like extradition. All we know for sure is that somebody is liquidating the assets of FGE."

"So what's being done?" Elizabeth asked.

"Oh, the obvious things. There's a list of the serial numbers the Federal Reserve Board turned over to First National. It may turn up in interesting places, but probably it's already been laundered. The American consulates are alerted for Fieldston's passport. But I don't know what we can expect from any of it. With four million dollars he can go pretty deep, if he's alive and on his own. If he's not, the possibilities are endless. We'll never hear of him or the money again."

"So what you're saying is that we're up against another dead end," said Elizabeth.

Brayer shrugged. "Maybe, but maybe we'll get lucky. The main thing is to keep on it. I'd say that as of yesterday Fieldston Growth Enterprises ceased to be a functioning entity. But that might be a break for us, if we can figure out who's carving up the carcass."

HE LEFT THE OFFICE and Elizabeth tried to return to the reports. The piles of information were getting bigger now. In another week it would be the size of a set of encyclopedias, and there would be nothing to show for it except paper. How many murders so far? A dozen? She began to leaf through the summaries, counting. Thirteen positive, and two more probable if you counted the two blood types found on the pavement in front of the Tropicana. And they still seemed no closer to an indictment than they'd been when Veasy the machinist blew up. And that too, she thought—the union. Veasy was dead, and the union's pension fund was somewhere in South America by now, maybe working its way northward through a dozen metamorphoses to become a certificate of deposit in some Caporegima's Swiss bank account. Even if the Justice Department knew about it, the laundering would be so complete they'd never be able to prove it. At least then they'd know whom to watch—but so what? By that time what they were watching for would already have happened. It was worse than hopeless. All they could do was keep score and try to figure out what was next, always hoping an agent might be on the scene when the hit men arrived. Only this time she knew where it would be, and there would be an agent on the scene. Because she had helped put him in front of the guns. If thine eye offend thee pluck it out.

246

27 Just before the five-o'clock rush reached its peak, a businessman carrying a briefcase walked out of the big Romanesque central post office in Peoria, Illinois. There wasn't anything about him to distinguish him from the surrounding crowds of people, except that he seemed to walk a bit more slowly than some of them. Only the most perceptive of observers would have said he had a slight limp. But they would not have had the time to feel sorry about the limp, because as he reached the bottom of the broad granite steps, a young woman pulled up at the loading zone in a small blue Datsun and opened the passenger door for him. He got in, set his briefcase on his lap, and smiled at her as they drove away. He didn't kiss her, but that wouldn't have seemed unusual, because there wasn't time. She was already off to make room for others at the loading zone, and a moment later the Datsun had disappeared in the traffic.

"Maureen," he said, "that was very good."

"I knew if you wanted to meet me it would have to be at the post office," said Maureen.

"Is the car safe?" he asked.

"Sure. It's rented. I wanted to spend my last few hours on this job in relative ease." She glanced over at him, as though she expected him to say something unpleasant.

He said, "Again, very good. We just aren't going to make it together." He took a package out of his coat and placed it in her purse on the seat. "You don't have to waste time counting it," he said. "It's all there—fifty thousand dollars."

"Fifty?"

"Yes," he said. "We'll get you on a plane tonight, but

247

first there are a few things I want you to get me. I'd better make a list."

HE WATCHED THE LIGHTS of the plane as it lifted into the dark sky and diminished to a pair of tiny blinking spots. The problem with airplanes was that they only looked that way—they were built in the shape of the prototypical image of untrammeled movement and freedom. But an airplane was only part of a complex of tubular corridors that moved you from one broad and brightly lighted lobby to another. There were no cutouts, no places to hide, no ways of modifying the predictability of their movement. A telephone call from one end meant that when you walked down the last tube at the other end there would be something waiting for you: maybe a quiet man who was carrying a box that looked like a present for grandma. But Maureen would be all right. They would have no idea who she was or where she'd come from, and they'd have to spot him again before they knew she was gone. He envied her. She was out of it.

He started the car and drove out of the airport parking lot. It was going to be a long trip, he decided, but the solitude and the darkness would give him time to think about what he was going to do. There was no question about his destination. The one thing he'd been sure of was that he could never go to Las Vegas again, but that had been before he'd realized how things were. They weren't going to forget about him. They had already devoted too much time and effort to finding him to let him sink out of sight into a comfortable retirement.

He had taken a couple of jobs for Orloff, and done them, and come to collect. It all seemed to have started with those two in the alley in Denver. As soon as he'd shown up with a few bumps and bruises, everything had changed. They all turned on him like sharks when one of them is bleeding. But that couldn't be it. It was too ridiculous. And they wouldn't

248

have killed Orloff just because the specialist he'd hired had a black eye. But they'd ignored the moratorium that had held in Las Vegas for years, and killed everyone they could find. Now they were after him and they weren't going to give up. That meant that whoever had killed Orloff still felt vulnerable—but to what? He didn't even know for certain who was paying Orloff. It might be Balacontano, or Toscanzio, Lupo, even Damon.

Whoever it was had sent soldiers all over the country looking for a single man, even with Castiglione dead. Even the death of the old consigliere hadn't distracted him, although the families would now be spending most of their time watching each other to see who moved first.

So he had to find out. The one who paid Orloff had too much juice to ignore; he'd used Little Norman as his errand boy, and had watchers waiting everywhere. But whoever it was was worried about something, and the soft spot had to be in Las Vegas. The link was Orloff.

The more he thought about it, the more angry it made him. It was stupid. Uneconomical. He had taken the contracts on the usual terms. He'd dealt only with Orloff and never inquired about who was paying the bill or why he wanted Veasy and the Senator. He hadn't been curious about it. He'd done his work and that should have been the end of it. He hadn't even been that curious about the killing of Orloff, although it had seemed bad luck that it had happened before he'd been paid. He'd behaved like a professional. But they'd gone too far. They'd panicked and shot down everything that moved. And that was stupid. Because they should have left him alone.

WHEN ELIZABETH AWOKE it was dark, but she had the disconcerting feeling that she was already late for something. It was a feeling of urgency; something had begun and she was

249

still in bed. She heard the knock on the door, and remembered the sound of it. Somebody had been knocking for several minutes. As she got out of bed she called, "I hear you," and the knocking stopped. She turned on the light and squinted at her watch on the nightstand—four thirty. It had to be Brayer, afraid to use the phone. Her bathrobe was draped across a chair, but even with that she felt naked. "Just a minute," she called. It was foolish, she thought, but was it more foolish than opening the door to a knock in the night? The gun fit into the pocket of her robe. She kept her hand on it when she unchained the door and opened it.

The man at the door was a stranger. He wasn't even as tall as Elizabeth, but he gave the impression that he was big because his broad shoulders and belly seemed to belong to someone taller. His hair was dark, but beginning to turn gray.

"What?" said Elizabeth, not sure whether she was angry or not, but positive she was uncomfortable.

"You're Elizabeth Waring," said the man. Elizabeth realized that it had somehow been intended as the answer to her question.

"I know that," she said. "It's four thirty."

The man said, "Please, can I come in?" He looked past her into the room as though he longed to be there. The look on his face startled her. Brayer hadn't sent him.

"What do you want?" she asked. Her grip on the pistol tightened.

"Please," he said, "I have to talk to you." She hesitated, so he whispered, "FGE."

She let him in and closed the door. He said, "Do me a favor, and take the gun out of your pocket. You can point it at me if you want, but in your pocket it might go off by accident and hit us both." He sounded sad, as though he had resigned himself to putting up with a great deal of incompetence.

Elizabeth obliged him. She aimed the gun slightly to his

250

side, but it was in sight. "What do you want?" she repeated.

"I want to be a material witness. Turn myself in and tell you stories."

Elizabeth said, "Stories?" But she was thinking, it's happening; he really is one of them trying to come in from the cold. But he's coming to me, and I don't know what to do with him. I can't even call for help because the telephone is tapped.

"Yes," he said, "I want to make a bargain with you. I want immunity, a new name, protection. In return I'll give you information about some people I know, testify in trials, the works."

"That all takes time," said Elizabeth. "And we hardly ever do it. How do we know your information and testimony are worth it?"

The man sighed. "If what I know wasn't enough to do them some damage, why would I want protection bad enough to come here?"

It hadn't occurred to her before, but it sounded true. If a man was willing to get involved at all . . . but she decided not to pursue it now, while she was still disoriented from sleep. "What's your name? Who are you?"

"I'm Dominic Palermo." He shrugged. "I don't imagine you know who I am. I was Ferraro's partner." He corrected himself. "Friend and partner."

Elizabeth understood. "So you're afraid they'll get you too. The way they got him in the gift shop. And that's why you came here, now. You didn't want them to know."

He nodded and smiled, then seemed to hesitate. "I came to you to turn myself in."

"All right," she said, "the problem is, I don't know when they'll be able to get the Attorney General to agree to your terms. When do you plan to actually come in for good?"

"For Christ's sake," he said, "I'm standing in front of you. I'm here. Now."

251

"But I thought you had conditions," said Elizabeth. "A bargain." She didn't understand.

"That's only for what I tell you," he said. "Not for going in as a material witness."

"You don't seem to understand, Mr. Palermo," said Elizabeth. "They won't consider you a witness unless you tell them something. You can't sit in a cell and bargain."

"I'll chance it," he said. "Meantime I'll be alive."

She thought about it. "All right. What we've got to do is get you over to the Bureau. You know you would have been smarter to go straight into the FBI office, don't you? What if somebody saw you come in here?"

"No," he said. "I'm not turning myself in to them. It's to you. The Justice Department, not the FBI. Remember that, it's part of the bargain."

"But it's exactly the same thing. The FBI is part of the Justice Department. We have to go there."

"I won't," said Palermo. "Look, honey. You don't seem to know how to do this, so I'll help you out. We'll help each other out. Whoever brings in somebody like me is going to look terrific—you'll get promotions, bonuses, whatever you people give each other. And your organization has control of the information. Like your boss can say to somebody—the police commissioner in New York, maybe—'I know who's running heroin in at Kennedy Airport. What have you got for me?' So believe me, it's to your advantage to hold onto me. Knowledge is the most valuable thing in the world."

She ignored the argument and decided to ground herself in facts. "But the Justice Department doesn't have field offices like the FBI. Most of them are just offices where lawyers work on federal cases, and it's usually civil cases at that. There's no place to put a material witness, and nobody trained for that sort of work."

"Look," he said, "I'm willing to talk, but you've got to go

252

a little way on this too. I picked the Justice Department because they give the best terms, for one thing. For another, it's the highest."

"Highest?"

"Yeah. If I have a deal with Justice, then five years from now the sheriff of Herkimer County can't decide he wants me for double parking."

She had to admit to herself he was smart. His idea of the way jurisdictions worked was bizarre, but he was right about the way they'd work for him. "All right," she said, "I can't give you any guarantees about what you're asking for. I can't even tell you if Justice will take you as a material witness. But I have to talk to my superior on this."

"Don't use that phone," he said. "It may be tapped."

She picked up the telephone and dialed Brayer. When he answered she said, "John, come to my room right away," and hung up.

"I'm not happy about that," said Palermo. "I'll go along with it because I'm stuck with it, at four thirty in the morning and all that, but I want you to know I'm not a happy man."

"What's wrong now?" said Elizabeth. She sat on the bed, keeping the gun trained on an imaginary spot a foot to the left of Palermo's chest. She could see he was telling the truth—he wasn't a happy man—but she wasn't sure if she wanted him to be. She wasn't sure what was supposed to happen now, but if he was unhappy she must be in control.

Palermo began to pace back and forth in front of the door. "Don't you people ever do anything on your own?" he asked. "There's always got to be a Mr. Brayer or Mr. Farquhar or some damn thing. No wonder none of you can find your own ass with both hands. You're taking a lot of chances with my safety."

Elizabeth said nothing, just let him walk back and forth, muttering to himself. Maybe Brayer could convince him to go

253

in to the FBI office downtown—or better still, maybe Brayer and a pair of armed field agents would take him there.

She heard the knock on the door and stood up. Palermo was visibly uncomfortable now. She could see a thin film of sweat was beginning to appear on his fat cheeks. He said, "Let me fling it open and stand behind. If it's anybody but your Brayer, blow his ass away."

Elizabeth ignored him. "Who is it?" she said.

"John, Elizabeth. Open up."

When she opened the door he slipped in and locked it behind him. "So. Who's this?" he said.

"John, this is Mr. Palermo. Dominic Palermo. He wants to turn himself in as a material witness on the FGE thing."

"And a hell of a lot more," Palermo volunteered. "But I want protection. Immunity, resettlement, the works."

"Why did you come to Miss Waring?" asked Brayer.

"I heard she was working on some things I know about," said Palermo.

"Heard?" said Brayer. "From whom?"

"I just heard, that's all. So what's the deal? Can you get me what I want?"

Brayer looked at him, then at Elizabeth, then back at him. He said, "That depends. If what you know is worthwhile and you're cooperative, and you tell us the truth, I might—just might—be able to arrange something like that. But a lot of people I don't have the authority to speak for would have to agree to it."

Palermo shook his head and stared at the carpet. "Christ," he said. "Another one. So you've got to call somebody too. And then he's got to call somebody."

"That's about the size of it," said Brayer, staring hard at the fat little man. "So take it or leave it."

Palermo looked at him in desperation. "What can you guarantee? Not what you might do if the President feels like it and the Attorney General's new shoes don't pinch his toes and there's enough humidity. Look, I'm no rummy. I got things you'd like to hear."

Brayer shrugged. "You came here because you think you've got something to sell. I can probably keep you alive, for one thing, and you wouldn't be here if you had the same offer from anyone else. So I'd say that's high bid."

Palermo sat down on the bed with his shoulders hunched and said nothing. Brayer turned to Elizabeth and drew her to the other side of the room. At first she hesitated, but Brayer said, "You don't have to watch him. What's he going to do to us?"

When they were out of earshot he whispered, "What's he told you so far?"

Elizabeth said, "He's a partner of Ferraro, the man they killed in the hotel gift shop, and he's afraid somebody's going to get him too. He's very particular about who protects him. He's set on the Justice Department. Not the police or even the FBI."

"Anything else? What about FGE?"

"Just that. The initials. But he must know something, or he wouldn't be here." She tried to remember the logic of it. "He wouldn't need protection unless—"

Brayer nodded and said, "Probably not. But if a war is on, it's hard to tell. He might be nothing. We can't take the chance, of course. The question is, how do we make the best use of him?" Brayer looked over at Palermo, who was sitting on the edge of the bed with his arms folded, staring at the floor.

"Why don't we get some guards and take him to the Bureau office?" said Elizabeth. "We could even call them to come get him. Then we could start making arrangements with Washington for the bargain."

Brayer's eyes narrowed. "You know, he may be right about the FBI. For one thing, we've got him and nobody knows it. If we take him to the Bureau headquarters openly, we lose the best part of him. If we don't, all his pals will know is that he dropped out of sight. See what I mean?"

Elizabeth nodded. "Sure, but how do we do it? We can't keep him here."

Brayer said, "What I'd like to do is get him to Washington, but I don't think we could do that very easily without either being spotted in an airport or driving, and that'd be worse. It would take a week before we got a word out of him. No, we've got to get him somewhere safe and quiet by morning."

"But where?" said Elizabeth. "We don't even have a field office in Las Vegas, and anyway—"

"No," said Brayer. "But how about the capital? Carson City. We've got one there, and it's within driving distance. Besides, it would convince him we're going to meet him halfway on his bargain. Go get dressed."

Elizabeth had a sick feeling. "We're not going to do it ourselves, are we, John?"

"What else can we do?" he asked. "If we start collecting agents here at quarter to five in the morning we might as well put an ad in the paper. In fact, if he's as valuable as he claims, he might even get killed."

Elizabeth went to the closet and began collecting her clothes. Palermo looked up and said, "So. You must have made a decision. What is it?"

Brayer answered, "We're going to do what you want, at least as long as you're cooperative. We're going to take you to the Justice Department's office in Carson City for now. If we can get you that far without anybody noticing, we can fly you to Washington later."

"Oh," said Palermo, "I get it. If I tell you enough in Carson City you're a hero and I get to go to Washington so you can show me off. If I don't, you don't have anything to show your boss, so you chuck me out."

256

Brayer said, "Could be. That's the chance you have to take. But don't worry. As you said, you've got things we want to hear. You're no rummy."

"That's right," said Palermo, his big, dark eyes glaring up at Brayer out of his broad face. "I've got nothing to worry about."

Elizabeth dressed quickly in the bathroom. Of course John was right. If they could get Palermo out of sight where he could be interrogated before anyone knew he was missing, it might be just the break they'd been waiting for. Whatever he knew would stay fresh as long as his bosses didn't know he was talking. As soon as they knew, things would begin to change, evidence would evaporate; they'd be raiding empty buildings and trying to arrest people who had already left the country.

She caught sight of herself in the mirror and shuddered. She must have been sleeping on her face; her eyes were puffy and her skin a sickly pale color she couldn't remember seeing on anyone who wasn't ill. A little makeup helped, but not enough, she thought. And if Brayer saw she'd taken the extra seconds to apply it—but that was something he'd have to let her decide. If he wanted her to be inconspicuous he'd have to wait.

When she came back to the bedroom, Brayer handed her a set of keys. "Take the rented car," he said. "It's parked almost at the side door by the casino."

"Aren't you going?" said Elizabeth.

"No. I've got to make the arrangements from here. And it's less likely to attract attention, just the two of you."

She was about to argue, but she stopped herself. She couldn't say she didn't want to go alone because Palermo gave her the creeps. He wasn't dangerous; she was his best hope of living the year out. And she couldn't ignore the fact that Brayer was doing her a favor, giving her a chance for a major coup.

257

At the car Palermo said, "I'll drive." When she hesitated he said, "Look, I know the way to Carson City. You don't even know the way out of town." It wasn't until he had established himself in the driver's seat that he added, "Besides, my nerves are shot already."

She resented it silently. In a way it was comforting. It seemed right that he should be thoroughly unpleasant.

He drove down a network of back streets. When he emerged on the highway she was surprised, but refused to be impressed. After all, he lived here. And this was the last driving he'd do for some time, she reminded herself.

Suddenly he said, "You don't care much for me, do you?" The formality of it seemed incongruous.

She was caught off-balance and only managed, "I don't know you."

He said, "I know. I'm a stool pigeon. Nobody likes a stool pigeon, even if it's a stool pigeon who gets them a promotion. I don't blame you. But I want you to know, I wouldn't have done it if they hadn't left me out here on a limb."

"No, I suppose not," said Elizabeth. She wondered how far away Carson City was. The world was supernaturally dark. She imagined desert on all sides, but could see nothing but the road.

"Damn right," said Palermo. "When Old Granddad was killed—"

"Old Granddad?"

"Castiglione. When he was killed they said they'd protect me. Told Ferraro that too. They protected the shit out of him, didn't they? Then I find out they've pulled out all the soldiers they had for some important project Carl Bala had on his mind. Nicky Palermo can go fuck himself. Well, we'll see."

"So you feel betrayed," said Elizabeth.

"Betrayed?" said Palermo. He drove in silence, staring off

258

into the darkness. "Yeah, I guess that's the word for it. For years it was Nicky, you're terrific, Nicky you're a real friend, Nicky, I owe you. All of a sudden the roof collapses and what do I hear? Who's Nicky Palermo?"

"What do you mean, the roof collapses?"

"Lady," said Palermo, "I don't know what you people do all day, but it must not be much. You must know about Castiglione, right? It was in all the papers, for Christ's sake."

Elizabeth said, "Of course."

"Well, he was the old consigliere. He kept the young bulls in line—Carl Bala, Toscanzio, Damon, Lupo, DeLeone, all of them."

"But I thought he was retired."

"He was, in a way. He had everything he wanted, so he wasn't interested in getting more. What he was interested in, I guess, was keeping the world quiet so he could hold on to it."

"But if he was retired, how could he do that? He didn't have any soldiers, did he?"

Palermo chuckled. "Neither does the Pope, honey. Or the head of the United Nations. When he made a decision it stuck. If it needed to be enforced, he'd get word to all the families and they'd do it. The smaller, weaker ones would be afraid the bigger ones would eat them up. The big guys like Toscanzio and Bala and Damon weren't interested in having twenty families come together against them. Besides, they couldn't trust each other. Castiglione they could trust. He didn't want anything but peace and quiet."

"So who wanted him dead?" asked Elizabeth.

Palermo drove on, shaking his head. "Figure it out for yourself, like I did. Who stood to gain anything? The little guys like Bellino or Lupo? Hell, they only existed because Castiglione kept the big fish off them. They're all scared shit-less. It had to be somebody who was big enough to think he

259

could step in and take over, gobble the small operations up."

"Then you think it was Toscanzio or Bala who did it. Or maybe Damon."

"No, I know who did it," he said. "There was supposed to be a meeting this week. Castiglione had called it. The only reason I knew was because it affected me in a way, or would have. I'd dealt with FGE a few times, and Castiglione wanted to talk about FGE."

"Why?"

"He didn't like it. It was practically in his backyard, and it had been used for some things he hadn't agreed to. Things that might bring a lot of weight down on him."

Elizabeth detected the slight shift in his tone. They were nearing some point he wasn't going to talk about: something he was planning to sell. She knew she had to steer him away from it or he'd stop talking entirely. She said, "So they killed him rather than give it up, and killed Ferraro and Orloff and would have killed you." He didn't react, so she took a stab in the dark. She had to get him back on the subject he was most interested in, himself. "Because you killed Senator Claremont and that man in California."

"The hell I did," said Palermo. "For Christ's sake, look at me. I weigh two thirty and I'm five eight. I'm over fifty years old. For the last twenty years I've cleared over two hundred thousand a year. Do I look like somebody who takes on wet jobs? Hell, they hired somebody to do that. A specialist."

"Who hired him?"

Palermo laughed. "I'm not going to tell you that," he said. "At least not now. Maybe later when I see what arrangements your boss made in Carson City."

"But these are the people who are trying to kill you," said Elizabeth. "And if you don't get them, they'll get you." She had stumbled into the spot he was protecting; all she could do now was pursue it until he refused to go on.

"No," said Palermo, "what they did was kill Castiglione

260

and leave me alone in the open when the war started. They didn't warn me, they didn't protect me. Nothing. It was the other families who killed Ferraro and would have killed me."

"Aren't you afraid?" said Elizabeth. "When they know you've come to us, won't they send this specialist after you?"

"They might, if you let them know," said Palermo.

"But we don't know what to do about a professional like that," said Elizabeth. "Look at all the assassinations. We can't protect you from that kind of killer unless we know who he is, or at least what to look for."

Palermo shook his head, solemnly. He said, "Jesus, you must think I'm stupid, pulling that on me. The specialist? Shit, him I'd give you for free if I could. Problem is, I can't. I never saw him, and I don't even know his name. When they talked about him they just called him 'the butcher's boy.' "

"Nice name," said Elizabeth.

"Yeah," said Palermo. "Isn't it?"

28

What he was most worried about was time. Las Vegas was probably the most difficult place in the world to hide in. It was full of people who were in the business of noticing every new face and searching it for the means of extracting a profit: greed, lust, gluttony, stupidity. Plenty of them had seen him before, and whoever noticed him first would feel fortunate—they didn't have to cajole or deceive him or cater to his sexual appetite. All they had to do was mention that he was there. The only things in his favor were the huge number of newcomers that arrived each day—tens of thousands of them—and the fact that he wouldn't be expected.

Even taken together, the two didn't represent much of an edge, he thought. He'd have to find a way to reduce the chance of his being spotted to practically nil. He'd have to stay away from the big hotels. No, any hotel, he decided. There was no way to predict who really owned what, and who was a friend of whom. The airport and the bus station and the restaurants were out too. It would have to be done by a quick visit to town in a single night, and then more forays later if they seemed productive. He had to keep the time he was visible to a minimum.

He wished there were some other way. If only he'd been more careless he'd know more, he thought. That was the irony of it. He'd always avoided personal connections with his clients. He never saw them more than once if he could help it, and never let them know where he lived. His post office box was all they'd known about him, and often he'd known even less about them. His lack of curiosity had been a form of protection. He let the middlemen, the brokers like Orloff, accept the danger of knowing. But now he wished he'd been curious, just this once.

Maureen had been helpful, he thought. Why wouldn't she be? She'd made fifty thousand dollars in less than a week. She couldn't have carried all that hardware on an airplane anyway. But it all helped, everything would help now that was done right. Weapons that couldn't be traced and hadn't turned up in a ballistics report would contribute something to his peace of mind, if nothing else. He knew the car was more important. There was no chance anyone would make a connection between him and a used car bought for cash by a single woman who'd just moved to Illinois to take a job in the local school system. The fact that in the fifteen-minute drive between the dealer's lot and the Illinois Department of Motor Vehicles the name A. Blake on the ownership papers had been changed to Mr. A. Blake would mean nothing to anyone.

He liked driving at night. He was a little disappointed when the sky began to acquire the blue luminescence that meant dawn would break soon. It was as though the sun were in a race with him, and now it was just behind him. In an hour it would catch up, and an hour after that it would be daylight in Las Vegas. He'd still be a day away.

IT WAS GETTING LIGHT now, and Elizabeth could see the pink, craggy mountains jutting abruptly around the flat, empty basin that seemed to contain nothing but the road and billboards. She hadn't noticed when the change had come. She'd gotten used to the advertisements for Las Vegas, and then she'd looked again and they were all for Reno and Lake Tahoe. The pictures were the same—a gigantic girl decorated with a few feathers and rhinestones, her impossibly long legs and ripe breasts taking more space than the suggestion of an opulent building behind her—but the location was different. They had left the gravitational field surrounding Las Vegas,

263

and entered the one that pulled cars into the complex in the north. They had passed some invisible boundary in the darkness.

She knew she should be feeling elated. Whatever value the man beside her turned out to be in court, he was a real asset already. At this moment she knew more than anyone about what was happening, and he hadn't even been interrogated yet. And what was more gratifying was that he'd confirmed most of the theories she and Brayer had developed. There was a war on between the families, and the key to it was Fieldston Growth Enterprises. One of the capos had even killed Castiglione over it. And Palermo knew who it was and might even be able to convince a jury. But almost as important for Elizabeth was that he knew what was going on at FGE. It didn't matter anymore that she'd let the company records slip away. She was bringing in something better, a man who could tell them anything the papers would have revealed, and more. Maybe she'd feel better after she'd eaten and slept.

Right now she felt a headache preparing to strike as soon as the sun rose high enough to pierce through the side window into her eyes. It had been over ten days since she'd begun shuttling around the country, and she'd gotten used to being exhausted. But the strain on her nerves had culminated in the arrival of Palermo in the middle of the night. And there was Palermo himself. She knew that was part of it. He was the break they'd been needing but hadn't dared hope would ever appear. He'd be more thoroughly protected than a visiting head of state, then resettled and watched and pampered for the rest of his life. In a way he was an admission of the hopelessness of it all. The Justice Department was just a better patron this week than whoever he'd been working for last week. And none of it seemed to change anything, really, she thought: if they weren't more afraid of each other than they were of the Justice Department, we wouldn't even have this man. And he's getting a free ride. The deal of a lifetime.

264

She felt the headache beginning to assert itself, and decided to think about something else. She was doing her job, and that was all anyone could do. There was another billboard. This time the girl was naked except for two pasties shaped like stars and a pair of net panty hose with a star on the crotch. It was the star on the crotch that made it ludicrous, she decided. Why couldn't the girl just be naked?

Palermo put on a pair of sunglasses. He was obviously prepared for the trip. There was probably a toothbrush in his coat pocket too. She turned away to watch for the next billboard. The drive was beginning to seem impossibly long. All of the proportions in the west were wrong. You could drive for hours and see nothing but empty, harsh, hot land populated only by smiling giantesses in their feathers and sequins.

"Oh, shit," said Palermo. "Oh, shit," he repeated.

"What's wrong?" said Elizabeth.

"Shit, shit, shit," he said in rising cadence. He had begun to accelerate rapidly, looking anxiously from the road to the rearview mirror and back. "Somebody's following us."

"Are you sure?"

He was still accelerating, his head bobbing frequently to look in the mirror. Elizabeth turned to see the car herself. In the distance behind them was a car, still tiny, but definitely gaining on them.

"They know," he said pitifully. "Who cares how?" She could see he was terrified. He had the gas pedal to the floor now, the car straddling the broken white line in the pavement. Elizabeth looked behind again. The car was still gaining. It looked from the front like a Cadillac or maybe a Lincoln or a big Chrysler. She couldn't tell the difference. But it must be going at least ninety, steadily gulping up the distance that separated them from it. The white line in the road was just a blurred ribbon that snapped and quivered in front of her. She didn't dare look at the speedometer but she knew they must be going about as fast as their car could go. Behind them, the other car was still approaching. She took the gun out of her purse and checked the load.

"Shoot the bastards," said Palermo. "Now, before they get close."

"But we don't know who it is," said Elizabeth.

"Jesus Christ, who do you think it is?" shouted Palermo. "They're going over a hundred. Shoot the bastards!"

The car was close now. Elizabeth could see it was a Cadillac. The dark green hood had an immaculate gleam that threw the sunlight back into the sky. It was drawing up behind now. There were two men in the front seat. She knew that at this speed all she'd have to do was hit the car. A punctured radiator or a blown-out windshield would stop them—maybe kill them. But what if it wasn't what Palermo said? What if it was just two morons opening up a big new car on a deserted highway? She said, "No. Wait a minute."

Palermo just repeated, "Shoot them! Shoot them!" as Elizabeth watched the big car pull up behind. The car honked twice, and then the driver leaned on the horn.

Palermo had subsided into a muttered litany: "Shit, shit, shit. Shit, shit, shit."

Elizabeth watched the two men. If one of them pulled out a gun, or even looked as though he were about to she knew she'd have to shoot. The car pulled abreast. Palermo yelled, "Hold on!" and stepped on the brake. Elizabeth saw the Cadillac flash past as her right shoulder hit the dashboard.

Palermo was gasping, slowing the car as the Cadillac diminished into the distance. Elizabeth managed to regain her balance, but only with difficulty. Palermo pulled to the side of the road and stopped.

The world sounded strangely quiet. Elizabeth watched as Palermo opened the door and walked out around to the back of the car. Her heart was pounding and her lungs didn't seem to be able to take in enough air. Then she heard it. She didn't have to look. Behind the car Palermo was throwing up.

266

When he came back to the car she didn't say anything to him. He sat quietly while she drove. When she saw the little outpost a few miles down the road she still didn't say anything to him, just pulled off the highway and stopped at the gas pump. Palermo climbed out of the car and disappeared into the men's room.

The station attendant was young, probably just out of high school. His long blond hair was still wet from his morning shower, and his blue work shirt was crisp and clean. He yawned as he topped off the tank. The station must have opened at seven, she thought. Probably there wasn't much business out here at seven. You'd have to leave home at five to get here from anywhere.

She paid the boy and looked for Palermo. She almost felt sorry for him. No doubt he was in the men's room, white and shaking, his stomach turning itself inside out. She wasn't feeling too great herself. She parked the car away from the pump and went to the ladies' room. It was too late to prevent the headache, but aspirin might make it bearable until Carson City.

When Elizabeth returned she expected to see Palermo sitting in the car, most likely in the driver's seat. He wasn't. She got into the car to wait, a little angry. The longer he took, the longer it would be before she turned him over to the section chief in Carson City and went somewhere to sleep.

She wasn't particularly surprised when the green Cadillac pulled around the building and onto the highway. It was perfect that they should go that fast, only to stop in that godforsaken coffee shop. They'd probably make up the time by covering the next hundred miles in less than an hour. She watched them accelerate rapidly, diminishing into the distance at a speed she didn't feel able to estimate. Idiots.

Palermo. What was keeping him? This is what men are supposed to be built for, she thought. Big feats of strength and speed in a momentary emergency. Quick action, the massive infusion of adrenaline, and then a long period of repose. Not like women, built to last, the damned extra layer of fat for heat and cold and hunger, the nervous system tougher to stand pain. Babies.

Elizabeth looked at her watch. It was almost seven thirty. She remembered what he'd looked like when he left the car— pale skin, gasping for breath, his heart probably racing—oh God, his heart. That would be just about right. A heart attack in this place, fifty miles from the nearest doctor, probably. And nothing to do about it. Coffee and doughnuts. Air in your tires, sir? Better let me check your oil.

She got out of the car. The sun was warming the still air already. She walked to the gas station, past the boy, who was in the garage staring upward in consternation at the underside of a car on the hydraulic lift. She knocked lightly on the men's room door, listening as much for the approach of another man as for Palermo's answer. She heard nothing, so she tried again, this time louder. There was something absurd about it—no, everything about it was absurd. If she'd been a man she could have gone right in, or even gone with him in the first place. Maybe she should have anyway. At this hour, in this place what difference did it make? But he wasn't really a prisoner. After the third knock she tried the doorknob. It was locked.

At the garage she said to the boy, "I wonder if you could do me a favor? The man with me went into the men's room. I'm afraid he may be sick. Will you go in and check on him?"

The boy looked at her with sullen disapproval, then stared back up at the undercarriage of the car. It must be his, she decided. Then he said, "How long has he been in there?"

She said, "A half hour."

The boy shrugged. "Okay." She followed him to the rest-rooms, and waited while he unlocked the door and sidestepped in, as though it were a tenet of his faith to protect the privacy of all men from the intruding gaze of the insistent woman.

From inside she heard the sound of his voice, "Agh!" In

a second he was back out, gaping at her in horror. He said to her, "We've got to call a doctor," and ran around the building toward the office.

Elizabeth rushed into the men's room. She could see Palermo's feet under the door of the stall, placed as though he were sitting on the toilet. But on the floor around them was a pool of blood. She slowly pushed the door open and looked at him. He was sitting there fully dressed, with his head hanging down on his chest as though he were engaged in some profound meditation. She didn't touch him, and didn't look more closely. She let go of the door and walked outside into the air. Then she remembered the boy. She knew she should go tell him to change the call. Anybody could see from Palermo's shirt what they'd done to his throat. The shirt had once been white. But there wasn't any hurry, really. She couldn't foresee any reason to hurry again. And out here the doctor probably doubled as the coroner anyway. The police would know. 47507Y. A blue license plate. Nevada.

269

29

It was just midnight when the sky above the black horizon began to glow pink, as though somewhere beyond this dark emptiness a city were burning. He was still twenty miles out when beneath the glow the impossible lights surfaced in a shimmering smear of white and blue and yellow and red.

His instincts resisted as the jumping, wavering apparition rose over the lip of the earth and began to resolve itself into the straight lines of bright streets and monolithic buildings bathed in color. He felt a strong urge to stay out here in the dark, empty desert, but he had to penetrate that eye of light. He had to have the name. Without it he could never be safe, because that man wanted him dead. The man wasn't to be distracted or fooled or misled by feints and sudden shifts because he wasn't even paying attention. He had signified the wish, and he was someone the others knew had the power to reward and punish at will, so it would remain a standing priority in a thousand minds until it was accomplished. That meant the name had to belong to one of fifteen or twenty men. That wasn't many, but each of them was like a celebrity or a petty monarch surrounded by retainers and sycophants and guards. There was no way to reach all of them, and each wrong guess would strengthen the one who wanted him dead. He had to have the name.

He avoided the exit ramp that led onto the Strip and its nearest neighbor. He took the third exit and moved up Flamingo Road across the Strip toward the complex of lesser streets beyond the lights. He had few choices. Little Norman knew, but there was no way to make him reveal the name. He had existed far too long by working for everyone and appear-

270

ing to know nothing about anyone. If he caught Little Norman alone the best he could hope for was to kill him. Little Norman was a professional. Orloff had known the name. Orloff was dead, but there was still Orloff's office, the place where they'd killed him. Fieldston Growth Enterprises.

He drove around the neighborhood, carefully covering the streets for three blocks on each side. If there were a competent team of watchers in the vicinity, they would have cars at the most likely points of access to the major highways, out of sight of the building itself. There might even be a building nearby with a dim light in an upper window that faced away from FGE.

When he had satisfied himself that there were no watchers he drove up the street toward FGE. The street was quiet. All of the buildings in the area were closed, their darkened windows reflecting only the lights of his car as he passed. He parked on the street behind, and set off on foot toward FGE. He carried Maureen's pistol with the silencer in his coat pocket. He hoped that a small building like FGE that consisted only of offices would just have a burglar alarm. If the place contained the kind of information he needed, there would be no night watchman—they wouldn't want to seem excessively worried about security.

He approached the building from the rear, prepared to look for the most likely window. But there were lights on inside. Damn, he thought. A watchman. He'd have to find the watchman first. And it would be nothing like he wanted, a quiet visit that nobody knew had ever taken place. Whatever Orloff had that would give him the name would be hidden in a place where only Orloff could find it. Nobody would have missed it. But now there would be a dead watchman.

He started to make a circuit of the building, looking for the window that would give him the best view of the watchman. At the parking lot he stopped. There were two cars there, parked side by side. He approached the cars, and looked inside the first one. It had to belong to the security guard service, he thought. It had a radio under the dashboard, just like the ones the police used. He moved to the other car. Small letters of a decal on the trunk said, "This car carries only bookkeeping material." He thought for a moment. The first car had to be the watchman. What was the other? He moved to the building and looked in the window.

Inside, there were three men in shirtsleeves, working at desks. One seemed to be scanning files and putting folders in a cardboard box and the others were going through the drawers of the desks. All three were wearing guns in shoulder holsters. He moved away from the lighted window and returned to the cars. This time he looked at the license plates. They were both white and said *U.S. Government*. He kept walking.

He kept himself in the shadows as he moved toward his car. He needed time to think. They had to be the FBI. Of course. Whenever there was a pretext, some possibility that one of these killings involved the crossing of state lines, the FBI moved in. But whatever they'd been doing in that office, it wasn't investigating Orloff's shooting. And the decal on the car had said something about bookkeeping. They were going through the files. What did they know?

He felt a sudden wave of panic, a surge of adrenaline. But the fear cleared his mind and subsided. No, it was all right. What Orloff had known about him was a post office box number. There would be a reference to him somewhere, but it would do him no harm. But the rest of it was disturbing. They knew that FGE was a blind. He hadn't counted on that. So now they were as likely to find the name as he was. But they were still looking, working through the night. And they were reading business files. Bookkeeping material, the car had said.

He smiled. There was hope. They were looking for the name, but they didn't know Orloff. They might figure out that

Orloff was moving money, and they might find out where some of it went. Unless they found Orloff's private ledger they wouldn't find out where it came from. Not the name. They were looking at whatever Orloff had prepared to throw off the auditors and the tax men, not what he'd prepared to keep track of the real transactions. Because there had to be a ledger: Orloff wouldn't have taken the chance that he'd make a mistake. They were looking in desk drawers and filing cabinets, not tapping floors and walls for hollow places. They'd walk out with their files and maybe they'd figure it out eventually. But by then he might have the name, and they'd be wasting their time.

He was concentrating now. FBI men in Orloff's office. They didn't know what they were looking for. Maybe they didn't even know yet what Orloff was. If they didn't, would they have searched his house? He'd never been to Orloff's house although he assumed there must be one. It had never occurred to him to wonder where Orloff lived until he'd hired the Cruiser to watch him. He had little interest in the brokers and middlemen. He knew and accepted the fact that he wasn't the sort of man they'd want to spend time with, even if it hadn't been dangerous. And if Orloff had invited him there he would have been insulted. He did the work and took the money, but he would have resented any presumption that he cared who gave it to him, or took any interest in the problems and personalities that provided him with a market for his services. Orloff had been a pig. He had noted it, as he noted whatever came within the range of his consciousness, because it might present a problem or a solution, but it evoked no emotional response. But now Orloff was important to him because Orloff had known the name.

He contemplated Orloff as he searched for the address in the telephone book. Orloff had been greedy. So the house would be large and opulent. He memorized the address and

273

returned to the car. But Orloff had been nervous and frightened most of the time, his greed conflicting with his natural cowardice to keep his fat body sweating beneath the custommade silk shirts in fits of excitement and terror. So the house would be difficult to break into, no doubt protected electronically from whatever phantoms Orloff's brain conjured up when it contemplated the possibilities of the night outside the windows. That part presented no problem, because Orloff was dead, and unless he had a family still living there, there would be no one to turn on the equipment.

When he neared Orloff's house, he followed the same procedure he'd used at FGE. He circled the block searching for signs that the house might be under surveillance. He saw nothing that was questionable, so he drove past the house. There were no cars at all in the driveway. Orloff's car had probably been impounded by the police in the investigation, he thought. Maybe because it caught some of the slugs from the shotgun, although there must have been more than enough in Orloff's body for any practical purpose.

He saw no lights in the windows. It was the sort of house he'd imagined. The low, T-shaped structure gave an impression of careless, sprawling expanse, the two wings sheltering gardens of close-cropped yew and juniper, and yucca. Another eye would not have noticed that anyone approaching either of the two doors in the wings could be observed from behind through opposite windows in what must be the same room.

He parked the car around the corner and walked to the house. The windows were all tightly latched and bolted, so he contented himself for the moment with examining them to see if he could discern the contact wires or the glow of an electric eye that would show him how to disengage the burglar alarms. He peered through each of the windows, seeing only the dark shapes of the furniture. It took some searching, but at the rear of the house behind a fan-shaped shrub he found the electric meter. He read the meter and sat down and waited patiently for fifteen minutes, then read it again. It was as he'd hoped. The police had either notified the electric company to turn off the power or simply gone through the house in their methodical, unthinking way and turned everything off. In any case, nothing was drawing electricity. Whatever alarm systems Orloff had installed were so much dead metal.

He thought about the house. Probably one of the doors would be easiest, and it would be less likely to show signs of his entry than the windows. He took another look at the electric meter and froze. The meter wheel was moving. Something had been turned on. His mind raced—at two thirty in the morning what could it be? The alarm system would take steady continuous power. A light? No. At this hour the person would have to have been sleeping in the house and awakened. He'd been here over twenty minutes and they'd have to have sat in the dark at least that long. Then he remembered. Of course, the refrigerator. It was the only thing that turned itself on and off. He was safe.

He went to the side door and used a credit card to depress the door latch and let himself in. The door had deadbolts and chains, he noticed, but you had to be inside the house to use them. Orloff would have hated that, he thought, but the alarms would have consoled him. Now that he was inside he could see the two black boxes of the electric eyes, their sensors turned off.

He listened for the refrigerator. He tried to remember where the kitchen window was. He had a mental image of the house plan, and followed it to the kitchen. The refrigerator was unusually quiet—he couldn't hear it at all. He felt for the handle, turning his head away in preparation for the glare of the light. He didn't want to destroy his night vision. There was no light, and in the darkness he smelled the unmistakable odor of rotten food. He closed the door silently and thought. Someone was in this house.

275

He crouched low and remained motionless. Superiority in the darkness was largely a matter of concentration and patience. "Get yourself a cat, like this one, and watch it," Eddie had said. "A cat will sit for an hour staring at whatever it's after and listening to it. As soon as the thing forgets what a cat is, the cat is on him, so fast you can hardly believe it. Forget all that jungle warfare shit they taught you in the service. You already know how to look like a fucking palm tree. A cat'll teach you how to look like a shadow, part of the house, a pile of garbage."

He waited until his watch told him it had been five minutes. If he'd been heard by whoever was in the house, they'd either discounted the sound or forgotten it. It was a matter of shaping time to dimensions that didn't fit the normal sense of pace. If they heard a sound they'd listen for a few seconds to hear another. If they didn't, they'd stop listening.

He moved out into the living room, keeping low and close to the wall. When he reached the first chair he settled down again to wait, crouching beside it in the darkness, listening. Whoever was in the house had been confident enough to turn on a light. That meant he had the only advantage he would need. Now that his night vision was at its best he could see that the living room was large—fifty by twenty-five feet, he estimated. It wasn't a room that Orloff would spend much time in. It was designed for receiving guests in a fashion that would appeal to Orloff's vanity—small tables and lots of chairs, but mostly arranged around the walls, without a focal point. And the shapes of the furniture weren't the sort of thing Orloff would feel comfortable in—too little padding. The furniture would be different in the room he was searching for: thick and leathery, and with seats that wouldn't cramp Orloff's fat ass. But there would be time for that after he'd found the man in the house. He had as much time as he needed.

He decided to move again. Past the living room was a

hallway leading to what must be bedrooms and bathrooms. That was where he'd find the room he wanted. Patiently he began to move himself by inches toward his goal, keeping himself low and close to the wall. His mind was cleared now of all thought except thoughts of sight and sound.

Years ago he'd done all of his thinking about what his body was now doing. Eddie had been wrong about cats—he'd learned that from Eddie's cat in the butcher shop. It wasn't that they shaped their bodies to imitate something else. All they did was make sure they didn't look like a cat. It was the eye of the prey that formulated the disguise. The instant that it would take the man he was stalking to decide that the shape in the hallway wasn't a chair, wasn't a shadow, was maybe a man, would be all the time he needed. That instant was the predator's moment, the cat's time.

At the first turning of the hallway he heard the man moving about in the darkness. He turned his head slowly from side to side to locate the exact point the sound was coming from. It was off to the left. It was then that the thin sheet of light shot out from under the closed door.

He stationed himself beside the door and listened. There was a sound of rustling papers, then a drawer opening, then a clicking noise. He listened, straining to sense the direction of movement, while someone walked from one end of the room to the other. There was another rustling, and then his ears detected the sound he was waiting for. The footsteps began to move away from the door. He snatched the door open and stepped into the room, his gun pointed at the sound.

A man whirled to face him, his expression the terrible mixture of animal and human that the instant of terror brought on him. A gurgling sound escaped from the taut muscles of his throat, and he dropped a briefcase on the floor. The instant passed, and the man said, "What?" Then the man said, as though correcting himself, "What are you?" His face be-

277

trayed the fact that he sensed that the question wasn't right. He tried "What do you want?"

He studied the man. He was about fifty years old, wearing a charcoal gray suit. Not a burglar. Police? He said, "Throw me your wallet and turn around."

The man seemed to be relieved. He reached into his coat and pulled out a long, thin black wallet, and tossed it toward him, then turned his face to the window.

He didn't bother to catch it. That would only give the man a chance to do something he'd seen on television. He had only asked for it to see if the man had a shoulder holster on or handcuffs, and there were none. He kicked open the wallet. There was no badge.

Keeping his eyes on the man, he said, "What's your name?"

The man said, "Please, take the wallet. There's over a thousand dollars in it."

He repeated, "What's your name?"

The man said, "Edgar Fieldston."

Fieldston. Of course. There would be a Fieldston. An Edgar or a Ronald or a Howard or a Marshall. He knelt down and opened the wallet. It was true. Edgar R. Fieldston. A driver's license, credit cards, a Blue Cross–Blue Shield membership.

He said, "Fieldston Growth Enterprises."

The man said, "Yes."

"What are you doing in Orloff's house?"

Fieldston's voice changed. He assumed an air of authority. He said, "Mr. Orloff worked for me. I needed some papers, and I have every right to be here. Now take the wallet and leave me alone."

He sensed the wrong note in the voice. It wasn't the bravado of a man trying to scare the sort of perennial loser that held people up for their wallets. And he hadn't said take the money and leave the wallet. He'd said take the wallet. And

278

to a man like this, the inconvenience of losing the license, credit cards, and identification could be more important than the thousand or so dollars. He said, "No thanks, I've got a wallet."

Fieldston's hands were in the air. Whatever resource he had been using to keep them from shaking now left him. When he spoke, it was with a slight tremor. "What do you want?"

He said, "You."

Fieldston turned toward him, as though unable to control himself. "No, wait a minute. You've got it wrong. I wasn't leaving the country. I'm here now, aren't I?"

He had to keep him frightened. He said, "Bullshit."

Fieldston pointed at the briefcase on the floor and said, "Look for yourself. I was going to give it to him. Four million dollars. Hell, that's fifty percent a year on his investment."

He had to get him to say the name. He just smiled and shook his head.

Fieldston was frantic now. His voice was shrill and strident. "Yes!" he said. "It's true. Here it is, and now we're even. I'll disappear where the police will never find me."

He said, "What were you doing in here?"

Fieldston said, "I knew Orloff. He would have kept something here to use against us if there was an investigation. I knew him. Before I left I wanted to find it."

He smiled again. Of course. He said, "No. You wanted it for yourself. To use against us. To save your ass."

Fieldston shook his head. "No. Honestly. I know better than that." He reached into his pocket and pulled out a checkbook. "See?" he said. "Here it is. It's a ledger of the transactions over the past five years. It's in his checkbook. I found it. We'll destroy it right now and you can tell them everything is okay."

He said, "You should have told them yourself."

Fieldston said, "But I was told never to use the telephone to talk to Mr. Balacontano."

279

The name. He wasn't surprised, just glad it was over. He decided to make it simple. He aimed carefully and placed the single shot in the center of Fieldston's forehead. The pistol spat once, Fieldston's head jerked slightly, and the body crumpled to the floor. He looked at his watch. Not even three o'clock, he thought. Plenty of time.

30 When Elizabeth awoke there was a moment before she remembered. It was like the moment the mind realizes that the foot onto which the body's weight is about to shift should already have touched solid ground, but didn't. Then there was the rapid succession of feelings—remembering, alarm, and the mind's recognition of an emergency that is somehow already determined and familiar—not less unpleasant for the recognition, but a mishap of a particular kind and consequence, and therefore accepted with frustration instead of terror. Palermo was dead.

She sat up in bed and looked at the alarm clock. It was almost three o'clock in the morning. She had slept for over eight hours already. The sheriff had driven her to Carson City, and she'd taken a plane back to Las Vegas after waiting until two o'clock for the first flight. It was nearly four by the time she'd made it to the FBI office.

Why hadn't Brayer called her? He hadn't been at the office or at the hotel. If he'd taken a plane to Washington he should have arrived hours ago. And Connors or Padgett would be there to give him the message: Elizabeth had done it again. Palermo was dead. Go back and try to pick up the pieces of the investigation. It had to be her telephone.

She turned on the light. There was no point in trying to go back to sleep. She had used up the eight hours of unconsciousness she'd purchased with the exhaustion, the disorientation, and the shame of the morning. Now she had to face whatever was left of the night. It was six A.M. in Washington.

Elizabeth dressed. If she was doomed to spend the next few hours thinking about it, then thank God it was Las Vegas.

Downstairs there would be something to eat, and crowds of people still gambling and drinking and living some life that didn't have to include an awareness of what sharpened metal did to flesh and arteries.

She took the elevator to the ground floor and walked through the casino. There were only a few tables open now, and people were playing blackjack and craps with a slow and leisurely alcoholic intensity in pools of light that swirled with blue-gray wisps of cigarette smoke. Elizabeth couldn't decide whether these were the serious gamblers who stayed on like permanent features of the landscape while the ephemeral hordes of tourists came and went around them, or just a straggle of losers who stayed on because there was nothing better to do than play away their last few chips, no place that offered more. It didn't matter. They were all here together at three o'clock in the morning—Elizabeth too.

She walked past the restaurants. They had closed hours ago. Nobody who was up at this hour wanted beef Wellington or sole bonne femme. The coffee shop was still ablaze with lights, but far off in the corner behind a stockade of upturned chairs a black man was following a vacuum cleaner in its jerky foragings beneath the tables. She picked a table away from the vacuum cleaner. She was only two tables away from a pair of beefy middle-aged men in gray suits, but at this hour it seemed best. It was inhabited ground, at least, and it made her feel less alone.

The waitress, she decided, had been pretty once. Maybe she was pretty still, but she looked tired and worn. The hairnet didn't help much either. She looked like a man wearing a beret. The waitress walked by on her way to the kitchen and slapped a menu on Elizabeth's table. In a few minutes she was back, standing over Elizabeth's table with her pad in her hand.

Elizabeth said, "I haven't decided yet. What's in a Donna Summer sandwich?"

"Pastrami. Chopped liver. Cole slaw."

It sounded about right, Elizabeth thought. She hadn't eaten in—how long? A whole day, at least. "I'll take that. And coffee."

The waitress nodded as she wrote. Her face retained its stony efficiency. In a very low voice she said, "By the way, do yourself a favor."

Elizabeth looked up, and saw that the waitress's eyes were sliding in the direction of the two men at the next table. Elizabeth said, "Favor?" in the same low voice.

The waitress said, "Don't try to sell it in here, honey." She tipped her head so slightly in the direction of the two men that even Elizabeth wasn't sure at first that it meant anything. Then she said, "Vice squad."

Elizabeth's mind sprinted to catch up. Of course. The only women she'd seen in the casino had been a group of four motherly ladies in pantsuits at a blackjack table together, all giggling and silly like the teenagers they'd probably been the last time they'd been out late in a pack like this. She said to the waitress, "Thanks," and the waitress disappeared.

Elizabeth looked at her watch. Almost three thirty. On some other night it might have struck her differently. But now it felt as though she'd been slapped. Was it her clothes? She wanted to tell someone something that would prove they were all wrong. Had they all been thinking that? But the words that rose to the surface of her mind were, "No, you're wrong. I got good grades, and worked hard!"

It was so peculiar it distracted her from the embarrassment. What had she stumbled on? Grades. Hard work and doing what they told you to do. Good girl. Ever so good. College. Scholarships. Business school. A government job. No mistakes, no flagging of attention, no momentary lapses, and you stayed at the top, the surface. Because just below the top it was dark and there was no way to see what lurked there. Something terrible. Everything terrible. And each step of the way was cumulative, like climbing up a ladder to avoid a

283

flood. It got you farther and farther away from whatever was down there. Humiliation.

The waitress returned with the sandwich and Elizabeth started to eat. It was so thick it strained her jaw to get her mouth around it, but she decided she didn't care. And she didn't care about the calories either. Bad girl. She smiled. So what? Today I'm a failure. A fat failure. Who looks like a prostitute.

She began to feel better almost immediately. In another hour or two Brayer would turn up, and it would be a new day. And Palermo had told her quite a bit, after all. When she finished eating she'd go upstairs and write it all down, so it was ready when Brayer returned. And there was still Edgar Fieldston. He couldn't stay out of sight forever.

She was aware of a voice beside her. She turned to see that it was one of the men at the next table, leaning his pink face toward her and smiling, the angle of his head making his tight collar cut into his shaven jowl. He said, "Would you like to join us for dessert?"

Elizabeth kept chewing and shook her head.

The man's smile only widened, his tiny white teeth like a string of pearls. "Oh, come on. I'll buy."

Elizabeth swallowed, then said, "Shut up and go away. I'm thinking."

HE KNELT OVER FIELDSTON'S body and placed the towels underneath the head. It wasn't bleeding much, considering. In a little while it would stop, when the body cooled. Meanwhile, there was plenty to do.

The briefcase was exactly as Fieldston had said. He'd never seen so much money, he thought. Hardly anybody had. What had he said? Four million. Must be all thousand dollar bills. So maybe he hadn't been running. He could hardly have expected to spend those bills without being noticed, and without Balacontano's organization to launder them. So what the hell was he doing? All right, take him at his word. He was planning to pay Balacontano and then disappear, with Orloff's checkbook as the threat that would convince Bala to leave him alone. Which meant the bookkeeping at FGE was perfect unless there was a key. But that was practically impossible. How could it be that good? The fool. Balacontano would have helped him disappear all right.

He made a quick search of the house. Fieldston apparently hadn't touched anything in the other rooms. He must have known Orloff well. Certainly Fieldston wasn't smart enough to have found the room without knowing, not if he'd been stupid enough to think he could blackmail Carl Bala.

He went back to the body and searched the pockets. There were no keys. He thought about it. Fieldston must have taken a cab from somewhere or walked. Probably the airport. And he hadn't planned to go home, ever again, because he no longer even had a key to his own house. And he hadn't checked into a hotel, he had no hotel key. Fieldston had been frightened enough to make sure nobody at all knew he was in Las Vegas.

There was a lot of work to do, so he had to move quickly. No mistakes, nothing he'd forgotten about that he had to come back later to correct. It all had to happen between now and dawn. He looked at his watch. Three thirty. Two good, safe hours and then another one before the people who worked the day shift started to get up. He went outside and drove his car into Orloff's driveway with the lights off.

He went back into the house and looked around for something to help. Orloff's desk chair was about right and it had wheels. He got down on his knees, put his hands under Fieldston's shoulders, and hoisted him into the chair. Then he went to the bathroom and took two more large bath towels from the linen cupboard. Whatever else they'd done, he was sure they wouldn't have counted towels. He wrapped one of

285

the towels around the upper part of the body and threw the other in Fieldston's lap. Then he pulled the office chair through the house to the door. He took the right arm and the body slumped forward onto his shoulders. He staggered with it to the car and shrugged it into the trunk. He arranged the towels as well as he could to keep the blood from escaping.

Then he returned to the house. He moved the desk chair back to Orloff's office, shuffling his feet on the carpet to remove the imprint of the wheels. He took a final look to see that everything appeared undisturbed, then put the wallet in the briefcase and went out. At the car he remembered. How had Fieldston gotten in? Fieldston hadn't had a key. He returned to the house and looked at each of the windows. It was the window to the guest bedroom, but Fieldston had been careful. There were no scuff marks on the sill, and the lock wasn't damaged, just scratched minutely. He took a last look around before he left the house. He pressed down on the trunk of his car just enough so the latch caught and drove off down the street. He took a labyrinthine route to reach the freeway without going down the Strip. As he felt the car accelerate onto the freeway, he had an impulse to laugh. By the time the sun came up he'd be in Kingman, Arizona, and maybe Flagstaff by the time the stores opened up. No telling how far a man might go after he'd been shot in the head.

THE BOOKS HE SELECTED were paperbacks. In the supermarket he bought three, all of which said bestseller on their covers. In the bookstore he picked classics—books he remembered being forced to read in school. In the drugstore he found two that claimed to be something called novelizations of movies. When he had enough, he sat in the parking lot to do the packing: one bill per page. It struck him as funny that the first of the paperbacks was worth over two hundred thousand dollars. It took more than an hour, but he couldn't afford to rush it. He was good at making packages, at tying and taping and arranging, and this was one package he wanted to make perfect.

By the time the post office opened he was there to watch the man unlock the doors. He sent the package fourth class, special book rate. It was a strange sensation to see the postman at the counter toss the package into the bin with a dozen others, all practically indistinguishable from one another. At that moment he knew there was no reason to think about it anymore. It was gone from his possession forever, and there was no way he could ever get it back. It was more money than he ever hoped to have, more than some towns were worth, probably. And now it was gone. He didn't linger at the counter to think about it. It had all been decided hours ago, while he drove through the cold air of the dark desert. It was the only way.

The sun was rising in the sky and he had to make every hour into miles. If he waited too long the bags of ice he'd bought would start to melt, and the seals on at least some of the bags would be defective. He couldn't afford to have water dripping from the trunk as he drove. If he kept at it he might make five hundred miles before he needed to change the ice, because the air rushing by would cool the surface of the car just as it cooled the engine. It was going to be a long time before he slept again, he thought. But there'd be plenty of time to sleep later on—twenty hours a day for the rest of his life, if he felt like it. All he had to do now was deliver Edgar. He said aloud, "Keep cool, Edgar. It won't be long now."

It was shortly after noon when he began to hear the sloshing sounds. Whenever he slowed down or accelerated there was a faint noise of water moving about in the trunk. By one o'clock he began to see drips of water hitting the pavement in his rearview mirror whenever the car gained speed too abruptly. When he stopped in Flagstaff to fill the gas tank he put his hand on the trunk and knew that his theory of air cooling had been wrong. The surface of the trunk was as hot as the metal fixtures on the gas pump. As he drove off he said, "Edgar, we've got problems. You're getting parboiled in there. Afraid we've got to make another arrangement."

It was in the Sears store that he bought the hacksaw and the shovel and the ice chest. He had to search another fifteen minutes before he found the ranchers' supply store. When he found it he shopped carefully for the lime, reading the labels on the big fifty-pound bags: calcium oxide—95 percent; magnesia—2 percent; total silica, alumina, iron—2 percent. Water content no more than 1 percent guaranteed.

He moved the bags to the car in a cart, and was back on the road again. The bags of Blue Ice he bought at a liquor store in Winslow, because it was the first place he passed through that looked as though they might sell it already frozen.

It was mid-afternoon now and so hot that the endless, straight highway danced and quivered. Off in the distance dust devils swirled crazily and dissolved, the only signs of movement. He took Route 77 through Snowflake and Show Low, and then swung east again through Springerville and into New Mexico on Route 60. It was already night before he found the place he was looking for between Quemado and Magdalena, about fifty miles past the Continental Divide. It was a back road not shown on the map, but he could see it went somewhere. It had been over an hour since he'd seen another car, and the local ranchers would be shutting themselves in for the night. He turned off on a dirt road that wound through rocky hillocks and barrows, and kept going until he found a spot that suited him. He parked the car on the side of the road and got out.

Looking around and studying the place, he saw nothing but the gigantic, bright expanse of the sky, the stars incredibly clear and close above his head. He took the shovel and set off up the side of the hill. It was pretty country, he decided, even at night—bigger and emptier and cleaner than the land the main routes passed through. And if he worked steadily he could probably still make Amarillo by the time the sun came up.

31 The first half of the day Elizabeth had spent dreading the return of John Brayer. It was the fact that he must have been in Washington when he found out about Palermo that bothered her. In the first place, he would probably already have set up the appointment with the Attorney General's office before he found out. That meant he'd have to explain to them why he no longer needed to see them. But more than that she hated the idea that he would be there when the anger and disgust settled on him. He'd be right there in the office where they handled personnel cases, where Elizabeth's file was kept.

Sometime during the afternoon her feelings began to change. The FBI agents were coldly polite, but she could feel the weight of their resentment and contempt. And they were right. If only Brayer had let her take Palermo here, he'd still be alive. He might not be happy at first, but it really would have made no difference in the long run. The trip to Carson City had served no legitimate purpose. Something could have been arranged to keep Palermo under wraps here in Las Vegas. But now Brayer was comfortably out of sight in Washington or somewhere, and Elizabeth was still here in the Bureau office, taking the force of their resentment alone. And of course they all knew about it. Her report had included the rationale for making a dash to Carson City. The ones who hadn't read it had been told. She could see it in their faces. At four o'clock Elizabeth decided she had been a fool. If Brayer filed a request for dismissal, or even so much as a negative performance evaluation, she'd demand a hearing and fight it.

He'd been the one who ordered her to handle Palermo that way, after all—a lone woman with an analyst's rating transporting a self-confessed criminal through an unpopulated area in the dark. She could have been killed too. If he filed any kind of reprimand, she thought, she'd make him regret it. By the time the hearing was over she'd have a special commendation.

At dinner Elizabeth began to wonder if she hadn't been too defensive. Nothing had come through from Washington all day that referred to Palermo's murder. Maybe Brayer was taking the blame himself, leaving her out of it for the moment. She'd seen him do that before, file a report in which somebody was just named as "the agent in place" or "the field agent." That would explain why he'd been out of touch.

When she went to bed she was already feeling worried about him. He was in Washington taking the blame for the disaster, and the fact that he hadn't returned meant Washington wasn't taking it well. And Brayer couldn't be more than five years from retirement.

The next morning Elizabeth was certain of it. Brayer was taking the blame, and it was going hard. The best thing for her to do was to make as much progress as possible while he was in Washington. If she could only come up with something big enough, Washington would forget about Palermo and they'd both be all right. What she needed was another Palermo, somebody who knew the name of the silent partner in FGE and could prove the silent partner was killing people to protect himself. What she needed was Edgar Fieldston.

At the Bureau office Elizabeth pored over the field reports. Palermo had hinted that it was somebody big, and the biggest were Toscanzio and Balacontano.

"10:08 P.M., Wednesday, February 21. Saratoga Springs, New York: Subject Carlo Balacontano AKA Carl Bala. Subject has been secluded in his country residence since Monday,

February 19. On Tuesday, February 20, he was joined by his wife, Therese Balacontano, his son Richard, and his daughter-in-law, Victoria, and their four children. Subject has received visits from a number of his associates. Key to: Lamborese, Antonio; Giambini, Robert; Montano, John; Guariano, August; DeFabiani, Daniel.

"9:15 A.M., Thursday, February 22, Evanston, Illinois: Subject Vincent Toscanzio. Subject has been in his home for four days. Subject's family, including subject's mother, Mrs. Maria Toscanzio, have arrived during that time and have remained on the premises. Members of subject's family were observed in the backyard making a snowman on Tuesday, February 20, but have remained indoors since then, possibly due to inclement weather. Frequent visitors, all employees of Diet Clubs of America, in which subject owns a controlling interest, except for the arrival on Wednesday of Antonio Damonata AKA Tony Damon, and two unidentified companions."

There was no question about what was going on, but that didn't help. They were circling the wagons around the women and children and giving orders to their lieutenants. But that didn't solve Elizabeth's problem. The one she wanted was the one who'd started it, the one who had killed Veasy and the Senator and Orloff and Castiglione. Because she wasn't foolish enough to believe she'd get the other one. If he fell it would be a freak accident. But the one Elizabeth wanted was vulnerable. He'd been using FGE for something. Whatever it was had to be bad enough to take risks to keep it a secret, to kill off everyone who came near it. And whoever it was had missed the key man. As long as Edgar Fieldston was alive Elizabeth had hope.

The secretary didn't bother to knock when she came into the office with the reports. Why should she? thought Elizabeth. It's their office. I'm the interloper, the outsider they have to treat with grudging tolerance. The one they have to cooperate

292

with who didn't cooperate with them when she had something to share.

It was the initial report on FGE's remaining papers. She scanned the inventory of records until she came to the summary. The papers weren't complete enough to prove anything yet. It would be like a problem in archaeology to figure out where the money came from and which accounts were padded. She supposed the FBI's accountants knew what to look for. Then she noticed the statement: *Recommended for intensive audit: Travel.* She leafed through the summary until she found the travel expenses. It was easy to see what had caught their attention. Calendar-year travel expenses were listed as $56,382.

She searched through the report for the breakdown. Most of it meant nothing to her. Orloff had gone to New York, Los Angeles, and Chicago. Fieldston had spent a week in Buenos Aires, then gone on for another week to Rio de Janeiro. Did they have investments in those places, she wondered? But they'd check it, of course. For one thing, they were looking for Fieldston, and it would help to know where he had contacts.

She moved down the list. The other travelers were unfamiliar to her. Probably they were salesmen or something. The FBI would be working on that too. She moved down to the final entry and stopped. *Edgar Fieldston, round-trip ticket to Nassau, Bahamas, February 16.* She gasped. Round trip. Why hadn't anybody noticed? But then she remembered. Of course he'd buy a round-trip ticket. If you had a return ticket the customs people didn't worry about you. They knew you wouldn't be stuck there when you'd spent your money. Damn! she thought. I'm seeing what I'm looking for, not what I'm looking at. Where the hell is Brayer?

THE PARTHENON MOTEL IN CLEVELAND had four Corinthian columns across the concrete slab in front of the office. They didn't support anything, but they looked as though they might have supported the motel's sign before it had been redone in neon and the wiring had gotten too complicated. It was after ten but he had no trouble renting one of the rooms with a kitchenette. People didn't travel through Cleveland much in February, and those who did had no use for a stove and refrigerator, certainly not those for rent at the Parthenon.

He had been driving almost continuously for over forty-eight hours, and now he knew he had to sleep. He parked the car outside his room and carried his suitcase inside. Then he went back to the car for his cooler. He brought it into the kitchenette and opened it. The Blue Ice he'd bought in St. Louis was still surprisingly cold, but he took it out and put it in the freezer to prepare for tomorrow. Then he said aloud, "You too, Edgar. Got to keep fresh." When he had finished loading the freezer he rinsed out the inside of the cooler, checked the locks on the door a second time, and lay down on the bed. He fell immediately into a nervous, troubled sleep. Late in the night he found himself partially awake, reaching for the pistol in his coat pocket. He took off the coat and laid it beside him on the bed. After that he slept soundly, dreamlessly, until the maid's morning knock startled him at eleven.

WHEN HE PASSED BUFFALO in the middle of the afternoon he thought of Maureen. He supposed she must be somewhere nearby, taking a rest and counting her money while she waited for the old man to offer her the next job. She'd been expensive, probably not worth that kind of money, but he didn't regret what he'd paid her. She'd caught him at a time when he was in the mood to be extravagant, so she was entitled to it. That was part of the business.

He knew exactly where he was going. He'd seen the place once, when he and Eddie had been trying to fill the contract

294

on Danny Lazaro. He'd owned a two-year-old filly named The Commodore's Pride, and Eddie had figured he'd come to Saratoga to watch her run. Eddie had been wrong, and they'd ended up watching the races and then driving around the area looking at the farms. It was a country composed of low, rolling green hills and small stands of ancient oaks and maples cordoned by the same white rail fences that lined the road.

"It's so the horses won't kill the trees," Eddie had said. "The fuckers are worse than beavers." He'd made a note to ask somebody about that who knew something about horses, but he'd forgotten about it until now. Eddie had probably made it up. Eddie had lived in big cities all his life. If he knew anything about horses it was probably from carving them up to look like prime rib.

They drove past a large farm with a low stone fence, partitioned into paddocks and pastures where tall chestnut-colored horses strolled in elegant leisure, and Eddie had said, "Know who owns that place?" He'd shrugged, and Eddie had said triumphantly, "Carlo fucking Balacontano, Esquire. That's who."

That night somebody else had collected on Danny Lazaro. They'd found him in New York in a little French restaurant on the West Side, and when Eddie read it in the papers he'd said, "No big thing. He missed a good race." Rochester and Syracuse and Utica floated by as green signs on the New York State Thruway. It was almost ten o'clock by the time he swung north on Route 87 at Albany.

At eleven he saw the sign that said Saratoga Springs 15. He thought, I'll make the call by one o'clock, from Plattsburgh. I could be in Montreal by three, or New York City by four or five. It won't matter where I am, because in another day there won't be anybody looking for me. By tomorrow night they'll all know it's no longer worth the risk. Because they'll all believe the man they hoped to please is beyond doing anything for them. Whatever he offered them will be just words. And they'll be thinking about something else. Some of them will lie low and wait to see who comes to the top in the five families and inherits New York, and some won't be able to wait for that: they'll run to Toscanzio or Tony Damon to anticipate the stampede.

He turned off at Saratoga Springs and drove to the farm. Even in the dark he recognized the white rail fences and the distant buildings. At the first boundary there was a small sign that said Montpelier Farms. And then in smaller letters, Arabians and Standardbreds. He wished he'd looked at the place in the daylight. Did horses get locked up at night? Did they even run loose in February? He drove along the fence studying what he could see of the acres beyond. There were three pastures, all empty snowdrifts and patches of frozen grass, and a smaller area near the stable that was trampled into mud. He decided that must be where they rode horses or trained them. Beyond that was a track, just like a racetrack only without a grandstand. On a knoll above the track stood the house. That was what power meant, he thought—so much empty land around Bala's house that he had to build a road to get to it, probably had to drive to see his own horses eating his own grass. He probably didn't come here more than a few times a year. And probably not at all in February. It was too cold out there for horses, he thought, too cold even to watch them.

It was going to be more difficult than he'd thought. There were at least two or three hundred yards of empty land between the highway and the house, and most of it was covered with snow. He couldn't drive it and he couldn't afford to leave footprints. And it was cold out there: the ground would be frozen solid. But there had to be a way. He'd come too far to give up.

He drove past the farm and thought about the problem.

296

There was only one way to do it, and he knew . accept that. But it wasn't going to be pleasant. He tur.. car around and drove back into Saratoga Springs. It took . a half hour to find a store that was open. It was a supermarke that seemed at this hour to deal mainly in beer, but he found what he needed—a pair of gloves, a knitted watch cap, a package of heavy plastic trash bags, and a roll of thick adhesive tape.

He parked the car a mile down the road from the farm in a closed gas station and made his preparations. He sawed the handle of the shovel off to the length of a foot and a half, then went around to the trunk. He shook out four of his plastic trash bags and placed them one inside of the other for extra strength, then opened the cooler. "Come on, Edgar," he said, "last stop." The walk was cold, but he knew it had to be done this way. Whoever Bala had to take care of his horses would be alarmed by a strange car parked close to the farm, and a car would be of no use to him now anyway.

When he reached the farm he walked along the white fence until he came to a point where another rail fence intersected it, dividing the two pastures. He was glad he'd bought the hat and gloves. He had to take off the gloves to fish out the adhesive tape. He put the shovel and gun inside one plastic bag, and taped the two bags together to form a sling, which he threw over his shoulder.

He climbed up on the fence, his feet on the bottom rail and his hands clinging to the top rail. He began to sidestep along the fence between the two pastures, moving in the direction of the farm buildings. He inched along, slowly at first, but before long he found he could make good progress by keeping as much weight as possible on his feet. The pastures were empty, but now he could see horse tracks in the snow. They must let them out sometimes during the day, he thought. He wondered how the horses felt about it.

297

It took him over ten minutes to reach the place where the fence intersected with the section that ran along Balacontano's private road. He stopped to rest and read his watch in the moonlight. It was already after midnight, and there was no telling how long this was going to take. If only it weren't so cold. As he approached the house, he realized something was wrong. From the pasture side it looked as though every light were on. Cautiously, he sidestepped closer along the rail. Balacontano's caretaker wouldn't have all those lights on, and grooms and stableboys wouldn't be inside the main house. In spite of the cold he began to sweat. He leaned over the fence and stared at the snow on the driveway. It was crossed with what looked like a dozen treadmark patterns. There were the thick jagged impressions of truck tires, at least two different patterns of studded snow tires, and a few ruts made by the smoother treads of road tires. Shit, he thought, he's here right now, and he's got some of his people with him. Of course he'd be here. Nobody can get within three hundred yards of the house without being seen. He looked at the house again and thought, there might be twenty or thirty of them sitting around in there to protect him. In New York City he'd have to make do with two or three.

He bent his knees and hung down behind the fence to keep from showing a silhouette. The area around the house was impossible. It had to be another way. He inched along the fence, with his body away from the house. It would have to be the stables. It was another ten minutes before he made it to the fence beside the long, low stable building. He studied the ground inside the exercise yard. There were only a few patches of snow, and the rest looked like mud. He cautiously tested the earth with one foot and smiled. It was mud all right but it was frozen solid into an uneven mold of hoofprints and footprints, ruts where wheelbarrows had passed, and tire tracks from what must have been a tractor. He set both feet on the ground and stood erect.

He walked along the fence across the yard to the stable. He could smell the strong acidic scent of the animals; he could feel their presence. He walked around the building and the scent grew stronger, almost overpowering in the cold, still, night air. He heard a horse's hoof clop on a wooden surface somewhere inside, and then a low neigh. They can smell me too, he thought. It's because I don't smell like horseshit.

He stood still for a moment to let the animals quiet down. As he waited he looked around. A few feet away was a mound of earth about ten feet high. No, he realized suddenly. That's not dirt. It's horseshit. That's why the smell is so strong on this side of the stable. It's a compost heap.

He moved away from the building to the other side of the mound. As he came near he sensed a very slight steam coming from the mound. He took off his glove and held his hand six inches above the mound. It was actually warm. Keeping low, he took out the shovel and began to dig. The manure wasn't frozen, nor was the ground under it. He dug down about two feet before he hit the frost. He thought, sorry, Edgar. This is it. He put the pistol inside the other plastic bag, tossed in Orloff's checkbook, and buried the bundle. He took the shovel and headed back the way he'd come.

When he reached the corner of the stable, he heard a horse neigh again, and then something else. He stood perfectly still. It was footsteps. A man. Suddenly, above his head, a light came on. The whole yard was bathed in brightness. He moved back into the shadow of the stable and waited. If only he'd brought a second pistol, he thought. I'm here, half a mile from the road, with a shovel, and the bastards are awake.

Suddenly he heard other footsteps behind him, coming along the back of the stable. He opened a door, stepped into the stable, and found himself standing next to a horse. The animal seemed gigantic. The horse turned its long, wise face to stare at him, its eyes rolling to fix him in its gaze. Outside, footsteps scraped on the frozen ground. They passed and he

299

could hear voices. One of them said, "I don't give a shit what he thinks. If Toscanzio sends somebody it won't be through the stable. If he's so worried he should come out here and slide around on the horseshit himself."

"Relax," said the other one. "We'll just make the rounds and go back inside."

Guards, he thought. Balacontano has them doing regular patrols. The horse seemed to be getting nervous. It blew out a sputtering sigh and edged away from him in the stall. Just a few more minutes and I won't trouble you, he thought. Just a few more minutes and I'll be out of here, you big dumb son of a bitch. He thought, you're supposed to talk to them to calm them down. I can't risk it. He decided that patting the horse would help. It seemed so huge, looming beside him in the dark. He reached out and patted the horse's flank gently. He felt the skin quiver beneath his hand, then settle, but it was too late. The horse in the next stall seemed to sense his fear or the nervousness of the horse beside him. It whinnied and kicked the wall behind it. The noise was like a shot in the still night air.

He heard one of the voices say, "What the hell was that?"

The other said, "We'd better look in the stalls. Something's bothering them."

He had no time to think. He opened the stable door and watched the horse turn and make its decision to go outside. As it passed him he leaped astride it and it trotted out into the yard. He was high in the air now, bouncing on the animal's back. Behind him he heard one of the men shout, "Look." He didn't know what to do, but he had to do something. He leaned forward. With his left hand he grabbed the horse's mane, and with his right he smacked the horse's flank with the flat of the shovel. "Go," he hissed. Before he was prepared for the response, he felt the animal's massive muscles tense as it

300

leaped forward, almost unseating him. He clung to its mane with a grip that wrenched the muscles in his hand, and his legs hugged the horse's sides.

The men had left the gate open and the horse headed for it. He hung on with all his strength as it galloped through the opening and out across the pasture. Behind him he heard a shot, and the horse, terrified at the sound, dashed forward still faster, out into the darkness. He didn't dare look back for fear he'd fall off. At the far side of the pasture he saw the fence looming before him, a white barrier getting closer and closer. He said to the horse, "Calm down, you bastard. Stop." But the horse seemed to pick up speed as it neared the fence.

He thought, if I jump off I'll be hurt and they'll find me. He thought of hitting the horse over the head with the shovel, but there was no way to know what the horse would do, so he just hung on. And then suddenly he was airborne, and the fence floated past beneath him. He braced for the shock, but the horse landed easily and kept going, out across the second pasture at full speed.

When he saw the second fence he thought, I'm in for it again. But this time the horse ran up to the fence, slowed down, and trotted along it toward the far corner of the pasture. It doesn't like the road, he thought. It just wants to be away from the lights and noise. When it reached the corner the horse stopped. He jumped off and climbed the fence. His legs were sore, and for some reason his rib cage hurt almost as much, but he managed to bring himself to a run.

The important thing was to cover as much ground as possible. He sprinted in the direction he'd come from, but as far from the road as he could go. He was already to the next farm before he saw the first headlights on the highway. They were moving fast, at least sixty miles an hour, racing for the entrance to Route 87. The second set of headlights moved

301

along the road at a slower rate. That would be the one search-ing for a parked car, he thought. He was careful to stay in the wooded areas now. A few minutes later more cars fol-lowed, but none of them stopped. There would be others mov-ing off in the opposite direction too, he knew. None of them would try to follow on foot.

32

When it came it wasn't the way Elizabeth had imagined it. She was sitting in the Bureau office going over the morning field reports when the secretary came through and left the first of the afternoon communications in a stack on the table beside the door.

Elizabeth stood up and walked to the table. She was getting tired of being the one who had to come in here every day and suffer the silent enmity of a building full of people. All morning nobody had found it necessary to speak to her. And now the secretary had taken to leaving the reports in a stack by the door, as though Elizabeth were a prisoner in solitary confinement, or a pet that had to be fed but didn't require attention.

It was the sheet on top of the pile. It said, "The following personnel will report to the office of the Organized Crime Division, Department of Justice, Washington, D.C., by 0800, February 28: Dornquist, William; Kellogg, Bertram; Smith, Thomas H.; Feiler, Eleanor; Goltz, Ann K.; Waring, Elizabeth. Travel authorized: air only."

She read it through a second time. February 28. That was tomorrow morning. And now it was already two thirty. She looked at the timer readout on the transcript—it had only come in at 2:15, which meant 5:15 Washington time. That would be fifteen minutes after most of the people in the Washington office had gone home for the night. At least it wasn't just Elizabeth. It looked as though they were pulling out everybody still on detached service in Las Vegas. So they weren't necessarily calling her home to fire her. They were giving up on the operation.

303

She picked up the telephone and made a reservation on the next flight, then packed up her reports and her notebooks. For a moment she thought of leaving without saying anything to anyone, but it seemed too crude somehow. She walked down the hall to the Bureau chief's office.

He said, "I heard you were leaving."

Elizabeth said, "Yes, it just came in over the wire."

He tapped a pencil on his desk and cleared his throat. "I suppose congratulations are in order."

Elizabeth shifted in her chair and crossed her legs so the heavy reports wouldn't slide off her lap. "Not that I know of," she said.

He stared down at his desk and said nothing at first, but she could see he was angry.

"Have it your way. But just let me say one thing off the record. If you people would be a little less secretive things would be a lot easier for everybody."

"I know," said Elizabeth. "I've been wanting to tell you too, off the record, that I was against taking Palermo to Carson City. It was orders and I tried to follow them and I lost Palermo. If it's any consolation, I think when I get back to Washington the first thing they'll do is—"

"Damn it," he said quietly. "I'm not talking about Palermo. That was two or three days ago. I'm talking about now. Do you think we're idiots?"

Elizabeth said, "Of course not. What are you talking about?"

"Your whole team gets jerked back to Washington on a priority call, and then twenty minutes later, as an afterthought, they send us this message." He tossed it on the desk and Elizabeth leaned forward to pick it up.

She read it aloud. "Re: Edgar R. Fieldston. Disposition: Take no further action." She said, "So what? They know he's not here."

Now he was almost shouting. "So the case is closed and

304

you're all on your way home. And nobody has the decency to tell us what in the hell's going on. Either we're in on it or we're not."

"How can it be closed?" Elizabeth said. "We don't know any more than we did a week ago, or at least I don't. And you saw every report I filed since I got here."

He sat in silence for a moment, then stared at her. Very slowly, his expression changed. He said, "All right. Maybe I was wrong." He looked as though he wished he hadn't spoken to her. He added, "If I was wrong I apologize."

Elizabeth stood up, cradling the reports in her arms. "I'm sorry about Palermo. But honestly, that's the only thing we didn't cooperate about."

He looked a little sad, and more than a little embarrassed. He said, "I guess there's something else I should show you. Or maybe I shouldn't, I don't know. But a few minutes ago, when I asked our own headquarters what was going on, this came back." He handed her another transcript.

Re: Edgar R. Fieldston, F.G.E., and related matters: Effective immediately, second copy all reports to: Department of Justice, United States v. Carlo Balacontano Trial Team, Attention Padgett.

Elizabeth felt as though she'd been slapped. She looked at him, and saw he was now staring down at the desk. She said, "They arrested Balacontano? I didn't know."

He said, "I believe you didn't. I'm sorry."

She said again, "They didn't tell me."

THE DEPARTMENT OF JUSTICE OFFICE BUILDING seemed quiet and cavernous at seven in the morning. The floors gleamed and sounds echoed and died among the out-of-date light fixtures along the high ceilings of the corridor. Post offices and museums had seemed this way to Elizabeth when she was a child. Even the smell seemed the same, a mixture of floorwax and dust and disinfectant and old paper; a substantial, official, governmental smell.

She walked into the empty office and over to her desk. It looked the way she'd known it would. When the accumulation of daily activity reports had grown too bulky for her desk they'd begun making a neat stack of them on the floor beside it. In a day or two somebody was going to have a lot of work to do.

She had only been there for fifteen minutes when she heard the first footsteps in the hallway, the purposeful clopping of male leather-soled shoes resonating in the emptiness of the building. In a moment she realized it was two men. And then one of them spoke and she recognized the voice. Padgett. "Just let me get a cup of coffee and—" He came through the door and stopped. He said, "Elizabeth! Terrific. Glad to have you back." He started to pour himself some coffee. It was then that the second man appeared. It was Martin Connors. He said, "Good morning, Miss Waring." Then he frowned slightly. "I'd like to talk to you for a moment, if you don't mind."

"No," said Elizabeth and stood up. He was already walking down the corridor toward his office. Elizabeth had to trot to catch up.

Behind her she heard Padgett say, "I'll bring you a cup, Martin." Then he added, "You too, Elizabeth?"

She didn't bother to answer. They walked in silence. He unlocked the door to his office and ceremoniously stepped aside to let her pass, then pulled a chair away from the wall for her. There was something about his manner that made her uncomfortable. It wasn't that he had the gestures of his own generation, but those of the generation before.

He sat down behind his desk, pursed his lips, and folded his hands. "I'm glad you're here early, because I want you to be ready to help with this thing."

Elizabeth thought, I'm not fired.

He leaned forward and said, "You're the one who is most

306

familiar with the case, and that makes it doubly important that you be here when it gets to the trial stage."

Elizabeth thought again, I'm not fired. Then she thought, most familiar? She said, "What about John?"

He said, "John?"

"Yes, John."

"You don't know?" Then he shook his head, and stared at his desk for a moment. "John Brayer is dead." He looked up at her again and said, "I'm sorry, I thought you knew. Stupid of me."

Elizabeth felt tears clouding her vision. She said, "When? How?"

Connors shook his head again. "Don't waste your tears on Mr. Brayer," he said. It was an order. "He was our informer and his friends decided he was too great a risk. It was in Las Vegas, shortly after the . . . the Palermo incident. He was found in the desert somewhere outside Las Vegas. It took quite some time to identify him."

"But nobody told me," she said. "Why didn't anybody tell me?" She was weeping now. Brayer was dead, and she'd been there, thinking—what? It was too wrong, there were so many things to remember. But she realized Connors had said something else too. Brayer the leak? She said, "John wasn't the leak. What are you talking about?"

Connors became the formal superior again. He spoke very slowly, as though he expected to say it once and never have to say it again. "When you and I spoke on your telephone we set certain wheels in motion. We both knew that. The result was that you and I both got an unpleasant surprise. The man who was killed was our John Brayer. So that's that. After he was killed we found he had a large amount of money in his home. Almost two hundred thousand dollars to be exact. And after that we received other evidence, which proves that John Brayer was the informer." He formed his hands into fists. "When I think of the things he must have told them—"

307

Elizabeth said, "No. You're wrong. I knew him and—"

Connors shook his head. "No, Miss Waring. The evidence I'm speaking of is conclusive. If you'll permit me to give you the most recent information, I'm sure you'll agree. I must caution you, however, that this information is sensitive. It must be released gradually and cautiously, at the right time. Some of it is very difficult to accept, but you must bear with me." He looked almost fatherly now, his white hair no longer in its customary order. In her detachment Elizabeth thought with surprise, this isn't any easier for him than it is for me.

She said, "All right." She would be quiet. It was all she could do. But she knew Brayer hadn't had that kind of money. It must have been planted.

He almost smiled. He said, "Good. Then let me fill you in. Early yesterday the police in Saratoga Springs, New York, received an anonymous telephone call telling them that they would find the remains of Edgar Fieldston buried on the estate of Carlo Balacontano. Actually, it's a place where they raise horses."

"A stud farm," said Elizabeth.

"Yes," he said. "On the strength of the call, the police got a warrant and raided the farm. What they found was, I'm afraid, not a pretty sight. It was the head and hands of Edgar Fieldston, and the pistol that killed him." Connors looked down again. "He was shot in the head."

Elizabeth waited.

"They also found the missing bookkeeping from Fieldston Growth Enterprises. It was a checkbook and we've been able to match the balances to the accounts of Harry Orloff and others."

Elizabeth said, "Wait, Mr. Connors."

He said, "Honestly, Miss Waring. There is no question at all. When you see the evidence for yourself you'll be amazed. Positively amazed. We have conclusive evidence that Carlo Balacontano was the silent partner in Fieldston Growth En-

308

terprises and that he was involved in the killing of Edgar Fieldston and had him buried on his farm along with the secret bookkeeping of the company. You know, he used FGE to invest illegal profits amounting to over two million dollars. And another thing. Yesterday he received the money Edgar Fieldston got for the FGE stock in the Bahamas. Four million dollars. The serial numbers all match the list the Federal Reserve people made when the money was sent to Miami. It was mailed to Balacontano inside a package of paperback books."

Elizabeth said, "Wait. It must be a frame."

"What are you talking about?"

"It's a frame-up. He wouldn't bury Fieldston's head and hands on his own property. He'd do the same thing with them he did with the rest of the body. Did you find the rest?"

Connors was flustered. "No, but—"

"And the gun and this checkbook. It's ridiculous. Mr. Connors, a man like Balacontano must have people killed all the time. Why would he be so stupid? He could hire experts. People so skilled we'd never find anything. And who made the call to the police?"

Connors said, "Miss Waring, I'm afraid you're asking questions that don't concern us. We have already compared the checkbook with what remains of FGE's records. What is there is genuine. The coroner has determined that Fieldston did die from a shot from the gun found with the, uh, remains. All on Balacontano's property. We have motive, body, weapon. Mr. Balacontano is going to prison. I don't care who made the telephone call or why."

"You know it's a frame," said Elizabeth. "I'm not saying he didn't own FGE, or even that he didn't have Fieldston killed. But somebody planted what was left of Fieldston, the gun, and the checkbook. That was who made the call. And come to think of it, that had to be the one who actually killed Fieldston."

"I know no such thing," said Connors. "And you're stepping very far out of line. I'll ignore it because of your distress over recent events. When you've looked at the evidence you'll see how clearly it implicates Carlo Balacontano."

Elizabeth just stood there knowing that anything she said would be wrong. Connors didn't want to hear the truth.

"I'll tell you what," said Connors. "You've had a hard time of it over the last couple of weeks. And you've built up a backlog of compensatory time off. I want you to take a few weeks. Go somewhere. Have you ever been to Hawaii? How about London?"

"I've been away a lot. It's good to be home," she said.

Connors repeated, "I'd like to see you take a vacation."

33

Elizabeth closed her eyes while the plane hurtled down the runway and lifted itself into the air. That was the only part of it she minded, the moment when it was going too fast to stop, but still seemed to weigh tons of metal. Whatever it was that converted it from a freight train to a bird was still essentially mysterious to her. The explanation given by people who understand such things sounded perfectly reasonable to the part of her mind that made decisions; to the part of her mind that controlled her pulse and her eyelids, it sounded like nonsense. But again the airplane defied common sense and rose into the sky.

In the airport she'd bought some magazines to read, but now they seemed to belong to a world that was foreign to her. Sometime she'd care about new ways to turn a strict diet into an adventure, but not now. Soon enough, when she returned from this mandatory vacation. When she'd done her time.

Elizabeth had picked London because she remembered it as cool and wet and densely inhabited. It was a place that looked as though people had always lived there, layers and layers of them, one over the other through time. From there, if she still felt restless, she could go on to the Continent. She wondered if it would be in the London newspapers when she got there. Probably it would. American scandals seemed to have a peculiar appeal to the English. When the Senator's staff turned up FGE, Balacontano had acted to protect himself. That had been the week poor Veasy had picked to write his letter to the Department of Justice Organized Crime Division. His careful, semiliterate, handwritten letter explaining why he thought his union's pension fund was being looted had found its way through the bureaucratic labyrinth to the desk of the one man who had any knowledge of Veasy's problem. John Brayer. The papers would love that part of it.

The letter had been in Brayer's desk when Connors had ordered the search. That was the part that still kept Elizabeth awake at night. Brayer.

She heard herself sigh. She would try to stay abroad during the trial, at least the first part of it with its sensational revelations. She already knew the strategy the department would follow. They'd arrange to have the trial in Saratoga Springs, where the evidence had been found. Just the head and hands—the parts used to identify a body—and the gun and the checkbook, all buried together a foot or two beneath the surface. But she knew the evidence wouldn't matter to the jury, any more than it did to Connors. If Balacontano wasn't the one who had killed Fieldston, everyone knew he had ordered the other murders. Fieldston was just the one they could prove. So they'd use what they had, and the jury would go along with it. If the prosecutors played according to Connors's plan the jury would even come to believe that the lack of a whole corpse was especially damaging. You had to be a monster to cut a man up like that. A monster, she thought, or a man who wanted to move evidence from one place to another. But Balacontano would be convicted. And maybe the prosecutors would generate enough heat to convict the men found with him at the stud farm at the time of the raid. It might be a week or more before someone else moved in to fill the vacuum he left in the Northeast.

Elizabeth was out of it now. She looked around her at the other passengers in the cabin. There were the usual tourists, an elderly couple seeing the world outside Iowa before it was too late, a pair of college girls in bluejeans, and three businessmen staring at papers resting on their trays. The only passenger within the limited range of Elizabeth's vision who wasn't immediately identifiable was the man across the aisle from her. She pretended to read one of her magazines while she studied him. He was wearing a comfortable sort of sport coat that she decided was too informal for a businessman trying to impress people in London. He was traveling alone and she couldn't see any carry-on luggage. He was just a quiet, solitary man with nothing special about him. He was probably a professor. He was a professor of English or history making one of those professorial pilgrimages to England, hoping perhaps that if he could stand where William the Conqueror stood or walk where Chaucer walked he would have insights unavailable to mere reason.

As Elizabeth watched the man leaned his head back on the seat and closed his eyes. She felt proud of herself for her perception. He was a professor. And right now he's thinking about the fun he's going to have prowling around in castles and cathedrals and libraries where musty old books have sat on the shelves for centuries. The man shifted slightly in his seat. Elizabeth thought she caught just the slightest suspicion of a smile on the corners of his mouth. She felt an involuntary instant of affection for him.

The man's smile faded and the skin at the corners of his eyes tightened in concentration. He was trying to remember. It was ridiculous, he knew, but once the problem had occurred to him, it had bothered him for days. What was the name of Eddie Mastrewski's cat?